pull you through

New York Times Bestselling Author
KAYLEE RYAN

Cover Design: Sommer Stein, Perfect Pear Creative Covers
Cover Photography: Sara Eirew
Editing: Hot Tree Editing
Formatting: Integrity Formatting
Model: Mike Chabot & Carolyn Seguin

dedication

To those who have served, are serving, or will serve,
and their loved ones who pull them through.

Slade

W HEN CLASS IS INTERRUPTED AND I'm summoned to the office, I know it's bad news. I feel it deep in my gut. There are two weeks of school left. Two more weeks of enduring high school, and then I'll be free of the drama of this day-to-day shit.

Grabbing my books and keeping my head down, I slide out of my too-small desk and stalk to the office. The receptionist gives me a sad smile and my anxiety ramps up even further. From the look on the receptionist's face, it's not good, whatever I'm being summoned for.

I assume I'm here because I was late, yet again. Tardy they call it. Gram was having a bad morning, and I couldn't just leave her, not until her friend Sheila got there. Sheila spends the day with her while I'm at school.

"Slade, you can go on in," she says, pointing to the principal's office.

Stepping into the room, I don't bother knocking. I've been here before, and he's always expecting me. This time though, this time it feels different. I can't quite put my finger on why or how, but there's a look on his face I haven't seen before.

"Slade, have a seat." He points to the chair across from his desk.

"What's going on?" I ask. He's never one to beat around the bush. It's usually, "Slade, are you aware you were late again?" or even, "Slade, you've missed too many days. I know about your gran, but you have to get here on time. I can't keep them at bay." "Them" being the state. Apparently, it's illegal and referred to as truancy. I get it, I do, but Gran is all I have in this world, and no way am I leaving her when she needs me.

"I got a call," Principal McCreary says cryptically.

"Okay. Look, there are two weeks left. I'm doing the best that I can," I explain. "Sheila was running late today, and I can't leave her alone. She's not well."

"Slade, Sheila called. I'm so sorry, son."

"What?" My stomach drops as my head swirls with confusion. "Sheila? Why would she call? What are you sorry for? Listen, it's two weeks, can you please just overlook this? Don't report it. Two weeks and I get my diploma. Please," I say, begging. I'm so fucking close to getting that piece of paper that I promised Gran I would get. It's something my dad, her only child, never accomplished.

"Slade." He stands, then takes the seat next to mine. "Your gran, she had a heart attack," he says gently.

I stand abruptly. "Which hospital?" I ask.

"Slade, sit down," he says, his voice stern.

"Look, I get it, my attendance sucks, but we're all the family each other has. I have to go to her. I'll just get my GED. It's the same thing, right? Or take summer classes or online classes. Hell, it doesn't even matter right now. Which hospital?" I ask again, my voice rising.

Mr. McCreary stands, and walks toward me. He places his hand on my shoulder, his eyes somber. "Slade, she's gone. It was fast. The paramedics announced her... at the scene. There was nothing they could do."

"No. No, no, no, no...." It's too much, and nothing makes sense. I saw her this morning. She couldn't have gone, have left me. "No. She was having a bad day, but nothing we haven't dealt with before. No, I don't believe you." Panic rises in my chest.

"Slade, I'm so sorry."

Turning, I punch the wall, over and over again. I barely register Mr. McCreary placing his arms around me from behind to stop me. My focus is on the pain, my throbbing hand, the jolts rushing up my arm. It's the only thing that's real.

"Can I call anyone?" the receptionist asks.

"No, Gina, I've got this."

"There is no one to call," I sob. The tears, no matter how hard I fight them, fall freely. "She's all I have." Twisting out of his hold, I drop to my knees and bury my face in my hands, one of which is now battered and bloody.

Heat registers on my shoulder. I don't have to look to know it's Mr. McCreary's hand. He doesn't say a word. He doesn't try to tell me it's going to be okay. He doesn't offer words of wisdom. He just lets me be me.

Broken.

Alone.

I don't know how long I sit there on my knees in his office. It's not until his phone rings, startling me, that I climb to my feet and move to the chair. I hear Mr. McCreary answer his phone, but I block out the conversation.

She's gone.

I knew she was sick. I take her to her doctor appointments, make sure she takes her medication. What I didn't know was that I was this close to losing her. Thinking back to this morning, relief washes over me when I remember I told her I loved her. I always let her know, multiple times a day. She saved me from my parents, her own son and daughter-in-law. Both had been so hooked on drugs, I'm not sure they even realized she took me. When she petitioned the courts for custody when I was twelve, no one was there to contest. It's been just the two of us ever since. Six years ago, she pulled me from my own personal hell.

"Slade." Mr. McCreary breaks me out of my thoughts.

"You're eighteen, son, but I don't like the thought of you being alone. Do you have a friend you can stay with? That can come and stay with you?"

I shake my head. I'm a loner and keep to myself. The first twelve years of my life were rough. I never had clean clothes or clothes that even fit for that matter. I was scrawny from the lack of nutrition. I was the outcast, the boy no one wanted to sit by at lunch, and was always picked last in gym class. I was good with it—disappearing in a roomful of people. At school, on the days I actually got to go, I was warm, was given a hot meal, and there were no fists being thrown at my face. I stayed in my shell and ignored them all. That didn't change when I moved in with Gran. Sure, my clothes were new, and fit me. I gained weight and grew into my tall, lanky body, but I was still quiet and brooding. I didn't need friends. I had Gran. She saved me and was all that mattered in my world.

I would sit in class and listen to my classmates bitch about lunch, how it was "so not good," or some other mundane complaint. If they walked a day in my shoes, they would know there's more to life, they would know to be grateful for the food you have, the new cars, the clothes. Gran always said I grew up way before my time.

"Well, then you're coming home with me."

My eyes fly up to him. "I'm not letting you spend the night alone after… today. We would love to have you."

"I'll be fine." I croak out the words. My voice is rough with emotion.

"Slade, you shouldn't be alone."

"That's my life, Mr. McCreary. I'm a loner." I stand from the chair. "I'll be here on time from now on," I assure him. "But I need to go today. I need to just… go."

He nods. I watch as he writes something on a Post-it and hands it to me. "Here's my cell number. You need anything at all, you call me."

"Yes, sir." With that, I turn and walk out of the room, down the hall and out to my old beat-up pick-up truck. I don't recall putting the keys in the ignition or the drive home, but when I pull into the driveway and see the ambulance, it's sirens deathly quiet, reality crashes back into me.

Gran is gone, and I'm alone.

chapter 1

Slade

TEN DAYS. TEN GLORIOUS DAYS of rest and whatever else we want to do. These past thirteen weeks have been intense, but I've lived through worse. Not eating for days, being slapped around as a kid, that's what I'm used to. Don't get me wrong. The vigorous intensity of what I and nineteen others went through over the past few weeks was some heavy shit. That's what makes us badass. We train harder, longer, and deeper. We're cut to the core, then built back up again. That's the Marine Corps.

"Where you headed?" Combs asks me.

Brandon Combs and I have become close during our thirteen weeks of hell. He's from a small town in Kentucky, and from the way he talks about them, they're a family unit who gives him nothing but love and support. I envy him.

"Not sure, man. I'm just going to pick a place and go. I've never really traveled." It sounds pathetic even to me, but it's my reality. It's also part of what drew me into the Marines. Getting to see the world. He knows my history. You don't spend every waking minute with someone, especially in the conditions we just completed, and not get close. These guys are my brothers, my family. We've been through hell and back, and we survived it together.

"Ever been to Kentucky?" he asks.

"No. This is my first time out of Michigan," I confess.

"No time like the present. Come home with me. We have the space."

His offer sparks more excitement in me than it should. "Nah, man, I'm good. Go home, see your family, spend some time with your girl. I'll see you when we appear for SOI." I know he's just trying to be nice, I don't want to impose on his time with his family. We only get a small number of days.

"School of Infantry." He holds his fist out for me to bump. "For real, come back to Kentucky. Let me show you around."

The thought of spending the next ten days alone, after being surrounded by my unit, does not sound appealing. Over the past thirteen weeks, Combs and I have created a bond, only those in our shoes can have. "You sure your folks won't care?"

"Nope. Like I said, we have plenty of room, and Mom and Dad have always been open to us bringing friends home."

Ten long, lonely days in a hotel room, or the chance to see where he's from, meet his family, and his girl that he never stops talking about? "All right, man, but maybe just for a few days." I don't want to wear out my welcome or intrude on his time with his family before we leave again. I know if it were me, I'd want the time with Gran. The familiar pain in my chest when I think of her makes itself known. I ignore it, push it aside and keep moving. That's all I can do.

"Grab your stuff. My dad will be here any minute to get us. Mom and Savannah left last night to go back home. Mom had to get back to work, and Savvy has class." I didn't get to meet them, I disappeared after graduation, knowing he would insist that I come with them to dinner.

"You're positive?" I ask as I finish packing up my bag. Not that I have much. I came here with the clothes on my back. There were a handful of pictures of me as a baby, as well as a few of Gran and Gramps before he passed. Those along with any important documents are in a safe deposit box at the bank.

Yesterday was graduation and was difficult for me. Not having family here… yeah, it sucked. I missed Gran something fierce. Combs wanted me to meet his family and his girl, but it was too much. I just needed time to myself, so instead of sticking around, I slipped away back to the barracks.

Bags over our shoulders, we walk out into the sunlight. It's a beautiful day in South Carolina. It's early fall, and temperatures are reaching to the low eighties. The sun is shining brightly and not a single cloud blemishes the sky. It feels like freedom. But while it's good to get a break, at the same time, I'm anxious for SOI. I'm ready to start the next phase of my career as a marine.

"There he is," Brandon says, heading toward a blue four-door pick-up truck. "Damn good to see you," he says, hopping in the passenger seat. "Dad, this is Slade. Slade, this is my dad, Eric Combs," he introduces us.

Reaching over the seat, I offer him my hand. "It's nice to meet you, sir. I hope it's not an imposition me being here."

"Slade, great to meet you. Our home is always open to you," he says kindly.

Feeling the worry slip away, I sit back, laying my head against the seat. I listen to them get caught up. Brandon is also an only child; the major difference being he seems really close to his parents. They talk about his mom and how his girlfriend, Savannah, has been hanging out at their place quite often while he's been gone. Brandon has talked about Savannah nonstop during boot camp. He showed me pictures, and she's a looker. Then again, so are her friends. The one picture he had was of her and her best friend, a gorgeous blonde with the bluest eyes I've ever seen. I remember thinking that I'd love to see them up close in person. Maybe I'll get the chance now.

I'm quiet most of the ride. I answer questions from Mr. Combs and fall into the conversation when Brandon prompts me. Although, I've always been quiet to a fault, my silence is mainly because I'm observing the two of them. If I'm honest with myself, I'm envious. I've never had this… bond they seem to have. I can't ever remember a time with either of my parents asked me about my day, or hell, even showed me an ounce of affection, unless you count their hands in anger.

The hours and miles pass by the closer we get to Kentucky. "We're almost there," Combs informs me. Not ten minutes later, we're pulling into the driveway of an old two-story farmhouse. It's dark, so I can't really see it, but I can see it in my mind. Brandon has described his home in detail. Field parties, sneaking his girl in and out... he's told me about it all. In turn, I told him about the day I lost Gran, that my parents are both a waste of sperm and egg, and how that led me to enlist.

"Home sweet home," Brandon says, climbing out of the truck. I follow him.

A screech erupts from the house. Before I can determine what's going on, a small brown-haired girl is launching herself at Brandon. He catches her easily as she wraps herself around him. A woman, who can only be his mother, from the way her eyes glisten in the moonlight, stands off to the side with her hands clasped to her chest. Her husband wraps his arms around her. Then there's me, leaning against the truck, taking it all in. This is what I've been missing.

When his mom notices me, she leaves her husband's embrace and walks toward me. I stand up straight and offer her my hand. She swats it away and pulls me into a hug. "Welcome home, son," she whispers.

I like to think that I'm hardened to life. I've come to expect the worst, and long ago came to terms that welcome home hugs are not in my future, but standing here in the moonlight, on a small farm in Kentucky, I'm proven wrong. I hug her back and swallow the lump that's suddenly formed in my throat. She pulls back and looks up at me a kind smile on her face.

"Hey, I'm Savannah." The brown-haired girl then leans in for a hug.

Awkwardly, I wrap my arms lightly around her. "Slade," I say as I pull away from her.

"Dinner's waiting. Let's get inside. Brandon, I made your favorite," his mom says.

"Are you for real? Baked steak, mashed potatoes, and gravy, corn, and mac and cheese?" he rattles off, with hope in his voice.

"Exactly that. There's also chocolate cake for dessert."

"You love me." He places one hand over his heart and the other around Savannah's shoulders, then follows his mom into the house.

"You hungry?" his dad asks me.

"Yes, sir," I respond. Thirteen weeks has it ingrained in me.

"None of that, Eric, or hell, Dad works. You're home now. Time to relax a little." He places his hand on my shoulder. "Let's eat." With that, I follow him into the house.

As soon as I hit the doorway, the aroma of dinner assaults me, and my stomach growls. It's been a long damn time since I've had a homecooked meal. The last couple of years, Gran was too weak, so I was in charge of cooking. We ate lots of spaghetti, grilled cheese sandwiches, and soup. It was nothing special, but it was a hot meal.

"Come, sit." Brandon's mom, Sarah, waves me into the dining room. "Sit anywhere." She points at the table.

Brandon and Savannah are already seated on one side. Eric rounds the table and sits on the end. I sit across from Savannah, leaving the spot next to his father open for Sarah. She surprises me when she takes the seat on the end, directly across from Eric.

"Dig in," she says, pointing to all the food.

"This looks and smells delicious. Thank you."

"The best way to thank the cook is to eat up." She smiles.

We fill our plates and dig in. Eric, Sarah, and Savannah ask lots of questions about boot camp, and I chime in here and there. I'm a little distracted. The dynamics of their family intrigues me. It's not sitcom-worthy, but it's... nice. You can tell his parents care, *truly care* about what we went through.

"So, Slade, where are you from?" Eric asks.

I wipe my mouth and take a drink of water before answering. "Michigan, sir."

"Eric, please. I've been up to Lake Erie a few times, finishing. Beautiful country," he says.

"It is. A lot of people say it reminds them of the ocean."

"Not you?" Savannah asks.

I shrug. "I've never seen the ocean."

"Never, but you were just in South Carolina," she says with disbelief.

"There was no downtime," Brandon tells her.

"When you go back, will you see it then?" Savannah asks Brandon.

"Nah, SOI isn't leisure either," he tells her. Savannah looks crestfallen at the news.

"So, ten days," Eric says. "Y'all got plans?"

Brandon laughs. "Sleep. Lots of sleep and more of this." He points to his now empty plate.

"What about you, Slade?" Sarah asks.

"No plans, ma'am."

Reaching over, she pats my hand. "Good, you boys will be around for more of my cooking. It's harder to cook for just two." Her willingness to include me without question, humbles me. I've never been privy to seeing a mother, one who loves her children in action.

"Thank you for dinner," I say, remembering my manners. "It was delicious."

She smiles brightly. "You're welcome. You make yourself home while you're here."

That ball of anticipation, it's back. "Thank you," I say quietly. How is it that I've been here a little over an hour and they're already pulling me into their fold? They're showing me what a real family should have been like. Gran tried her best, but her health wasn't good when I went to live with her, and she declined quickly from there.

"I told Reeves I'd show him small-town country life," Brandon says, referring to me by my last name. Something we've gotten used to.

"What part of Michigan are you from?" Sarah asks.

"Detroit, a suburb of Detroit, far from the country life."

"We're not so different," Eric says. "You can just see the stars here, and it's a hell of a lot quieter."

"That's not a bad thing," I tell him.

"Not at all. Sure, we have to drive to the store, the post office, even the gas station, but we like our little piece of heaven out here in the country," Sarah says wistfully. "Nothing is within safe walking distance, but we love it."

"I should probably go," Savannah says, standing. "I have an early class in the morning." Brandon stands as well, lacing her fingers with his as they disappear into the living room.

"And I need to get on these dishes." Sarah stands, as do I to help her. "Sit." She points at my chair, or better yet, Eric, show him to his room. Take a break, Slade. You've earned it."

"Yes, ma'am. Thank you for dinner and the hospitality." I'm overwhelmed by how welcome they're making me. Not that I expected otherwise. Truthfully, I didn't really know what to think. I know that spending ten days all alone wasn't alluring. Trying my luck going home with Combs for that time sounded way more appealing. It took little effort for him to convince me. Now that I'm here, I'm glad I came.

"You're welcome. Please make yourself at home."

"Let's go grab your bags," Eric says.

I nod and follow him outside. Brandon and Savannah are leaning against what I assume is her car. Brandon's dad doesn't blink an eye as we pass them to his truck. He hands me my bag and then grabs Brandon's as well. "Goodnight, Savannah," he sing-songs as we pass them for the second time. I hear a muted, "Oh my God," in a female voice, and chuckle.

"I just couldn't resist," Eric says conspiratorially when we're back in the house. He heads for the stairs, so I follow him. "This is the guest room, which will be yours anytime you come to visit."

"Thank you, sir."

"Don't know your story, son. I do know that my home is always open to you."

I nod. Not really wanting to get into my history. Not tonight. Witnessing the way their family interacts together, the love they all share, it's cut me to the core. I'm lost in my own thoughts, thinking about my life. Gran saved me and did the best she could, but she couldn't give me this: a mother and a father fully invested in my life. I envy Combs in that aspect.

"Make yourself at home, Slade. Get a good night's rest."

"Yes, sir." I watch as he leaves the room, shutting the door quietly behind him. Setting my bag on the bed, I remove my boots and place them neatly at the foot of the bed. I'm just getting ready to strip down when there's a knock on the door, and Brandon then comes inside.

"You good?" he asks.

"All set."

"All right man, I'll see you in the morning. Here's to sleeping in," he says holding his fist out of me to bump.

"Good luck with that." Our internal clocks are set, I can't see that habit breaking anytime soon. Not to mention that it will be the same routine once we're back from leave.

With a tired smile, he nods, wishes me good night, turns on his heel and leaves.

Once I've stripped down to my T-shirt and boxer briefs, I lie down on the bed, and the softness has me sighing in relief. After sleeping on a hard-ass mattress for the last thirteen weeks, this is heaven. Pulling the covers up over me, I fall into a deep sleep.

chapter 2
Austyn

AT EXACTLY TEN O'CLOCK, I rush to the door and flip the sign to Closed. Chase laughs from behind me. I turn at the sound and give him a warning look. "Seriously, Chase?"

He laughs harder. "What's the rush?"

He knows damn well what the rush is. "Oh, I don't know. Maybe because I worked on my own tonight because your plaything couldn't bother to come to work tonight."

He shrugs. "I'm not her keeper. I told you to call Savannah."

"You do realize that Brandon came home today, right? This is the first time they've seen each other in thirteen weeks."

"And?" he asks.

"Gah! You're such a jerk." My outburst causes more laughter. Rolling my eyes, I start putting the chairs up on the tables so we can sweep and mop and get out of here.

"You're supposed to wipe those down first, Austyn," he points out.

"No shit, Sherlock. I already did that. I also already filled all the salt and pepper shakers and the ketchup bottles. While you did what?"

"Hey, the kitchen is my domain." He points over his shoulder at the kitchen.

"Great, then you better get back to your domain and out of mine."

"You seemed stressed, babe. I can help with that." He wriggles his eyebrows at me.

This is nothing new from Chase. He's a serial dater and an epic flirt. I wouldn't go as far as calling him a playboy, because well, I don't see that he has much game. He's not a bad-looking guy. He's average height, blond, and blue-eyed. I bite back a smile when I remember Brandon referring to him as "that pretty boy we work with." That sums up Chase. "Now, Chase. You know you can't handle me," I retort.

His eyes light up, and I groan. "Nope. Not ever. Not going to happen, so just erase it from your mind. Nope," I say again.

"I'm wearing you down," he says, pointing at me.

With a snort, I carry on lifting the chairs. "Keep telling yourself that, bud. Now, can you please get back to work so we can get the hell out of here?" It's been a long day. My feet are killing me and I'm exhausted. I just want to go home and shower off the smell of diner and go to sleep.

He looks at his watch and his eyes widen when he sees the time. He now realizes his bullshit is delaying us even further. He doesn't want to stay here any later than I do. I quickly place the chairs on the tables, then get to work on sweeping. It amazes me how people will drop things, such as napkins and cutlery and not pick it up. I get dropping some crumbs... it's a restaurant. But the napkin on the floor that they had to step on, or over, to get out of your seat. Come on.

It's eleven by the time we leave. It's usually twenty to thirty minutes' tops, but with one waitress and dealing with Chase, it took longer tonight. I'm exhausted and my feet hurt. I just want to go home, take a hot shower and wash off the grime of the day, and go to sleep. I'm just pulling into the house when my cell rings. I know it's Savannah without even looking. The two messages I received while driving I'm sure were her as well. My lack of reply has prompted a phone call.

"Hello," I say, turning off the ignition.

"I've texted you twice, you okay?" my best friend, Savannah, asks.

"Yeah, I'm good. Autumn called in tonight, and then Chase was, well, being Chase, so it took forever to get out of there. I didn't want to reply while I was driving.

"You should have called me. I would have come in."

"I know you would have, which is why I didn't. How's Brandon?"

"He's great. It was so good to see him. Oh, and he brought one of his marine buddy's home with him. He's hot."

I laugh. "Good to know. Wait, are you still with him talking about his friend? That's wrong," I say, giving her a hard time. After all, what are best friends for?

"No. They're exhausted from traveling, and I'm on the morning shift with you tomorrow."

"You are? I thought you took today and tomorrow off?"

"I did, but then Margaret called and asked if I could work. Apparently, she scheduled herself but forgot about a doctor's appointment."

"She's had quite a few of those lately."

"Yeah, she says it's all routine, but I worry about her."

"Me too." Margaret is the owner of The Home Place Restaurant where Savannah and I both waitress. We started the same day our junior year of high school. The job is part-time, and Margaret works with our class schedules now that we're in college. It's a great gig for extra cash. I hate the thought of asking my parents for money all the time. It makes me feel like a bum.

"So, I hope you don't have plans for tomorrow night."

"Nope. What's up?"

"I kind of told Brandon that we'd go to the county fair with him and Slade."

"Slade," I repeat the name. I don't know about the guy, but

the name is hot.

"That's his friend, who came home with him. You'll go, right? I don't want Slade to feel like a third wheel."

"Sure. We always go to the fair," I remind her.

"I know, but not with me fixing you up."

"Hold up, you didn't say this was a fix-up. Savannah, you didn't." I love my best friend, even though she romanticizes everything and thinks I need to find someone so I can be as deliriously happy as she and Brandon are.

"Calm down, I didn't, but he's hot and seems like a really nice guy."

"Right, how much time did you spend with him?"

"Just a couple of hours, but I can tell," she replies.

"I'll go, keep the guy company while you two lovebirds do your thing, but don't go getting any ideas in that head of yours. It's a favor. Nothing more."

"You're the bestest best friend ever," she says excitedly.

I can already tell she's not listening to a word I just said. "I mean it, Savannah."

"Got it. I'll see you at work in the morning." She hangs up before I can say anything more. I love her, but sometimes she's a handful. Shaking my head at her antics, I climb out of my car and head inside. The shower and my bed are calling my name.

"Good morning, Sunshine," Savannah greets as soon as I walk into work.

"You're chipper," I say with a yawn.

"Of course I am. Brandon's home."

I smile at her. "How's he doing? He seem okay?" I'm such a bad friend. I forgot to ask last night.

"He's great. You can tell they worked them hard. His muscles are even more defined than before." She wags her eyebrows.

"He was a pretty fit guy to begin with," I comment.

"Right?" She beams, then opens her mouth, but I hold up my hand to stop her.

"I know what you're going to say and I don't want to hear it."

"What?" She feigns innocence.

"I don't need details, Savvy," I tell her.

She huffs. "Fine, but as my best friend, you're supposed to want details."

I laugh. "I've heard it all from the two of you. I'm good for a lifetime of details."

"Ladies, ladies, there is no need to fight over me. There's enough Chase to go around," Chase says, coming in through the front door.

"You're not on the schedule and no. Just no," Savannah says.

Her refusal doesn't faze him. "Margaret called me this morning and said RJ called in. Asked me to cover the morning shift." He comes over and stands between us, placing an arm around each of our shoulders. "You know, sharing does have its benefits." He grins.

"Get off," we say at the same time, ducking out from underneath his arms. His laughter follows him into the kitchen.

"What time are we leaving tonight?" I ask her once we've made our escape. I'm hoping there is time to go home and grab a nap before we go.

"I don't know for sure. I'll talk to Brandon later and let you know."

"Sounds good." Glancing at the clock, I see it's a few minutes before eight. "We better get moving. Only a couple of minutes until we open." We rush to get the chairs off the tables and the salt, pepper, and ketchup back in their rightful places. We're just finishing the last one when old man Harris ambles up to the door. He's a regular, a widower who comes in for breakfast seven days a week. "Hey, Mr. Harris," I say, opening the door for him.

"Austyn, dear, how are you?" he asks, carefully maneuvering his frail body with his cane.

"Can't complain. Savannah and I are going to the fair tonight."

"Oh, I remember when my Rosie and I would go to the fair. You girls behave." He tries to act stern; he's anything but.

"Oh, I'll keep Savvy out of trouble, don't you worry," I tell him, taking his cane and sitting it in the seat across from him.

"Don't listen to her, Mr. Harris, you know I'm the good one," Savannah says sweetly as she sits down a black coffee and a glass of orange juice. "What sounds good today?" she asks him.

"Two eggs, over easy, bacon, and wheat toast," he tells her without even looking at the menu.

"Coming right up." Savannah goes to put his order in while I finish opening up the front counter and making another pot of coffee.

The morning flies by. The Home Place has been in our town for over thirty years. Known for its homemade recipes, we stay busy, but the weekends are our busiest, thankfully it's not the weekend. I'm standing at the counter, making what feels like the one-hundredth pot of coffee today, when I hear a deep, familiar voice behind me.

"Good help is so damn hard to find these days."

I can't help but smile. Brandon is Savannah's boyfriend and has been since freshman year, but he's also my friend. We all went to school together since we were little. I take my time, knowing it's him, and finish making the coffee.

"Is she ignoring you on purpose?" I hear another deep voice ask.

This voice is different, and it sends tingles down my spine from the deep rumble. This must be the marine friend Brandon brought home with him. Sexy name, sexy voice, and Savvy's seal of approval. I've got to see this guy. Grabbing a towel and drying my hands, I slowly turn to face them. My eyes land on Brandon and a grin spreads across my face. "You're home!" I say, rushing around the counter and hugging him. So much for playing it cool.

"Hey, Aust, how are ya?"

"Me? How are you?" I release him and step back.

"Good. Stopped by to have some lunch. Where's Savannah?"

I point over my shoulder. "She was in the back grabbing more pie for the case."

He nods. "Hey, there's someone I want you to meet. Austyn, this is Slade. We went through boot camp together."

Turning to face the deep, sexy voice, I have to bite my bottom lip to keep my mouth from dropping open. He's tall, at least a head taller than my five foot four. With broad shoulders, dark black hair, and scruff to match, he's handsome. That combined with deep brown eyes, so dark they appear to be onyx, this guy is the complete package.

Holy hell.

chapter 3

Slade

"HEY," I SAY, HOLDING MY hand out to the blonde. It's the same girl from the picture. Her blue eyes are striking, so much so that the picture did not do them justice. She's a fucking knockout. "Slade, it's nice to meet you," I add, remembering my manners.

"H-Hi, Austyn." She places her hand in mine.

Her hands are soft, a contrast to mine that are rough from the last thirteen weeks of hardcore training. I'm standing there holding her hand, staring into those ice-blue eyes, when Savannah comes around the corner.

"Hey, what a nice surprise." She stands on tiptoes and kisses Combs on the cheek. "I see you two have already met." She smirks.

Austyn pulls her hand back and lets it hang at her side. I didn't even realize I was still holding onto her, not that she appeared to be complaining. I don't have a whole lot of experience with this kind of thing. My dating experience is slim to none, but I'm wise enough to know attraction. I can see it in the way her eyes darken, and I can feel it in the crotch of my jeans.

"What are you doing here?" Savannah asks.

"Can't a guy just stop and see his girl?" Combs grins.

Her eyes light up and her smile grows wider. I chance a glance at Austyn and find her eyes on me. Quickly, she turns away. I don't. I take her in. She's about a foot shorter than me, with blonde hair just below her shoulders, and a tight little body if her black pants and T-shirt are any indication. And then there are her eyes. Ice-blue and piercing, as if she can see straight into your soul.

"Laying it on a little thick there, B." Austyn busts his chops.

"I wanted to see you," he says with a laugh, pulling Savannah into him. "And we were hungry. I also needed to see this one." He puts an arm around Austyn and tugs her to him as well.

I envy him, this easygoing banter. It's not something I've experienced. Admittedly, I'm suddenly really glad I agreed to come home with him. When Austyn glances my direction and gives me a shy smile, I know it's the right decision.

"We missed you," Austyn tells him. "This one," she points to Savannah, "has been a pain in my ass without you here."

I can visibly see Combs soften at her words. His shoulders slack, and he gets this dopey smile on his face. He places his lips next to Savannah's ear. Her face turns a slight shade of pink. Whatever it is he's saying to her, it's affecting her. "Love you," I hear him whisper before pulling away.

"All right, lovebirds, we have to get back to work. You guys grab a table, and one of us will be over in a minute," Austyn says, waving her hand around the dining room.

Combs kisses his girl quickly on the lips and motions for me to follow him. He leads me to the very back of the dining room to a small booth in the corner. "Everything is good here," he says, handing me a menu.

"We have a diner similar to this back home. The small mom-and-pop places are always the best."

"It doesn't hurt that the help is easy on the eyes." He jokes, holding his fist out for me to bump.

"What can I get ya to drink?" Austyn says, stopping next to

our booth. Combs looks over her shoulder, and she laughs. "She's in the back. She had an order come up. We're both going to be taking care of y'all," she explains.

Combs orders and then she turns those blue eyes to me. "Slade?" The sound of my name from her lips, that soft southern drawl of hers, has my cock twitching in my pants. "I'll have the same," I say. I have no idea what Combs ordered, but I'm not a picky eater. The entire time he was ordering, I was watching her. I guess I should have been paying attention. She smiles at me, then turns to put in our orders. I watch her go, unable to take my eyes off her. It's not until she disappears behind the swinging door that I do.

"She's a looker," Combs comments.

"She's a fucking knockout."

He nods in agreement. "Austyn is one of the good ones, like Savvy. They're the kind of girl you take home to meet the folks."

I raise my eyebrows, silently questioning him.

"I just mean, she's not one to play around. She's got a good head on her shoulders and is worth more."

"What are you saying exactly?"

He sighs. "Listen, Austyn, Savannah, and I grew up together. She's not a fling type of girl. I see you watching her, and I don't blame you; she's gorgeous. I mean she's not Savannah." He smiles. "I don't know what you're thinking, but I don't want you to use her while we're here."

"That's not who I am," I tell him. Of course, we've only known each other for thirteen weeks, but he knows me, well, just what I've told him. The only information I've given him about my dating life is that I'm single.

"I just wanted you to know. I'm not against you starting something with her, but you need to keep in mind that she's special. They both are," he says, just as Savannah stops next to our table and drops off our drinks.

"Here you go." She smiles brightly. "Austyn is coming with us tonight. What time do you want to leave and where do you want to meet?" she asks Combs.

"We'll pick y'all up. I'm thinking around seven."

"That works. That will give us time to take a nap and get ready. I'll just have Austyn come to my place."

"That works, babe," Combs tells her.

"Your food should be out soon." With that, she turns and walks away.

"I've been thinking," he says, once she's out of earshot, "I want to ask Savannah to marry me."

My eyes widen. "You're eighteen," I remind him.

"Nineteen next week," he counters with a smirk.

I laugh. "What are the chances that we have the same fucking birthday?"

"Right? I thought you were fucking with me until you showed me your paperwork," he says with a laugh.

"I know you're not used to big celebrations, but this year, we're doing it up big."

"Don't even tell them it's mine too." It's his day and his family's. I'm not moving in on that.

"Hell yes, I am. That just makes it even better."

"So, proposing?" I change the subject.

"I know we're young, but fuck, I love that girl. I hate that I'm going to be gone for five months and then, who knows where we'll end up. I can't bring her with me unless we're married."

"Is that what she wants? You said she's in college, right?"

"Yeah, but damn, man, I want her as close as I can get her."

"You got a ring?" "Not yet."

"That might be your first step there, bud." I smirk.

"What did we miss?" Savanah asks, placing a plate in front of each of us.

"Nothing, babe," Combs says.

"Uh-huh." She chuckles. "One of us will be back with some refills."

"Slacker." Austyn hip-checks Savannah while laughing.

"Here you go." She sets a fresh glass of sweet tea in front of us. "Good help is hard to find." She tilts her head toward Savannah and winks.

"Hey!" Savannah lightly smacks her arm, causing both girls to laugh.

I can't take my eyes off Austyn. Her blue eyes are sparkling with her laughter, her smile lighting up her face. I'm transfixed by her beauty.

"Let us know if you need anything else," Savannah says, and just like that, they're walking away.

"I think you're drooling." Combs snorts.

I grab my napkin and wipe at my chin, just in case. "Do you blame me?" No point in denying it.

"Not at all, my man, not at all."

We finish up our lunch with a few more visits from the girls to see if we need anything. Savannah brings us our bills, and we both hand her money, telling her to keep the change.

"We'll split it." She smiles. "See you soon." She blows a kiss to Combs and waves to me.

I wave back, then seek out Austyn. She's standing at the counter, talking to an older gentleman as she pours him a cup of coffee. She must sense me staring. Her eyes lift to mine, and she gives me a small wave before focusing her attention back on her customer.

"You'll see her tonight." Combs pulls my attention from the blonde beauty.

With one more quick glance, I follow him out of the diner.

chapter 4
Austyn

WHEN SAVANNAH TOLD ME BRANDON'S friend was hot, I believed her. I did. But I didn't expect... that. Tall, broad shoulders, dark hair, intense dark eyes, and five o'clock shadow.... That's every girl's dream guy, but on Slade, it's so much more. It's the intensity in his eyes. The way they follow me, assessing me. It's hot as hell.

"So?" Savannah stands next to me at the counter. I know it's been killing her that I spent time with Mr. Harris. He stopped in for lunch; it's not uncommon for him to do so. He's a lonely old man, and if I have a few extra minutes, I give them to him while he's here. I feel bad for him.

"So what?" I play dumb. I can't look at her while I wipe off the counter. I know she'll see right through me.

"Don't give me that, Austyn." She lightly smacks my arm.

"Fine," I groan, as if it's an inconvenience to admit. "He's hot."

"Uh-huh, tell me more," she says sweetly, causing me to laugh.

"He's hot. He likes double bacon cheeseburgers, fries, and sweet tea," I rattle off their order.

"Okay, if that's all, I suppose you don't want to hear that he couldn't keep his eyes off you," she goads.

"Whatever," I say, knowing it's true. I could feel his stare. Although, he wasn't the only one who had a hard time looking away. Thankfully, the diner started to pick up, so I placed all my focus there. It could have been embarrassing.

"So what are you wearing tonight?"

"Honestly, I don't know. I wasn't worried about it until now, so thanks for that."

"You're welcome," she sing-songs. "Just fulfilling my duty as best friend."

"This is crazy," I tell her. "He's leaving in a few days. There's no point trying to impress him." Even as I say the words, I know I'm full of it. "Where's he even from? Somewhere far away from Kentucky, I'm sure."

"I didn't ask, but that doesn't mean he can't be your soul mate."

"Really, Savvy?" I laugh at her. "I wonder how your brain works sometimes."

"Stranger things have happened. Besides, I have this feeling," she admits.

"A feeling? Like the time you told me that there was no way your parents would find us sneaking out to go the field party with Brandon? Or how about the time you had a feeling that your parents were going to be gone all night, so you snuck Brandon into the house and up to your room? Like those feelings?" I ask her.

"This one is different." That's what she always says.

"No more soul-mate talk. He's a hot guy, who's here for a short visit. End of. I'm tagging along tonight so that he doesn't have to be the third wheel with you and B."

"What are you wearing?" she asks again.

"Ugh! Fine. I'm going to wear my skinny jeans, my black Hunter boots, and my gray and black sweater."

She nods. "That works. It might be chilly so don't bring a

jacket. Slade will have to keep you warm." She grins and waggles her eyebrows.

"I'm not going to do anything that's going to put him or me in an uncomfortable position. You just focus on your man and getting as much time in with him as you can before he leaves."

Her face falls at the mention of him leaving. "Yeah, this small break he has is going to fly by."

"I'm sorry," I say, pulling her into a hug. "I know it's hard on you, on both of you. I shouldn't have brought it up."

"No, it's fine." She pulls out of my hug. "We talked about it before he enlisted. This is his dream. I support him. It's hard to be away from him, but this is the path that we chose, together. No way could I have asked him to stay, to not chase his dream."

"Come on, let's get through the rest of our shift, and then we can go take a quick nap before your big date tonight."

"Our big date," she corrects me, and I roll my eyes. This causes her to break out into a fit of laughter. Customers turn their heads to look at us, but we pay them no attention. Once we get ourselves under control, we return to work. Luckily, we stay steadily busy, and the time flies by.

"You coming to my house to get ready?"

"I can. I just need to run home and grab some clothes first. I'll probably just go ahead and take a quick power nap, try to anyway, then head over."

"Sounds like a plan. Brandon said they'll be at my place at seven."

Hitting the button on my phone, I see that's it's four now. "I'll be there around five thirty, if not a little before."

"Sounds good." She turns to walk toward her car, and I head toward mine. On the outside, I'm cool, calm, and collected. On the inside, I'm freaking out just a little. Okay, a lot that I'll be hanging out with him tonight. "Austyn," she calls out. Stopping, I turn to look at her. "Make sure you wear some sexy undies." She winks and turns back around. Shaking my head, I climb into my car and head home. This favor I agreed to is turning out for my benefit after all.

No matter how hard I try, I can't sleep. The excitement of tonight is keeping me awake. After thirty minutes, I give up. Sifting through my closet, I pull out the black and gray sweater and my skinny jeans. I pull my black Hunter boots from the rack on the closet floor. I grab a T-shirt and boxers to sleep in, just in case I end up sleeping at Savannah's, not sure what she and Brandon have planned. They might be extending their night. In the event that doesn't happen, it's better to be prepared.

Tossing my sleep clothes on the bed with the others, I grab a clean bra and underwear for tomorrow, leaving me to decide which set I'll be wearing tonight. I know no one will see them but me—I push aside Savannah's words swirling through my head—but they make me feel confident, pretty, maybe even a little sexy. Reaching into the back of my drawer, I pull out my black lace matching bra and panty set from Victoria's Secret. I have a few sets of these, but I like sticking with the black theme. It's been a while since I've added to my collection. Maybe Savannah and I need to plan a trip to the mall to remedy that situation.

I also grab my makeup bag. Savannah will have everything else that I need. I pack everything in my Vera Bradley tote and open my bedroom door to find my little brother, Dawson, with his hand raised, ready to knock.

"Hey, Mom wants to know if you're going to be here for dinner?" he asks.

Dawson is eight, ten years younger than my eighteen. "No." I reach out and run my fingers, through his sandy-blond hair. "Savannah and I are going to the county fair."

"I want to go," he whines.

"Sorry, bud. How about I take you later this week? Deal?"

His eyes light up with excitement. "You promise?"

"I promise." I hold my hand out for him to shake. He shakes my hand up and down so hard I think my arm might fall off. He giggles when I let my whole body shake as if he's the one doing it.

"Thanks, Aust," he says, letting go of my hand and wrapping his arms around my waist.

"You're welcome." My parents tried for years to have another baby after I was born without luck. They finally gave up, believing it just wasn't in the cards for them, and a few years later, Dawson surprised us all. I have to admit, being a big sister is pretty cool.

"Come on," I say, releasing him. Dawson flies down the stairs, which prompts me, and my mom, yelling for him to slow down before he falls and breaks his neck. "Hey, Mom," I greet her.

"Hey, sweetie." She eyes the bag on my shoulder. "Going to Savannah's?"

"Yeah, Brandon's home so we're all going to the county fair."

"That's right. How is he?"

"He's good. He came to the diner today for lunch with a friend of his he brought home with him from boot camp."

"Good. You make sure you tell him to stop by and say hello before he leaves again. How long is he home for?"

"I think Savannah said ten days. Then he goes back for some other kind of training. I'm not really sure."

"So this other guy, is he cute?" Mom asks.

I can feel my face heat, which is a dead giveaway. "I don't know if cute covers it," I tell her honestly.

"Tell Brandon to bring his friend too," she says with a laugh.

"Who's bringing who where?" Dad asks, coming in from the garage.

"Brandon's home and he brought a friend with him. How was work?" she asks, turning to face him. He places a kiss on her lips.

"Good. How is he?" Dad asks me.

"He seems well. Happy to be home and see Savvy, I'm sure. We're going to the fair tonight."

"You kids be safe. Will you be home tonight?" he asks.

"Not sure yet. I might stay at Savannah's. I'll be sure to call or text and let you know for sure."

"Be safe," Dad says again, rounding the counter and pulling me into a hug. "Love you, Aust."

"Love you, too, Dad. I better go. Love you, Mom, Daws," I say to them. A chorus of "I love you, toos," follows me out the door.

When I pull into Savannah's driveway, she rushes out the front door. "I couldn't sleep," she confesses, grabbing my bag from the back seat.

"Yeah, I gave up. I need a shower," I tell her.

"Spare room is all yours. I'm going to hop in too. Have you eaten yet?"

"No, I just figured we would eat at the fair."

"Good. That's what I was thinking too. Mom and Dad just left to go out to dinner with some friends, but I could throw us a frozen pizza in the oven or something."

"I'm okay for now. Just a shower. I need to wash the diner off me." Pulling my shirt to my nose, I give it a sniff. I smell like coffee. Not necessarily a bad smell if you drink coffee. I, however, do not.

"Me too."

Following Savannah inside, I make my way to the spare bedroom. Savannah is an only child, so this room is for guests, which more often than not is me. I take my time showering, knowing we're early. I'm just stepping out of the shower when Savvy is banging on the bathroom door.

"You okay in there?" she yells through the door.

"Yeah, what's up?"

"Will you curl my hair?"

"Sure, let me get dressed and I'll be right over." I make quick work of drying off and getting dressed. Standing back, I take a look in the full-length mirror that's hanging on the back of the bathroom door. I turn left and right, then all the way around, looking over my shoulder. Savannah says these jeans make my ass look good; it's why I bought them. I can't help but wonder what Slade will think. Shaking my head to detour that train of thought, I slip my sweater over my head, which is not an easy feat with my hair still wrapped up in a towel.

I find Savannah sitting at the vanity in her room, the curling iron plugged in and ready to go. "It always looks better when you do it," she says in greeting.

"It looks the exact same as when you do." I smile her.

"I just want to look good for him, you know? It hit me on the way home, really hit me that I only have a few short days with him. I want to make the most of them, and part of that is looking good for him." Although she tries to hide it, I can hear the sadness in her voice. She's not her chipper, bubbly self, and I hate that for her.

I pick up the curling iron and start adding loose curls to her hair. "Savvy, you know he loves you, right? Not just "oh that's my girl, and I love her," you two are the real deal."

"I know he does, and I love him, too. I want him to be excited about what he has to come home to."

"What's going on with you?" My brows dip in concern, and I place a hand on her shoulder, squeezing lightly. "Where's all this coming from?" When Brandon left for boot camp, I expected this kind of reaction. She surprised me with how well she dealt with him being gone. I know thirteen weeks of no contact was hard for her, but she never let it show.

"This is hard, Aust. So damn hard. I did okay, you know? After a few days, I adjusted, and I know I will this time too, but now my heart knows what it feels like to be away from him." My heart squeezes in my chest at her admission. Reaching out, I wrap my arms around her and hug her tight.

"You've not had any time to spend time with him since he's been home. Last night it was his parents and Slade. Today we were working. Tonight, you will get some time with him. I'll entertain Slade so you can soak up as much of Brandon as you need to. When he leaves, I'll be here to lend a shoulder, or distract you, whatever you need. This is a great thing he's doing, but that extends to you, too."

Her eyes find mine in the mirror of the vanity. "How is being the girlfriend of a marine a good thing?" she questions.

"He needs you, Savvy. He's fighting for his country, but also to keep those he loves safe. That's you. You give him something to fight for, something to come home to. He knows he doesn't have to worry about you sleeping around. Remember all those online forums we found when he first left for boot camp? The distance is hard on a relationship, only a love like what you two have will beat the odds." Tears well up in her eyes. I was worried the forums would scare her, but instead, I think she found strength. I can still remember one of them she read to me. It basically said that even though your marine is away, you're their rock, their foundation. They need to know their foundation is solid to do what they do. Savvy took that to heart and was a rock star the last thirteen weeks. "Now," I change the subject, "how many curls are we talking?"

She laughs, knowing exactly what I'm trying to do. "Just a few. I just want a little bounce."

"I mean, maybe you should be talking to Brandon about your bounce, that's really not up to me." I school my features, trying my hardest not to laugh. When Savvy bursts out laughing, I join her. I finish her hair and then go back across the hall to blow dry mine. I'm leaving mine straight tonight. I'm just me. I should probably add some curl too, but I don't want it to look like I'm trying too hard. Besides, I meant what I said earlier. He's leaving when Brandon does, hell, maybe even sooner for all I know. No point in starting something we can't finish. My shoulders drop and some of my earlier excitement diminishes. The gorgeous marine is leaving in a few days. That pretty much sums up my luck with guys. The good ones are always taken, and the ones with potential are just passing through.

chapter 5

Slade

COMBS PULLS UP IN FRONT of a small two-story house just outside of town. There are two cars in the driveway, both nicer than anything I've ever driven. Hell, this truck I'm sitting in is my dream truck. It's ten years old, but it's a four-door Ford F-350, a man's truck.

"You coming?" he asks, parking the truck and climbing out.

Not wanting to look like a tool, I follow him. I know Austyn and I are not on a date, but this kind of makes it feel that way. Not that I would know; there was no time for dating when I had an ill grandmother to take care of. I know it's not a date; she's just there as filler to keep me from being the third wheel. I'm sure of it. I know this, yet my palms are still sweaty. Quickly, I wipe them on my jeans just as Combs knocks on the front door.

"Come in!" a female voice yells.

I follow him inside and come face-to-face with both of the girls. Savannah jumps into Combs's arms while Austyn and I stand there just staring at each other. "Hey," she says finally.

"Hey," I say, shoving my hands in my pockets.

"You ladies ready to go?" Combs asks, his arms still locked around Savannah.

"All set," Austyn tells him, and takes a step toward me.

Taking that as my cue, I turn on my heel and walk back outside. I walk straight to the passenger side back door and open it. Turning, I smile at Austyn and tilt my head toward the truck.

"Thank you," she whispers as she passes me, and climbs into the truck. I make my way to the other side and climb into the back seat beside her.

"Slade, I could have sat back there," Savannah says once they're both inside the truck.

"No worries. You two have been separated long enough." Her face softens and she mouths, "Thank you," before turning around in her seat. I watch as Combs reaches over and grabs her hand.

A smile lights up her face, and I know in this moment, that all the stories I've heard about this girl are true. Combs talked about her nonstop, but one thing that stood out to me was the way he described her smile. He claimed that one look from her, with that smile on her face, and he would give her the world, just to keep it there. I thought it sounded kind of sappy, but I didn't question him. I've never had a girlfriend, so what do I know? Seeing her face light up when she looks at him, though, not only do I get it, I envy it. What would that feel like, to have a love like that? To not be alone in the world? Maybe one day I'll be lucky enough to find out.

"So, Slade," Savannah turns to face me, as much as her seat belt will let her, "you have county fairs where you're from?"

"We do, but I have a feeling that the county fairs I've been to are nothing like the one we're about to see." This causes everyone to laugh.

"Where are you from?" the sweet voice next to me asks.

"Michigan, just outside of Detroit."

She nods. "I've been to Michigan on vacation with my family."

"Yeah? What part?"

"We got a house on Lake Michigan, right on the water. It was nice."

"Slade's never seen the ocean," Savannah chimes in, remembering our conversation at dinner last night.

"No?" Austyn asks.

I shrug. "Just never had the opportunity."

"Hopefully one day, in your travels with the Marines, you'll be able to."

"I'm not sure, but that would be nice."

"We should plan a trip," Savannah says. "Spend a week at the beach."

"Savvy, babe, it's September." Combs laughs.

"It's warm in Florida," she counters, sticking her tongue out at him.

"Babe, we'll be gone for five months," he reminds her gently.

"Yeah," she concedes. It's obvious by the somber tone of her voice it's not something she's looking forward to. I know for a fact it's been eating at Combs as well.

"Maybe we can plan it in between? I don't know how much leave we get after SOI, but maybe we can figure something out. What about school?"

"At that time we'll be out for winter break, but it doesn't matter. We can make it up, right, Austyn?"

"Wait? By *we,* you're including me in this little adventure?"

"Of course I am. Both of you," she says, looking at me. My pulse races thinking about spending more time with her. On the beach, in a bikini, hell yes. Sign me up.

"Yeah, we can make it up," Austyn readily agrees.

There's relief in Savannah's eyes. Glancing at Austyn out of the corner of my eye, I can see that she sees it too. She smiles, knowing she's just given her best friend an opportunity to spend the week at the beach with her boyfriend. Well, possibly fiancé; I'm not sure what Combs has planned. I'm don't know why she needs her best friend by her side, but she's happy to know that's the outcome either way.

Pulling into the fair, we park in a big field. I quickly climb out of the truck and hurry to the passenger side and open both the front and rear door for the girls.

"Reeves, man, you're making me look bad," Combs jokes as he saunters around the front of the truck, taking his sweet-ass time.

Savannah laughs as she rushes toward him, linking her arm through his. "Thank you, Slade," Austyn says, stepping back so I can shut the door.

"Y'all have everything you need? I'm gonna lock it." Everyone checks and gives him the okay, and then we're off. We trek through the field to the main gate. The sounds of the rides, kids laughing and screaming float through the air. The smells that make a fair what they are assault my senses.

"Fair food." Austyn moans from beside me.

"You hungry?" I ask her.

"Yeah, but even if I wasn't, I'd be indulging," she says, laughing. "The fair only comes around once a year, and I have to get my fill."

"What's your favorite?" I ask.

"All of it." She throws me a grin. "I mean, how am I supposed to choose? French fries with vinegar, and ketchup, caramel corn, candied apples, deep fried Oreos, elephant ears, pork tenderloin sandwiches, mmmm," she moans, causing my dick to twitch.

"That's all?"

"No, that's just the start, and oh, freshly squeezed lemonade," she says, stopping beside said lemonade stand.

I'm thankful for the break so I can adjust myself. When she steps up to order, as discreetly as I can, I make things more comfortable. Combs and Savannah keep walking, and I should probably tell them that we stopped, yell ahead to them, but I don't. I'll take all the time I can get with this girl. She's down to earth, not at all like the girls I've been around. She doesn't think she's better than everyone around her. She's just her, just Austyn, and that's endearing as hell.

"You want one?" She turns to look at me.

"Why not," I say, and reach into my pocket for my wallet. She waves me off and hands me a long, slender cup with lemons all over it, and a yellow bendy straw. "Thank you, let me give you some money," I offer again.

"Nah, you can get the next round," she says, placing that bendy straw in her mouth.

I can't take my eyes off her lips as they wrap around it. Her cheeks pull in as she sucks and just like that, I'm no longer twitching, I'm hard as a rock. I don't know what it is about her, but she's affecting me. Stirring up all kinds of emotions I've never felt before. "What next?" I ask, pushing myself to not think about how sexy she looks standing before me.

"Hmm, I'm thinking pork tenderloin and fries." She looks around us, and I know who she's looking for.

"They went on ahead."

She shrugs. "Their loss. You ready?" She turns and starts walking in the opposite direction of where Combs and Savannah just disappeared into the crowd.

"Lead the way," I tell her. What she doesn't know is that I would follow her anywhere. I don't know her, but my body's reaction to her tells me that I need to.

We walk down the strip—as she calls it—several people, mostly guys, call out to her. She gives them a wave but keeps on walking. "So I'm thinking we split up," she suggests when we reach the end of the strip. "Over there," she points to the right, "are the fries, and there," she points to the left, "are the sandwiches. Divide and conquer. Meet back here." She points in front of us as some picnic tables that are set up.

"What's back there?" I point just beyond the picnic tables.

"That's where they hold the demolition derby and the tractor pulls."

"You a fan?" I ask her.

She shrugs. "I've watched a time or two with my dad and little brother."

"How old?"

"My brother?"

I nod.

"He's eight. How about you, any siblings?"

"Only child as far as I know," I say, letting that last part slip.

She raises her eyebrows in question. She doesn't ask, just waits for me to tell her. "My grandma raised me from the time I was twelve. I haven't seen my parents since. So, as far as I know, it's just me."

"Their loss," she says. "Now, you go left for the sandwiches. I'll go right for the fries. You have to get the vinegar-to-ketchup ratio just right." She smiles up at me.

I'm grateful she takes my words at face value and doesn't pry for more details. It's not something I like to talk about. "Here." I pull my wallet out and try to hand her some money.

"You can buy dessert," she says, walking backward toward the fry booth.

I stand there and watch her go. I don't move until she makes it to the booth and finds her place in line. Even then I have to force myself to pull my eyes from her to go order our sandwiches. I order four, not sure how hungry she is. I know I can eat two easily on my own.

"You ready for an Austyn fair fry experience?" she asks, once I join her at the picnic table.

"You hold the secret to fair fries?" I smile at her.

"I told you, it's the ratio of ketchup to vinegar that makes all the difference." She slides a small cup of fries my way. "Go on." She nods toward the cup.

Not willing to disappoint her, I grab a couple of fries and pop them in my mouth. The combination of flavors burst on my tongue, and I have to admit, she's onto something. "Good," I say, swallowing and taking a drink of my lemonade. "Here." I push two sandwiches toward her. "I wasn't sure how hungry you were."

"Starving, but one is plenty. I have to save room. This is just the start of the list," she reminds me.

"Take the other one home to your little brother," I tell her.

She looks up from unwrapping her sandwich and smiles softly. "That's sweet of you. We'll see if the others want it, or you can have it."

"Two and fries is plenty, and it sounds like I've got more to try. I'll be paying for this when we get to SOI. I'm going to need to go for a run in the morning to work this off."

"What's SOI?" she asks, taking a big bite of her sandwich.

"School of Infantry."

"It's a great thing you're doing, serving our country. Thank you."

I nod. I have my reasons for doing what I do. Sure, I want to serve my country, but the Marines are giving me something I need, a family. A camp of brothers. "What's next?" I ask, pushing past the subject. I don't like to, nor do I want to talk about my past. Not right now. I just want to spend some time with her. She makes me feel... normal. That's not something I've had much of growing up.

"I say we walk around, let this settle a little before we dive into anything else. I don't want to get sick."

"I think that's a wise decision."

We make small talk when we can, several people stop by our table to say hi, again mostly guys, some just shout out her name as they walk by. "You seem to know everyone."

"Downfall of a small town."

"I don't know. It does seem to have its appeal." This is unlike our fair in Michigan. Then again, it's been years since I've been. The first year I went to live with Gran, she took me. I rode rides, and we shared cotton candy and caramel corn. By the next year, when the fair rolled around, her health had declined so much, it was too hard for her to walk around. She declined fast.

"It's not bad, makes you wonder what else is out there though. I'm sure the Marines will take you places you never imagined you'd see."

"Yeah, some I'm sure I'll be fine never seeing," I admit

quietly. "I'm hoping it's a good mix of both."

Her face softens at my words and she offers me a small smile. Her cell then rings, interrupting the moment, and I stand to gather our trash and throw it away while she answers.

"You left us," she says in greeting. I don't hear the other end of the conversation, but when she says, "We're good," I stand a little taller, glad to know that she's having at least an okay time with me. "We've already hit up the food booths. We're going to walk around a little then go for round two." She pauses. "Yeah, we might. I'll ask Slade and text you."

"Everything okay?"

"Yeah, that was Savvy. She wants to know where we wandered off to. They're going to go back to the grandstands and watch the demolition derby later. She wanted to know if we wanted to watch it with them."

"I'm yours for the night. Whatever you want to do is what we'll do."

"I say we take a walk." She steps next to me and links her arm through mine, leading us through the crowd.

If I stood taller when she said she was good, I'm as tall as the fucking Jolly Green Giant now that she's linked her arm through mine. She doesn't let go when people she knows calls out to her. When the guys yell out her name, this time, envy doesn't raise its ugly head. I'm the one she's with. Pride fills my chest to have her on my arm. It's a feeling I could get used to.

chapter 6

Austyn

I DON'T KNOW WHAT CAUSED me to slip my arm through Slade's, but he didn't pull away, and I like the warmth being close to him provides. "How do you feel about rides?" I ask him.

"Rides? As in, do I ride them?" he clarifies.

"Yeah."

"Honestly, I haven't been to a fair since I was twelve. That was my first and last time there. I went on a few rides."

"What about an amusement park?"

"Nope," he says popping the p making me smile.

"Are you afraid of heights?" I ask.

He turns his head to look at me. "I'm a marine," he smirks.

My face heats with embarrassment. I knew that. "Well, then you and I have a date with some rides. Which one do you want to ride first?"

"You choose."

"Hmmm," I ponder the idea. "The Scrambler!" I say excitedly. "I love it. Wait, you're good with spinning, right?" It's a legit question. Every year I see at least ten different people stumbling off and vomiting.

He chuckles. "Yeah, I'm good with spinning."

Tugging on his arm, I pull us to the line for the Scrambler. "You want inside or outside?"

"Is one better than the other?"

"Oh, my dear, dear Slade. The enjoyment you've missed out on." When the gate opens and they let us in, I rush to an open cart. I'm excited to share this with him. From the little I've learned, his childhood was lacking in the fun department. My heart breaks for him, but I don't show it. I'm sure he doesn't want my pity. The next best thing is showing him some of the things he missed out on. Getting to experience that with him is a bonus for me.

"Wait, which side is worse?" he asks.

"They're both pretty even. Some say one side is worse than the other, but I've ridden both more times than I can count, and they're both the same."

He nods and climbs in beside me, locking the bar. He's a tall guy, all muscle, and I'm just me, at least a foot shorter than him; I only come up to his shoulders. "I can take it," I tell him when I see the worried look on his face.

"I don't want to hurt you. I'm a big guy. I could squash you." His voice is deep, and his dark eyes are filled with concern.

"It's fine, trust me. This is all in good fun. Promise." I place my hand over his on the bar. It's meant to be comforting, and it is, but it's more than that, especially when he turns his hand over and entwines our fingers. I try not to freak out that he's holding my hand. I mean I've held hands before, but I barely know him. He's all dark and sexy, and is so unlike anyone I've ever met before. Brandon is the only guy who even comes close, but he's never made my insides shake from nervous energy. That's all Slade.

When the ride starts, we begin to spin and pick up speed. When the ride throws Slade into me, he releases his hold on my hand and puts his arm around my shoulders. He holds me next to him as we twirl around and around, back and forth. The chilly September night air washes over us, but I'm not the least bit cold in his embrace. When the ride stops, he releases his hold on me, and I immediately miss his warmth.

"Well?" I ask once we are off the ride.

Looking down at me, he raises his hand and helps smooth out my hair. "Time of my life."

"Right, okay." I look away, breaking our connection. He's giving me all of his attention and that makes me nervous. "Time for the next one. Have you ever been on the Tilt-o-whirl?"

"That one I have ridden."

That's how our night goes, more rides, more laughs, and it's the best time I can ever remember having at the fair. When I take him to the line for the merry-go-round, I thought for sure he would protest. He's a big guy. Nope, he walks straight on and lifts me up onto my horse, and stands behind me. Wrapping one arm around my waist, the other grips the pole, his hand on top of mine. That's how we ride the entire time, with me wrapped up in him and trying to convince myself that the flutter in my chest is from the nostalgia of this ride from when I was a kid. I try to convince myself it has nothing to do with his hold on me or how good it feels.

"One more," I say, pulling him to the Ferris wheel." My intention was to meet Savvy and Brandon back at the demolition derby, but we've been having too much fun. I don't really want our time alone to end.

"What about all this fair food we were supposed to try?" He lightly bumps his shoulder into mine. As the night goes on, he seems to relax more and his smile, it's potent, and threatens to knock me to my knees. Luckily for me, the first time I witnessed it we were standing in line and I was able to lean against the fence for support.

"The fair's here all next week."

He's quiet and standing close to me in line. "Maybe we can come back," he offers.

I link my arm through his and rest my head on his shoulder. "I'd like that." I would. I really like him. In just a few hours, I can tell he's a good guy. I know he's leaving in a matter of days and that he lives in another state, so there's nothing that will come of this. My stomach dips at the thought, but I refuse to allow our short time together to be dragged down by my sadness. Instead, I'm just going to enjoy hanging out with a hot guy who treats me like a human being not a piece of meat. Something most men around here, at least those our age, tend to do. Slade is an anomaly.

When it's our turn to climb into the car, Slade places his hand on the small of my back and lets me go first. Once we're in, he double checks that the bar is locked and then stretches his arm out on the back of the seat. I want him to wrap it around me, but I'll take what I can get.

"This your first time?" I ask.

"Yeah, my gran, she wasn't much for heights."

"So I get to be your first." The words are out of my mouth before I even realize it. My hands go to my mouth to cover it to keep more word vomit from spewing.

"Austyn," he says. I can feel his stare. "Hey," he says softly. Gently, he places his index finger under my chin and guides me to look at him. "I'm glad it's you." He leans in as if he's going to kiss me.

I close my eyes, wanting, waiting for it to happen. Then the car jerks, causing us both to sway along with the car. Opening my eyes, I see that the moment is broken. It's not completely lost though. Slade moves his arm to rest across my shoulders and pulls me next to him. I snuggle in close and enjoy the ride.

As soon as we are off the Ferris wheel, my phone rings. Pulling it out of my pocket, I see Savvy's name light up my screen. "Hey."

"Where are you guys?"

"We just got off the Ferris wheel."

"Are you coming back to the derby?"

"Savvy wants us to come back to the derby," I tell Slade.

"I'm with you," he replies looking at me intently.

"We'll head that way." After ending the call, I slide my phone back in my pocket. Slade surprises me when he offers me his elbow and a smile that I fight hard not to swoon over. I don't hesitate to slide my arm through his. "I'm thinking we stop and get a refill on our lemonade and get an elephant ear. You want to share?"

"We can share."

Making our way to the other side of the fairgrounds, we stop and get refills on our lemonade, and luckily the elephant ear booth is right beside it. Slade refuses to let me pay. I don't argue with him. This isn't a date, not really, but it feels like one. He's sweet and attentive, and... everything I've never had on a date.

Walking in front of the grandstands, I look for Savvy and Brandon. I spot them at the very top and head their way.

"Finally," she says. "We thought y'all were lost."

"Not lost, just enjoying the fair." I take a seat beside her where she sits in front of Brandon, leaning back against him. Slade takes the seat beside Brandon, directly behind me. Turning, I hand him his lemonade, and in turn, he hands me our gigantic elephant ear. "Try it," I say, pushing it back toward him.

"You first," he insists.

Reaching out, I tear off a bite and hold it up to his lips. His dark brown eyes seem to grow darker as he opens and takes the bite I'm offering. His tongue flicks against my fingers, and it takes everything I've got in me to not squirm in my seat.

"Good?" I'm barely able to get the word out.

"Very," he says, and offers me the plate. I tear off another bite and shove it in my mouth and moan at the taste. Too bad we only get these once a year.

"That looks good," Savvy says smirking, and I know she just witnessed me feeding him. I'm never going to hear the end of this.

"You want some?" I offer, not making eye contact.

"Nah, I'm stuffed. We had pork tenderloin and deep-fried pickles."

"Damn," I say, turning to look at Slade. "I forgot about deep fried pickles."

He laughs from deep in his gut. "We'll make a list for our next trip and hit them all," he assures me.

Satisfied, I turn back around.

"Next time?" Savvy whispers, leaning in close.

"Later," I whisper back.

She looks at me hard, making it clear she wants to know all of the juicy details. I grin in response, just before she says, "Take a picture," and pulls away. She hands me her phone and leans back into Brandon. He wraps his arms around her, and they both give me a big cheesy smile. "Thanks," she says when I hand her phone back to her. "Now you two."

I turn to look over my shoulder at Slade. "You up for a picture?"

He nods. "With you." The way he says it leaves zero room for interpretation. He'll take a picture with me. That's it. Butterflies take off in my stomach knowing it's only me.

I scoot back on the bench seat thinking he'll just lean in and we'll take the picture. He surprises me when he opens his legs, and I fall back into him. He rests his chin on my head as Savannah tells us to smile. I smile, but it's not for her. It's for him, for this moment. It's for the way he makes me feel, as if we're together and taking this picture is the highlight of his day. She snaps the picture, and even though I hate to, I move back to a sitting position. "More?" I hold up the elephant ear for Slade to grab another bite, and he does. I turn back around just as quickly; I can't watch his full lips lick the powdered sugar from his fingers. I have no idea what is going on with me. I've never reacted this way to a guy. It's exciting to feel this connection, but it's nerve-racking at the same time.

Savannah distracts me by talking about everyone she's seen since we've been here. Most of our friends from high school went away to college, unlike Savannah and me. We opted to stay close to home. I can hear Slade and Brandon talking behind us, and I try to block it out, but his deep timber calls out to me. I'm so focused on listening to him, but not hearing a word his says that I'm ignoring Savannah.

"It's starting," Savannah says, leaning her shoulder into mine, pointing to where the first heat of the large derby cars are pulling into the arena. She's all chipper and happiness because Brandon is home, as she should be. It's going to be hard on her when he leaves.

The night goes on, and we each pick a car to win each heat. We cheer as if the driver is our best friend. By the time the feature rolls around, I'm exhausted and unable to stifle my yawns. Strong hands grip my shoulders and pull me back. I don't fight it. Instead, I rest between his legs and tilt my head back to look at him.

"You look like you're going to fall asleep any minute."

"I didn't nap."

He glances over at Savannah, who is leaning into Brandon, his arms wrapped around her. "Looks like you're not the only one."

I have to admit, she looks tired but comfortable. I'm certain there is no place she'd rather be, well, unless it was just the two of them. "It's been a long day."

Slade bends down so only I can hear him. "Rest, Austyn. I've got you."

Not able to resist, I relax fully, letting him hold my body weight. The heat from his body surrounding mine takes the chill out of the night air.

When the feature ends, we all stand and stretch. I lead the way down the grandstands, the others following. I get ahead of them and then stand off to the side. I see Savannah and Brandon walking toward me hand in hand. Slade is behind them, hands tucked in his pockets. He doesn't stop until he's next to me.

"Ready to head out?" Brandon asks. Savannah yawns, and he laughs. "Yeah, you're exhausted, babe. Let's get you home." She nods and steps into his hold. He puts his arm around her, and they head off toward the parking lot.

"Ready?" Slade asks, offering me his arm once again.

I'm not so tired that I need to hold onto him, but even if was wide awake, there's no way I'd pass up the chance. I slip my arm into his, and we follow our friends. It's no surprise when we reach the truck that he opens my door for me once again. I also don't miss the fact that Brandon has stepped up his game and opened Savvy's door. The ride back to Savannah's is quiet, just the soft lull of the radio filling the cab of the truck.

"You guys want to come in?" Savannah asks when we pull into the driveway.

Brandon turns to look at Slade and me. "You two cool with that?"

I know her parents aren't going to be home until later, and Savvy desperately misses Brandon. No matter how tired I am, I can't say no. Besides, I'm off tomorrow; we both are. I have a class at eleven, so I'll be able to sleep in. I know that they want time alone to… connect if you will, and I don't want Slade to feel awkward or like a third wheel. Not to mention, I'm not ready for this night to end. I've enjoyed spending time with him, getting to know each other.

"I'm staying here, so I'm good with whatever," I tell him.

"I'm down," Slade says from beside me.

The butterflies in my stomach go crazy at the thought of spending more time with him. Suddenly, I'm not as tired as I thought.

chapter 7

Slade

T RYING TO KEEP MY COOL, I climb out of the truck and head for her door. She's faster than me this time and is hopping down when I get to her. Her foot slips on the running board, and she begins to fall, but I catch her. My hands land on her hips and I hold her close to my body a little longer than I need to. It's as if this is where she is meant to be, in my arms. Always. When I finally help her get steady on her feet, she looks up at me, and I'm captivated. Her blue eyes, crystal in color, are shining in the moonlight. With her blonde hair a halo, she looks like an angel.

"Thanks." Taking that as my cue to let her go, I reluctantly remove my hands from around her waist and step back. "Looks like they left without us," she says, looking over at where Savannah and Combs disappear into the house.

"Lead the way," I say, stepping back so she can close the door. My voice is gravelly as I fight against my desire for her.

We walk side by side up the front steps and onto the porch. Our hands brush against one another we're so close, the warmth of her skin sweeping against mine. That's intentional on my part. I want to reach out and hold her hand, but I'm not exactly sure what the protocol is for this. I'm not exactly an expert on dating, not that this is a date, but I would like to think that if it were, it was a good one. I'm letting her lead me through this, whatever it might be.

"Slowpokes," Savannah says when we join them in the living room. "We're thinking a movie downstairs. Why don't you guys go on down? We'll make some popcorn. There are drinks in the fridge," Savannah says.

Combs pulls her into a kiss, whispers something to her that causes her to giggle, then releases her. "You ready to sit through a chick flick?" he asks me as we head down to the basement.

"Honestly, I'm good with whatever."

"I bet you are. I saw the two of you getting cozy. Remember what I told you," he warns.

"She's nice. Not like most girls I've met."

He nods. "Not sure why someone hasn't snatched her up yet. All the guys in school wanted her. She just never gave them the time of day."

I don't comment and keep my features schooled. Internally, I'm smiling and fist bumping. "Nice place," I say, changing the subject.

"Yeah, we've spent a lot of time down here."

"You two seem solid," I tell him. "Have you thought any more about what you mentioned?" I'm vague on purpose, in case the girls can hear us.

"Yeah, man. I don't—" He looks over his shoulder at the stairs. "—have it yet, so maybe after we finish SOI. I want to find the right one, you know?"

I nod. "I could imagine if I were in your shoes, I'd want the same thing."

"Did you find a movie?" Savannah asks.

"Nope, we were waiting on you," Combs replies swiftly, not missing a beat.

I watch as Savannah sets a big bowl of popcorn on the table and holds her hand out for him. "Y'all make yourselves at home. We're going to go to the back room to… catch up," she says, not taking her eyes off him.

He stands, taking her hand, and follows her down the small hallway. I watch as they disappear behind a door.

"You do know what she means by 'catch up' right?" Austyn laughs. "We better pick an action movie. Something loud, where they blow stuff up."

I throw my head back and laugh. "I'm surprised he's waited this long."

"Me too to be honest. They've always been that way, unable to keep their hands off each other."

"They've been together a long time." It's not really a question, more of a statement. I already know because Combs gave me a play-by-play at boot camp.

"Yeah, they've always just clicked. Anyway, movie. Here." I watch as she pulls up Netflix and then hands me the remote. "Pick something."

"Go ahead." It doesn't matter to me what we watch. Chances are sitting next to her, I'll be too damn distracted to pay attention anyway.

"Let's see what Savvy has on the DVR."

I watch her as she points the remote at the TV and scrolls through the recordings. I'm staring, but I can't seem to help myself. She must feel my stare because she turns to look at me. I'm busted. Quick to recover, I say, "I'm good with anything."

She chuckles. "You're a pretty easygoing guy, Slade."

"Am I?"

"You seem to be."

"I've always been a more... 'to myself' kind of guy."

"I can see that from you, but there's also more. I can't exactly put my finger on it."

"More?"

"Yeah, I'll let you know when I figure it out." She grins.

I smile back at her. Maybe we'll spend more time together while I'm here and she can figure it out. One can only hope. "You serious about going back to the fair?" I ask her.

"Sure, if you want. I have class tomorrow, but it's over at one. After that, we could go. I don't have to work tomorrow either."

I wipe my sweaty palms on my jeans, something that seems to happen quite frequently around her. "We should go, I mean, if you want to." Shit, I sound like a tool.

"You did promise me more junk food," she says. "How's this?" She points to the screen.

"What is it?"

"Lip Sync Battle. They have different celebrities come on and lip sync. It's pretty funny. We can turn up the sound." She motions her head toward the hallway where Savannah and Combs disappeared.

"Sure."

I watch as Austyn pulls a blanket off the back of the couch we're sitting on and throws it over her legs. I want to volunteer to keep her warm, but I barely know this girl. She'd probably junk punch me or something.

"So, I'll pick you up tomorrow after class? I'll need to run home and change so maybe we should touch base when I'm done?"

"I'll be ready," I tell her with conviction.

"Thirteen weeks is a long time. They might be in there for a while."

"Yeah, it is," I agree. "I'm good here watching TV if you have something to do or want to go to bed…." I say the words but inside, I pleading for her to stay down here with me.

"I have nowhere to be," she says. We're both quiet for a few minutes when she speaks again. "Why the Marines?"

I debate on how much to tell her. It's not that I hide my background, plus I already let some details slip earlier, but it's not something I like to talk about either. Although, sitting here in the dimly lit basement with her, all cuddled-up and sleepy-eyed, I find that she's the exception. "Life growing up was… not normal. My parents are both addicts. My grandma, she got custody when I was twelve. It was just the two of us after that."

I'm glazing over the details as I don't want to see pity in her eyes. "Gran passed away two weeks before graduation," I rush on, not wanting to let my emotion take over. "That last week there was a career day for those of us who were still undecided about our futures. There was a marine recruiter there."

"So you signed up, just like that?"

"Gran was all I had, so yeah. They offered me a way to be a part of something, give me a family of sorts. The skills training and the education are all a bonus, too."

"Have you really never heard from your parents?" There's no pity in her eyes, just genuine interest.

"No, not since the day I was taken from them. I don't know where they are or even if they're still alive." I stare at the TV, trying not to think about the last time I saw my parents. It's not something I think about often.

"Hey." I turn to look at her as she pulls her hand out from under the blanket and rests it on my arm. "What you and Brandon and everyone else enlisted are doing is brave and a true sacrifice. It seems like a courageous decision you made to me."

"Don't get me wrong, I agree with you about the others, but for me, I had no one. It was kind of a no-brainer. I have less to lose than the others."

"I'm sure you have friends, a girlfriend maybe?"

My heart stutters at her question, hoping she's asking for more reasons than general curiosity. "Nope. I was always the scrawny, dirty kid with clothes that didn't fit growing up. When Gran got custody, that changed. I gained weight, had clothes that were clean and fit, but kids are cruel and don't forget, you know? I stayed to myself during school, and at night, I went home and took care of Gran."

"Was she sick?" she asks softly.

"Yeah, bad heart. It was hard for her to get around. I would make us dinner, do the grocery shopping, laundry, and cleaning. Whatever we needed done."

"Most guys our age don't even know how to do laundry. I

assume you're my age," she says.

"Eighteen, nineteen next week. Combs, I mean, Brandon and I have the same birthday."

"Really? How cool is that?"

I can't help but smile at her enthusiasm. "Yeah, it's pretty cool."

"So you'll be here then, for your birthday?"

"Yeah, I'm here until we leave for SOI."

"So you get to learn to shoot guns and stuff?" she asks. I raise my eyebrows in questions and she grins. "I know how to use the Internet," she defends.

"Something like that." I grin at her. The door to the room Combs and Savannah disappeared into opens.

"I love this show," Savannah says, taking a seat on the other couch. Combs sits right next to her and pulls her into him.

"Done already?" I tease them.

"Oh, we're not done, just taking a break." Brandon smirks.

That's how we spend the next couple of hours. Savannah's parents come home and seem nice. They came downstairs to say hello, and that was it. We watch what has to be a DVR of every episode of Lip Sync Battle. We don't leave until both of the girls are sound asleep. I watch as Combs kisses his girl on the cheek before standing and covering her with a blanket. He doesn't seem to be upset that his plans for a short break were changed by her falling asleep. I make sure that Austyn is covered as well. Although I forego the kiss, I wish I didn't have to.

"Austyn and I are going back to the fair tomorrow," I tell Combs on the way back to his place.

He glances over at me, before turning his attention back to the road. "Taking one for the team," he says, chuckling.

"Something like that."

"Thanks, I appreciate it."

"Yep." I don't offer any information, and he doesn't ask. He's already given me the speech. Not that he needed to. Anyone who spends any kind of time with Austyn would know she's not just your average girl. When we get back to his place, I mumble goodnight before closing myself in the guest room. Sleep evades me as I picture the blonde-haired blue-eyed angel. When I do finally drift off, she's still all I see.

chapter 8
Austyn

I WOKE UP THIS MORNING with a stiff neck, and it's been a pain in my ass all damn day. I had to forgo my morning run because of it. To make matters worse, I was rushing and running late for class since Savannah and I stayed up late last night with the guys. When I got to class, the auditorium was full, meaning I had to sit down front. The professor decided to use the projector, and of course, it was as high as the damn thing would go on the wall. This means I had to tilt my head back to look at it. Yeah, not a good day.

As I'm walking out to my car, my phone rings. Looking at the screen, I see it's Brandon. "Hey, stranger," I greet him.

"Uh, hey, Austyn, it's Slade."

Damn, that voice. "Hey, Slade. What's up?"

"I just wanted to see if we're still good for the fair later on, or a movie or something? I just want to be able to tell Co—Brandon he's off the hook for entertaining me."

"Old habits, huh?" I ask him.

"What?"

"Calling him by his last name."

"Oh, yeah, it's a hard habit to break."

"I know him both ways, so it's all good," I laugh. "I think a movie is out, I have a stiff neck, I must have slept wrong last night. Unless of course, we can get the very back row."

"We don't have to do anything," he backpedals. "I just thought, you know, since I'm the odd man out and Brandon brought me home to be nice, that I could give him and his girl a night together without me tagging along, but I know he won't leave me here alone. His parents are great, and all, but I know he won't," he rambles on. If I didn't know any better, I'd think he's nervous.

"Why are you using Brandon's phone?" I blurt out the question, my own nerves getting the best of me.

"I don't have your number."

"We'll have to fix that," I say, trying not to let the excitement show in my voice. I don't want to sound too eager.

"Yeah," he says huskily. "We need to fix that for sure."

"The fair?" I ask him, needing to get this conversation back on track and my reaction to him in check.

"Definitely the fair."

If he only knew the things his sexy voice made come to mind. "So, I'll swing by Brandon's and pick you up around what? Seven?" This gives me time to take a quick nap, shower, and shave—you know, just in case.

"That sounds great."

"I'll be there at seven."

"I'll see you soon, Austyn."

He doesn't wait for me to reply; instead, the line goes dead. Climbing into my car, I look at my reflection in the rearview mirror. My eyes are shining and the smile that tips my lips is unmistakable. This day is looking up after all.

I wait until I'm home to text Savannah.

Me:	Slade and I are going back to the fair tonight.
Savvy:	So I heard. I knew there was something there.
Me:	Just giving the lovebirds a night alone.

Me:	You're welcome.
Savvy:	Excuses! But I love you for it.
Me:	ove you, too. I'm picking him up at Brandon's at seven.
Savvy:	You're the best! I can't wait for some time alone with him. Just the two of us.
Me:	Have fun!
Savvy:	Don't do anything I wouldn't do.
Me:	LOL! You know better.

I've listened to Savannah all these years talk about how great sex is. I'm envious of what she has with Brandon; she was lucky enough to be in love her first time. Those two are the real deal. It's not that I'm saving myself for marriage or anything. I've just never really been serious enough about a guy to get to that point. I refuse to have a random hook-up just to mark it off the list. There's only one first time. I want it to mean something.

As luck would have it, Savannah is so wrapped up in Brandon — as she should be — she didn't question me when I told her that Slade and I made plans to head back to the fair tonight. I can imagine she was wearing a knowing smile when she read my text. Lady luck is definitely on my side. My best friend can and has always been able to see right through me. I don't really know what I'm feeling about Slade and seeing him again. I just know he's a really nice guy, easy on the eyes, and the idea of spending more time with him makes me giddy with excitement.

How I make it through class today is beyond me. I don't remember one single part of the lecture. I groan internally, knowing I'm going to have to read over the chapter and ask for notes. No matter how hard I tried to focus, I just couldn't, not with knowing that in just a few hours, I'd be spending more time with him.

When I walk in the front door, the house is quiet. Mom and Dad are both at work. My stomach growls so I make a quick sandwich. It's not as good, as the fair food that is calling my name, but it will hold me over. I attempt to settle down for a nap, but my mind keeps racing with thoughts of Slade. When the alarm on my phone alerts me that it's time to get moving, I realize I've lain here awake for a couple of hours, just daydreaming about spending more time with him. I quickly change into jeans, another pair of skinny jeans, not my fave but a necessity for wearing my Hunter boots. I throw on a T-shirt and grab a flannel out of my closet. It was warm out today, but the night air will be chilly.

When I pull into Brandon's driveway, the guys are sitting on the front porch. My eyes immediately go to Slade. He's wearing faded blue jeans and a tight-fitting marine T-shirt. He looks every bit the badass marine. His muscles are tight around the arms of his shirt. When he raises his hand in a casual wave, I realize I've just been sitting in my car staring at him. *Get it together, Austyn.*

Turning off the engine, I climb out of the car. I take my time making my way to them. I keep my eyes on my phone as if it's the most interesting thing in the world.

"Hey, Aust," Brandon says once I reach the edge of the porch.

I look up and focus on Brandon. "Hey." On their own accord, my eyes pass over him and land on Slade, again. Oh my, up close is so much better. "Hey, Slade."

"Austyn," his deep, sexy voice greets me.

"What have y'all done today?" I ask, turning back to Brandon. I'm afraid if I keep looking at Slade, I'm going to embarrass myself even further.

"You see it," Brandon laughs. "We've pretty much just chilled out all day. It's nice to get a break. Hell, we both slept in this morning."

"You deserve it," I tell him. If anyone deserves a break, it's these two. Not that I know much about being a marine, but from the videos that Savvy and I watched online, these guys have very little, if any, downtime while at boot camp. A car pulling into the driveway pulls my attention. Looking over my shoulder, I see it's Savannah.

"There's my girl." Brandon jumps over the railing of the porch to greet her.

I know I should look away, give them space, but I can't. The love that they share is one that most dream of. Sure, they're young, but they've beaten the odds of failed high school sweetheart relationships, and are still together. There's not a single doubt in my mind that they will stand the test of time.

"You ready?" Slade asks.

I turn to face him. "Depends, you ready to be seen with me?" He tilts his head to the side, confused. "I'm starving, and we're headed to the fair.... I can't be held responsible for my overeating actions," I warn him.

He smiles, and his face lights up. "I'll take my chances."

I grin back at him. "All right then, don't say I didn't warn you."

He stands and joins me at the bottom of the steps. He stops and leans down, his lips next to my ear. "It's going to take more than that to keep me from spending the evening with you, angel."

I stand there, letting the feel of his hot breath and the meaning of his words wash over me. He called me angel. Be still my heart.

"You guys heading out?" Brandon asks when I turn to face them.

"Yeah," I say, trying to get myself under control. Slade affects me like no one ever has. "I tried to warn him," I say, looking at Savannah. "I'm starving."

She laughs. "Be strong, Marine." She pats Slade on the arm. Slade throws his head back and laughs. The sound washes over me like a caress.

"I think I can handle it."

"Let's see what you got." I hip-check him, trying to get back into the playful banter. I can't be staring at him with stars in my eyes all night. What fun would that be for him? We say a quick goodbye and head for my car.

"Want me to drive?" Slade asks.

"What? Big badass marine can't be seen riding with little ole me?" I ask.

He grins. "By all means, chauffer me around. I was just trying to be a gentleman."

"Uh-huh," I say, not believing him.

"So, Austyn, do you have a last name?" he inquires.

"I do." I don't offer it.

"Are you going to tell me?" I can feel his eyes on me.

"Depends."

"On what?"

"Why you want to know?"

"What? Am I not allowed to know the name of the gorgeous girl I'm spending so much time with?"

"Smooth," I smile. "You go first."

"Slade Joseph Reeves."

"Wow, busting out the middle names."

"Hey, go big or go home, right? I mean, I am a big badass marine," he jokes.

"I see how it is." I smile over at him, before putting my attention back on the road. "Austyn Michelle Wilson." I hesitate then continue, "Michelle is my mom's name. My little brother, Dawson, his middle name is Lee. That's my dad's name."

"It's beautiful, and that's really cool, to have that family connection."

"What about you, family connection?"

"Not that I'm aware of. Who knows what they were thinking when they named me. I mean, Slade?"

"What? I like it. It's hot," tumbles out of my mouth before I can stop it.

"Really?" he asks, amused.

I can feel the blush coat my cheeks. "I mean, yeah, it's unusual, and it fits you."

"Fits me, huh?" Humor lifts his words and I daren't look at him.

"You know, big badass marine," I admit. Thankfully, we arrive at the fairgrounds before I can continue to embarrass myself by describing his hotness. "Front row," I say, as I pull into a front row parking spot. "That's really kind of awesome considering I'll more than likely be too damn full to walk to the south forty."

Laughing, he says, "I'd carry you." Before I can reply, my stomach growls. "Let's get you fed," he declares, climbing out of the car. I rush to get my door open before he can get to me. He gives me a look, one that says, "that was my job." I feel... weird having him opening the car door for me all the time.

"I was coming to get you," he informs me.

"You don't have to open my door for me."

"Wait for me next time."

I don't argue. The look in his eyes tells me he means business. Besides, a girl could get used to being treated this way. "What do you want first?" I ask him once we're through the gate.

"I'm down for anything. You have what? Deep fried Oreos, cotton candy, caramel corn, and candy apples on the list, right?"

I stop in my tracks; he does the same and turns to look at me. "You remembered?"

"You talk, and I listen." He shrugs. "What's first?"

"Actually, I'm thinking a walking taco."

"Walking taco, it is," he says with a laugh. "Lead the way." He holds his arm out for me, just like last night. I don't hesitate to grab onto his elbow and lead us toward the taco stand.

"Well, what do you think?" I ask once we've finished off our tacos. I can tell by the way he devoured his, just as I did mine, that he liked it.

"They were good. What's next?"

"I'm thinking deep fried Oreo's for dessert. We might have to end up taking the other stuff home with us. I don't know if I can eat all that." I sigh in defeat.

"What?" The arm that I'm not holding onto covers his chest. "Where's this girl who's going to embarrass me from all she's going to eat?"

"She's feeling full." I laugh. "My eyes are bigger than my belly."

"We'll just have to come back."

Turning my head, I look up at him. "You want to come back?"

"What? Am I boring you?"

"No, not at all…." I start to defend when he chuckles. It's a rumble from somewhere deep in his chest. I smack his arm.

"Hey." He laughs even harder. "I was just messing with you." He gets himself together. "Our time here is limited. I can't think of a better way to spend it than with you."

I try to act cool, calm, and collected, as if his words don't affect me. "You're assuming I can fit you into my schedule," I tease.

When he leans in and his nose brushes across my cheek, I know he can see right through me. "We can do anything you want, angel. I'll be on my best behavior. I promise," he says sincerely, his lips next to my ear, his words for me and me alone.

"Deep fried Oreos," I say, because what do I say to that? Slade is intense, more… mature maybe than the guys I'm used to.

"Grab us a table." He points to a small row of picnic tables. "I'll get our Oreos. What do you want to drink?"

"Water, please. Here, let me give you some money."

He gives me that look again, the one that tells me he's paying and that's that. "Thank you, Slade." The words are a whisper from my lips.

He nods and walks away. I watch him go. He makes those faded jeans look good. When he reaches the line, he turns to look at me and catches me staring. He winks, and I turn quickly and walk toward the picnic tables and grab us a seat.

"Hey, Austyn," Mark Lake says, stopping beside the picnic table, just as I'm sitting down.

"Hey, Mark, hey, Lawrence."

"You here alone?" Mark asks.

"No, actually, I'm not. I'm here with a friend."

"Savannah?" he asks, turning to look around for her.

"No, Savvy's with Brandon. He's home for a few days."

"Got ya, why don't you ladies join us?" Lawrence says.

"What makes you think it's a girl friend?" I ask him.

"Isn't it?"

"Nope," Slade says, walking up behind me.

He places two bottles of water and a large dish of deep fried Oreo's in front of me. I expect him to sit down across from me, but he surprises me when he rests his hands on my shoulders. Anyone else and I would be rolling my eyes, but this... show from Slade has me feeling all warm inside. "Guys." I clear my throat. "This is Slade. Slade, this is Mark and Lawrence. We went to high school together."

"Nice to meet you," Slade says politely, but he doesn't remove his hands from my shoulders.

"Didn't know you were dating, Austyn," Mark smarts off.

"Babe, did we forget to send out the announcements? Damn, wait, no, we did. You just weren't on the list," Slade quips.

I can't see Slade, but I can imagine he's standing tall, with those muscles on display, his chiseled jaw set from clenching too tight. "It was good to see you," I say, trying to diffuse the situation. Not because I care—Mark and Lawrence are both players out for a good time, one they both know they're not getting from me.

"Catch ya around, Austyn," Lawrence says, putting his hand on Mark's shoulder and pushing him to walk away.

Once they leave, Slade takes the seat across from me. I lift my brows at him. "What was that?"

"I don't know," he says. I can tell from the clipped tone of his voice, he's not impressed.

"You don't know?"

He looks up and his eyes lock on mine. "I don't know, Austyn. That's not me." He pauses a moment. "I've never felt like that before. When I saw those guys talking to you, I just… reacted."

"They're harmless."

He nods. "I'm sure they are, but I didn't want them taking my time with you."

What do I say to that? Reaching across the table, I place my hand over his. "I'm here with you, Slade. They were just saying hi."

"I know, and you're not mine, I'm sorry." I want to tell him that I could be. That I don't see anyone but him. That thought alone is depressing considering he doesn't live here, and who knows if he will ever come back. This is just a passing in time for us.

"Our Oreos are getting cold." I point to the tray in front of us. He gives me a smile and hands me a fork. Ever the gentleman, he waits for me to take a bite before he does. "Good, huh?" I ask, covering my mouth.

"So good," he says, never taking his eyes off mine.

chapter 9

Slade

"SAVANNAH JUST TEXTED ME," AUSTYN says as we head back toward her car.

My arms are loaded down with caramel corn, cotton candy, and candy apples. We decided to take them to go. Austyn suggested we take them back to her house and sit around the fire pit. I don't care what we do as long as I get to spend more time with her. It's unreal the way I react to her. I've never been possessive or jealous, but then again, I've never had anything or anyone worth feeling that way for.

"What are they into?" I ask. I glance over at her and can't help but smile. She's clutching the huge teddy bear I won for her and trying to text Savannah and walk at the same time. "Let me hold that." I reach out for the bear, and she stops and turns away from me.

"Not happening, Reeves." She mock glares.

Placing my hand on the small of her back, I lead her to the side of the gateway we're currently stopped in the middle of, as we head to her car. Looking over her shoulder, I see that Savannah wants to get together at Combs's house tonight.

"She wants to." She turns and ends up looking up at me reading over her shoulder. She laughs when I blow her bangs out of her eyes. "What do you think?"

"I'm with you, angel. We'll do whatever you want."

She nods as her fingers fly across her phone and she texts Savannah back. "I told them we'll meet them there."

"Sounds good." She slides her phone back in her pocket, and I follow her as we walk back to her car. When we reach it, she unlocks the doors, and I unload my arms into the back seat. Turning, I reach for her bear, but she shakes her head. "You drive," she says, tossing me the keys. Without another word, she climbs into the passenger seat and buckles up.

After adjusting the seat, we're on our way. "You need directions?" she asks.

"No, I've got it."

"Is that some kind of super marine thing? Remember where you are and how to get back to where you were?"

I chuckle. "Staying alert and aware of your surroundings. I've been here a few days, and this is a small town," I remind her.

"Yes, it is." She sighs heavily.

"What made you decide to stay close to home for college?"

"There are colleges here that have great education programs."

"Teacher, right?"

"Right. Wait? Did I tell you that?" she asks.

"No, Combs did. He mentioned that you and Savannah had the same major. He never stops talking about her."

"So you feel my pain?" She laughs. "Not that I blame them. I can't imagine how hard it is on them. I mean, Brandon and I are just friends, and even I missed him. That has to run deep for the two of them."

"I imagine it does." I wouldn't know. Everyone I would miss has already left this earth.

"Can I ask you a question?"

"Shoot." I find myself wanting to open up to her. There's just something about Austyn that makes me want to bare my soul.

"Why do you call me angel?"

That's an easy one. "Because that's what you remind me of. With your blonde hair and those crystal blue eyes. Not to mention you have a heart of gold," I tell her.

"H-how do you know that? I could be the biggest bitch ever."

"Right." I laugh. "The biggest bitch ever who took pity on a guy who tagged home with his fellow marine because he has nowhere else to go. The girl who gave that guy two days that were the most memorable he's ever had. Does that sound like a bitch thing to do to you?"

"It's not like it's a hardship to spend time with you, Slade," she confesses.

"That's good to know, angel." I use the name again, just to see how she reacts. Her words make it hard for me to not reach out for her and pull her into me, smashing my mouth to hers.

"Although I'm not sure it's deserving, I like it," she admits, a soft blush coating her cheeks.

"It's deserving. Trust me on this one."

"It's intimate."

Not able to help myself, I reach over and lace my fingers with hers. "It is," I agree. I don't say anything else and neither does she. I'm out of my element here. I'm going strictly on feeling, letting my emotions feed off hers and guide us through this. I know I'm leaving in a few days, and the more time I spend with her, the more I know that she's going to be my someone who I'm going to miss.

I don't know what these small touches and caresses mean, but I do know that I'm soaking up every fucking minute of them while I'm here with her. I don't know if I'll ever see her again after this, and the thought alone takes some of the wind out of my sails. I want to remember every word, every touch, every feeling that courses through me when I'm with her.

"Looks like they beat us," she says when I pull in behind Savannah's car.

"I'll get your door," I tell her. Quickly, I jump out and rush around her car and pull open her door. She climbs out still holding onto the bear I won her. "This guy needs a name," I tell her.

She looks down at the bear in her arms and then back up at me. "Knight," she says softly.

"Knight?" I question.

"Yeah, you know this guy, he won him for me, and that's what he reminds me of. This strong knight that takes care of everyone. My knight in shining armor." She smiles.

"That's not me, angel."

"No? I've just met you, and you're already doing more for me, looking out for me more than guys I've known since kindergarten. That's pretty knightly, Reeves."

"I'm just doing what feels right," I admit. "This is all new to me."

She surprises me when she stands on her tiptoes and presses her soft lips against my cheek. They're soft and warm, and leave me wanting more. "Could have fooled me," she says, dropping back on her feet and ducking under my arm.

I watch her as she walks away and fight the urge to place my hand on my cheek right over the spot her lips just touched. That would be a pussy thing to do, so instead, I shut the passenger door and open the back to pull out all the fair snacks, as Austyn called them.

"Sheesh, Austyn, make the poor guy carry your loot why don't you," Combs laughs.

"Hey, my hands are full." She holds up her bear with two hands as proof.

"What is all that?" Savannah asks, taking a bag of caramel corn from my hands.

"Fair snacks. We ate too much so we got some to go. We were just going to chill at my place until I got your text, so now we'll share the loot with the two of you."

"Cotton candy." Combs grabs a bag from my hands.

"Where do you want the rest of this?"

"Just sit it in here," Combs says, and I follow him into the kitchen.

"I can't believe she has you packing around all her shit," he says, laughing.

"Have you seen her?" I ask him. "Besides, I insisted she let me carry it."

He laughs again. "Yeah, I've seen her. She's got you hooked already, huh?"

I don't answer him, and luckily, I don't have to as the girls come into the room, effectively changing the conversation. "You want any of this now?" I ask Austyn.

"No, thanks." She holds her stomach with one hand while the other still holds onto the bear I won her. I've never done that, won a girl something; it's a heady feeling to know that something I did, something I won, put that smile on her face. It's one that I know that I can quickly become addicted to.

"I'm gonna go start the fire pit." Combs kisses Savannah and walks out the door.

I set the rest of the items on the island and turn to follow him. "Slade!" Austyn calls out to me.

I stop and look over my shoulder. "Thank you for today." My lips turn up in a smile. I wink at her, turn back around and walk out the door.

What I really want to do is stand next to her, put my arm around her, and hold her hand. I want to know if her soft lips feel the same against my lips, as they did against my cheek. The list goes on and on of things that I'd like to experience when it comes to Austyn.

The girls join us not long after. We all take a seat around the fire, and they begin talking about high school and all the crazy times they've had. I sit back quietly and listen to them, wishing I could have been there with them. I have no crazy stories to tell, no parties, no football games. Nothing in my life would be even remotely interesting to any of them.

"What about you, Slade?" Savannah asks.

I'm just about to tell her what I was thinking when Austyn speaks up. "You know what we haven't done in forever?"

"What's that?" Savannah immediately turns her attention to her friend.

"Hide and seek."

Combs throws his head back and laughs. "Aust, the last time we did that we were what? Sophomores? And we'd snuck beer from my parents."

"That's right," Savannah chimes in. "It was their Fourth of July party. That was a blast."

"We're not drinking," Combs reminds them.

"Come on, Brandon. Where's your sense of adventure?" Austyn asks, standing up. She holds her hand out for me. "Slade, you coming?"

I take her hand and stand. She walks to the edge of the deck and stops, turning to face me. She's bathed in the moonlight, and I want nothing more than to kiss her right now. "Thank you, angel."

"For what?" she whispers.

"You saved me back there."

She shrugs. "I didn't want you to be uncomfortable. From what little bit you've told me and by the look on your face, we were heading into uncomfortable territory."

Not able to resist her, I tug on her hand, and she falls against my chest. I wrap my arms around her and place a kiss on her forehead. "Thank you."

"If we're doing this, we're doing guys against girls," Combs voice booms into the night. Austyn steps out of my hold, and I let her.

"You're on," Savannah says. "Aust, we got this." She links arms with Austyn, and they step off the porch. "We hide first. Let's make it interesting. Brandon, you have to find me, and Slade, you have to find Austyn."

"Savvy, it's too damn dark. How are we going to do that?" Combs complains.

Savannah laughs. "Humor me. Besides, you're marines now. Don't you have some kind of super-secret training?" She smirks.

"Woman," he growls, and barrels down the steps. Austyn lets go of her arm just in time for Combs to pick Savannah up and twirl her around, causing her laugh to echo into the night. "Fine," he says, placing her feet on the ground. "What do I get when I find you?"

"Hmmm, you'll have to find me to find out."

"What about Slade, what's his prize?" he asks.

Savannah looks over at Austyn. "Bragging rights," Austyn says automatically, causing us all to laugh.

"There you have it," Savannah says. "Now, count to one hundred," she says, linking arms with Austyn as they jog off into the darkness of the yard.

I watch them disappear into the darkness before turning to Combs. He's got his head tilted back, and his lips move silently as he counts. "You really counting?" I ask him in disbelief.

He ignores me and continues to count. He speaks, "One hundred," and turns to look at me. "Dude, have you never played hide and seek?" he asks. "You must count. Trust me, my girl will know," he says, dead serious.

"Only played in elementary school when we had to," I admit.

His mouth drops open. "We'll get to that another time. Right now, we have ladies to find." He descends the final steps of the deck and disappears into the darkness.

Realizing that time is wasting, I follow along behind him. He goes left and I go right. I take slow steps and keep my breathing even. Stopping every few feet, I listen to what surrounds me. I'm almost to the field with the tall hay or straw, not sure which one, but I'm pretty sure neither of the girls would venture out that far. I turn to head back to the house, and that's when I see her. Her blonde hair reflects off the old truck she's hunkered down beside. The moonlight lighting her up, she looks every bit the angel I've pegged her to be. The purpose of the game is to find her first, but I can't seem to stop watching her. I take her in. She must hear me. She whips her head around and stands, knowing she's been found. My feet move toward her, hers doing the same. We meet in the middle of the darkened backyard, just the light of the moon guiding us.

"You found me," she whispers.

"I did," I whisper back.

"But you were just watching me?" She phrases it as a question, sounding confused.

"I was," I tell her honestly. I can't see it, but I know her face is a light shade of pink.

"Why?"

"It's not every day you get to see an angel glowing in the moonlight," I tell her. "You're beautiful." I sound like a fucking sap, but the words just seem to fall from my lips before I even realize it. She has that effect on me.

"Slade," she whispers.

"Angel."

She takes one step closer, and I do the same. We're now standing toe-to-toe. "You won bragging rights," she says. Her voice is so soft I'm not sure I could have heard her if I were not standing mere inches from her.

"Bummer," I say. "Combs gets a kiss."

"Is that what you want?" she asks. Her tongue comes out and licks across that full bottom lip.

"I do. But go easy on me, you're my first," I confess.

"What?" she breathes.

Slowly, I raise my hand and cup her cheek. "I told you, I was a loner. Didn't have time to date, not that I was considered a good prospect in my hometown."

Resting her hands on my hips, she stands on her tiptoes and presses her lips to mine. It's short, just a peck, but the shock is anything but. Sparks of electricity surge through me. I lick my lips, desperate to taste her. I want more of her, more kisses, just more.

"Game!" Combs yells, causing us to step away from each other. "Where are you guys? I found her and claimed my prize," he boasts.

"Over here!" I yell out. I place my hand on the small of Austyn's back, and she shivers. "You cold?" I ask her.

"It's a little chilly out here."

"Let's get you back to the fire." I lead her back up to the deck to find Combs and Savannah kissing. I lead Austyn over to one of the wooden chairs. "I'll be right back," I whisper next to her ear. Rushing into the house, and up the stairs, I go to my bag and pull out my marines sweatshirt. It'll swallow her, but the idea of her in something of mine is overwhelming. I've seen it in movies, heard Combs talk about his girl in his clothes, but I've never really gotten the appeal. Not until Austyn.

"Here." I hand her the sweatshirt and take my seat next to her.

"Thank you, Slade." Her voice is soft yet raspy, as if she's overcome with emotion from my gesture. Maybe it was the kiss?

The rest of the night we stay around the fire. Combs ends up going inside and getting Savannah a sweatshirt too. They share more stories of them growing up, and we chat about stories from boot camp. When it's time for them to leave, we walk them to their cars. I want to kiss her goodbye, but I don't. I settle for "Drive safe, and I'll see you soon," followed by a wave. I hate it. I hate that I can't show her all of this want, this need that I have for her. It's sudden and I have no explanation other than, it's Austyn, and any man would be a damn fool to not fall under her spell.

chapter 10
Austyn

OVER THE PAST FEW DAYS, I've spent a lot of time with Slade. We've hung out as a group, and he and I have gone off on our own, giving Savannah and Brandon time to themselves. The more time I spend with him, the more I like him. I've tried to talk myself out of it a million times, but then there are the looks he gives me, like I'm the only person in the room. The light touches, nothing crazy—his hand on the small of my back, leading me into a room, touching my arm in passing, things like that. Then there was the kiss. It only happened once, and it was short, too short, but the electricity that sparked when I pressed my lips to his still zings through me. It's heightened every time he touches me. Every time it's just us, I tell myself I'm going to do it again, but I always seem to chicken out.

It's better this way as he's leaving in four days and at this point, I don't even know if I'll ever see him again. I know he doesn't have any family, none that he's willing to claim as family anyway, that much he confessed to me. I try to not get my hopes up that he'll make this his home, here where I can see him. But maybe if he does, we can be... more. My mind races and my heart is reeling. I need to get myself together.

Today's their birthday. Brandon's parents are having a little get together at their place, with grandparents and other family members. This way, everyone will get to see him before they leave for SOI. Savannah and I are invited, of course. Afterward, there are going to be some friends from high school stop by and a few Savannah and I've met in college. I feel bad for Slade. It's his birthday too, and there's no one really there for him. Well, me, I'm there for him, but I'm too afraid to tell him that. I can't imagine what it must be like for him. I'm going to stick with him tonight. I don't want him to be alone on his birthday.

Picking up my phone to check the time, I see I've a missed text message from Savannah.

Savannah:	Hey, you want to ride over with me?
Me:	What time are you going over?
Savannah:	Getting ready to leave now. Thought I could help set up.
Me:	I'll meet you there. That way if you want to stay longer, I won't be the third wheel.
Savannah:	Right. LOL. Like Slade would ever let that happen.
Me:	What do you mean by that?
Savannah:	Please, that boy doesn't take his eyes off you.
Me:	How would you know? You're too busy with your man.

My heart races knowing that she's noticed too. We've been so busy with the guys, and she's spending every spare minute with Brandon, we've not really had time to catch up. But I know she's right. I can feel his stare; it's as if I can feel him anytime he's close. I know that sounds like I'm a crazy person, but it's true. I don't know how else to explain it.

Savannah:	I may be focusing on B, but I see things. I also notice he's not the only one looking.
Me:	If you're looking for denial, you're not getting one.
Savannah:	LOL. Go for it. He's hot and he seems like a great guy.
Me:	He's not from here, Savvy.
Savannah:	He's a marine, Aust. He's going to be all over the

world. He can be from wherever in the hell he wants to be.

Me: I'm leaving now. I'll see you there.
Savannah: Avoiding!
Savannah: Drive safe.

She's right. I am avoiding. We both know it. Grabbing Slade's hoodie and one of my own, I then scribble a note to my parents on the dry erase board on the fridge and head toward Brandon's.

When I pull into the drive, Savannah's car is already here. After I grab my keys and my phone, I head around back, assuming that's where everyone will be getting ready for the party. What I find is Slade. He's sitting on the steps of the deck, looking out into the backyard. From the looks of it, he's lost in deep deliberation.

"Penny for your thoughts," I say, and then inwardly scold myself. I sound like my mother.

Slowly, he turns to look at me. A lazy smile tilts his lips. "My gran used to say that."

Great. Just what I was hoping for… to remind the super-hot guy of his grandmother. "Yeah?" I ask because it's already out there. I might as well own it instead of letting it get to me.

He slides over on the step making room for me. "Yeah," he says as I take a seat next to him. "She had things she said that never really made any sense to me, but it was her." He shrugs.

"Tell me about her."

He shocks me when he reaches over and laces his fingers through mine, letting our joined hands rest on his lap. I don't let him see it though. I just sit still next to him waiting for him to say something or make the next move. "I miss her. She fought so hard for so long. Her heart just couldn't keep up with her spirit."

"I'm glad you enlisted," I say to break the silence.

He turns toward me, and our faces are close, so close I can feel his breath mingle with mine. "Yeah?"

I nod. "That brought you here." I give his hand a gentle

squeeze. "I know that sounds crazy but, it would have been a shame not to have met you."

"That brought me to you." His words are so soft that if he were not this close, I would have missed them. "You're unlike anyone I've ever met, Austyn."

"How's that?" I ask. He has my full attention as I hang on every word.

He turns back to face the yard. "You're genuine. You say what you mean and mean what you say." He laughs, and I smile at the sound. "I'm messing this up." He looks down at his feet. "The girls in school, they worried about what they look like, who they hung out with to get them to the next social status in the ladder of popularity."

"That's just city girls," I say, trying to lighten the mood.

He throws his head back in laughter. "Maybe you're right, but to me, it will always be you who's different, special."

"Hey, you two," Savannah says, walking out on the deck. I try to pull my hand away, but Slade isn't having it. "I didn't know you were here yet." She walks toward us and takes the step just above us. "Brandon's in the shower. He'll be out in a minute."

Slade nods, but keeps his grip tight on my hand. I turn to look at her, and she raises her eyebrows in question. I give her a look that warns her not to mention the fact that we're holding hands. "Y'all need help setting up?" I ask.

"Nope, I think we've got it. It's just going to be us, his grandparents, his aunt and uncle, and his two little cousins."

"How are they? I have not seen them in forever."

"Growing like crazy. I was over here a few weeks ago when they stopped in. They asked about you," she says.

"Of course they did. They're my boyfriends." Slade stiffens, his grip tightening on my hand. "Jonah and Noah are Brandon's little cousins. How old are they now? Eight?" I ask Savannah. Slade relaxes, and I fight a smile.

"Yeah, they just turned eight. You've got some competition."

She nudges Slade's shoulder.

He turns to look at me. "That's what the knight does, right? Fights for the princess?"

His words are low, just for me, but when Savannah places her hand on my shoulder and squeezes, I know she heard him. "I don't know," I say, trying to lighten the situation. "I mean, they are adorable twins. That's double the trouble."

"I'll take my chances," he smiles, looking back out over the backyard.

"There you are," Brandon says. "What are we doing out here? It's cold as hell."

Savannah laughs at him. "Maybe if you had a shirt on you wouldn't be freezing."

"I was looking for you," he says, sitting down next to her on the top step and putting his arm around her. "What are we doing?"

"Just chatting. I was telling Austyn the twins are coming today."

"Oh yeah." He grins. "They're going to be happy to see you."

"I should be jealous. They both want Austyn," Savvy says with a laugh.

"They know you're mine. She was their only option. You're taken."

"Oh yeah, well what if Aust is taken too?" she asks.

"Austyn?" Brandon leans forward, and I know the minute he sees my hand enclosed in Slade's. "Well damn. Those little buggers are going to be heartbroken. Break it to them easy." He throws me a wink, and I try my hardest to control the heat threatening to pinken my cheeks.

Before I can tell him it's not like that, his mom, Sarah, comes to the door, letting us know everyone's here. Savannah and Brandon rush to their feet and head inside. "You don't want to go in, do you?" I ask Slade after we stay put.

He shrugs, rubbing his thumb over my knuckles. "It's a family moment."

"Then stick with me." I stand, pulling him with me by our joined hands. "Ready?" He nods, and we head inside.

chapter 11
Slade

I SHOULD PROBABLY LET GO of her hand, but she acts like it's no big deal as she pulls me behind her into the house. I'm not about to let go if I don't have to. I don't know what came over me, but reaching for her felt like the most natural thing to do. To my surprise, she didn't pull away. Now, I don't ever want to let go. That's some crazy shit I'm feeling, and I don't know how to handle it.

"Austyn!" Two little boys with heads full of shaggy brown hair rush her, and she releases me to catch them. They wrap their arms around her, and she does the same to them.

"Hey, guys."

"We missed you," they say at the same time.

Austyn beams down at them. "I missed you, too. You're getting so tall," she exclaims.

"When we get tall like Brandon, we get to take you on a date, right?" one of them asks.

"I don't know, buddy. This guy might have something to say about that." Brandon joins them and points at me.

"Who are you?" they ask again at the same time. Stepping back from Austyn, they place their hands on their hips and stare me down. I have to fight back a grin.

"This is my buddy, Slade. He's a marine like me," Brandon explains.

They're eyes grow wide. "You're a marine, too."

"I am," I tell him.

Their little eyes look from me to Austyn and then back to me. "Are you her boyfriend?" they ask.

"Boys!" their mom scolds them.

"Mom, he's a marine and Austyn's boyfriend," one of them whines.

"Hey." Austyn drops to her knees and pulls them both close. I can't take my eyes off her as she talks to them. "You two monkeys are going to make two ladies very, very happy when you get older. We've talked about this, right? How I'm too old for you?"

"But you're really pretty and nice to us," one of them says. I can't help but agree with him. Only, she's not just pretty, she's fucking gorgeous.

"You're sweet," she says, kissing him on the cheek. I swear the kid puffs his chest out when her lips touch his skin. Again, I know the feeling. Austyn's kisses make you feel ten feet tall and bulletproof.

They share a look and step away from Austyn, and she stands back to her full height. The twins come to stand in front of me, causing Austyn to step and stand next to me as well. They cross their little arms over their chests and glare at me. I want to laugh at them, but I bite it back, knowing this is serious to them. "What are your intentions with our Austyn?" one of them asks me.

Austyn grabs onto my arm and leans into me, hiding her face. Her body's shaking with her silent laughter. Brandon doesn't try to hide his, and neither does anyone else in the room. That doesn't seem to faze the boys. They keep their eyes locked on me.

How am I supposed to explain to these boys without hurting their feelings? She's obviously tried to tell them before that she's too old for them. I try to think like an eight-year-old, which is hard for me. I never really got to be a kid. My mind races like a highlight reel of my time with Austyn, and that's when it hits me. Austyn gets herself together at the same time and lifts her head from my shoulder. I slip the arm she was just holding onto around her waist. "She's my princess," I tell them. Their eyes grow wide at the same time Austyn relaxes into me, causing me to hold her a little tighter.

"You're a marine like Brand?" one of them asks.

They look just alike, so the chances of me telling them apart are slim to none. "I am."

"So you'll protect her and us, just like Brand. That's why he went away to protect us and Savvy," the other one says.

"Yeah, little man. I'm a marine to protect America, and Austyn." I turn to face her as I say her name. Her eyes are on me immediately. I'm shocked when they both step forward and hold their hands out to me. "Thank you." They look over their shoulders at their mom. "What else are we supposed to say?"

She gives them a watery smile. "Thank you for your service," she reminds them.

They turn back to me. "Thank you for your service," they say in unison.

Not gonna lie, I'm a little choked up. Not knowing what else to do, I hold my hand out and shake both of theirs. Once that's done, they turn, but then one of them stops to face us. "You know where to find us if you get tired of him," he says. We all bust up laughing, no longer able to hold it in.

"All right then," Brandon's mom, Sarah, laughs. Let's eat."

We all gather around the dining room table. The twins are sitting at a card table just beside us. Conversation is light and easy; apparently, the twins took care of the heavy. After dinner, we all help clear the table and head outside to play some badminton with the twins. All in all, today is another day for the memory books.

After Brandon's family leaves, the four of us climb into his truck and head to an open field behind the house. Brandon and

I cut up some firewood yesterday while the girls were in class to be ready for tonight.

"What time is everyone coming?" Austyn asks.

"Told them around eight," Brandon says, tossing a match onto the pile of brush that immediately goes up in flames.

"Show off," Austyn yells out to him, and the three of them roar in laughter.

"What am I missing?" I ask Austyn. She pulls down the tailgate of the truck and tries to jump up, but falls short. Taking any opportunity to touch her, I grip her hips and lift her. Her hands brace on my shoulders.

"Thank you."

There's a pinkish tint to her cheeks from the glow of the fire. "You gonna fill me in?" I ask her. She drops her hands from my shoulders, and I'm cussing myself internally. I should have kept my mouth shut, and maybe she would have kept her hands on me.

"We've been doing this for years, and one year, Savvy and I said we were taking care of the fire. Well, we had no clue what we were doing. It was well after nine before we admitted defeat. Brandon waltzes over, throws some lighter fluid on, tosses in a match, and bam, instant fire. Savvy and I give him a hell every time he starts a fire now."

"Got ya."

"Oh, hush," she says, pushing on my shoulder that's resting next to her where I lean against the tailgate. "I guess it was one of those 'you had to be there' moments."

"There she is!" a deep booming voice carries over the field.

I pull my eyes from Austyn and see the two guys we ran into at the fair. "Come here you," the tall dark-haired one says.

Austyn kicks her legs out in front of her to stop him. "Like I want your cooties," she says, laughing.

"Cooties, woman, I'll give you cooties." He wags his eyebrows.

I place my hand on her thigh, my not so subtle way of

showing them she's mine. I'm just as shocked as she is apparently. Her head whips toward me, and a slow smile graces her lips. "Guys, you remember, Slade."

Stepping away from the tailgate to stand in front of her, I offer them my hand. "Good to see you," I say. I don't mean it, but I know it's the polite thing to say. Not that they've done anything to me, but I can tell that they want her, and that's just not gonna work for me.

"You're a marine, too, right? With Brandon?" the one who seems to be less of a douche asks.

"Yep."

"Austyn, save me a dance later." Douche, who I think is Lawrence, winks.

She surprises me when she wraps her legs around my waist from her seat on the tailgate and pulls me back toward her. Not that it takes much effort; it's as if I gravitate toward her on my own. I rest against the tailgate between her thighs. Going for casual, as if this is us, I rest my forearms on her thighs.

"Not sure my guy here would be okay with that," she says sweetly.

"Is that how it is?" Lawrence asks.

"Yep," she says, popping the P.

"Catch you around, Austyn," Mark, the not so douche one, says and pulls his buddy to the other side of the huge-ass fire that's blazing in front of us.

"Sorry about that," she whispers in my ear once they're gone.

Turning, I place my hands on the tailgate on either side of her. "What was all that?"

She shrugs. "Lawrence is a flirt. He's harmless but relentless. I thought that if he thought we were, you know, together, he would chill."

"Is he bothering you?" I ask, standing up taller.

"No, not like that. He's more like an annoying gnat that won't go away. He's not the kind of guy to go after someone who's… attached."

"I see. So you used me to keep him at bay?"

Worry crosses her face. "I'm sorry, Slade. I wasn't thinking."

"Hey." Unable to resist, I lift one hand and cup her cheek. "If it helps you, I'm good with it." She nods. "But what about when I leave? I'm only here for four more days."

"I wasn't thinking that far ahead."

"Just tell him we're still together. He knows I'm a marine, right? So he'll know that we're going to be gone a lot. Just tell him it's me." What I really want to say is I want it to be me. I want to ask her to try this with me, a long-distance relationship. It's just my luck I'd find her when I'm already committed to the Marines.

"He'll figure it out eventually, when you don't come back."

Her voice is small and laced with sadness, if I'm not mistaken. "Who says I'm not coming back?" My mind is calculating the next time I might be able to come to Kentucky to see her.

"I just assumed. I mean, I know you aren't from around here."

"I'm not from anywhere, not anymore," I tell her honestly. I don't know why, but I end up spilling the truth when I'm around her.

"Slade," she whispers, leaning in, and all I can think about is kissing her. Pressing my lips to hers, feeling their softness, tasting her… Austyn could quickly become my addiction.

"What did we miss?" Savannah asks. She turns her back to the tailgate, and Brandon lifts her just as I did Austyn earlier.

"Nothing much," Austyn tells her.

Brandon grabs us each a bottle of water. He holds his up as if we're toasting. "Happy Birthday, brother," he says to me. The four of us click our plastic water bottles together, causing the girls to laugh.

"Not drinking tonight?" Savannah asks him.

"Not tonight, babe. We're underage, and if they test or some shit, it could be bad. The risk isn't worth the potential punishment."

I'm still resting between her legs when I feel her shiver. "You cold?"

"Just a little." She smiles. "I actually brought your sweatshirt back to you and brought me another. They're in the back seat of the truck."

"I'll be right back." I walk around the truck and see the two hoodies lying there. I grab mine and shut the door. "Here," I say, holding it out to her.

"I brought one. At least I thought I did."

"You did," I say, handing her mine again. Her blue eyes light up with the glow of the fire and I can see recognition in them. She gets what I'm saying. I want her in mine. I wait until she has it pulled over her head and her arms in the holes before I take my spot back resting between her thighs.

"What about you? Are you cold?" she asks.

"No, but if I do get cold, I'm depending on you to keep me warm," I say, keeping my voice low, just for her.

She doesn't reply, but she does move her hands to rest at my sides, right under my arms. To anyone looking on, we're a couple. If only that were true. The night goes on with the four of us shooting the shit. I'm introduced to all kinds of people whose names I will never remember. The girls ate me up with their eyes, while the guys sized me up with theirs. However, all of them seem surprised to see Austyn and me so close. That's exactly how we were, close. I didn't leave her side all night. I asked her several times if she wanted to go say hi to her friends, but she declined. So did Savannah. The four of us stayed where we were and let them come to us.

The party dies down. Apparently, we're boring since we're not drinking. Brandon doesn't seem to mind, and neither do I. I prefer to remember every minute I have with Austyn. The four of us hang out until the fire dies down. We play some song trivia game that the girls made up. They have to sing a line of the song and Combs and I had to guess the title and the artist.

When we get back to the house, we walk the girls to their cars.

"Thank you, Slade," Austyn says, not looking at me.

Reaching out, I place my finger under her chin and lift gently until her eyes land on mine. "Never thank me for spending time with you."

"That… and letting them think we're together. I know I was wrong, but—"

"But nothing. I'd be one lucky son of a bitch to be able to call you mine, Austyn." She opens her mouth to reply but quickly shuts it. "You're beautiful." I step closer to her. Her back is now resting against the side of her car. When her tongue slips out and wets her lips, I lose my resolve. Leaning in, I press my lips to hers. I want to fucking devour her, but I find my restraint and pull back.

"Drive safe," I tell her, stepping back to open her door.

"I-I almost forgot." She leans down and grabs something out of her car. When she stands, she shuts the door. "Happy Birthday, Slade," she says, handing me an envelope.

"You didn't have to," I say, without even opening it. The only other person in my life I've ever received a card from, hell, a gift from is Gran. It's unreal—the fluttering in my chest from a piece of paper. Then again, maybe that's just Austyn.

"It's not much."

"Thank you." I lean down and kiss her again. Just a quick touch of my lips to hers, but a kiss all the same. It doesn't lessen the way my lips tingle, or the way I long to kiss her for hours.

I start to pull open the envelope, and she places her hand over mine. "Wait, just until I'm gone."

"Austyn, whatever it is, it's from you, so it's perfect." I can't see her blush with the darkness that surrounds us, but I know it's there.

"Goodnight, Slade."

"Goodnight. Text me when you get home," I say, opening her door for her. When she's buckled in, I close the door and step back. I watch her until I can no longer see her car. Not wanting to share whatever it is she's given me, I slip the envelope under my shirt. I walk past Combs and Savannah; they're too lost in each other to notice me, but I keep the envelope under my shirt anyway.

When I get up to my room, I pull out the envelope and carefully slide open the seal. Austyn has no idea what this means to me; it could be a blank piece of paper and just the fact that she thought of me. No one has thought about me before, except for Gran. Pulling out the card, I open it, and something falls to the floor. Reaching to pick it up, I see it's two of the pictures we took from the fair on Austyn's phone. She and I are making silly faces in one, and she's kissing me on the cheek in the other. She's so fucking beautiful she takes my breath away.

Realizing there's more, I focus back on the card in my hand. It's just your average birthday card, but it's the note inside that gets me.

Slade,

Happy Birthday! It's not much, but I wanted to give you something to remember your trip to Kentucky. I can't imagine what it's like, being a marine, but when times are tough, I hope that this will help lift you up.

Always,

Austyn

Without even knowing it, she's given me a gift that I will forever treasure. There have been so many moments in the last seven days that I want to commit to memory. All of them involving her. Sitting on the edge of the bed, I look at the black and white photo of the two of us. I can't seem to tear my eyes from her until my phone vibrates. I know it's her.

Austyn: I'm home.

Me: Thank you for the card and the pictures.

Austyn: It's not much.

Me: It's everything. Goodnight, angel.

Austyn: Goodnight, Slade.

I don't even bother to change my clothes. I just kick off my shoes, turn off the light, and lie back on the bed. The moonlight filters in through the blinds, but it's not enough light to see the picture, or to see her smiling face or the kiss she's giving me. I hold the picture to my chest and close my eyes. I don't need to see it because it's ingrained in my memory. Every moment with her is.

chapter 12
Austyn

HAVE YOU EVER BEEN SLEEPING and wake up because you feel like someone is watching you? You're in the state of being half asleep and half awake. You don't want to open your eyes, but you know you should because someone is watching you. That's me, and the culprit is my little brother, Dawson.

"Morning, Aust," he says, giving me a toothy grin.

"Morning, bub. What are you doing up so early?" I ask with a yawn.

"It's not early. It's almost lunchtime."

Groaning, I reach over and grab my cell phone from the nightstand. I see it's a little after eleven and that I missed a message four hours ago from Slade.

"Can we go to the fair today? You promised," Dawson says, bouncing on the bed in excitement.

I reach out and ruffle his hair. "Yeah, bud. Let me get a shower, and we can go. What are Mom and Dad doing?"

"They are going on a date since I'll be with you. A day date, Mommy said."

I smile. My parents are still so in love it would be sickening if not for the fact that I've watched it all these years. "Okay, make sure you get some old shoes or boots, and get a hoodie."

"Yay!" Dawson cheers and races out of my room.

I take a minute to rub the sleep from my eyes before lifting my phone and unlocking the screen.

Slade:	Morning, beautiful. What are your plans today?
Me:	Sorry, I slept in. You were up early.
Slade:	Hazard of the job, I'm afraid. You get rested?
Me:	I did. I probably would still be asleep if it were not for Dawson.
Slade:	Ah, the little brother was tired of being quiet.
Me:	LOL. Nope, I promised him I would take him to the fair today.
Slade:	Want some company?
Me:	You want to hang out with me and my little brother.
Slade:	I leave in two days.
Me:	I thought it was three.
Slade:	We have to be there on Tuesday.
Me:	Give me an hour or so and we'll swing by and pick you up.
Slade:	I'm ready when you are.

Rolling my lazy ass out of bed, I grab some clothes and head across the hall to the shower. Twenty minutes later, I find Dawson in the living room, old boots on his feet, and a hoodie in his arms as he watches cartoons. I smile at his excitement and make my way to the kitchen.

"Morning, sweetie. He's excited." She motions her head to the living room where Dawson sits.

"I can see that."

"This is all he's talked about all week. I left some money for you under your keys by the door."

"Thanks, Mom."

"Dad and I are going to lunch and run some errands. We should be back before or around the same time as you."

"Don't rush. I've got nothing else going on today. I'm driving by Brandon's and picking Slade up. He's going to hang out with us today."

"You've been spending a lot of time with him."

That's Mom; she's questioning without questioning. "Yeah, started out so he wouldn't feel like a third wheel, but he's a nice guy."

"Nice, huh?" she asks, taking a sip of her coffee. I swear she drinks that stuff all day long.

"Yes, nice." I hold back my laughter.

"Do we get to meet him?"

I shrug and finish chewing my bite of Pop-Tart before answering. "They leave in two days, so I'm not sure."

"Bring him with you when you bring Daws home."

"Maybe." I shake my head and smile. "Where's Dad?" I ask, changing the subject.

"He ran over to the hardware store."

"I thought the two of you were running errands."

"Oh, we are, but he wanted to knock that one off the list and I didn't argue," she says with a laugh.

"I don't blame you." I finish my Pop-Tart and rush back upstairs to grab myself a hoodie. When I see Slade's hanging on my desk chair, I remember I have one in the car still. I grab his so I can return it, then head back downstairs. Dawson is waiting for me on the last step. "You ready?"

"Yes!" He cheers, grabbing my hand and pulling me to my car. He climbs in the back and buckles himself in. I wait and watch him to make sure he's secure before buckling in and heading toward Brandon's. "Austyn, this is not the way to the fair," he says from the back seat.

I laugh. "I know that, bud. I'm bringing a friend of mine today. He's a marine like Brandon."

"He is?" he asks, eyes wide.

"Yep. He's going to hang out at the fair with us today. That okay with you?" I'm not sure why I ask him if it's okay; it's happening regardless.

"Sure. Is he nice?" he asks. "I mean, Brandon's nice to me and he's a marine, but the Marines on TV are big and scary."

"Scary?"

"Yeah, they can kill people with their bare hands," he says, wide-eyed.

I glance into the rearview mirror, and he has a look on his face that says *Duh, you should know this.* "He's nice, Daws." The rest of the ride to Brandon's, my little brother rambles on about how cool marines are. He repeats everything my parents and I have told him since Brandon left. Brandon and Savvy and I spend a lot of time together and a lot of the time includes Dawson after school. He was sad when Brandon left. Dawson is also good friends with Brandon's twin cousins, Noah and Jonah. They're all in the same class, so to these little guys, marines are their heroes, just because of Brandon. I don't think their little minds process that all military, not just Marines, are our heroes.

We pull into Brandon's drive, and as soon as the car is turned off, Dawson is throwing off his belt and bolting from the car. He's up the steps and knocking on the door before I can get my door shut. "Brandon!" I hear him yell and see him launch himself at him.

I feel bad. I should have made sure that Daws got to see him sooner. I've been so caught up in Slade, it almost didn't happen. "Hey," I say, walking in the front door to find Dawson on Brandon's hip. It's something that he is too big for, at least for me. Slade stands beside him, and from the sounds of it, I'm just in time for the introduction.

"Daws buddy, this is my friend Slade. He's a marine like me," Brandon tells Dawson.

"You're big like Brandon," Dawson says.

"Dawson!" I scold him.

"Aust, he is," he defends.

Slade's deep rumble of laughter pulls my attention from my

little brother. "Nice to meet you, Dawson." Slade holds his hand out for him to shake. Dawson takes it, his tiny hand disappearing into Slade's.

"Aust," Dawson says, letting go of Slade's hand.

"Yeah, bud?"

"Come here." He motions for me to come closer. "I forgot," he whispers, but not really. We can all hear him.

"Forgot what?" I whisper back.

"What I'm posta say." He jerks his head toward Brandon and points at Slade.

"You lost me, bud." I'm super confused right now.

"When I meet the men like them, I'm posta say something, and I can't remember."

Now I get it. I lean in close, and this time, I do whisper in his ear, just for him. "Thank you for your service."

His little head bobs up and down. He turns to Brandon and wraps his arms around his neck, giving him a big hug. "Thank you for your service, B," he says.

Brandon smiles over at me and hugs him back. Dawson lets go of his hold on him and wiggles out of his arms. Brandon sets him back on the ground and Dawson walks to stand in front of Slade. He stares up at him. I try to see him from his eyes. He's a little taller than Brandon, my guess is a couple of inches, and his shoulders are broad, more so than Brandon's. To a little boy like Dawson, I can see how he would be intimidating. Without a word, Dawson walks closer and wraps his little arms around Slade's waist. "Thank you for your service," he says softly. He lets go of him and comes to stand beside me.

Placing my arm around him, I bend down and whisper, "Good job, buddy." He smiles up at me. Standing to my full height, I see both Brandon and Slade standing a little taller at my little brother's praise. Both wear looks of pride, as they should. "You ready?" I ask Slade.

"When you are," he says, stepping next to me.

"What are you and Savvy getting into today?" I ask Brandon.

"Hanging out here." He smirks, and I read through the lines. Alone time it is.

"Right, let's go, Daws."

He grabs my hand and we walk out to the car. I open the back door for him and make sure he's buckled in. When I get into the driver seat, I see Slade's knees are hitting the dash. "You can scoot your seat back," I tell him.

He looks back and sees that he has room. "Didn't want to squish him," he explains, moving the seat back.

All the way to the fair, Dawson rambles on about the animals he wants to see, the rides he wants to ride, and the food he wants to eat.

"He gets it honest." Slade laughs.

I don't even bother denying it. "Yep."

"What are we doing first?" I ask Dawson once we're through the gate.

"Animals!" he says, jumping up and down.

"Animals it is." I hold out my hand, and he takes it, leading me toward the barns. When I feel Slade's hand slide into my other one, my heart stutters. I grip his hand once our fingers are entwined. We make it to the barn, and Dawson let's go. "Stay close!" I yell after him. He turns and nods, his smile brightening his face as he moves several feet in front of us to look at the sheep.

"He's excited," Slade says as we leisurely walk through the barn, keeping a close eye on Dawson just up ahead.

"He is. He asked to go with me earlier in the week. I promised him I would bring him. Mom and Dad usually do, but not until the weekend. They're spending the day together while I occupy Dawson. I'm pretty sure the three of them will end up back here tonight for the truck pulls."

"Alone time." He chuckles.

"Stop it." I smack him with the hand that's not laced with his. "I don't need to hear that or think about it." I give an exaggerated shudder.

"Easy, killer," he jokes, reaching over to rub where I just smacked him.

"Austyn! I need a lift," Dawson calls.

When we reach him, he's trying to look over a tall wall. Standing on my tiptoes, I look over and see it's a wash station where they are bathing the sheep before their shows. I release Slade's hand, and he stops me.

"I got him." He steps up behind Dawson. "I'm going to lift you so your sister doesn't have to. That okay with you?" he asks Dawson.

"Yeah!" he cheers. He doesn't have a care in the world, his focus on seeing over the wall in front of him. Without effort, Slade lifts him and steps closer to the wall. "Wow! I can see everything," Dawson exclaims.

Slade shifts Dawson to one arm and holds the other one out for me. I take it and step closer to them. "That's better," he whispers, placing a kiss on my temple. Butterflies ignite in my belly and a warmth washes over me. Whether it's his actions, or his words, they both make me feel… content.

I stand there and listen to my little brother go on and on about the sheep and don't comprehend a word he's saying. Each day I spend with Slade is better than the last. The simple touches, the kisses.… Is it possible to fall this hard for someone in a week?

"Let's go on some rides!" Dawson says, bringing me out of my thoughts.

"You have all the other animals to see first," I remind him.

"I know, but I'm ready for rides."

"All right then." I hold my hand out for him, and he takes it. That's how the rest of the day goes. Slade rarely lets go of my hand, and when he does, it's not for long. No matter who we run into, where we are, he keeps my hand in his. Not that I'm complaining. It's a great day, but I can't help but wonder what it all means. If it were up to me, it would mean we're starting something. I know he's leaving, but it's not like he has a choice. He's serving our country.

"I think he's done," Slade tells me a couple of hours later when Dawson gets off the scrambler. He's lost the pep in his step for sure.

"You ready to head home?" I ask Dawson.

"Yeah, I'm tired."

Decision made, we head home. When we get there, my parents aren't home yet, and Dawson is sound asleep. "I'll carry him in," Slade offers.

"Thank you. He's getting too big for me to carry."

Slade climbs out and has Dawson in his arms before I can make it to the other side of the car. I shut the door behind them and race to open the front door. "Let's take him up to his room." I lead the way upstairs and step into Dawson's room.

"Austyn," Dawson asks sleepily, once he's lying on his bed.

"Yeah, bud?"

"Thank you." He holds his arms out for a hug.

"You're welcome."

"I like your marine," he mumbles rolling over.

I look up at Slade. "I like him too."

Slade's eyes soften, and he holds his hand out for me. I stand and take it, letting him pull me out of Dawson's room. "Which one is yours?" he asks.

I point to the room across the hall. He pushes open the door. Once we're both inside, he closes it behind us. Turning to me, he places his hands on my hips and moves me to stand in front of him. He steps forward and I step back. We continue this dance until my back hits the door. Leaving one hand on my hip, the other slides around the back of my neck. Leaning close, he rests his forehead against mine. "Angel," he rasps. My hands find their way to his neck, and I lock my fingers together. "Can I kiss you?"

"Please." Slowly, painfully so, he presses his lips to mine. I rise up on my toes and pull him into me, needing to be closer. His tongue traces my lips seeking entrance, and I don't hesitate to open for him. I'm not sure how we manage to do it, but without breaking the kiss, he lifts me, his hands on my ass, my back still pressed against my bedroom door. When he grinds his hard length into me, causing me to moan. "Slade." I murmur his name, needing something, but not able to voice what it is. Hell, I don't even know what it is. Just more. More, of his lips on mine, more of his hard body pressed into me. Just more.

Like a bucket of ice being poured over us, the front door closes and I hear my mom calling out for me. "Austyn!" she calls up the stairs.

Frantic, I scramble out of his arms. My chest is heaving for the breath that his kiss took from me. My only saving grace is that my bedroom door can't be seen from the bottom of the steps. Taking a deep breath. I hold my finger up to Slade telling him to wait just a minute. Opening my door, I walk to the top of the steps and peer down. She's not at the bottom. Looking over at Slade, I motion for him to join me.

He adjusts himself.

Right. There. In. Front. Of. Me.

Feeling the flush hit my cheeks, I turn and head down the stairs, leaving him to follow. I find my parents in the kitchen unloading groceries. "Hey, Dawson is sleeping. We just got home," I tell them.

"You carried him upstairs?" my dad questions.

"No, Slade did."

"Slade?" he asks.

"Brandon's friend from the Marines, catch up." Mom hip-checks him and laughs.

"Thanks for letting me use your restroom," Slade says, walking up beside me.

"Dad, Mom, this is Slade. Slade, these are my parents, Lee and Michelle."

"It's a pleasure to meet you, sir." He shakes my dad's hand. "Ma'am," he says, releasing Dad and offering his hand to Mom.

"You as well."

"Right, honey, we better get the rest of those groceries," Mom says.

"I got it." Slade gives my arm a gentle squeeze and heads outside. Blood is pulsing through my veins. I don't know if it's from being interrupted or if it's from what we we're on our way to doing. What I do know is that I just had the hottest moment of my life and now I have to stand here with my mother and act as if it didn't happen.

chapter 13

Slade

AS SOON AS I GET outside, I suck in a lungful of air. There was no way I could go downstairs and face her parents with my cock hard. I needed a minute to get myself in check. Luckily, Austyn caught on and the bathroom story passed. At least I hope it did. I was more than willing to collect the groceries to get some air, not that I wouldn't have done it otherwise.

"You like my daughter?" a deep voice asks from beside me. I'm standing on the porch, eyes closed, willing myself to calm the fuck down.

I freeze. I'm not sure I'm even breathing. I've never met *the* parents, so this is all new to me. Opening my eyes, I exhale. "Yes, sir," I say, going with honesty.

I don't look at him, but I can see him shake his head from the corner of my eye. "You're leaving soon?" he asks.

"Yes, sir. Two days."

"Thank you for your service, son." I nod. "Don't hurt her. Marine or not, she's my baby girl, and I will hunt you down."

"No, sir. Austyn… she's special."

"Damn right she is. You'd do well to remember that."

"Always, sir."

"Good talk," he says, gripping my shoulder. He lets go and

steps off the front porch. "You coming?" he asks.

Jumping into action, I follow him down the steps and to the SUV. We're able to get the remaining bags in one trip. I follow his lead, setting the bags on the counter. I was prepared for more of an interrogation, not that I'm complaining. I'm glad that Austyn has people in her life who care about her. That she has friends and family who are willing to go to bat for her and warn a guy like me to treat her right. She deserves that, and so much more.

"What are you kids doing tonight?" her mom asks.

Austyn looks over at me and shrugs. "No plans. I reserved the day to take Daws to the fair."

"Thank you for that. He's been talking about it all week."

"I had fun," she says.

"I'm making chicken stir-fry for dinner if y'all want to stay and eat."

"I'm not sure. Slade might have plans," Austyn says, looking over at me.

Is that hope in her eyes? She gives me a subtle nod, and there's my answer. Of course, I would have accepted regardless, unless she made it clear she didn't want me here. To be honest, I'm not sure I would have left then if the invitation still stood. I have two days, one if you want to get technical, and that's not enough time to spend with her. It figures I would meet her now, at this time in my life when I can't give her all of me, all of my time. That's how my luck goes. "I'm wherever you are," I say, not even bothering to keep my voice low. Her dad knows I like her. Why hide it?

"Okay, then I guess we're staying for dinner. You need help?" Austyn asks her mom.

"Slade, I could actually use your assistance if you don't mind. I'm building a new workbench out in my shop, and could use a hand unloading the materials I bought this morning," her dad asks.

"Sure thing." My eyes find hers for a brief moment before I

follow her dad outside. I'm not sure if he wants to grill me some more or if he really does need the help. Outside, he leads us to a flatbed trailer with a stack of lumber on it.

"I was gonna have a buddy of mine stop over tomorrow when he had time, but since you're here, I thought I'd take advantage of the situation."

"I'm happy to," I tell him. We work in silence lifting the boards and then the heavy sheets of plywood and carrying them into the garage. "You're building a workbench?" I ask him.

"Yeah, well, that's what I'm calling it. I like to tinker out here, and sometimes you just need a solid surface to work on."

"Need some help?" I offer.

"You ever built anything like this before?" He eyes me skeptically.

"No, sir, but I'm willing to learn."

"Well, dinner will be at least thirty more minutes. We can maybe get the boards measured and cut." I watch him as he grabs a measuring tape and pencil and starts measuring and marking boards. "Grab that end, will you?" he asks when he gets to the longer boards. We work in silence, measuring and marking each board.

"What next?" I ask once we've marked all the boards.

"Next we cut."

"What are you two doing out here?" Austyn says from behind us.

I turn to look at her. She's leaning against the side-entry door to the garage, arms and ankles crossed. All I want to do is go to her, wrap her in my arms and repeat what we did up in her room. I can still taste her.

"Manly things," her dad, Lee, replies.

I grin at his answer.

"Well, can you two put your manly things on hold and come and eat dinner?" she sasses back with a grin.

"Slade, you're in for a treat," he tells me. "My wife makes a mean chicken stir-fry."

"Hey, I helped." Austyn acts as though she offended. She's anything but, judging by the smile she's wearing.

I can't seem to take my eyes off her. It's not until I hear her dad chuckle and his hand clamps down on my shoulder that I'm brought out of my Austyn trance. "You got it bad, son," he says, his voice low. He moves toward Austyn and wraps his arm around her shoulder. "I know you did, sweetheart," he tells her.

"You coming, Slade?" she asks.

I nod and follow along behind them. I can't help but think what it would have been like to have parents like hers. So open and loving. Supportive. They're good people, and it shows in the kids they've raised. I know I sound like someone well beyond my years, but living the life I've lived, you grow up fast. If that's not enough, thirteen weeks of Marine boot camp will finish the job.

In the house, Lee motions for me to follow him. I do as I'm told, and he leads me to the laundry room with a big washtub. Again, I'm reminded of all these moments that I never had with my sperm donor. We each wash up for dinner. Back in the living room, Dawson is up from his nap and bouncing with energy.

"Slade!" he exclaims, and rushes toward me. He wraps his little arms around my waist. "You stayed." He looks up at me with a big toothy grin.

"Sure did."

"Let him go, Dawson." Austyn prods him.

"Will you sit by me?" he asks me.

"Sure bud." No way can I say no to this kid. He's cute as hell. Grabbing my hand, he guides me to the dining room table.

When I take the seat that Dawson instructs is mine, I'm sitting right across from Austyn. If I can't sit next to her, this is the next best thing. Although, I'm going to have to make a conscious effort to not stare at her the entire time. Her dad's already caught me once today. With a flurry of activity, we're all seated and filling our plates. The food is delicious, and the company's even better. It's a novelty for me to be a part of a normal loving family. I've seen it all week with Combs and his parents as well and have enjoyed it.

"Thank you for dinner," I tell Michelle, as I stand to help her clear the table.

"You're welcome. Sit, you're a guest."

"I don't mind helping." I pick up Dawson's plate and mine and follow her and Austyn into the kitchen.

"What are you kids planning for the rest of the night?" Michelle asks us.

I look over at Austyn for guidance. "Plans?" I ask her.

"I don't know. Daws wore me out today." She laughs.

Her mom laughs, and it sounds a lot like Austyn's. "We're taking him back," she tells us. "He wants to see the truck pulls, and you know your dad, he's all over that."

"I'm out on that," Austyn tells her. "I've had my fill for the day."

"Well, whatever you kids get into, you be safe." She closes the dishwasher and turns to face me. "Slade, thank you for helping with Dawson today, and then with Lee, and the dishes. I'm not sure when I'll get to see you before you leave." She steps toward me and wraps her arms around my waist in a hug. "Thank you for your service, young man. You're always welcome here," she whispers.

Emotions swarm me, so many I'm not sure which is stronger. I'm angry at my parents for being the addicts they are. I'm mad at the universe for taking Gran from me, my one cheerleader in life. I'm humbled to be receiving generosity from this family, as well as Brandon's, and then there's Austyn and the long list of things I feel about her.

Want.

Need.

Comfort.

Happiness.

The list goes on and on. My heart beats double time whenever she's near. I've done nothing but think about her since the first day I laid eyes on her in the flesh. Then there's the worry of leaving, and never seeing her again. I had nothing, no one... so I gave my life over to my country, to serve and to protect. I had nothing to lose when I signed up. Now, *now* I feel like I have everything to lose, and I don't know how to deal with it, with leaving her when I feel as though I might need her to breathe.

chapter 14
Austyn

THE SOUND OF FEET TROMPING down the steps wakes me up. Dawson has one speed in the mornings. Gotta love little brothers. Rolling over, I see Savannah's still asleep. She and Brandon came over last night. We hung out in the basement watching movies. Since I picked Slade up and Brandon had picked Savvy up, she stayed the night with me. The girl is a bed hog though. I have a queen, and she takes up more than her half.

Grabbing my phone from the nightstand, I hit the home button and see a message from Slade.

Slade: Morning, angel.

My heart flutters in my chest and I'm grinning like a fool. How is it that in such a short amount of time, just a simple text, two words from him can brighten my day?

"What's got you all smiles at the ass crack of dawn?" Savannah grumbles sleepily.

Looking over, I see her eyes are open, but barely. "It's hardly the ass crack of dawn, Savvy. It's nine."

"It's Sunday," she counters.

"It is. It's also your last day with Brandon before they leave tomorrow."

"I know. I'm not ready for him to leave."

"I know you're not."

"What about you? I assume Slade is the reason you're grinning at your phone like a fool?"

I turn the screen to face her so she can read his message. "He's hard to resist," I admit.

"Why does he call you angel?" she asks. "I've heard him call you that but haven't had the chance to ask you."

I give her his reasoning and now she's smiling. "He likes you, and I know you like him."

"What's not to like? But he's also leaving and has no roots here," I remind her.

"I don't know how much the two of you have talked, but Brandon says he doesn't have roots anywhere, not really. He didn't really explain, just that Slade is a good guy who was dealt a rough hand."

"Yeah, he's told me a little. I like him, Savvy. I really like him."

"I know," she chirps, more awake now. "So go for it. From what I can tell, he's just as into you."

"But he's leaving."

"Don't let the fact that he doesn't live here stop you. He's a marine and will be stationed for at least the next four years. You know I plan to go to wherever Brandon is. Are you willing to do that?"

"Today? No." I laugh. "If things progress, I think so. That's his career. He doesn't get to decide. I can finish school anywhere. I can teach anywhere."

"That was a big part of my decision making. I love kids, but it's also a career that I can do anywhere."

"Have you talked more about your future?"

"Not really. He's mentioned it, but I tell him to focus on getting through his training and then we can talk. I want him to stay focused on what he needs to do."

"I can see that."

"So, I say go for it. Put yourself out there. You always keep yourself in the shadows. You put all your energy into work and school. I've seen you turn down guy after guy. Take a chance, Austyn. You're beautiful and have so much to offer."

"I'm not going to throw myself at him, but regardless of that fact that he's leaving, if he wants to see where this goes, then so do I."

"He *so* wants you," she says, laughing and climbing out of bed.

I watch her walk out of my room and to the bathroom before opening up the message and texting him back.

Me:	Good morning.
Slade:	What are you doing today?
Me:	Depends.
Slade:	On?

I take a deep breath and know that with this admission, I'm in this — on the ride that is marine life. You can't date a marine and not go into it knowing what that means: a lot of worry and a lot of time alone. I've thought of nothing but that since the day Brandon left. Trying to put myself in Savannah's shoes so I could understand her emotions. I've lived it with her, and now that could be me. If it means being with Slade, I'm good with it.

Me:	On you.
Slade:	Today is my last day.
Me:	I know.
Slade:	I want to spend it with you.
Me:	You tell me when and where and I'll be there.
Slade:	Let me talk to Brandon, see what his plans are. Hold tight.

"What are you and Brandon doing today?" I ask Savvy when she comes back into the room.

"I'm not sure. He said he has something planned. He told me

to keep the day and the night open. Not that I would make any kind of plans on his last night here."

"I'm glad we're both off today," I confess.

"Yeah, me too. I hate that they have to use a day for travel, but I get it they need to be there early the next morning."

Her phone rings. "Hey, babe," she answers.

Giving them time, I climb out of bed and grab some clothes, heading to the shower. Fifteen minutes later, I find her on my bed still talking. I busy myself with brushing out my hair. Sitting at my vanity in my room, I plug in my flat iron and start putting on my makeup. I want to look my best for him; it's his last day here after all.

"Brandon says we have plans, but he won't tell me what they are. He said be prepared to not be home tonight."

I turn in my seat to look at her. "What are you going to tell your parents?"

She shrugs. "I'm eighteen, a legal adult, not to mention we've been together for years. I'm going to tell them I'm staying with him."

Before I can answer my phone pings with a message.

> **Slade:** Can you get away tonight?
>
> **Me:** Away how?

My belly does flips because I'm pretty sure he means all night, just as Savvy is with Brandon.

> **Slade:** All night. I can talk to your parents if you want.

"Is that Slade?" Savannah asks.

"Yeah, he… uh, he wants to know if I can get away tonight, all night."

"Yes!" she exclaims. "What did you tell him?"

"I didn't. He offered to talk to my parents."

"Wow, he's serious."

"I've known him a week. Brandon's only known him a couple of months. This is crazy."

"Not crazy. You're a good judge of character, you always have been. He's a good guy."

"We don't know that," I say, starting to panic. "I'm not ready for that, Savannah."

"Look, Austyn, you don't have to have sex with him. Just be upfront with him. If he gives you vibes, you can come home. Drive your car. Hell, I'll leave with you."

"You don't even know what we're doing."

"You don't either."

Before I can say anything more, my phone rings. "It's him," I tell Savannah.

"Answer it." She wriggles her brows.

"Hey," I greet him.

"Hey, angel," his deep voice rumbles. "You didn't reply. I was afraid that my last text freaked you out."

"Kind of," I admit.

"Don't tell Savannah as Combs wants to surprise her. He's getting a room at a hotel so they can spend his last night here together. I'm doing the same, but I just want to hang out with you. Spend my last night with you."

"Slade, I'm not ready for —"

"I just want your company, Austyn. Nothing more. You have my word."

"I'm not much of a rebel," I say softly. "I don't want to lie to them."

"I understand that. That's why I offered to talk to them. Give them my word. Savannah and Combs will be there too. You can drive your car and leave at any time. If you don't feel comfortable, we can figure something else out, but I really want this time with you before we leave tomorrow. We have to be up and on the road early. This is my last chance to spend time with you."

"Can I think about it?"

"Yeah. In the meantime, you ladies feel like going to a movie?

Combs says there's some chick flick that Savvy's been wanting to see."

"We both have. She was waiting until he left, not wanting to take time away from him while he's on leave."

"So you'll go?"

"Yes." I can hear Brandon talking to him in the background, while Savannah hangs on my every word.

"Can you ladies be ready in an hour?"

"Can you be ready in an hour?" I ask Savannah. She nods and flashes me a beaming smile. "Yeah, we'll be ready. We're still at my place."

"We'll be there soon," he says, ending the call.

"What? What are we doing?" Savannah asks.

"We're going to the movies."

"Really?"

"Yep, B said there's a movie you've been wanting to see. I hope it's that new romantic comedy. I've been dying to go see it."

"I mentioned to him that you and I were going to go, so that must be it."

"Get ready, woman!" I say, motioning for her to get in the shower. She walks to my closet and grabs her bag of clothes that she keeps here. I do the same at her place. We never know where we're going to end up when we're together, although we still end up taking each other clothes. That's just what we do. I finish getting ready while Savannah showers. Heading downstairs, I find my parents and Dawson sitting in the living room.

"Hey, honey," Mom greets me.

"Hey." I take a seat next to Dawson and ruffle his hair. His eyes are glued to the TV on some cartoon he's watching. Mom is reading a book and Dad is playing a game on his iPad. "Can I talk to you guys?" This gets their attention, and they both look up and nod. Tilting my head toward the kitchen, I stand and head that way. I hear the recliner close, and I know they're right behind me.

My dad's the first to speak. "What's wrong?"

"Nothing, I just want to talk to you guys about something." Before I can get another word out, there's a knock at the door. I know it's them without even looking. Dad answers the door, which is right off the kitchen, and in walks Brandon and Slade. I was hoping to do this on my own, but then again, I'm sure they would have wanted to talk to him anyway.

"Hey," Brandon says, taking a seat at the kitchen table. Slade stands just inside the door.

"Hey, angel," he says when our eyes meet.

My face heats, but I don't know if it's from his attention or my parents; I can feel their eyes boring into me. "Hi." I wave awkwardly. "So, I was getting ready to talk to them. I want to stay." I point to the table where my parents are now sitting. He nods and follows me to the table. He pulls my chair out for me, and I know that my parents are taking in his actions. "Right, so Brandon and Slade leave tomorrow morning to go back. This time to to North Carolina, right." My parents nod. I have their full attention. "Brandon, he... uh... got a hotel room, so that he and Savvy can spend some time together, just the two of them before they leave."

"You did that before you left, right?" Mom asks.

"We did. I just want to soak up as much of her as I can before I leave," Brandon says sincerely.

"Instead of staying with Mr. and Mrs. Combs, I've rented a room too," Slade speaks up. "I've asked Austyn to hang out with me. She's welcome to stay. I want her to stay, but not for the reasons you're thinking. I like your daughter and the thought of leaving and not getting to see her...." He shakes his head. "I just want to soak up as much of her as I can before I leave." He uses the words Brandon just used.

"Austyn is technically an adult and can do as she wishes. I have my reservations. We don't know you. You've known my daughter a few days at best." My dad speaks up.

"Yes, sir. I understand that. Austyn is unlike anyone I've ever met."

"Lee," Brandon intervenes. "I've only known Slade for a couple of months, but when you've been through what we have, we're brothers. I love Austyn as if she were my sister. I would in no way put her in harm's way."

"Austyn, what do you want?" Mom questions me. She's using her "I'm your mother, but I also understand what you're feeling" voice. Serious yet compassionate, that's my mother.

I take a deep breath. I can't believe we're having this conversation. "I'd like to stay. I'll drive. That way I have my car, and if I change my mind, I can come home." I know that they can't tell me no, not really. But I've never been one to lie to my parents. I would also spend the night worrying I was going to get caught and not be able to enjoy his company.

"Slade, she's my baby," my dad says. "You seem like a good kid and so is my Austyn. I trust her judgment. Let me tell you something, if you hurt her in any way, force her into anything, I will find you. Don't forget our talk," he threatens.

If the moment were not so tense, if I were not holding my breath waiting for their reactions, I would laugh.

"Are the two of you… together?" my mom asks. I can see the worry etched across her face. She's concerned things are moving too fast. If her facial expression didn't give her away, her stiff posture would have.

"No, ma'am," Slade answers. "I like your daughter very much. I don't think it's fair to her to start something and me leave."

My heart drops at his confession, but at the same time, I get it. It's going to be hard enough when he leaves tomorrow with what we have now, whatever that may be. I can't imagine him leaving and us being an official item. I watched Savannah go through it so I can guess.

"Hey," Savannah says, bounding down the steps and into the kitchen. She's oblivious to the conversation we're having.

"Austyn, it's your call," Dad tells me. It looks like it pains him to do so, but they raised me to be responsible and even though they wish they didn't have too, they let me make my own decisions. They've always guided me, and given me advice, but have let me be my own person at the same time.

I nod. "I'm not sure. I need a little more time," I confess. I want to stay, I don't know why I can't just make the final decision.

Slade lays his hand over mine that's resting on the table. "No pressure, angel. I told you that."

I nod. "I know." It's out there now. I just need to decide. Needing to change the subject, I look over at Brandon. "What time does the movie start?"

He looks at his phone. "We actually need to get going. We can go to a later show, though," he suggests.

"No, this is your last day. Let's go."

"What are you all seeing?" Mom asks. I'm sure she's trying to lighten the mood. My dad is sitting with his arms crossed, staring at me and then Slade.

"That new one with Zac Efron," Savvy chimes in.

"You got them to see a chick flick?" Mom asks, amused.

"Pretty sure they could get us to watch paint dry," Slade mumbles, but we all hear him. Even my dad cracks a smile. How could he not?

chapter 15

Slade

W E RIDE IN BRANDON'S TRUCK to the movies. Austyn is by my side looking out the window. I want to pull her into me, wrap my arms around and just... keep her close. I leave in less than twenty-four hours, and I don't know if or when I'll see her again. Hell, I don't even know if she wants to see me again. I don't know if I overstepped with her parents, but fuck, I wanted her to know she wasn't alone in this. I'm not trying to lure her into fucking me all night. I just want to be with her, spend as much time with her as I can. The time I've spent with her has been the best I can ever remember. No one can blame me for wanting to hold onto it.

After getting our tickets and some snacks, we find our seats. Brandon leads us to the back row of the theater. He sits, then Savannah, Austyn, and I follow. "Tight quarters," I say when our elbows connect on the armrest. Austyn laughs. I love that sound.

"No kidding. At least the cup holders are in the back of the seats." She leans forward and places her bottle of water in the slot.

We opted to share popcorn. I'm currently holding the large tub on my lap. I wait for direction from her, not wanting to do something that will have her not wanting to stay with me tonight. We've shared simple touches, held hands, and shared a kiss or two, but that's it. I don't really know where we stand, and that bothers me. I want to wrap my arm around her and bring her as close to me as possible.

"You can set it here. I have more room than you do," she says, taking her arm from the rest."

"What? Are you saying I'm fat?" I raise my brow at her.

She scoffs. "Right, your muscles have muscles."

The lights go down, and the previews begin to play. It's perfect timing; otherwise, Austyn would see just how her words affect me. I don't know that I've never blushed before, but I can feel it in my cheeks. Not to mention the stiffening of my cock. That's nothing new though, not this past week. That happens anytime she's near. Just the thought of getting to see her makes me hard as steel.

I need to get us back to how we used to be, carefree She's been quiet since we left her house. Leaning in, I whisper, "I'm sorry if I overstepped."

She turns to look at me. "Not at all," she whispers back.

"I promise you, Austyn, I don't expect anything but your company. I-I'm having a hard time knowing that I leave tomorrow morning and I don't know if I'll ever see you again," I confess. "It's eating me up."

"Do you want to see me again?" she asks softly. She's now leaning into me, our shoulders touching.

"More than anything."

"Then we'll make it happen." She smiles. It's one that says she's happy.

It's enough for me. I set the popcorn on the armrest. "Can you hold this?" I ask. She does without complaint, and I lift my arm, placing it over her shoulders. She leans in a little closer, and that's how we stay for the entire movie. We share popcorn, our hands often touching in the bucket.

"What did you think?" Austyn asks as we exit the theater. Our hands are linked.

"He got the girl," I say, giving her hand a gentle squeeze.

"He did. The book was better," she tells me.

"Right?" Savannah chimes in. "The books are always better."

"What now?" Austyn asks.

"Babe," Brandon tells Savannah. "I got us a room. It's going to be longer this time, before I get to see you again, and I wanted to spend my last night with you. The hotel has an indoor pool. I thought we could hang out there, for a while. Then some dinner?" Brandon states it as a question.

"I need to run home and grab some clothes," Savannah says, not missing a beat. The smile on her face tells us all we need to know—she's more than on board with the plan.

"Why don't you drop us off at my house. I need to do the same. We can meet you there." She looks up at me for confirmation.

Bending down, I press my lips to hers. It's soft and quick, but I hope the kiss tells her what I'm feeling.

Elated.

Excited.

Nervous.

It's as if my heart is now about to beat out of my chest at the idea of her lying next to me all night.

"That works," Savannah responds to Austyn.

This time in the truck, Austyn sits in the middle of the backseat, right next to me. Her hand's locked firmly with mine. *This,* this is where she should have been on the way to the theater. This is where she should always be.

When we climb out of the truck, she keeps her hand in mine until we reach the front steps. We walk into the kitchen to find Dawson at the table eating a bowl of cereal.

"Hey, D," I say, holding my fist out for him.

He grins at me. "Slade!"

"I was here earlier," I tell him.

"I know, but I was watching *Teenage Mutant Ninja Turtles*," he says, like I should know what that means.

"He's obsessed," Austyn explains. "Where are Mom and Dad, Daws?"

"Dad's in the garage and Mom was upstairs folding laundry."

"I'll be right back," she says to me.

I nod and pull out a chair beside Dawson. "So tell me about these turtles."

He abandons his cereal and starts talking animatedly about his favorite cartoon. "They're so cool," he exclaims.

"Are you boring Slade with your turtle talk?" her dad asks from behind us a few minutes later.

"He asked," Dawson defends.

"That I did." I throw him a wink.

"Daws, go on in the living room for a few. I need to talk to Slade."

Dawson grabs his bowl without complaint and heads toward the living room. He stops when he gets to the door. "You leave soon?" he asks.

"I do. In the morning."

Dawson walks back toward me and sets his bowl on the table. The next thing I know, his little arms are around my neck, giving me a hug. "Thanks for hanging out with me. I hope I get to see you when you come back."

"Anytime, Dawson." I pat his back awkwardly. It must be good enough for him, though, as he pulls away, grabs his bowl and goes to the living room.

"Will you be?" her dad asks.

"Will I be what?" I ask him.

"Back? Are you coming back here?"

"That depends on your daughter, sir. I can tell you that I couldn't handle being here and not being with her."

His face is void of emotions as he stares at me. "Does she know that?"

"No, sir. I don't want to pressure her."

"Where will you go?"

I shrug. "I don't have a home, not anymore. My parents are addicts. My grandmother raised me. She passed away two weeks before high school graduation. The Marines, they're my family." I lay it all out for him. I really like his daughter, and he should know who she's spending time with.

"Respect her," he says sternly.

"Always." I don't hesitate with my reply.

"Almost ready!" Austyn calls down the stairs. I look at them, following the sound of her voice. I can't seem to help it. I know she's still up there, but I gravitate toward her, even her voice.

"Slade."

Her dad pulls my attention away from the stairs. He holds his hand out to me, and I take it. "I want you to know, regardless if you end up with my daughter, as long as you treat her right, you're always welcome here. No matter what your relationship status is."

There it is, that lump in my throat. The one I get when I think about leaving Austyn. "Th-thank you, sir."

"Hey," Austyn says, clearing the bottom step, a bag on her shoulder. "I'm going to stay. I'll have my phone," she tells her dad.

He holds his arms open, and she falls into him, hugging him hard. I watch as he kisses the top of her head. "Be safe, Aust. Call me if you need anything."

"We'll be fine, Dad."

I don't miss that she says we'll not I. She's probably talking about her and Savannah, but I'm going to go ahead and put me into that equation as well. I can't imagine being anywhere else.

"Ready?" Austyn asks.

"If you are." I hold my hand out to her dad. He takes my offered hand and gives me a firm shake. "I'll take care of her. You have my word."

I follow Austyn out to her car and open her door for her, pulling the bag from her arm. "I got it," I tell her.

"Slade, I can open doors," she says with a light laugh.

I can tell that it makes her happy, even though she tries to hide it. "I know, but this is my last chance to do this for you, for a while," I add, hoping I'm telling the truth. "I leave tomorrow, and I'll be gone for five months. I need to know I took care of you when I had the chance."

She nods, her shoulders slumped, and climbs in the car. I wait until her seat belt is buckled before closing her door. I open the back door, toss in her bag, then make my way to the passenger side. Once I'm buckled up and we're pulling out of the driveway, I see her parents sitting on the front porch. Her dad has his arm around her mom's shoulders, and they're both wearing soft, nervous smiles. I didn't know they were watching, but it looks like they're pleased with what they see.

When we get to Brandon's, he and Savannah are already there. Austyn doesn't bother knocking. She walks on in announcing our arrival, with me hot on her heels. "You ready?" she asks Savannah.

"Yeah, we just got here. Brandon's packing up his things." She sniffs, and I can see the moisture in her eyes.

I place my hands on Austyn's hips and step in close to her. Her body is aligned with mine. "I need to do that too. I'll be back," I say, my lips next to her ear. She shivers, and I let her go. Devouring her mouth in the foyer of the Combs's house is not what I need to be doing. I need to pack up my shit and get to the hotel. That's where I can kiss her until our lips are bruised. Kiss her enough to last me months, hell a lifetime. I have no idea what we are, but I'm hoping tonight we can clear that up.

When we get to the hotel, I check us in. Grabbing our bags and tossing them over one arm, I hold my hand out to Austyn with the other. My palms are sweaty, and I know she has to be able to hear the rapid beat of my heart as it drums against my chest. She doesn't hesitate to put her hand in mine as we walk toward the elevators. As if spending the night with me is the most natural thing in the world. We're both quiet on the ride up to our room; this is new for both of us. At the room, I hand her the keycard. For some reason, it feels like it's important for her to unlock the room. Like I'm giving her the choice to be here with me. I'm still astonished that she is, that she wants to spend this time with me.

"Wow," she says, holding the door open for me.

The room is spacious with a king-size bed sitting in the center of the room. There is a small table and a couch that pulls out into a bed. I made sure of that. The king is big enough for both of us to have our own space, but if that makes her uncomfortable, I can take the couch. My hope is that she won't want space between us. That I can hold her in my arms, have the memory of what that feels like to take with me.

"This is too much," she says, coming out of the bathroom. "The shower is huge."

I can't help but laugh at her. "I'm going to be living on base without these kinds of luxuries. We have twin-sized beds, and some of us are in bunk beds."

"Is it bad?" she asks.

"Boot camp was us in a room together, lots of bunk beds, a trunk for our personal items. The barracks are better, more like bedrooms that we share. We're allowed more personal items: our phones, computers, things like that."

"That's good."

"Come here." I hold my arms open.

She walks toward me slowly, hesitantly. As soon as she's close enough to reach, I pull her into a hug. I hug her tightly, remembering the feeling of her in my arms, storing it in my memory. "I'm going to miss you, angel," I tell her honestly. She doesn't reply. Instead, she wraps her arms around my waist and holds on tightly. We stand there for I don't know how long, neither one of us willing to pull away. That is until my phone rings. I groan.

"You should get that," she murmurs breaking our embrace.

Reluctantly, I pull my phone out of my back pocket and swipe my thumb across the screen. "Hello."

"Reeves, we're headed down to the pool. Are you guys in?" Combs asks.

"You want to go down to the pool?" I ask Austyn.

"Yeah, I just need to change." She goes to her bag and picks it up, carrying it into the bathroom and closing the door.

"Yeah, we'll be there. We just need to change. I don't have trunks," I say as an afterthought.

"Open the door."

"What?" I ask, walking toward the door. Pulling it open, I see Combs and Savannah standing there. I end the call and shove my phone back into my pocket.

"These are for you. I figured you didn't pack any for boot camp," Savannah says. "I had Brandon grab an extra pair."

"Thank you." I smile, touched by the thought. "Austyn's getting changed, so we'll meet you down there." After closing the door, I sit on the edge of the bed and wait for Austyn to come out. Part of me wants to stay locked in this room until the moment I have no choice but to leave, but the other part wants this memory with her too. I want it all, every single moment we can create before I leave.

chapter 16
Austyn

I'M CHANGED. THAT PART WAS easy. The hard part is walking out of this bathroom and facing Slade. Staring at my reflection in the mirror, I'm regretting grabbing my bikini. Not that I'm ashamed of my body; that's not it. The problem is there's not much to the thin scraps of material. I already feel this magnetic attraction anytime he's near. How is that going to be with me barely dressed? Debating on what I should do, I reach into my bag and dig for my cover-up. I know I shoved it in here. It's black and sheer, but it will give me some semblance of modesty. At least I hope it does. Finally, I feel the thin material and remove it from my bag. Sliding it over my head, I take a deep breath. I'm spending the night with him in this room. Maybe that's the root cause of my apprehension. Grabbing one of the hotel towels, I then shove everything back into my bag and open the door.

Here goes nothing.

I walk out of the bedroom with my head held high, much more confident and a whole hell of a lot less nervous than what I actually feel.

"Combs, just...." His voice trails off when he raises his head and looks at me. He stares. His eyes roam over every inch of me, from my head to my toes before his eyes lock with mine. "You're fucking gorgeous."

His deep timbre washes over me. Goose bumps break out across my skin. The combination of his deep voice, the fact that he called me gorgeous, and the way his eyes are cataloging every inch of me, has butterflies breaking free in my belly. "Y—" I clear my throat. "You were saying something about Brandon?"

"Yeah." He stands and walks toward me. "They're down at the pool." He stops to stand in front of me.

He leans in and I close my eyes, waiting for his lips to connect with mine. When I feel them press against my forehead, I'm surprised. "You okay?"

"Yeah, angel. I'll be out in a minute." He steps to the side and closes the bathroom door behind him.

As soon as I hear the click of the door closing, I exhale slowly. I didn't even realize I was holding my breath. This thing between us is intense and is so unlike anything I've ever felt. I don't know what to do with it, but I do know I'm not ready to say goodbye to him. How did I let this happen? How did I fall for him in such a short amount of time? How are we going to navigate the waters that lie ahead, even more so, does he want to?

"Ready?" he asks, placing his hand on the small of my back. I jump, not realizing he was there. I was so lost in my thoughts I didn't hear the door open. "You okay?"

"Yeah, did you grab a towel?" I ask him. He holds it up and shows me. "Room key?" I ask.

"Damn." He chuckles. Stepping away, he grabs his wallet, phone, and the room key. "Now I'm ready."

We walk hand-in-hand to the pool. "About time, slowpokes!" Savannah calls out as soon as we enter the pool area.

"You were ready when you invited us," I counter.

She laughs, cupping her hands and splashing. I step back, and my back hits Slade's chest. "Careful," he says with a laugh. His hands rest on my hips and with a small tug, he pulls me closer, my body aligning with his.

"Y'all getting in or what?" Savannah taunts.

"We better join them, or she's going to soak us regardless," I tell him.

"She's a pistol," he says.

"You have no idea." Keeping his hands on my hips, he turns me to the table and chairs that Brandon and Savannah have occupied for our stuff. We reach the table and he lets go of me. He takes my towel from my hand and places mine and his on the table. He slides his wallet and phone underneath them.

"You have your phone?" he asks me.

"No, I left it in the room."

"Austyn!" Savannah yells.

"She's relentless." I grin. Knowing he's about to see all of me, with little left to his imagination, I school my features and reach for the hem of my cover-up. Like a Band-Aid, I pull it up and remove it quickly. I take my time folding it and place it on the table next to our towels.

"Jesus," he murmurs.

I lift my head and turn to look at him. His dark eyes are smoldering as he strokes them over my body. I feel the heat from his gaze. "Ready?" I ask, ignoring his comment, his eyes, and the heat that's pouring from the combination of the three.

Reaching out, he snakes his arm around my waist. The feel of his rough hands on my skin causes me to shudder. "Austyn." He tugs me closer. My hands rest on his bare chest while both his arms move around my waist. The stroke of his thumb brushes just above the waistline of my bikini bottoms. The heat of his skin mingles with mine, and my breath catches. Tilting my head back, I look up at him. Without a word, he presses his lips to mine. It's brief but no less intense.

"Come on lovebirds!" Brandon calls out.

"Why didn't we stay in the room?" he asks me.

I smile widely. "Because we wanted to swim."

"Did we?"

"We did. Let's go." Stepping back, I clutch his hand and lead him to the steps of the pool. Together, hand-in-hand, we immerse ourselves in the heated water.

"Finally." Savannah grins. She swims toward us and latches herself onto my back. "I missed my bestie."

"What am I?" Brandon asks, hands in the air.

"Swim," she says low, just for me to hear her. Without question, I let go of Slade's hand and swim away from him. When we reach the opposite end of the pool, she slides off my back, and we both hang onto the side of the pool. "That looked intense." She doesn't elaborate, but she doesn't have to. I know what she's referring to.

"Little bit," I confess.

"You okay with staying with him? I don't want you to do it because of me, because I'm staying with Brandon."

"He's sweet, and I can trust him."

"You sure about that?"

I look over at Slade and Brandon who are deep in conversation. "Yeah, he's been nothing but great. I have my car if things change."

"Call me. I'll keep my phone on. Hell, scream. Our room is beside yours."

"I'm fine, Savvy. Promise."

"I know. I just feel like I pushed you into this."

"Trust me, if I didn't want to be here, I wouldn't be. I really like him."

"So, are you two an item?"

I shrug. "I don't know if we're anything at all. He leaves tomorrow."

"So? Brandon and I are doing it."

"Yeah, but y'all have been together for years. We all grew up together."

"When you know, you know. Remember freshman year

when I told you after my first date with Brandon that he was the man I was going to marry?"

I smile at the memory. "I do. I thought you were crazy."

"Look at us now. Over four years later and we're still going strong. The heart doesn't know distance, Austyn."

"Who said anything about my heart?" I counter. I've never lied to my best friend, and by the look on her face, I'm not doing very good job of it now.

"Please," she draws the word out and rolls her eyes, "I'm your best friend. You don't do casual. The men in this town with cracked hearts are proof."

"What's that supposed to mean?"

"Just that you've turned them all down. No one's ever gotten to you, not until Slade."

I don't argue because she's right. "We're just going slow, playing it by ear. He asked me if I wanted to see him again, and I told him yes. But I don't know what that means really? I mean, how does that work? It's not like we have four years to build whatever this is before he left, like you and B."

"If you both want it bad enough, it will all work out. Have a little faith, Aust."

"How about a game of chicken?" Brandon calls out.

Savannah wags her eyebrows at me, causing me to laugh. We swim toward the guys, and they meet us halfway. "You're going down, Wilson," Savannah taunts me.

Slade moves to stand in front of me. "Climb on." He disappears under the water, and I put my legs over his shoulders. When he stands, I smooth his wet hair out of his eyes for him. His hands are gripping my thighs. "You ready for this?" he asks.

"As I'll ever be."

Turning his head, he kisses my inner thigh. It's just a peck, but it lights my body on fire. The intimacy of it all has me reeling. That's why I don't hear them say we were starting and I'm not ready when Savannah comes at me, knocking me off his shoulders. She cheers in victory while I spit and sputter from the water intake.

"You okay?" Slade asks. His hands are on my hips, holding me up.

"Yeah, I wasn't ready. You distracted me."

"Me?"

"Yes. You. That kiss distracted me."

"Now you know what to expect."

"I've played chicken before," I tell him.

A look crosses his face, but it's gone before I can determine what it means. "The kiss, you know to expect the kiss. I can't have you wrapped around me like that and not… kiss you."

Oh.

"Ready for round two?" Savannah calls out.

Nope. Not even a little. Slade winks, releases his hold on me and turns around. He disappears under the water and I climb on his shoulders. Again, I push his wet hair out of his eyes, and this time, *this time* he kisses both thighs, effectively driving me crazy.

We spend the next couple of hours laughing and swimming. Savannah and I tied with chicken, so we decided to race. Slade and Brandon, of course, blew us out of the water.

"We can't let them keep winning. I wonder how fast they are with us on their backs," Savannah muses. "We're going to line them up against each other. They've tied so far. You jump on Slade. I'll jump on Brandon."

"Why do we want to slow them down?" I ask, confused.

"Oh, my sweet Austyn." She shoots me a wicked grin. "We don't want to slow them down, but we do want to wrap ourselves around them. This is our excuse."

I have to admit, it's a solid plan. So when she lines the guys up, I sneak up behind Slade and look over at my best friend. She nods, and I wrap my arms around his neck and my legs around his waist. He grips my legs, holding me to him. Not once does he ask what I'm doing or get pissed that I'm messing with his race. He just holds onto me.

"Try your luck now." Savannah laughs loudly.

The guys exchange a look. I can't see Slade's face, but from the look on Brandon's, having us on their back is nothing for them. Of course it's not, they're marines and have been through rigorous training for this sort of thing. We didn't think about that.

"Don't let go," Slade tells me. He releases his hold on me and gets ready.

"Go!" Savannah yells.

Slade takes off with a jolt, and I squeal with laughter. Water sloshes over us as his wide strokes move us to the opposite side of the pool. I'm too engrossed in him, the feel of his muscles rippling under my touch from the effort of his strokes against the water to pay attention to our friends.

"Tie!" Brandon cheers.

Slade laughs, and I can feel the rumble in his chest. "Come here," he says, looking over his shoulder. I'm not sure how we manage to do it, but I slide from his back to his front. My legs still wrapped around his waist, my arms around his neck. "You're my good luck charm, angel."

"Hmmm… an angel and a knight," I muse, causing him to grin.

"Opposites attract and all that."

"Attraction, is that what this is?" I ask. Being wrapped in his arms makes me feel bold. That, and we have hours left before he has to leave.

"I'm not sure," he confesses. With me still holding onto him, wrapped around his body, he moves us away from our friends. "I've never felt anything like this, Austyn. I've never had my heart race so hard that it feels as though it could explode just by looking at someone." He presses his forehead against mine. "It's attraction, yes, but I'd like to think that it's more than that."

"It's more," I confirm.

"I'm leaving."

"You're a marine."

"I can't ask you to wait."

"You didn't. That doesn't mean I'm not going to."

"This is crazy."

"It is."

"You guys want to grab something to eat?" Brandon calls over, interrupting us.

"Can we talk more about this?" he asks, lifting his head to look at me.

"Later.' I press a kiss to the corner of his mouth. "We have the rest of the night."

"Not long enough," he mutters.

My heart stumbles. He's right; it's not long enough. We just need to make every second count, that's all. We climb out of the pool and dry off. Brandon and Slade work out that we're just going to meet at the hotel restaurant. None of us really want to leave the sanctuary of this place, knowing that the next time we do leave, they will be gone for a long time. It's not something any of us really want to face, even though we have to.

chapter 17

Slade

THE HOTEL RESTAURANT IS GOOD, the company even better. Once Brandon and I have paid the bill, we decide it's time to head back to our rooms. It's a little before seven, and I have twelve hours left with her. Twelve hours to memorize the sound of her voice, the feel of her soft skin, the smell of her hair and learn everything I can about her. Although I can't ask her to wait, I want to. I want to beg and plead for her to be mine. I know that's selfish, but it doesn't stop me from wanting it all the same.

"Dad will be here at seven to get us," Brandon tells me on the elevator ride up to our rooms.

"I'll be ready," I assure him.

Our rooms are side-by-side. The girls walk ahead, and I see Austyn nod. Then they hug. "Take care of her," Brandon says.

"You know I will. Besides, we're not going to be doing anything that she needs care for." He looks at me skeptically. "I can't fuck her and leave her." That doesn't mean I don't want to. Just the thought alone has my cock hard. The thought of leaving her physically causes my chest to ache.

He nods. "See you in the morning, brother."

We walk the small distance to our rooms. Austyn is leaning

against the door looking a hell of a lot more relaxed than she did earlier. Without saying a word, I pull the key card out of my pocket and unlock the door. "After you."

She steps inside with a smile. "I can't believe how nice this room is." Once inside, she turns, a small smile on her lips. "I thought we could watch a movie or something, I mean, unless you have something else planned?" she rambles, and looks ridiculously cute doing so.

"A movie's good. You pick. I'm going to go change." I grab some gym shorts out of my bag and disappear into the bathroom to change. "Find something?" I ask her.

"No." She tosses the remote on the bed. "This is your last night here, you pick. I'll change."

I watch her as she grabs her bag and takes it with her in the bathroom. It takes her longer than me. I scroll mindlessly through the channels. I couldn't care less what we watch, as long as I'm spending time with her. When the bathroom door opens, I turn my head. She's in a tank top and a pair of short shorts. Nothing too revealing, but I can easily see the swell of her breasts, and then there are her long tan legs.

"Find something?" She throws my words back at me.

"Nah, we can scroll through and look together." I slide back on the bed and rest against the headboard. Austyn climbs in the opposite side, doing the same thing, leaving plenty of space between us.

Remote in hand, I scan through the stations. We settle on *Family Feud,* both of us trying to answer the questions. Out of nowhere, a loud crack of thunder booms, causing her to jump. Wind and rain pelt the window of our room.

"I love to sleep when it rains."

"Do you? What's so different about it?"

"I don't know really. I guess maybe it's the soothing sound as it hits against the roof or the windows. As long as I don't have to worry about tornados, I even like the storms."

Pointing the remote at the TV, I turn it off. The room is dark, and all we can hear is the wind, the rain, and the cracking of thunder. Bolts of lightning shining through the window is our only source of light, coming at short intervals. "Austyn," I whisper her name, but even through the storm, she can hear me.

"Yeah."

"Can I hold you?"

"Slade, I—"

"Nothing else. I just want to hold you. I want to experience what it's like to listen to the storm with you in my arms." She doesn't reply, but I can see her shadow as she moves closer. Scooting down, I lay my head on the pillow and open my arms to her. She slides in close and rests her head on my chest. Still and quiet, listening to the storm rage outside, she remains in my arms. Unfortunately, it's not the only storm brewing. The one inside me is raging as well. The one that wants to hold onto her and never let her go. The one that wants to rebel and say fuck the Marines, and just be here with her or wherever she is. The one that roars to life when I think about leaving this amazing girl when I've just found her.

"You're changing it." She breaks the silence.

"Changing what, angel?"

"The storm."

"Changing it how?"

"Every time it storms, I'll forever think of this moment. Think of you."

"Will you?" I ask hesitantly. "Will you think of me?" I sound like a pussy, but I need to know. I need to know how she feels, what she wants before I leave.

"Every day."

Closing my eyes, I let her reply sink in. "I can't ask you to wait for me." I repeat my words from earlier, my stomach a knot of unease.

"Did you ask?"

"Smartass." I tickle her side.

"What do you want, Slade?"

"You."

"What does that mean? You want me until tomorrow morning? You want me when you come home on leave? This isn't your home."

"I don't have a home to go to, Austyn. I have no one in my life who I care to see, at least I didn't until now."

"How long are you gone?"

I know she already knows the answer, but I tell her anyway. "A while. SOI is months of training without leave."

"So we go slow."

"That's not fair to you. You didn't sign up for the Marines. I did. Why should you put your life on hold?"

"You do realize what you do it's incredibly selfless, right?"

"It's not. I had nothing, no one. The Marines gave me purpose."

"Slade." She lifts her head to look at me. "You put your life on the line to defend our country. You have to go away for months at a time from those you care about. You sacrifice yourself for our country. I get to go to college and hang out with Savvy on the weekends because you and all the others enlisted. You're giving me and every other American that freedom."

"I didn't care about anyone when I signed up," I admit. It's true I didn't. I had nothing to look forward to. Sure, I could have managed on my own, but my grades were shit, so college was out of the question. Plus it's expensive, and even with selling the house, I couldn't afford it. Then I would have needed a place to live. The Marines gave me a family, gave me a home.

"And now?" she asks hesitantly.

I run my fingers through her hair. "Now, there's you. I have my marine brothers, and I expected that, but I never expected you. I never expected to feel as though I'm walking away from everything good in my life by going back."

"You're not. I'll be here."

I think about what she's saying, and I want that. I want her. I want to call her mine. But that would be selfish. I need her to be certain. "Let's go slow. See how this works with me being gone. You might change your mind."

"I'm not that shallow," she fires back.

I pull her closer to me, worried she'll pull away. "That's not what I meant." I'm quick to diffuse the situation. "It's hard, Austyn. Brandon, he was miserable all through boot camp being away from Savannah."

"She was too."

"I don't want that for you."

"You don't get to make the choice. That's up to me. What about you? Are you saying you're not going to miss me?"

"You know better than that. I'm here thinking about how bad it would be if I didn't go back. What would the punishment be?" I let my words sink in. "What do you want, Austyn?"

"You."

I release a heavy breath. "How do we do this? I'm out of my element here, both with my training and with you. I don't know what to expect. I just found you but I'm going away for months. It's not just a short vacation. It's long periods of time."

"We take it one day at a time. Savvy said Brandon gets his phone now and his computer."

"Yeah, we have more liberties now we're beyond boot camp."

"We talk, we text, we e-mail, and there are these really cool inventions, I don't know if you've heard of them, but they're called pen and paper. They even have these nifty things called envelopes that you can put them in and send them to someone."

"Ha ha, smarty pants."

"If we want this, we can do this."

I have to be certain. "Is this what you want?" I hold my breath waiting for her to answer.

"I want to get to know you better. I want to see what this crazy intense flutter is in my belly. I get it every time I'm around you, get a phone call or text message from you. I want to explore that."

"That's just it, Austyn, you won't be seeing me."

"I didn't say it was going to be easy." Her thumb brushes against my arm. I don't even think she's aware she's doing it, but with every caress, heat pulses through me. "Nothing worth having ever is. At least that's what my mom always says."

"Regardless of what does or doesn't happen between us, I'm grateful to have met you. You give a guy hope." I struggle to keep the emotion out of my voice.

"Hope?"

I close my eyes briefly before looking over at her. "Hope that my future isn't as bleak as I once expected it to be."

She shimmies up the bed, my hand still in her hair. She's watching me. I can't see her eyes, but I know their color. I know the way they sparkle when she looks at me. Without saying a word, she inches closer. Her sweet breath brushes past my face. She stills, her lips mere inches from mine. With my one hand still buried in her hair, the other cups her cheek. It's the exact moment she leans in and presses her lips to mine. The kiss starts slow, a molding of our mouths as we take our time savoring the moment. It's not until her tongue presses between lips, seeking entrance that the game changes. I open for her, my tongue accepting hers as if this could be our last chance. I need her closer. Removing my hands from her hair, I grab her hips and guide her to straddle me.

"Slade?" It's a question. I can hear the insecurity in her voice.

"We're not going there," I tell her. "Not tonight, not when I leave you in a few short hours." My words must ease her fears as she throws one leg over my hips and straddles me. "I wish I could see you," I whisper into the darkness.

"I—we could turn on a light."

"You okay with that?"

She laughs nervously. "Honestly, I don't know. This is new for me. I've never been alone with a guy like this, in this position.

I don't know what I'm doing."

I relax into the pillow at her words, her confession both surprising and welcome. "Can I confess something without losing my knight status?" I ask playfully. That makes her laugh. The room is still bathed in darkness which is going to make my confession easier. "I've never been here either. It's all been with you."

"How is that possible?" she asks.

"I told you I was a loner in school. I didn't go out, I had Gran to take care of and spend time with. I felt guilty leaving her alone after everything she did for me. She saved me. Nothing else really mattered to me. No one ever caught my attention like you have."

"Guys at my school, aside from Brandon, they only want sex. I've grown up watching my parents and the love they share for each other. I never wanted to be the "hit it and quit it" girl. Savvy and Brandon are proof its possible at our age. I want that. I want a relationship, not a guarantee of marriage and a future, but the hope of one. You can't get that hooking up. I've held out, not willing to settle."

"And yet you're here with me, the night before I leave for months."

"I'm here because I want to be. In the time you've been here, you've shown me what kind of guy you are. You've not once tried to sleep with me, use me as a hookup. You're more than that. I feel it here." She raises my hand and places it over her heart. "My instincts have never steered me wrong."

"What are your instincts telling you?"

She pauses, lacing our fingers together on both hands, resting them on her thighs that are still straddling me. "They're telling me that I'm where I am supposed to be. They're telling me that you're worth it, that what we could be is worth it, and no amount of distance can change that."

"Is this how it happens, Austyn? We've known each other a little over a week."

"I'm not saying I'm in love with you. I'm saying I think I could be… with some time, getting to know you."

My heart's in my mouth when I reply, "We don't have time."

"Slade, we don't have to be in the same state or same country to get to know each other. We communicate. That's the key, right? Good communication?"

"Communication, huh?" I ask with a smile.

"Mmm hmmm." She hums her reply.

"I guess I should communicate with you that I want to kiss you."

I can hear the smile in her voice. "Is that so?" She sits forward, and I know she can feel my rock-hard cock beneath her. "Oh!" She moans her surprise.

I raise my hips, not bothering to hide what she does to me. "Can I kiss you, angel?" I want more than that. I want all of her. But I meant what I told Combs. No way can I fuck her and leave her. And that's not just to spare her feelings, but mine. I'm slowly becoming addicted to her, and the thought of leaving is tearing me up. I can't imagine what it would be like if I was able to feel her from the inside. I don't know if I'd be strong enough to walk away.

"Please," she whispers as she leans in, and presses her lips to mine. Her hands that were gripping mine let go and she braces her hands on either side of my head.

The kiss is slow, just like all the others we've shared. I run my fingers up and down her back, stroking softly, letting her take the lead.

"I want more," she whispers against my lips."

"Tell me."

"Can we take your shirt off?"

I lift, and she moves back at the same time. She climbs off my lap and watches as I pull my T-shirt over my head and toss it on the floor. Lying back on the bed, I wait for her next move. I wish I could see her, we never did turn the lights on, but I imagine that's where some of her boldness is coming from.

"I want…." Her voice trails off.

"Tell me."

"Savvy, she talks about skin to skin, that after, that's her favorite. I've never felt that."

Fuck. "You want that?"

"Yes."

A simple, straightforward answer that makes my heart sing. Sitting up, I reach out to her. Finding the hem of her tank top, I pull it up, slowly, gently, giving her time to stop me. She doesn't. "Lift your arms," I say into the darkness. I feel her raise them and I pull her tank over her head and toss it on the floor. I lie back on the bed and place my hand on her back, guiding her down with me.

"Wait," she murmurs.

Keeping my hand on her bare back, I give her time. It's not until I feel her arms moving, reaching around her back and the bed dip that I realize what she's done. She just tossed her bra onto the floor with all her other clothes. There is not a single item of clothing covering our top halves. When she lies down this time, it's nothing but her smooth, soft skin and her full naked breasts that press against my chest. I run my hand up and down her bare back, memorizing the softness of it. I'm lost in the feeling, of her half-naked against me, trying to keep my dick under control. An action I'm not doing well with at the moment. When her soft lips press against my bare chest, I fight the urge to devour every fucking inch of her.

"Savvy was right," she says into the darkness.

"Yeah," I agree, because nothing has and, I'm certain in this moment, nothing will ever feel this way again. "Can I touch you?" I ask, needing my hands on her, all over her, more than I need my next breath.

"Can I touch you?" she counters.

"I'm all yours." I say the words, but I inwardly send up a silent prayer that I can keep from losing control. If she touches my dick, it's over. I won't be able to hold back, not with the feel of her naked breasts pressed against my chest and my hand on the soft skin of her back. Her hands find their way to my abs. With her index, finger she traces every line, every curve of my muscles. "Austyn?" I ask, because I need to touch her too.

Instead of answering, she takes hold of my hand that's not on her back, the one that I have fisted at my side—the one trying to play it cool that this isn't the single most intense interaction of my life. That's the hand that she grabs. Propping herself up on her elbow, she places my hand on her bare breast, and I groan.

"Please."

My hand trembles, but I don't let that stop me. Gently, I squeeze, testing their firmness. Austyn lies back on the bed, presenting both breasts to me. "I need to see you."

"Okay."

Scrambling, I jump out of bed. I just need enough light to see her, to remember how she looks in this moment. The bedside lamp will be too much. I rush to the bathroom and turn on the light over the sink, then pull the door closed. A small sliver of light peeks through the crack. I turn my gaze toward the bed and take in the beauty before me. Her eyes are on me, as she remains on her back, hands gripping the sheets beside her.

"You're beautiful." My voice is deep and gravelly. Slowly, I walk back to the bed, my step uncomfortable with my erection. I've never been this hard in all my life. I slide my hand down my shorts and adjust myself. Her eyes follow my hand, and her mouth opens and then quickly closes as she licks her lips.

"You coming back to bed?" she asks.

Not needing to be asked twice, I climb back in beside her. This time it's me who's on my side, propping myself up on my elbows. My cock is throbbing, but I ignore it. I put all my focus on her. Hesitantly, I reach out and pinch her nipple between my thumb and index finger.

"Slade." Her voice is breathy, and it turns me inside out knowing she's turned on, that my touch does this to her.

"Yeah, angel."

Her hand reaches out for me, and her nails scrape across my abs. She continues onward until she reaches the waistband of my shorts. She slips her index finger under the thick band, and the tip of her finger brushes the head of my cock.

"Is that?" There's disbelief in her voice.

"Yeah," I groan. Leaning in, I capture her nipple between my lips. She moans and her hand grips the back of my head.

"Do that again," she gasps.

Not willing to disappoint her, I do it again. This time, I nip the stiff bud with my teeth, not hard, just enough to cause her to arch her back off the bed. Her hands dig into my hair and hold me to her. And as if my mouth has a mind of its own, I lavish her breasts with attention. Between my mouth and my hands, I can't seem to get my fill of her. She's writhing on the bed beneath me, and that does nothing but spur me on and makes lying in this position, with my cock hard as steel, uncomfortable as hell, but no way am I moving. Not until she tells me to. I can do this all night, until I have to leave in the morning.

"I need," she breathes, and I pull my head away, letting her wet hard nipple fall from my mouth.

"What do you need?" I'll give her anything in this moment.

"I want to touch you," she says shyly.

"Fuck," I mutter under my breath. I'm wracking my brain, trying to come up with a way to tell her that if she gets her hands on me, things will get... messy. Before I can find the words to explain it, without looking like the inexperienced ass that I am, she pushes on my chest, causing me to fall back on the bed. She moves over, resting her head on my chest. Instinctively, my arms wrap around her, settling on her hip.

The only sound in the room is our breathing, the rain, and the thump, thump, thump of my heart as it beats against my chest. Her hand roams again over the dips and valleys of my abs. This time, she doesn't stop at the waistband of my shorts. This time, she slips her small hand underneath and cradles my hard length in the palm of her hand.

"It's hot," she murmurs, scooting further down the bed.

"Austyn." Her name is a warning, one that I can't seem to complete with her hands on me.

"And smooth. It's not at all what I expected." She moves even further down the bed, sitting up and pulling my shorts down over my erection. I lift my hips, because what else would I do in this moment? I need to tell her that much more, and I'm going to lose my shit, but the feel of her hands on me, the way she's watching as she gently strokes me from root to tip, that's all her, and who am I to say she can't touch me? I told her that I was hers and I meant it.

"Austyn."

"I don't want to hurt you. Show me what feels good."

"Shit," I hiss. "Everything. It—" I swallow hard on her downward stroke. "—feels good," I finish with a huff.

"Are you, I mean, do you think you can come like this? I know it's not sex, but do you think?"

"I know," I manage to croak out.

"Really?" she asks, surprised.

"Mmm-hmm."

She gets even closer. "It's soft and hard at the same time, I wonder…." Her voice trails off.

Closing my eyes, I focus on taking deep, even breaths and not coming. I want this to last as long as possible—her hands on me. This is not a situation I want to rush through. When her hot wet tongue swipes across the tip, I rise from the bed. "Woah."

"Did I hurt you?" she asks, turning to look at me.

I tuck a loose strand of hair behind her ear. "No, but I was close with your hands on me. You do that again and it's going to be over."

"You mean this?" she asks, bending, and this time, she takes the tip in her mouth.

"Fuck," I breath, placing my hand on the back of her neck. I don't push her; instead, I just rest it there, loving the connection.

I stare down into my lap and watch her take more of me with every bob of her head. When she takes all of me, my balls tighten. "Austyn, babe, you need to… fuck you need to stop. I'm close," I try to warn her. She ignores me and continues. Her mouth is hot and perfect. And fuck, it's the most incredible sensation I've ever had. "Austyn," I groan. "Babe." I move my hand from the back of her neck to her shoulder, trying to warn her. She shrugs me off and keeps going. The sensation is overwhelming, and on her next downward stroke, I spill into her mouth. My entire body is on fire, as if electricity is coursing through my veins. I struggle to catch my breath. My eyes are closed, but I doubt I could see clearly anyway. Flopping back on the bed, my hand on her bare back, and soak up the most intense orgasm of my life. Of course, when you're a one-man show, it's bound to be mediocre.

chapter 18
Austyn

I CAN'T BELIEVE I JUST did that. I've listened to Savvy talk about sex for years, about doing this exact thing, and I could never seem to wrap my head around the fact that she also enjoyed it. Now... I get it. He's smooth and hard, and the thrill alone, knowing that I was the reason he was coming undone, pushed me to finish. The finish, though, is not such a great thing. He tastes hot and salty and... thick. I guess it's something I'll get used to.

Maybe.

Possibly.

"Austyn," he pants my name. "Come here."

My cheeks are hot and my lips are swollen, and the rush of what I just did still courses through my veins. Slowly, I move up the bed, lying down beside him. I'm breathing heavy from the excitement. Slade rolls onto his side and props himself up on an elbow. He reaches out and traces his index finger up my stomach. He takes his time traces each breast, making sure to run the pad of his thumb over my nipples. Closing my eyes, I bask in the joy of having his hands on me. It's going to be a long time before we're here like this, together again. When his finger slips under the waistband of my shorts, my eyes pop open. He's watching me.

"I need to do that for you."

"D-do what?"

"Make you feel it, the bliss that you gave me." I don't say anything because of the lump in the back of my throat. I'm nervous. He takes my silence as the acceptance that it is and pushes his hand beneath the waistband. "Lace," he murmurs.

"I've never…." My voice trails off. I don't want to ruin the moment, but my nerves are getting the best of me.

"Me either." Gently, he runs his thumb over me, the thin piece of lace doing nothing to mask his touch. "You, this night, all of it is new for me too. This entire trip."

A few more strokes over my panties that are now soaking wet and I'm ready to beg for more. He must read my mind because he slips his hand under the thin scrap of lace. His fingers are a ghost of a touch that sends shocks of desire through my system. "Slade." His name is a plea.

"Yeah, angel?" He gazes down at me, his eyes dark with need. The look he gives me causes my heart that's already beating erratically to thump harder against my chest. I open my mouth to speak, but nothing comes out. So, I do the next best thing. I lift my hips. He doesn't hesitate to pull my sleep shorts and panties to midthigh. I try to open for him, wanting him to touch me, but I'm restricted. "Off." Knowing what I need, he slowly peels them down my legs. I kick them off, not caring where they land. Feeling brazen with need, I slowly widen my legs, giving him access. When he sucks in a breath, I try to shut my legs, embarrassed, but his large calloused hands stop me.

"Fuck, Austyn." His deep voice rumbles as he leans in close, so close I can feel his breath… there.

With rapt attention, I watch him as his head lowers and he presses a kiss just above where I need him. The feel of his lips against my skin, so close to my slit, has me writhing beneath him.

Slade moves up the bed, hand resting between my thighs, his

thumb lightly rubbing, driving me crazy. When he reaches me, his mouth fuses with mine. His tongue seeks entrance, and I open for him at the same time he slides his fingers through my folds. I gasp into our kiss, but that doesn't stop him. His tongue strokes against mine as his fingers continue to explore me.

"More?" he asks against my lips.

I can't speak, so I bury my hands in his hair and hold him to me. I need his lips on me, his hands on me. I need it all—anything and everything he's willing to give me. Slade takes that as his answer and kisses me deeply, as if he needs our kiss to survive. When his finger slides inside of me, I moan in the back of my throat.

He pulls back, but barely. "Talk to me, angel. Am I hurting you?"

"N-no."

"The last thing I ever want to do is hurt you. I need you to tell me what you need. What feels good." He presses a kiss to my neck, just under my ear. "We'll learn together," he whispers. Lazily, he moves his finger. In. Out. In. Out. I lift my hips, and he chuckles. "Good?"

"So good," I sigh.

"Another?" he asks, pressing a chaste tender kiss to my lips.

"I-I'm not sure. We can try." I don't know if another is too much, but I know what he's doing is driving me crazy and I don't want him to stop.

"Tell me if it's too much." His lips that are next to my ear bite down lightly on my lobe. His lips trail across my cheek until they land on mine once again. "Ready?" I nod, and as he slides in two fingers, he kisses me again, deep, his tongue commanding mine, the way his fingers are commanding my body.

"Slade," I pant.

"What do you need?"

"I don't' know." I don't. I can't tell him, but I know I need something. I can feel it... the electricity pulsing through my veins.

"Slower?" he asks, slowing his movements.

Immediately, I know that's not it. "No." I lift my hips, seeking out his touch.

"Faster then?" He increases the speed of his fingers.

"More," I plead. Fast is better, so much better.

"This too much?" He nips my bottom lip.

"No." My hands move from his hair to his shoulders, and I grip him tightly. I can feel it; it's as if pressure is building. "There," I gasp.

"God, you're beautiful," he says.

Opening my eyes, I see he's watching me. The expression on his face is full of... wonder? I'm too wrapped up in the sensations washing over me to define it. Watching me intently, he thrusts faster, causing my nails to dig into the skin on his shoulders. When he starts to slow, taking my pleasure for pain, I force the words, "Don't stop," past my lips.

He nods and goes back to it, his eyes locked on mine. It takes seconds before I feel it. The intense, overwhelming sensation takes over. I'm hot and my eyes close as I succumb to the overpowering waves of pleasure that crash through my body. It's there, and then it's gone, leaving havoc in its wake. I've never felt anything as intense, as powerful as what just happened. My eyes are closed, my legs shaky, and my heart's racing; it's intense. When I feel his hand leave my core, I lazily open my eyes. He's still looking at me.

"I—" He swallows hard. "I've never," he starts again, "seen anything as beautiful as you when you lose control. I could feel you, Austyn. Your body gripping my fingers. Fuck, I wish I had the words to explain it to you.'

"You were pulsing in my mouth," I tell him. My voice is weak as I struggle to catch my breath, but I need to tell him that I know what he's feeling.

"Yeah." He buries his face in my neck. "How am I going to leave tomorrow? How am I going to survive not being able to touch you? Kiss you? Feel your skin against mine? Fuck, I'm going to miss you."

I don't say anything. I can't. Instead, I wrap my arms around him and hold him close to me. I can't answer because I'm thinking the same things. I just found him. We just found this, and he has to leave. I know better than to say anything. He's doing it enough for the both of us. I don't want to make tomorrow harder for him, or for me. He has a job to do, and if we're going to be together, it's my job to stay strong for him.

"I should… uh, go take care of this." Heat spreads across my cheeks with embarrassment.

"You're coming back, right? You're not going home?" His voice is soft almost shy as he asks.

"Yeah, just need to… clean up a little."

He presses his lips to mine then releases his hold on me. I'm quick to climb out of bed and rush to the bathroom. Once I'm behind the locked door, I exhale, resting my palms on the counter. Looking into the mirror, I realize I'm still naked. Wild hair surrounds my flushed face, and bright eyes stare back at me. I can't believe I'm here with him, staying the night with him, that we just did that. I fight the urge to cry that he's leaving in the morning. I don't want him to go. I want him to stay here so we can spend more time together, get to know each other better. I know what he's doing is selfless and if I want to be with him, I need to be strong. It's just so damn hard.

Standing tall, I square my shoulders and steel my resolve. I can do this. *We* can do this. Suddenly, I need to be next to him, soak up these last few hours. I rush through cleaning up, hit the light, and blindly feel my way to the bed.

"You okay?" he asks when I slide under the covers.

"Yeah, just a little chilly in here." It's not a lie. Of course, I'm naked, so if I had some clothes on, this might not be the case.

"Can I get under there with you?" he asks from his side of the bed. My answer is to lift the covers. It's dark, but he can sense what it is I'm doing as he stands and pulls up the part of the cover he was on and slides underneath. He moves to the middle of the bed. "Come here, Austyn."

I move over and rest my head on his bare chest. His strong arms wrap around me. I feel his lips press to the top of my head and my heart swells. I'm a romantic. Growing up watching my parents share the love that they do, I truly do want that. I never wanted to settle for less than, which is why I haven't dated much. I've never let another guy get this close. Not until Slade. He's the first to treat me as something more. He makes me feel special. The fact that he didn't press me for more and that he's willing to hold me, skin to skin and not push or pressure me proves my instincts were right. He's one of the good guys. The phantom gentleman I was fearful no longer existed.

"What are you thinking about?" he asks.

"You," I tell him honestly.

"Oh yeah?" He moves his hand lovingly up and down my spine.

"Yeah, you're unexpected, but I'm glad to have met you."

"You make it sound like you're never going to see me again."

"I'm not here with expectations, Slade."

"Well, you should be. The first chance I have to get away, this is where I'm coming. To see you. Nothing can keep me away."

I try to tramp down the excitement his words cause. "We said slow, right? I'm not going to hold you to that because of what we just did. Things change with time."

"They do," he agrees, and my excitements wanes a little. "But I know this won't." My heart stutters as it picks up speed. "I know we need to get to know each other better before we can make promises to each other, so this is my promise to you. There will be no one else while I'm gone. I'll write with that paper stuff you mentioned earlier." He chuckles and presses another sweet kiss to my head. "I'll call when I can, e-mail. I can text you, but it's going to be erratic. I don't know when I'll be able to or how often, but you need to know that no matter the amount of time between all of those things, you are and will be the only thing on my mind."

"You need to stay safe," I tell him.

Another kiss on the top of my head. "This is training, and I will be. I have to be. I have something too precious waiting for me not to be."

"I know I shouldn't say this, but I really don't want you to go."

The hand that's tracing my back wraps around me, and he holds me tight. "I'm with you, Austyn. Every day I'll be with you. I might not be able to hold you or kiss you, but my mind and my heart are always with you."

My own heart sputters in my chest at his words.

"You're the best thing that ever happened to me."

I snuggle into him closer, and this is how our night goes. We talk about anything and everything. We spend the time getting to know one another, breaking up our conversation with lots of kisses and subtle caresses. Neither one of us willing to let sleep claim us, not wanting to miss a single second of our time together.

"I probably need to get in the shower," he says eventually.

The sun's already peeking through the curtains, so I know it's already time. "What time is it?" We've just been lying here the last hour or so and holding onto one another.

"Just after six. Combs said we'd grab food on the road. His dad will be here at seven." He kisses my temple. "You stay in bed. I'll be out soon." His voice is low, and I can hear the hesitation—he doesn't want to leave. Reluctantly, he releases his hold on me and climbs out of bed. He ruffles around in his bag and then disappears behind the bathroom door.

As soon as I hear the shower turn on, I climb out of bed and rush to my bag. I pull out the notebook and pen I shoved inside and begin to write him a letter. I had one ready, but so much has changed since then. I now have more to say. The words pour out of me, and I fight tears. When the shower shuts off, I seal the envelope and hide the letter in the bottom of his bag, shoving the paper and pen back in mine. I pull on my sleep shorts and tank and sit cross-legged on the bed.

"Hey," he says when he steps out of the bathroom. "I thought you were staying snuggled in bed?" he asks sweetly.

"Nah, I'm not going to stay here, not without you."

"You can. I have the room until eleven."

"No, I think I'll just head home. I just... don't want to be here without you," I confess.

He steps in front of me and cups my cheek. "Can you tell me something? Can you tell me that it's only me? I mean, until we figure this out, see if the distance is something we can tackle, can you not see anyone else? I know it's selfish and it goes against everything we've said up to this point, but fuck, Austyn, I can't leave here not knowing that you're mine."

I scramble to climb up into my knees to be closer to him. His hands grip my hips, holding me steady. "Are you mine, Slade Reeves?" I ask him.

"No question."

"Then we're good. I want you to know that it's only you. If that changes, you'll be the first to know. I need you to have a clear head when you're training. You need to learn those skills to stay safe. To come home to me."

He pulls me into him and hugs me tightly. "Fuck, this is harder than I thought it would be."

I don't say anything. I can't. If I try to speak, my tears will fall, and I can't let him see that. I need to stay strong for him.

His phone vibrates on the nightstand, and he pulls back, kissing my forehead before grabbing it. "That's Combs. His dad's downstairs waiting for us." I scramble off the bed and dig for a hoodie. "What are you doing?"

"I can't walk you down like this."

"Hey." Reaching out, he grabs my elbow. "Let's do this here, okay? This is our moment. I want to remember you just like this." I nod. The tears are close, and I'm fighting hard to keep them at bay. "I'll miss you, angel," he whispers before kissing me softly, and that's all it takes. No matter how hard I fought them, tears fall unchecked as he kisses me.

"I'm going to miss you, too," I say through my tears when he pulls away.

Using the pads of his thumbs, he wipes my cheeks. "I need your e-mail address. I don't have one, but I'll make one. I need your address too." He unlocks his phone and hands it to me.

I search through his contacts and stop when I see there are four contacts. Recruiter, Realtor, Combs, and Austyn. My heart breaks for him and all that he's lost. I type in my information and hit Save before handing it back to him. "If you change your mind about us—" His lips press to mine, stopping me from saying more.

"I want us, Austyn. I'm coming for you as soon as I get leave. This is where I'll be."

"Stay safe," I say, hugging him tightly, burying my face in his chest.

"You too. I need to go."

"I know." I say the words, but I don't bother letting go, and neither does he.

"Come on," he finally says. He grabs his bags, shoves in his clothes from yesterday, and opens the door. We find Savannah and Brandon in the hallway hugging. Slade drops his bag and turns to face me. He cups my face in his hands and presses his forehead against mine. "My angel," he whispers, and a sob escapes my lips. I can hear Savannah crying too.

"My knight."

He chuckles. "I'm always with you."

I nod. "Take care of you."

He presses his lips to mine, and I know he can taste the salt from my tears.

"See you soon, angel,"

"See you soon."

He pulls away, picks up his bag and turns for the elevator.

Brandon does the same. Savannah is next to me, and we wrap our arms around each other, holding on for dear life as we watch them wait for doors to open. They step inside and Slade waves, giving me a sad smile. I wave and fight the urge to run to him, to latch onto him and keep him here.

When the doors close and they disappear, Savannah sobs against me. I hold her close. I lead her into my room, and we collapse on the bed, holding onto one another. Her sobs break my already fragile heart. My tears are for her and Brandon, my two best friends who have the real thing, the love that you're lucky to find in a lifetime. They're also for me, for Slade, and the hope that we can find our way.

"I don't want to be here," Savannah says finally.

"I couldn't agree more. Go pack up. We'll check out and head home. You're off today, right?"

"Yeah, you?"

"Yeah, I traded with Beth."

"Let's go back to my house, take a nap because I know neither of us slept a wink last night. Then we'll go see Brandon's parents or go shopping. Anything you want."

"What would I do without you?" she asks.

"You'll never have to find out." I hug my best friend and then push her out of bed. "Go pack up. Meet me in the hall, fifteen minutes." She gives me a watery smile and walks out the door. I'm zipping up my bag, doing a final walk of the room to make sure I didn't forget anything when my phone vibrates in my back pocket. Pulling it out, I see a message from Slade.

> **Slade:**   I miss you already.

Tears well in my eyes.

> **Me:**   I miss you too.

I hesitate for a minute wondering if I should let him find the letter or tell him about it. I decide to tell him about it. What if he doesn't unpack right away?

| **Me:** | I left you something in the bottom of your bag. |
| **Slade:** | I might have left you a little something too. |

I drop my phone on the bed. Unzip my bag and turn it upside down. Everything falls into a pile on the bed, and there it is, a small white envelope sitting on top of the pile. I smile, knowing we both had the same idea. I grab my phone and text him a picture of the pile, the envelope on top.

Me:	Great minds think alike
Slade:	Did you dump your bag?
Me:	Yep, I was just getting ready to meet Savvy to check out, but I couldn't wait.

His reply is a picture of my envelope lying on top of his bag.

Slade:	We're more alike than I thought.
Me:	Text me when you get there. I have some reading to do.
Slade:	I can do that. Get some rest.
Me:	You too.

Grabbing the envelope, I sit on the edge of the bed and slide my finger under the seal. It's a postcard from the hotel. Flipping it over, I read the back.

Austyn,

Just the first of what I hope are many keepsakes from our time together.

These past nine days have been the best of my life.

Thank you for giving me that.

I'll see you soon.

Slade

chapter 19

Slade

I'M STARING AT THE LETTER in my hands. I've been gripping it for the last hour. Part of me wants to tear it open and devour her words, the other part wants to wait until I'm alone. As if anything she has to say should be sacred between the two of us.

Combs is sleeping in the front seat. I imagine, like Austyn and I, they didn't sleep. His mom was there today, to say goodbye to him, and she commented that he looked tired. He assured her he would catch up on the drive. That was my intention too, but I can't seem to shut my mind off. I keep replaying last night. Hell, every minute that I've spent with her is on a highlight reel.

"You okay back there?" Eric asks.

"Yeah, too tired to sleep I guess." I laugh it off.

"We have a lot of miles ahead of us."

"Yeah," I say, looking out the window.

"I'm glad he met you," he tells me. "It makes his mother and me a little less anxious knowing he has a friend with him."

"We're brothers," I tell him. We are. We might not be blood, but there's more to family than blood. We formed a bond during boot camp. Other than Combs, Spiller and Jeffers are my other two closest friends. The four of us are rooming together on base.

Silence surrounds us, just the soft croon of whatever song is in the background and the sound of the truck tires traveling down the road. Looking down at the letter, I decide to go for it. With Combs, Spiller, and Jeffers around, this is probably the most privacy I'm going to get.

I angle my body toward the door, slide my finger under the seal, and pull the letter out of the envelope.

Slade,

I don't have much time. You just got in the shower, and after what we shared last night, the letter I had ready just isn't good enough. I didn't expect you. I knew Brandon was bringing a friend home with him. I thought we'd hang out, give them some time, but what I got was so much more. I got the honor of meeting the guy who charmed me, treated me with respect, and gave me so many firsts.

No matter what our future holds, I'll always have that. The time with you, the firsts. Thank you for that, for the nine days of amazing.

It's important you know there's someone at home waiting for you. We haven't defined us, but regardless of how that turns out, I don't want to lose you as a part of my life.

So when times get rough and you feel alone, remember that. I'm here waiting for you. Let that memory pull you through until I see you again.

Stay safe,

Austyn

Folding the letter, I place it back in the envelope and grip it. Tilting my head back against the seat, I close my eyes. For years, I've wondered *why me?* Why was I dealt the hand of having drug-addicted parents? Why did the one person who I had in the world have to die? It's now, as I hold her letter in my hands, her words and the memories of our time together, I think that maybe it all happened to lead me here. To lead me to Austyn. Gran was always big on saying things happen for a reason. No one knows God's intention. I never really believed her, not until Austyn. Maybe all the pain, the sadness, the loss, the suffering, maybe that's what I had to do to be here, in this moment — to be a marine, and to have the honor of defending my country, and the privilege to fall for the blonde-haired beauty with mesmerizing blue eyes.

My angel.

Maybe Gran guided me here. Maybe it's fate. I don't know the reason, but I know I'm incredibly grateful for Austyn and the time I've spent with her, and the time I hope to spend with her in the future. It's going to be hard as hell. It's going to be five long, lonely months without her kiss, her touch. I'm a prick for asking her to wait, but I had to. No way could I have left her not knowing she was mine. At least for now. I have to hold onto that, hold onto the hope of us. That's my last thought as I drift off to sleep.

When the truck stops, I open my eyes. Looking around, I see we're in the parking lot of a restaurant. Rubbing my hands over my face, I yawn, trying to wake up.

"Thought you boys could use some food, and I need to stretch my legs," Eric says from the front seat.

"Yeah," I reply, because stretching my legs and my back is sounding pretty good about now. I'm a tall guy at six foot three, and this back seat has modest legroom, but being cramped in a truck for over five hours, sleeping at that, is not my idea of a good time.

"Food is good. Then more sleep," Combs says groggily.

"Stay up late, did ya?" His dad smirks.

"All night. Didn't want to miss it," he tells him honestly.

"What about you?" he asks me once we're seated at a table. "You stay up late too?"

"All night."

"Let me guess, you didn't want to miss it?"

"No, sir. I just found her, and now I have to leave her. Co—I mean Brandon, he's been with Savannah for a long, long time. They have that bond, one that will carry them through. I'm not sure I have that. I'd like to think we could, but only time will tell." I don't tell him that I couldn't sleep for the fear that it would be the last time I'd see her. That my heart is hers, but I was too afraid to tell her that after only nine days. I don't tell him that I would have given anything to have more time with her.

"No matter how much time has passed, a week, a year, hell, even a decade, it takes work. You have to want it and have to be willing to give it one hundred and ten percent every day."

"Yes, sir." I let his words sink in, and I know without a shadow of a doubt that I want her, want there to be an us for a long damn time, if not forever. I'm keeping that to myself, but the thought is there.

"So it's five months this time?" Eric asks, changing the subject and I'm grateful. We spend the entire time at the restaurant talking about what comes next. Combs, Spiller, Jeffers, and I are all going into combat engineering. Basically, we're going to be the guys clearing demolition, potential land mines, and building bridges.

"Yeah, then we'll find out where we're going to be stationed," Combs tells him.

The rest of our time is spent talking about what their next steps will be. Where we think we will be and hope to be stationed. Eric is one of those dads who listens to what you say. He's not asking because it feels like the right thing to do. He's asking because he actually cares what's going on in his son's life.

Back in the truck, I pull out my phone and text Austyn.

Me:	Hey, how's your day?
Austyn:	Hi! Good. Savvy and I came back to my place to take a nap.
Me:	Wish I was there with you.

Austyn:	Me too, but you have great things ahead of you, Slade Reeves.

I don't know how she does it, but she manages to always say what I need to hear.

Me:	What are the plans for today?
Austyn:	Nothing much. We're going to go visit Sarah in a little while. Keep her company.
Me:	We're a little over four hours away. I'll text you when we get there.
Austyn:	Be safe.

Sliding my phone back in my pocket, I rest my head against the window and let sleep claim me once again. When I wake again a few hours later, we're in North Carolina.

"Almost there," Eric tells me, glancing in the rearview mirror.

"I can't believe I didn't think of it," Combs grumbles from the front passenger seat.

"Think of what?" I ask, still a little groggy and trying to get in on the conversation.

"We're staying in a hotel tonight. We could have had the girls come with us."

"Damn," I mutter to myself. However, I must be louder than I think because Eric laughs and Combs grumbles, "Exactly" agreeing with me.

"I'm sure it was hard enough on them to say goodbye. That's why your mom stayed home as well," Eric chimes in.

"It was," we both say at the same time. I can still see her tears as I kissed Austyn goodbye. When I signed up for this, I had no one. No one to miss me, and no one to miss. I was destined to a life with the Marine Corps. I don't regret signing up, not for a minute, but I do wish I had more time with her, that she could have been in my life sooner. Then again, maybe if I had met her sooner, things wouldn't have worked out like they have, like they are. I just keep hearing Gran telling me, "Everything happens for a reason." I get that. I do. I just hope this reason keeps her in my life.

When we reach the hotel, we grab our bags and check in. I opted for my own room, even though they offered to let me stay with them. This will give them some father-and-son time, and well, it gives me time to call Austyn. We have to report in at eight in the morning, so we call it a night and head to our separate rooms. It's just after seven, and I don't know if she's home yet, but I have to call her. Even if it's to hear her voice for a minute or two.

She answers on the first ring. "Hey."

My shoulders immediately relax at the sound of her voice. "Hi."

"Are you at the hotel?"

"Yeah, just got in my room. How was your day?"

"Good, we went and had dinner with Sarah. I actually just got home."

"You skipped classes today?"

"Yeah, I can make it up."

"Thank you for the letter."

"I meant it. I know you're in training and the danger's not as imminent, but it's still dangerous. You're learning how to shoot guns and clear freaking minefields."

"I'll be fine."

"I know, but I thought you know, reminding you that I'm here might make you be extra safe."

"I don't need the reminder. You haven't left my mind for a single second since the minute I laid eyes on you."

"You nervous?"

"Not really. Boot camp gave me a pretty good idea of what's to come. We have more free time now that we've made it through that initial phase. I actually meant to buy a laptop but forgot."

"Can you order one online and have it shipped?"

"There's a place on base. It's like our own little village. I'll get one as soon as I can and set up an e-mail and text it to you."

"Do you know your address yet?"

"Not yet. I'll find out tomorrow."

"Send it to me when you can."

We're both quiet. I know what I want to say, but I'm not sure if I should. I don't want to make this harder for either of us, but I really want her to know. I want her to know that when I tell her she's all I think about, that it's the truth. "I miss you," I say, my words barely a whisper, not able to hold the truth back.

"I miss you, too."

"I'll call and text as much as I can. I don't really know what 'free time' means, but as soon as I do, you'll be the first to know."

"I'll keep my phone on me at all times, work, school, it doesn't matter. I'll answer. I don't care if it's the middle of the night. I'll answer."

"If I could, I would."

"I know that, Slade. You just worry about you. Stay safe, learn all the skills you need to stay safe. I'll be here when you have time."

"I hate that, that you're just waiting around for me."

"That's how this works. It's military life."

"Yeah, I get that, but you didn't sign up for this. I'm struggling with pulling you into this life."

"You didn't. I mean, I guess you did when you made me fall for you with your charms." She chuckles softly, and my breath hitches at her words. "I knew who you were, what your career was, and that didn't stop me. I support you, Slade."

"You… incredible." She really is. She's taking all of this in her stride, letting me stake claim on her and then leave her.

We talk for another hour, just about everything. Dawson wants to draw me a picture and send it, and her parents reminded her to tell me I'm always welcome there, and for the first time in my life, I feel like I'm surrounded with support. It's a heady feeling.

"I better let you go. You have to be up and at it early in the morning, and you didn't sleep last night," she says.

"I slept in the truck on the way here."

"That's not true rest. You need to be in your best form. A good night's sleep will do you wonders."

"I know you're right."

"Call me in the morning?" she asks. "Just you know, I don't know when I'll get to talk to you again and I just… want to hear your voice."

"Sure, angel. I'll call when I get up."

"Night, Slade."

"Night, Austyn." I end the call and pull up the picture app on my phone. I scroll until I find one of us at the fair. Her blue eyes are sparkling at the camera. I don't need the picture to see them, but it's my fear that in five months, when I get to see her again, I might forget. Austyn Wilson is not someone I ever want to forget.

chapter 20
Austyn

I T'S BEEN EXACTLY ONE WEEK today since he left. We've managed to send a few text messages here and there, but he's been busy settling and with training. I miss him. How is it that I was with him for not many more days than the amount he has been gone yet my heart aches for him? I fell hard and fast, something I never thought it was even possible. I was a naysayer, until Slade.

Working on a paper for my history class, it's almost midnight, and since I can't sleep, I figure I might as well use my time wisely. I don't have class until tomorrow afternoon, and I work after that. I figure I can sleep in tomorrow to make up for my late night.

I'm flipping through my history book when my phone vibrates from the nightstand where it's charging. I lean over in a rush to get to it, and it falls off the nightstand. I try to lean over the edge of the bed to get to it and end up rolling off my bed. Finally, I reach it and swipe the screen, "Hello," I say quickly and out of breath.

"Austyn?" his deep, sleepy voice asks.

"Hey." I take a deep breath and slowly exhale, moving the phone away from my mouth, trying to calm down.

"Are you okay? What's wrong?"

Great. Nothing like embarrassing yourself the first time I've spoken to him in a week. "Yeah, I'm good, I… um, kind of… sorta fell off the bed?

"What? Are you okay? How did that happen?" I can hear the concern in his voice.

"Well, my phone was charging, and I tried to reach it and knocked it to the floor. When I tried to lean over and get it, I kind of fell out of bed."

His deep laughter comes across the line. "I would have liked to have seen that."

"Hey! Leave me to wallow alone in my embarrassment. Enough about that. How are you? It's so good to hear your voice."

"Good, it's been crazy. We've been in the classroom." He pauses, as if gathering his thoughts. I wait him out, knowing he'll eventually say what he has to say. "I miss you," he murmurs. "I knew I would, you know. I just didn't know how it would feel, to have you agree to be mine and then not be with you."

"Hey, you're with me always, remember?" I throw his parting lines the day he left back at him.

"You know what I mean."

"I do, but this is us. This is our future. We have to stay strong. *You* have to stay strong. I can't have you getting hurt."

"There are safety precautions all over this base, not to mention we're just in the classroom right now. We have fields days, well, more like weeks planned, and then we have classroom time. It's split up. This first session is four weeks. Then we have fourteen weeks of our OSUT."

"What's that?"

"One Station Unit Training. That's where we gain our skillset for our permanent position within the Marines."

"Combat engineer, right?"

"Yeah. Hey, I didn't wake you, did I? I'm sorry it's so late.

Combs, Spiller, Jeffers, and I, we got out early today and went and bought laptops. We had to have the secure network installed by the IT guys, but I'm up and running. That's why I called. I wanted to tell you that."

"That's great. Will you have more time to check it?"

"Hopefully. Things should start to slow down. The first week is a lot of getting back into the swing of things, testing, things like that."

"That's good to hear. How's the base?"

"It's good. Kind of like our own little world. We even have a hotel where family can stay when they come to visit."

My mind races immediately. Savvy and I need to plan a trip to North Carolina. I wonder if you have to be family, if girlfriends are allowed into that equation. Am I his girlfriend? I told him I was his. "That's great that they offer that," I finally say.

"It is. Look, I know it's late I won't keep you, I just wanted to tell you about the computer. I'll send you a text of my e-mail address. And selfishly, I just wanted to hear your voice. I knew if you were sleeping I'd at least get your voice mail."

I melt at his words. "Not sleeping. I have a late class tomorrow and then work after that, so I'm busting out this history paper and making it a late one."

"School going okay?"

"Yeah, it's school." I laugh. "Classes are same old, you know? Kind of a means to an end to get where I want to be," I say with a yawn.

"I'll let you go. Goodnight, angel."

"Night."

As soon as we end the call, my phone beeps with a text alert.

> **Slade:**   HerKnight@directmail.com

Did he really?

> **Me:**   Look at you getting all creative.
> **Slade:**   You like that?

| Me: | I'm sure you'll get shit over it. |
| Slade: | From who? You're the only person I care enough to give it to. |

Holding my phone to my chest, I grin like a fool. That's when the idea hits me. I have an e-mail address, but I'm going to make a new one. Just for him. This way, I'll be sure to never miss a message lost in the madness that is my inbox. Pulling up Direct Mail, I type in the address that I want and cross my fingers that it's available. When the screen prompts me for a password, I squeal, and then realize what time it is. I listen to make sure I didn't wake anyone up before finishing my account. Once I'm in, I hit Compose Message and fire off an e-mail.

To: HerKnight@directmail.com
From: HisAngel@directmail.com
Time: 01:15
Subject: New E-mail

I thought I'd send you a quick message giving you my new e-mail address. I can't let you be the one having all the fun. It was so good to hear your voice earlier. I miss you. Have a good day tomorrow. I hope we get to talk again soon.
Yours,
Austyn

After hitting Send, I close down my laptop. No way can I concentrate on my history paper after my call with Slade. Instead, I pull up his picture on my phone. One of the many we took, or I took without him realizing it during our time together. This one is my favorite. He's sitting on the back porch at Brandon's and looking out across the yard. A small smile tips his lips. I like to think that I had something to do with that. He's responsible for mine, even when he's not here. I grin, because I know that he's thinking of me like I am him. There's not a doubt in my mind. Reaching over, I plug my phone back in and turn off the lamp on my nightstand. I drift off to sleep with thoughts of our time together.

My plans for sleeping in fly out the window when my cell rings at eight. Reaching over, I grab it and look at the screen. Any other time I would turn the ringer off and keep sleeping, but that was before Slade, before there was a chance it could be him calling. It's not him, not that I really expected it to be at this time. It's Savannah. "Why are you up?" I greet her.

"I have the morning shift."

"I thought you were off today?"

"I was, but Kara asked me to switch with her."

"Oh, so why are you calling me at the ass crack of dawn?"

"Because I have an idea I want to run by you. It was either call at one o'clock this morning when it hit me or call now."

"I was up then."

"Why?"

"Working on a paper and then Slade called."

"I was up, too, talking to Brandon."

"How is he?"

"Good. They're in training. I guess it's long days, but they have more free time than boot camp, so that's something."

"That's what Slade said, too," I say with a yawn.

"Anyway, after I hung up with Brandon last night, an idea hit me. I think we should take a road trip."

"Okay," I say cautiously. You never know what you're getting into with Savannah. "Where are we going?"

"North Carolina." She gives her words time to sink in. When I don't reply, she forges ahead. "To see the guys."

My heart leaps in my chest. This is exactly what I thought last night. "Can we do that?"

"We can. They get weekends off, and there's a hotel on base."

"Don't you have to be family or something? To be able to stay there?"

"We are family," she counters.

"Legally, not just in heart."

"Easy, we call the guys, have them meet us off base. They take us to get a visitor's pass, and voila."

"Do they know about this grand plan?"

"Nope."

"So what if we get there and they can't have visitors or have training or something?"

"Damn, I didn't think about that."

"Yeah, so maybe we can surprise them with the trip before we get there? Maybe see if we can get them together and call them or do a video chat or something?"

"I like where you're going with this. Does that mean that you'll go with me?"

"Yeah, it sounds fun. When are you thinking?"

"Thanksgiving. It's about five weeks away and even though they have a long weekend, they have to stay on base."

"Your parents cool with that?" I ask her.

"Don't know, don't care. I don't know if his parents are planning on going down or not."

"You thinking we could ride with them if they are?"

"No, I thought we could use a girls' trip. I feel like we've both been playing catch up with school and work since the guys have been gone. I don't know where your head is at with Slade, nor what's it is that's going on with the two of you. Plus, I miss you. Not to mention I didn't get to tell you that Brandon is talking about getting engaged. I don't know if it's for my benefit because he knows I miss him, as reassurance, but he should know me by now that I don't need reassurance. I just need him to come home safe."

"He loves you." He does. They're as thick as thieves, and I'm not at all surprised that Brandon's talking about getting engaged. Once they're married, she can live on base with him. And as far as I know, that's always been the plan.

"I know, but it's all so real, you know? We would sit and talk about what our life would be like once we graduated and he enlisted. It's surreal that it's all playing out so far just as we'd planned. Well, aside from my bestie falling for one of his marine brothers. I could not have planned that better if I tried."

"Who says I'm falling?" I counter. We both know damn good and well that I am. I fell fast and hard. We both did.

"Keep telling yourself that, my friend. Anyway, I'm at work. What time do you work tonight?"

"I'm there from five to close."

"Call me when you get off and we'll brainstorm. In the meantime, I'll call his mom and see what their plans are. I don't want to take away from anything they might have planned."

"Sounds good." I end the call and decide that I might as well get out of bed and get moving. Maybe I can finish my paper before I have to leave for class. I need to stay on top of things and not let them slip just in case he gets a leave, or we plan another spontaneous trip. I don't know how this marine life works, how often he gets leave, or if they're even allowed visitors like Savvy seems to think they are. It's a lot to learn. I have a feeling I'm going to be spending a lot of time on Google in the coming weeks. Maybe I should ask Brandon or Slade if there's some type of manual for families. On second thought, Brandon is the safer bet. I'll have Savannah ask him. I don't want Slade to think I'm a stage five clinger.

chapter 21

Slade

CLASS TODAY WAS BRUTAL, AND then we ran five miles. I'm dead on my feet. We all are. It took more effort than any of us wanted to put forward to grab something to eat.

"My toes hurt," Spiller says from his spot on his bed.

"My everything hurts," Jeffers pipes in.

"Toughen up," I say, even though I want to whine just like they are.

Before Combs can chime in, his phone's ringing. He answers immediately, and from the way his voice gets soft, I know it's Savannah. Jeffers and Spiller razz on him, making kissing noises and asking if she has any hot friends. That's when I perk up and take notice. Savannah does have a hot friend, gorgeous in fact and she's mine. I'm just ready to make that known when Combs does it for me.

"She does, but this guy," he points to me, "has already called dibs. Now leave me the fuck alone so I can talk to my girl," he says with mock rage, all the while wearing a smile on his face.

"So what's up with you and the friend?" Spiller asks.

"We hung out most of the time we were on leave. We're seeing where things go."

"She know that?" Jeffers asks, wagging his eyebrows.

"Yeah, she knows. I made sure we were on the same page before I left."

"What's her name?" Spiller asks.

"Austyn." I can't hold back my smile even if I wanted to.

"You got a picture?" Jeffers chimes in.

"Yeah." I dig my phone out of my pocket and pass it over to him.

"Not bad, Reeves," he says, passing the phone to Spiller.

"Fuck, man, she's a looker," he says, handing me back my phone.

I take a quick glance, making sure I haven't missed any messages, and slide it back in my pocket. "She's gorgeous. That picture doesn't do her justice."

"Not you too." Spiller sighs. "We already hear it from this guy about missing his girl. We were supposed to be the three Amigos, showing him what he was missing by being tied down."

"Maybe you two are the ones who don't know what you're missing," I counter.

"You've known this girl, what, a month at best? You really already that lost for her?"

It's taking little effort for my mind to pay the highlight reel of my time with her. "Yep," I say, not giving a shit how it makes me look.

"Damn, must be some good —" Spiller starts, but I stop him.

"Don't fucking finish that sentence." I glare at him, my fists balled at my sides.

He holds up his hands in surrender. "Didn't mean any disrespect. It's just odd that you're so into her in such a short amount of time."

"It's none of your business what I am or how I feel about her. What you need to worry about is not disrespecting her."

"Looks like it's just the two of us," Jeffers intervenes, no doubt trying to diffuse the situation. "And then there were two," he jokes.

I don't get a chance to reply because my phone vibrates in my pocket, taking my full attention. Digging it out, I see her name on the screen.

Austyn:	Just wanted to say hi. I hope you had a good day.
Me:	Hey, angel. It's better now.
Me:	How was class? Work?
Austyn:	Just another day. Nothing exciting. You?
Me:	It was a long one, but it's finally over.
Austyn:	I won't keep you. I just wanted to say hi.
Me:	I miss you.

I wait for her reply. I see the little bubbles appear and disappear several times before finally, her message comes through.

Austyn:	I miss you, too.

I read her words over and over, and will my heart to slow its rapid pace in my chest. I know the guys are watching, well, except Combs; he's still on the phone with Savannah. I want to call Austyn. I want to her hear her voice and not just rely on the memory of her sweet Southern drawl. I'm just about to when I overhear Combs tell Savannah that he's sure I'm up for it and that he'll text her later and let her know. He now has my full attention.

"What's up?" I ask as soon as he pulls the phone from his ear. I sound eager as fuck, and I am.

"Savvy was asking about the girls coming to visit in a couple of weeks."

"No shit?" I ask. I try to keep my cool to not let my excitement show.

He laughs. Apparently, I failed. "Yeah, I guess they wanted to surprise us and then realized that they weren't sure if we could have visitors or were sure where to stay really."

"Here, on base."

"That's what I told her. I told her I'd see how you felt about Austyn coming and then I'd book them a room. They just need to tell me when."

"You know damn good and well how I feel about Austyn coming, and we're going to need two rooms."

"Yeah, I don't want Austyn to have to suffer through Savvy and me spending time together and not have a place to go. You know I'm going to need some alone time with my girl."

"Two rooms because I need some alone time with mine." I wait for him to give me shit. It doesn't happen.

"I'll get the dates and then take care of the room."

"On second thought, let me take care of mine."

"Yours?"

"My girl and my room. Just give me the dates, and I'll handle it." Excitement courses through me knowing I get to see her, hold her, touch her soft skin and taste her sweet lips.

"We'll book them at the same time. I'm sure the girls will want to be close for the times we can't be with them."

I nod. I want this trip to be something special for her. I want to dote on her and spend as much time with her as I possibly can. I'm not going to let her out of my sight for a single fucking second.

Unable to table my excitement, I grab my phone and send her a quick text.

Me: Can you talk?

Austyn: With you? Always.

Standing from my bed, I walk outside. I hear the guys call out for me, asking me where I'm going. I raise my hand and wave, not bothering to turn around and give them an explanation. I walk to the side of the building where there's a row of picnic tables set up. I take a seat, pull up her name, and hit Call.

"My knight," she answers.

"My angel," I counter, making her laugh.

The sound washes over me, settling in my bones. What I

wouldn't give to make her laugh like this every damn day. "I hear you're planning a road trip."

"More Savannah than me, but she asked me to come with her."

"I don't know where I'm going to be stationed once we're through training so I don't know when I'll get to see you."

"Slade Reeves, you act like you miss me or something."

"I'm not a very good actor," I tell her, relieved she can't see my big-ass grin. She laughs again. "So you're coming with her? Do you know when?"

"We were thinking around Thanksgiving. We have a break from school. Savvy said you get a long weekend."

"We do, but we have to be here on base."

"That works for you guys, then?"

"Yeah, that works for me. The only issue I see is that it's too far away." I hear a guy say her name and she tells him she'll be right there. I open my mouth to ask her where she is when she beats me to it.

"Sorry, I'm at work and they're getting backed up in there. I need to go."

"Okay. We'll talk soon?"

"Yeah, Savvy and I will get the dates to you, and we can go from there." I hear her name called again. "I really have to go."

"I know. Can you text me when you get home?"

I hear her moving and the sounds of the restaurant growing louder. "It might be late."

"Don't care."

"I can do that. Bye, Slade," she says softly. It's so soft I almost don't hear her over the roar of the restaurant.

"Bye, angel." The line goes dead and although I wish I had more time to talk to her, maybe even a video chat, I'm still stoked she's coming to visit. It's more than I expected would happen. It gives me hope that she and I can do this. We can be together despite my career path and the distance between us.

We can still fall even further into this and come out happier, together.

When I get back, Combs is still on the phone talking quietly, and I know he's still chatting to Savannah. I've never been one to talk on the phone, but I can see the appeal, especially being this far away from her. I can't help but wonder if we'll ever get to that point? Better yet, do I want to be?

Grabbing my laptop, I pull up our last e-mail exchange. I feel like I know her, yet there is still so much I don't know. Without overthinking, I hit Compose and begin to type.

To: HisAngel@directmail.com
From: HerKnight@directmail.com
Time: 20:03
Subject: You

Although I feel like we know each other, there's still so much to learn. We jumped into this head first, and I'm glad we did. I have no regrets, but I want to know all of you.

We're new, but I know that I want to see where this goes. I know that I don't want either of us to see anyone else, which we agreed to before I left. I also want to know your favorite flower, your favorite movie. What do you do when I'm not there taking up all of your time besides school and work?

Who are you, Austyn Michelle Wilson?

Slade

chapter 22
Austyn

IT'S LATE BY THE TIME I get home. Work was crazy tonight, and clean up took longer than it normally does. We had customers still inside well past closing. Margaret never turns anyone away. No matter if they walk in one minute before closing, the grill is still hot and we still serve. It's a good move business wise, but for me, on a night when I just want to go home and fall into bed, not so much.

Now I'm home, all I want to do is fall into bed, but I can't. I have to wash off the stink of fried food. Stopping in my room, I grab some clothes and then head to the shower. I rush through getting the restaurant smell off my skin. I dress quickly and leave my hair in a towel. I'll let some of the water soak up then tie it in a knot on top of my head. I'm too exhausted to worry about going to bed with wet hair. We were short a waitress the second half of the night. Autumn left right after I talked to Slade; she was sick. The only upside is I killed it in tips. That will go a long way to my trip to North Carolina to see Slade. To say that I'm excited is an understatement. We're really doing this. We're making it work. I want that more than anything. When I dream about the future, it's always Slade I see. The weeks are going to crawl by until then.

In my room, I grab my laptop and sit on the bed. I'm going to send him a quick e-mail telling him goodnight. I know he's probably already in bed as his day starts before the damn chickens wake, but at least when he gets my e-mail, he'll know I was thinking about him. That's all that matters.

Once I'm logged in, I'm surprised to see his name sitting in my inbox. Quickly, I double click, and his message fills my screen. It's short and to the point, and my heart soars. He wants us to get to know each other, even more than we do. I find that refreshing. He's unlike any other guy I've ever met. I hit Reply and begin to type.

To: HerKnight@directmail.com
From: HisAngel@directmail.com
Time: 23:54
Subject: RE: You

Hey! I just got home from work. It was brutal. Autumn called in and I was left the only waitress. Sorry I had to rush off the phone. It was good to hear from you. How was your day?

So you want to know me, huh? I hope you know that goes both ways. We did happen really fast, but I don't regret it.

Now to answer your questions:

Favorite flower: Lilly

Favorite movie: That's harder. There are so many. I'm going to have to go with Sweet Home Alabama.

What do I do? School and work are it. Savvy and I go to the occasional party someone from school is throwing, but that's a very rare occasion. We do go to the movies a lot, go shopping. I love to read, and then there's Dawson. I help my parents with him on the days I don't have to work.

I'm just your average girl, leading a boring life. Nothing exciting ever happens here or to me. Well, until the day I met you.

I'm exhausted and calling it a night. Have a good day tomorrow. I can't wait to see you. Savvy and I are going to get some dates together tomorrow. She's going to send them to Brandon. Do you want them, too?

XOXO

Austyn

I hit Send, close my laptop and climb under the covers. I think I'm asleep before my head hits the pillow. I sleep all night and am woken by my alarm at eight for my nine o'clock class. I want to lie here in bed, but I know my hair that I forgot to take out of my towel, is a hot mess. Reaching up, I run my fingers through it, and it's knotted chaos. Feeling around I find the wet towel and reluctantly climb out of bed.

I'm ready with a few minutes to spare, so I pull up my e-mail, hoping to see a reply from Slade. When I see his name, my stomach flutters with excitement.

To: HisAngel@directmail.com
From: HerKnight@directmail.com
Time: 05:02
Subject: RE: RE: You

Austyn,

Sounds like you had a rough night. I crashed early. We have to report at five thirty for our morning run, then off to class. I don't know your schedule yet, but I think maybe you have class early today?

I don't regret a single second of the time I got to spend with you. It was fast, but it feels right. The only thing that could make it better is if you were here with me.

I guess turnabout is fair play. I'll tell you anything. All you have to do is ask.

Favorite flower: Lilly because it's yours. I'm not much of a flower kind of guy.

Favorite movie: Tombstone. Grams had a thing for Kurt Russell, and you know cowboys are badass. At least when I moved in with her, that's what I believed at the age of twelve. Now, it's a good movie, but the best part about it is that it reminds me of her.

What do I do? Work, the Marine life is not my own. I work hard, follow the rules, learn how to be the best marine I can be. Wash, rinse, and repeat. We stay busy, and up until I met you, I was good with it all. Now, I worry that the time and the distance will be too big of a factor for us. I worry that now that I've found you, I'll lose you.

Enough of the sappy.

I can't wait to see you. Yes, send me the dates too. Not that Combs won't tell me, but it gives me an excuse to hear from you.

Missing you.

Slade

I close out of my email and shove my laptop into my bag. I don't have time to reply before class. Rushing downstairs, I grab an apple and a bottle of water out of the fridge and hurry out the door. I can't keep the smile off my face all the way there. When I pull into the lot, I reach for my phone and send a text to Savannah.

Me:	Hey, we still meeting up this afternoon to talk dates?
Savannah:	You know it. Are you are in class?
Me:	Just getting ready to go in. You?
Savannah:	I still have thirty minutes. Getting ready to leave the house now.
Me:	Be safe. See you at my place around two?
Savannah:	I'll be there. I'm so excited about this trip!
Me:	Me too!!!

Shoving my phone down in my purse, I grab my bag and head inside. I barely pay attention in class, thinking about our visit to the guys in NC. I hope we can work out a date that's sooner rather than later. I know the time we've been away from them is short, and in reality, I know that's nothing compared to how it will be if and when he gets deployed. It's not like I can just fly to wherever he is across the world for a weekend getaway. I hate it, but I get it. I need to squeeze in as much time with him as I can before that happens. It's still a few months away, maybe longer, but that thought still lingers. It scares me a little how much I care for him already, and the fact that he's putting his life on the line every day. It's overwhelming. We're both in class. I'm learning how to teach kindergarteners; he's learning how to clear land mines.

Big difference.

After back-to-back morning classes, I can't tell you what was covered in either one of them. I need to get my head together, or I'll be flunking out of college, all because I can't stop thinking about seeing my maybe boyfriend. We didn't exactly label what we were, just that we both agreed to not see other people. Great, something else to think about. Maybe I should just ask him. That will be a lot easier than face-to-face rejection. Not that I think he would reject me, not in the slightest, but the fear of rejection still lingers. We're so new, and with the distance between us, it's hard not to have fear about pretty much everything.

I swing by the store on my way home and grab a huge bag of pizza rolls. Dawson will be home from school not long after Savvy is supposed to come over. It'll be a good afternoon snack for all of us.

I'm just sliding the pan into the oven when I hear a knock at the door. "Come in," I yell out, knowing it's Savannah.

"Hey, I'm a little early. Class ended early." She grins. It's always a good day when class lets out early.

"I just put some pizza rolls in the oven. Daws will want a snack when he gets home."

"What time does the bus drop him off?"

"Two forty-five, but I'm starving. All I've had today is an apple. He won't care that they're cold or he can pop them in the microwave."

"I had a granola bar before class so yeah, I'm starving too." She takes a seat at the island and pulls out her phone. "Dates!" she says excitedly. "Have you thought about what works best for you?"

"Not really. I'd prefer not to miss class. My dumb ass will fall even further behind."

She tilts her head, studying me. "What's up with that? You're the most 'on top of things' person I know."

"That was me pre-Slade." I laugh. "I couldn't tell you what we talked about today in class. Neither one of them. I drifted through the entirety of both lectures thinking about this trip."

She throws her head back and laughs. "Welcome to my world. That's how I was a few days before they came home. That's all I could think about. It had been too damn long since I'd seen him."

"You went to his graduation," I remind her.

"I did, but it's not the same. He was all professional marine graduate the entire time, which I get. I wanted him here. Just Brandon, hanging out, no prying eyes."

"And the truth comes out." I snort.

"Oh, hush. Just you wait."

I don't say anything to that. If I did, it would be my admission to her that I've thought about my first time being with Slade. Of course, since she's my best friend, she can see right through me. Doesn't mean I have to confirm or deny, though, so instead, I evade.

"So when were you thinking?" I ask her.

"I don't really want to miss class either. I'm thinking the parents might have something to say about that since they're paying for our educations."

"Good call."

"So, Thanksgiving is our best bet? I know it would mean we're away from our families, but the guys get a four-day break. No class, no training, nothing. However, they can't leave base."

"What about his parents? Are they going down at Thanksgiving?"

"No, which is another reason that's the best time. I talked to his mom last night, and they're going to go down at Christmas. They were thinking of doing both, but decided against it.

"They could go too," I say, feeling guilty keeping them from their son on the holidays.

"I told her that. I guess some friends of theirs want to go on a cruise. They need one more couple to get a group rate, so they're going."

"Good for them."

"Do you think you'll go with them at Christmas?" My heart constricts thinking of Slade being alone at Christmas. He's been through so much and to think of him being alone, it breaks my heart.

"Maybe, I guess if they offer me a ride."

"You know they will."

"Probably. So, what do you think?"

"I think it sounds good to me. I'm sure my parents will understand."

We get lost in planning, even though we're not sure the dates work for the guys. Savvy assures me they will. We also talk about the pitch to Mom and Dad about me being gone. Legally, I'm of age so they can't stop me, but I would rather them be on board with my decision. It just makes life easier.

chapter 23
Slade

ANOTHER DAY OF TRAINING IN and we're all exhausted. Getting up hours before the sun rises does that to you. Spiller and Jeffers are arguing over Juicy Fruit and Big Red. Boredom has set it. I'm clutching my phone in my hand, waiting to hear from Austyn. She said she would send me dates. I checked my e-mail as soon as we got in, but nothing yet. I'm hoping that she calls. When my phone vibrates in my hand, I look at the screen and see her smiling face. Only she's not calling; she wants to video message. I fumble to swipe at the screen and accept the call.

"Hey!" she and Savannah say at the same time.

"Trouble." I shake my head and laugh.

"Is Brandon with you?" Savannah asks.

"That my girl?" Combs asks from his bed beside me.

Before I know what's happening, the great debate about gum flavor is long forgotten as the three of them huddle in behind me to get a look at the girls.

"Hey, ladies." Jeffers lays on the charm. When I hear an "umpf," I know that Combs has given him an elbow or something equivalent for flirting with them.

"What are you two up to?" I ask them. I'm not looking at

Savannah; I can't take my eyes off Austyn.

"Just finished dinner," Austyn answers. "Dawson made spaghetti, well attempted to. We had to help him here and there."

"Hey, babe." Combs waves to the screen.

"What are you four getting into?" Savannah asks.

"Just got in and doing a whole lot of nothing."

"We have some dates if y'all are ready for them."

"Fuck yes," he says, as if he's been waiting a lifetime to hear her say those four words. I know how he feels. I've been waiting all day, and trust me, it feels like a lifetime.

"We were thinking around Thanksgiving," she says.

Mentally I calculate the how long that is. Weeks are better than the original five months. I didn't expect to see her this soon. It's more than I could have hoped for.

"Perfect. Will you drive?" he asks.

Savannah looks over at Austyn, and she shrugs. "Yes. We're out of school that Monday and don't have to be back until the following Tuesday. We were thinking road trip."

"I'll buy you a ticket if you want to fly," I say. Austyn's eyes soften at my words.

"Thank you, but we were kind of liking the idea of a road trip."

"It's safer to fly. The two of you don't need to be traveling alone."

"I agree," Combs chimes in. "Not to mention, if you fly here Monday and leave Monday, that's seven days we get with you."

"I thought you only got a four-day break?" Austyn asks.

"Got any friends that look like either of you that might want to join you?" Spiller interrupts, apparently bored of our planning.

"Times two," Jeffers adds, sticking his head in front of all of us so that the girls can only see him. They smile and laugh at his antics.

"We do," Comb continues as if the guys aren't here, "but you'll be staying here on base. We can meet up after our day ends. We can't stay with you, and we have to meet lights out, but we can still see you. Have dinner or something."

"Yeah, but there wouldn't be much for us to do during the day."

"You're allowed to leave base. You could go explore the area," he suggests.

"We wanted to make sure those dates worked. We'll talk about it and work out the details then get back with you."

"I'll book you a room," I tell Austyn. "I'll go ahead and book it for the entire week, and we can adjust it from there. I don't want you staying off base where I can't see you."

"What he said," Combs says.

"Friends," Spiller repeats. "You have to bring friends. I'm a great guy. Ask these two." He points to Combs and me.

"What about me?" Jeffers asks.

"Meh," he says, causing all of us to laugh.

Austyn's smile is wide and her blue eyes are sparkling, just how I remember her. It's good to see her, and with us being so far away, I'll take as many of these video chat sessions as she wants. However, the issue is privacy. My current situation is case in point.

"Whatcha doing?" I hear in the background. I know from the sound of the voice that it's Dawson.

"Hey, Daws." I wave when his face comes into view of the camera.

"Slade! Brandon!" he says loudly. From the way the girls cringe, I'm guessing it's even louder in person. "Are you coming home?" he asks.

"Not for a while, bud," Austyn tells him.

He nods. "I made pasketti for dinner."

"Spaghetti," Austyn corrects him.

He turns to look at her. "That's what I said."

"We're working on it," she says affectionately. "Why don't

you go upstairs so Savvy and I can finish our call."

He looks at the screen. "Who are they?" he asks.

"These are my friends, Corey Jeffers and Troy Spiller," I explain.

"Are they marines too?" he asks wide-eyed.

I bob my head. "They are."

"Cool. See ya." He waves and rushes out of the room.

"Sorry about that," Austyn apologizes.

"Babe, you going home?" Combs asks Savannah.

"I thought I'd hang out here for a while, why?"

"I was going to call you."

"You still can," she tells him.

"Austyn, I'll call you right back." I'm down with this plan. I might not be able to see her, but at least we can have some level of privacy with a phone call.

"Got it." She smiles. That smile turns me inside out.

We end the call, and immediately the guys start yapping. "Fuck me, how did you two get so lucky?" Jeffers asks.

"Seriously, do they have friends they can bring with them?" Spiller asks.

"I'm not sure, but I thank God every day that I did. Not sure about Slade here." Combs points to me. "As for friends, hell no. No way are you two going to have a fling with one of their friends and cause trouble for either one of us. You're just going to have to go chasing your pussy somewhere else. You're not getting it here."

I don't comment, even though I agree with everything he just said. Including thanking God every day for bringing her into my life. I'm the lucky one indeed. Ignoring them, I hit her name on my contact list and put the phone to my ear. Looking beside me, I see Combs doing the same thing. I block Jeffers and Spiller out and count the rings. I don't make it past one before she picks up.

"Hey, you," she greets me.

"Hey, angel. You have a good day?"

"I made it through it." She ends with a chuckle.

"What's so funny?"

She groans. "Well, I was a little preoccupied during both of my classes today. There's a good chance... in fact, I'm certain I didn't retain anything from either lecture."

"Something on your mind?" My shoulders tense up as I wait for her to tell me that this is too much for her, to wait for me. I wait for her to tell me that she's changed her mind about all of it.

"You."

"Me?" I ask hesitantly.

"Yeah, I got your e-mail right before I left for class and I was thinking about the trip and getting to see you. I knew Savvy and I were meeting this afternoon to discuss dates and well, I just kind of zoned out."

Relief washes over me. "Yeah?"

"Yep. I'll need to go back and read the chapters again, just to pick up anything that I missed."

"I know I should probably tell you I'm sorry for distracting you or at least tell you that you need to stay focused on school, but I'll admit, it's a boost to my ego hearing you say you were thinking about me. I was afraid you were going to tell me that you changed your mind... about us."

She laughs, and the musical sound washes over me. "Nope. Just me being a flake because I was excited."

"You're hardly a flake."

"I was today."

"Well, you're my flake." I curse inwardly at my sappy comment. I can't seem to stop the words from falling from my lips. She brings it out in me.

"How does forever sound?" she asks softly.

"That's a long time."

"It is."

"You sure you're up for that?"

She's quiet, as if she's really thinking about her answer. "I'd like to think I am. I like where things are going so far."

"Me too, Austyn, me too." We go on to talk about random things including the answers in our earlier e-mails. It's not until the guys turn out the lights that I realize I need to let her go. We've been on the phone for over an hour. "As bad as I hate to say this, I need to let you go. Five o'clock comes early."

"That it does. Savvy's still here. We'll decide dates for sure, and I'll send you a message or e-mail or something," she rambles.

"Sounds good, angel. Goodnight."

"Night, Slade."

"Night, angel," Spiller mimics and then snickers. "Dude, she's got you by the balls already."

"I mean she's hot as hell and her eyes are wicked blue, but come on, man, don't let her control you," Jeffers says.

"Is that what you think I'm doing?" I ask into the darkness of the room.

"You don't get it," Combs speaks up.

"You gave your balls away a long fucking time ago, Combs," Jeffers jokes.

"Damn right," Combs agrees.

"It's not about her controlling me or having my balls as you call it. I can't even really explain it, other than the fact that calling her mine is worth any ribbing you all want to dish out."

"Is she though? You just met this chic," Spiller points out.

"Just wait, fuckers," Combs says. "I can't wait to ride your asses when you find someone you're willing to give up the random lays for. Remember this moment." Combs laughs.

I don't say any more. They can laugh it up all they want. At the end of the day, I get to call her mine, at least for now. We're going to see where this goes with the distance between us. See if we can make a go of it. I want it to work out more than I've ever wanted anything. In just the short time I've known her, I'm certain of that.

chapter 24
Austyn

I CAN'T BELIEVE HOW FAST the weeks have gone by. After some begging and promises of spoiling, Savvy and I gave in to the guys and decided to spend a full week in North Carolina. Even if we get an hour a night with them those first few nights, that's more than what we would have if we stayed here in Kentucky. The day after we agreed, we confirmed we'd stay Monday through to the following Monday. That same day we both received e-mails with our flight info. They took it upon themselves to book us a round-trip flight. I argued of course, but Slade said it was safer and this way we wouldn't be exhausted when we got home. After he very sternly turned down my offer to reimburse him for my ticket, I decided to just roll with it. Savannah was good with it, so I let it go.

Our parents are thrilled we're not driving that far on our own, which makes the fact that two nineteen-year-olds leaving for a week to spend with a bunch of marines easier to swallow. Well, almost nineteen. Savvy turned nineteen three weeks ago and me, well, my birthday is Friday. Slade seems excited I'll be there for my birthday. I know I am.

"You all packed?" Mom asks.

"Yep, I just did another check to make sure I have

everything."

"You have money?" Dad questions.

"I do. I have plenty saved up, and I have my one credit card that you all helped me get to build my credit. There's nothing on it, so if there's an emergency, I'm covered."

"You call us as soon as you get there," Mom instructs.

"I will."

"And every day, as often as you want," Dad adds.

"Guys, I'll be fine. I promise to call you when we get there and check in each day."

"You need us, you call, no matter when or what for you call, you understand?" His voice is stern.

"I love you, Dad, both of you. I'll be fine."

"You sure we can't take you to the airport?"

"Brandon's parents' flight leaves close to ours, so we're all riding together. However, we'll need a ride home when we get back."

"Just send me your flight info and we'll be there," Dad assures me.

"Thanks," I say as a horn honks, letting me know they're here. "All right, I'll see you guys in a week."

"Be safe, honey," Mom says, hugging me tightly.

"Be safe, Aust, and I mean it. You call me no matter what you need. I can get you in a matter of hours by hopping on a flight."

"Dad, I'll be fine. Please don't worry."

"Have a safe trip," Mom says as I pick up my suitcase, carry-on, and purse, and head outside.

They step out onto the front porch and wave as we load my bags and pull away. "Your parents give you warnings of checking in and calling if you need them?" I ask Savannah.

"Yep." She laughs. "I take it yours did the same."

"They did."

"That's because as your parents, we worry about you. No matter how old you get, that never stops," Sarah, Brandon's mom, explains.

"Damn right. I expect a text message at the least telling me that you girls are with the guys safe and sound," Eric adds.

"Yes, Dad," we say at the same time.

"So, what do you have planned for this week?" Sarah asks.

"Not sure really. The first few days we're going to just explore the area. The guys are in training all three days. After that, it's up to them."

"I'm sure they have plans for you for your birthday, Austyn," Sarah says. That's the great thing about growing up in small towns and being friends since kindergarten. Your friends' parents remember big milestones in your life like your birthday. Then again, maybe I just got lucky to have kickass friends who have kickass parents. Either way, it's a win for me.

We spend the remainder of the ride to the airport talking about their cruise and all the places they'll be stopping. It's the first time either of them have been on one this long, but they don't seem worried. I, for one, don't know if I could go days without seeing land.

"All right girls, we're headed to our gate. Call or text when you get there," Sarah reminds us. "And give those boys a hug from me."

"We will," I say, giving her a hug. I love how she included Slade. My heart breaks for him knowing he has no family. Although, family is what you make of it. I'm more than willing to share mine. No matter what happens with us, he needs that. Hell, he deserves it.

We make it through security without issue and let the waiting begin. "You nervous?" Savannah asks.

"Kind of."

"You two have been talking and writing for weeks. There's nothing to be nervous about."

"Easy for you to say. You and Brandon have had years to get over the nervous energy. This is all new to me, to us."

"That's what you need to remember. This is all new for him

too. From what you've told me, you're both on the same page in that aspect."

"We are. That's a good point. You think he's nervous?" I ask her.

"Maybe a little, but he doesn't strike me as the type to get nervous."

I sigh. "You're probably right. That's most guys. They have it easy."

"Right?" She laughs.

"They'll be in training when we get there, so we're going to have to kill some time. We can't get on base and check into the hotel without them meeting us at the visitors' center to get our security pass."

"We can grab something to eat, pick up some snacks for the room."

"Can you believe those two? Plane tickets and room reservations?"

"Slade said he's banking his money and has money saved and invested from selling his grandmother's house."

"Brandon has been too. We're saving for whatever happens in the future."

I turn in my seat and look at her more fully. "Have y'all talked any more about that?"

"Yeah, he wants me to move with him to wherever he's stationed. We've looked at what it would take for me to transfer colleges. Luckily there are a few to choose from that have good education programs, near each base."

"And?" I prompt.

"I don't know. Part of me thinks it's better to stay at home, close to my family, but if I stayed close to base, I could see him."

"What about marriage? Any more talk about that?"

"A little. If we get married, we can live in married housing. That means I see him more, can sleep with him at night, all those kinds of things. But, if and when they get deployed, I'll be alone."

"I get what you're saying, but as a marine wife, that's what you do, right? Make friends with the other wives and hold down the home front?"

"You telling me you'd be okay with it?"

"Honestly, I've not thought about it, but yeah, I think I would be okay with it."

"You'd leave your family to live alone?"

"Not alone. They only deploy for what six-to-seven months at a time? The rest of that time it's a normal life. He comes home to you at night. How is it different than if he were an accountant and y'all moved out of state?"

"I guess it's not really." She sighs. "It's scary, you know? Thinking about him being deployed and me staying in our home, not really knowing if he's going to make it home."

"I get that too, but no one said it would be easy. Are you having second thoughts about the two of you?"

"No." Her answer is immediate. "I just... I don't know. He's been talking more and more about it, and it's all so sudden." Her voice is wary, as if she's afraid to believe it's finally happening.

"Savannah, you've known for what, two years now that he was going to enlist?" I don't know where this sudden hesitation is coming from.

"Yeah, but now it's all happening and so fast."

"I get that, I do. Savvy, you have to sort this out, babe. You can't let him think all is well if it's not. If you're second guessing being with him, you have to tell him."

She shakes her head. "It's not that," she says emphatically.

"Think about this," I say gently. "He gets deployed, and he leaves knowing you're on the fence about things, how do you think he's going to handle that? Where is this coming from? It's been the two of you against the world since freshman year."

"I'm not second-guessing us," she says quickly. "I'm not. I'm just... overwhelmed I guess. It's so damn hard being away from him."

"You've never led me to believe you were anything but ready to jump at the chance to move to wherever he gets stationed."

"I am. I was—" Before she can say anymore, we're called to board our flight.

We grab our bags and stand in line to board the plane. Once we're seated, I reach over and grab her hand. "I'm here for you no matter what. You can talk to me."

"I know. I'd be lost without you. You're part of the problem." She laughs, wiping a tear from her eye. "I'll miss you, too, so damn much. You're my support system, always have been. It's just hard to wrap my head around that everything we've talked about is finally coming true."

"I'll come visit."

She smiles. "What about you? If you and Slade get serious, are you willing to leave?"

"Yes," I answer without hesitation. "I thought a lot about that when we met and in the past several weeks since he's been gone. That's something I wanted to be sure about before we took this, whatever we are, any further." I've done nothing but think about it for weeks. Can I handle it? Can I truly deal with him being gone? Can I live with the fear that when he's deployed, hell, even when he's not… that his job is extremely dangerous? I've spent hours talking about this with Savvy listening to her talk about it with Brandon. Not once did I consider what I would do if I was in her shoes. That all changed when I met Slade. I knew from her struggle with Brandon enlisting, that I too needed to dig deep and decide if I could handle it. I knew that I need to make a firm decision and move forward with it. When I think about not being with him, not having the chance to see what we have, the answer is clear. Yes, I can do it. It's going to be hard, but this is Slade. And he's worth it.

"I suck," she says, resting her head back against the seat. "I've been with Brandon for going on five years now, and you and Slade just started talking or dating or whatever, and you're on board. What's wrong with me?" she asks, defeated.

Resting my hand on hers, I try to console her. "Nothing's wrong with you. It's change, and you've never done well with change, Savannah. Besides, all of our talks when Brandon first decided to enlist helped me get to where I need to be."

"I know, and I want everything he and I have talked about, but it's scary as hell." Her voice shakes as she fights back her emotions.

"It is, but it's you and Brandon. You can't ask him to give up his dream while you get to live yours. Brandon would never ask you to drop out of college and not become a teacher. As for us, no matter where you live, you'll always be my best friend. I'll come and visit and spoil all my nieces and nephews."

"And what about my nieces and nephews?"

I laugh. "You've got a few years on me there. Let's see if we can navigate being in a relationship before you add babies to the mix. You and Brandon are light years ahead of us. But who knows, maybe one day."

"Light years, yet you've thought about moving to be with him." I can tell by the tone of her voice she thinks I'm talking shit.

"I knew going into this being a marine is who he is. He had nothing and planned his life around his career. I knew that if I wanted to be with him, to really see where this goes, I have to be okay with that. I thought I was while he was here. It seemed like no big deal, then he left, and I got to see a glimmer of what life will be like. We're just starting this relationship, so I can only imagine how hard it is for you and Brandon." I take a drink of water. "But yes, these last several weeks, I've done nothing but think about it. I don't want to lead him on any more than I want him to do that to me."

"You're so responsible." She chuckles. "I need to be more like you."

"No, you don't." I reach out and squeeze her hand. "You just need to be you. Besides, my mom is the one that mentioned it to me. It's not like I got there on my own. Right after they left, she sat me down and told me I really need to think about moving things forward with him. The consequences of moving constantly, him being gone more than he's there, it was all things I'd considered briefly. But I only really started to pull the scenarios apart after she mentioned it."

"So you're all in?" she asks me. Her voice is lighter, and I know it's because she's happy for me.

"Yeah. I think he and I both are, but this week should help determine that." She nods, and I change the subject by asking her about her classes and the crazy full loads we've both taken on. It's our attempt to get through our courses as quickly as possible. We've had enough of the heavy for one flight. That's how we spend the rest of the trip.

When we land, we take a cab to a local restaurant and have a late lunch. We have two hours to kill before the guys can meet us at the visitors' center. We end up spending the entire time at the restaurant. When Savannah's cell rings, her face lights up, and I know it's Brandon. I listen to their conversation, trying to figure out what the plan is, but she gives nothing away.

"They're going to meet us there in thirty minutes."

We gather our bags, pay our bill and call a cab. I'm nervous and excited to see him. My stomach feels like there are a hundred butterflies flapping their wings. I can't wait to see what this week holds.

chapter 25

Slade

C OMBS COMPLETED HIS VERBAL SKILLS assessment early. They go in alphabetical order, so while he's a free man, I'm waiting for my name to be called. He catches my attention and holds his phone up in the air. He's going to call the girls. I look at the clock on the wall and see that it's four thirty. We're supposed to meet them around five. I hope all these fuckers in front of me hurry the hell up so I can get out of here. It's been hard as hell to concentrate today, knowing they're arriving. Austyn texted me to let me know they landed and I was able to reply quickly, but other than that, it's been nonstop all day long. I get it as it's why I'm here, but my girl is here now too and my concentration's shit.

I'm standing still at attention, waiting to be called, and it's killing me. I want to pull out my phone and text her. Hell, I want to run out the door and go to her. "Reeves." My name's called, and I almost do a little jig from my excitement. Instead, I proceed to the front of the room like the trained, disciplined marine I am. Most days that is. When it comes to not seeing my girl for almost two months, well, discipline flies out the window. I complete my assessment and rush out of the room. Combs is leaning against the wall right outside the door.

"Hey, they're meeting us at the visitors' center in—" He looks at his phone. "—five minutes."

"What are we waiting for?" I clamp a hand down on his shoulder, and we begin to walk, hell, I would almost call it a jog over to the visitors' center. Luckily for us, we're in shape, and it's only about a half a mile to the front of the base.

As soon as we walk through the door, the girls spot us. Immediately, they're both on their feet and headed our way. I don't know about Combs, but I don't stop moving until I have her in my arms. I hold her tight against me and spin around in a circle. Her vanilla scent washes over me, reminding me of our time together.

She's laughing as I spin us in circles. When I finally come to a stop, her feet are still dangling in the air as I hold her in my arms. "Glad you could make it." I smirk.

"Oh, you know, there's this guy. He and I kind of have a thing going, so I thought I would tag along see if he's interested in spending some time together." Her smile is contagious.

"Sorry to disappoint you, sweetheart. You're gonna have to call him and tell him there's been a change of plans," I say, staring into her eyes.

"Oh yeah?"

"Mmm-hmm." I lean in a little closer, my lips hovering over hers.

"Why's that?" she asks. Her voice is barely a whisper.

"Because you're mine. I don't plan on sharing you. Not this weekend, not ever." Closing the last slither of distance, I press my lips to hers. I want to fucking devour her, but I can't. Not here. But I will for the next seven days.

"Yours?" she asks, pulling out of the kiss.

Her face is flushed and her eyes are sparkling. "Mine," I say, before pressing my lips to hers one more time. While I missed her, I hadn't realized just how much until this moment. Part of me felt as though our time together was a dream. It was a short amount of time I've got to be with her, yet in that time, she became the most important person in my life. Standing here with her in my arms, the way my heart is thundering in my chest, the way my arms lock around her and refuse to let go, I have the sudden urge to run away with her.

"You two ready?" Combs asks.

Reluctantly, I set her back on her feet. "Yeah," I tell him. Grabbing her bags in one hand, I hold hers with the other as we follow them out the door.

"This is like your own little town," Austyn says as we reach the hotel.

"It is in a way, I guess. It's nice for times like this." I give her hand a gentle squeeze. I step up to the counter and check her in. Combs and I talked about it, and we got separate rooms. We figured that would give us alone time even the nights we have to go back to the barracks. He needs time with his girl, and I need time with mine. I, however, stepped it up a notch. Friday is Austyn's birthday, and she's spending it with me. I want this trip to be special, memorable for both of us. I reserved a suite. It has a small kitchen and two bedrooms. Not that I think we'll need two rooms.

"I'll text you our room number. You guys want to grab something to eat?" I ask Combs.

"Yeah, give us… some time." He smirks.

I nod my agreement. Time with Austyn is music to my ears. In the elevator, I hit the button for the top floor.

"I bet we can see most of the base from the top floor," she comments.

I've never thought about it. "Hopefully." Not that I really care what the view is like. I just wanted to do it up big for her birthday. I also thought that with the second room, if Savannah wanted to stay with her until we can be with them, she could. Admittedly, that was an afterthought, but it's a possibility. I know how close they are.

Reaching the door, I slip the keycard in the lock and push it open. Stepping back, I allow her to walk past me and enter first. She gasps and I grin.

"Slade, this is too much," she argues.

"It's my girl's birthday weekend, and I haven't seen you in

longer than I care to think about. It's not too much." I place her bags by the couch and go back to the door, making sure that it's locked. Turning, I watch her as she takes in our surroundings. She runs her fingers over the island that separates the kitchen area from a small living area.

"Two bedrooms?" she asks, peeking into each door. "Why would we need two bedrooms?" she asks.

Good to know we're on the same page. "We don't," I assure her. "That's just what comes with the suite."

"This is too much," she says again, this time facing me.

"It's not." I hold my hand out to her, and she takes it. I pull her into me and wrap my arms around her. "Have I told you how happy I am to see you?"

"I guessed." She laughs.

I rest my forehead against hers. "So fucking good to feel you in my arms, angel."

She sighs. "How is it that I crave you when I've only just found you?"

"So it's not just me, then?"

"This is crazy, Slade."

"It is, but I wouldn't change it."

"No, me either."

Keeping one hand on her waist, I place the other against her cheek. Instantly, she leans into my touch. Moving in closer, I touch my lips to hers. I mean for it to be a quick kiss, but when she opens for me, I slide my tongue past her lips. My grip tightens on her hip, and I use my hand that's resting against her cheek to tilt her head. I devour her, my tongue exploring her mouth, tasting her for the first time in way too damn long. By the time we pull away, we're both panting, our breaths rapid and heavy.

I'm just about ready to go in for more when there's a knock at the door. "You two ready?" Combs calls out.

"Shit," I murmur.

Austyn giggles. "Time flies when you're having fun."

We take the girls to the food court at the exchange. They're not hungry, but it's been hours since Combs and I have eaten. I kept Austyn close to me for multiple reasons: one, that's where she belongs always, and two, I see the way my brothers are checking her out. We're just finishing up when Spiller and Jeffers walk up to the table.

"Ladies," Spiller says, winking at both of them."

"Aren't you going to introduce us?" Jeffers asks.

"Nope," Combs says, and I bite back my laugh.

"I'm Savannah." She holds her hand out to Spiller. He takes it and brings it to his lips for a kiss, causing her to laugh. Combs growls. At least that's what it sounds like.

Spiller drops her hand, and she offers it to Jeffers. "Pleasure's all mine." He winks at her, holding onto her hand longer than needed.

Spiller turns to Austyn. "I'm Austyn." She waves. He reaches for her hand, but my girl drops it to her lap.

"You know," Spiller says to her, "you get tired of this guy, I can show you around town."

"Actually, I'm the better option of the two," Jeffers adds.

Austyn stiffens a little beside me. "That's cute." She releases a forced laugh; it's one I've never heard before. Spiller opens his mouth to say God only knows what when she beats him to it. "That's cute that you think you can compete with Slade."

They both stare at her, mouths hanging open. This time I don't hold back my laughter, and neither does Combs. I put my arm around my girl and pull her into me, kissing her temple.

"We should probably get going," Combs says. "We'll drop y'all off and then meet up with you tomorrow after training."

When we get back to the room, I walk her in. "You got everything you need?"

"I'm all set. We're going to call a cab and go explore tomorrow. You get out at five?" Warmth spreads through me from her hands that are pressed against my chest.

"Yeah, we can go have dinner again." I pull her into my arms.

"I can't wait until Wednesday at five."

"Oh yeah? What happens Wednesday at five?"

She knows, but if she needs to hear me say it, I will. "I get four entire days with you. No training, no class, nothing will keep me from you."

"In that case, I can't wait until Wednesday at five either."

"Thank you for coming here to see me. I missed you," I tell her, kissing her neck.

"I missed you too. None of that," she groans, stepping away. She sounds as reluctant as I feel. "You have to leave, and that's going to make it harder. Let's get through the next two nights, and then I won't leave your side for four days. You'll be sick of me."

"That will never happen."

"Never say never."

"Angel, that will *never* happen." I kiss her softly.

Breaking the kiss, she says, "Goodnight."

"Night." After a kiss on her forehead, I lace my fingers through hers and lead her to the door with me. It's a few feet at best, but I'm soaking up every second I can with her while she's here.

"Call me in the morning… if you want."

"It'll be early."

"I'm on vacation. I can go back to sleep."

"Okay." One more kiss and I have to force myself out the door. I'm ready to knock on Savannah's door when Combs appears.

"Two more fucking days," he says, grinning.

"My thoughts exactly." We head back to the barracks, making it just in time. Spiller and Jeffers start yapping their jaws about the girls, but we just ignore them. We know what we have. We know that yes, they're beautiful, but that's not all they are. I couldn't care less about the ribbing. My girl is here, and I get four days with her. Nothing can tamper with my good mood.

chapter 26
Austyn

SO FAR, SAVANNAH AND I have been tourists during the day, and then having dinner with the guys at night. Today, our plans are to just hang around at the hotel. The guys are hopeful they'll be out of training a little early, so we want to be here just in case.

"You know what we should do?" Savannah asks.

I turn to look at her from my lounge chair. "What's that?"

"We should get food to make dinner tomorrow."

"Ummm, do you know how to make Thanksgiving dinner?" I ask her.

"I've seen Mom do it every year. I think I can handle it."

"You know how to cook a turkey? A ham?"

"Well, no, but honestly, how hard can it be?"

I laugh. "I'm guessing it's more complicated than our mothers make it look."

"We have to learn sometime. Might as well start now." She moves to sit on the edge of her lounger. "What kind of cooking utensils do you have in that kitchen of yours?"

"Honestly, I don't know. I just have a couple of bottles of water in the fridge."

"We need to check it out." She stands and wraps her towel

around her waist. "We need to get to the store and be back in case they get out early."

"Savvy, come on, do you really think this is a good idea?" I can handle a couple of side dishes, but a turkey, I have no idea where to start.

Her face looks resolute. "Absolutely. We don't have to make a huge spread, just some basics. Besides, I'm sure the guys would appreciate a homecooked meal."

"I'm sure they would as long as it's edible." I chuckle.

"Oh, hush." She grins. "We've got this. Come on." She holds out her hand for me, and I take it, allowing her to pull me from my lounger chair.

We head to our rooms to shower and get ready for the day. A knock comes at my door, and I open it, not bothering to ask who it is. I know it's Savannah. "Have you checked out the kitchen yet?" she asks.

"Nope. I went straight to the shower." Reaching out, she grabs my hand and tugs me toward the small kitchenette.

"We need a menu so we know what dishes we need. I called Mom, and she suggested we could buy those disposable aluminum pans to use."

"That's a good idea. So, what are you thinking?"

"We need a turkey obviously." She raises her hand and holds up one finger and then others as she lists items. "Mashed potatoes and gravy, macaroni and cheese, rolls, and a dessert. Oh, and stuffing. I would say sweet potatoes, but Brandon doesn't like them."

"Yeah, Slade doesn't either."

She looks at me with raised brows. "How do you know?"

"We talk, all the time. We've had weeks of talking and getting to know one another."

She nods. "Okay, so what else?"

"For the four of us, that's plenty. I can handle all the sides, but I don't have the first idea of how to cook a turkey. As far as dessert, we can just grab a pumpkin pie from the freezer section and some whip cream."

"I thought we could make one from scratch." She almost pouts.

I snort and shake my head. "Let's not bite off more than we can chew. This is our first attempt. Besides, the guys couldn't care less if it's frozen. It will be the effort, and they get to spend the day with us. It'll be fine. Trust me."

"Fine." A soft sigh escapes her lips. She pulls her phone out of her pocket and makes a list of things we'll need as she sifts through the small kitchen. "They don't give you much," she says, opening and closing cabinets.

"I'm sure not many people plan to make Thanksgiving dinner from their suite."

"Really? Surely we're not the only ones who come to visit and plan to cook during the time the base shuts down."

I shrug. "I don't know what they do, but I know what we're doing."

She grins. "Yes. Let's head to the store here on base. I hope they have everything that we need."

Fifteen minutes later, we're in the store with Savannah's list pulled up on her phone. We take our time walking down every aisle, tossing items in the cart. By the time we make it to the checkout counter, the cart is full. We check out and push the cart outside and realize our mistake. We have no car to load them into, and there are no taxis on base. We look at the cart, then each other, then back at the cart, clearly at a loss for what to do next.

"You ladies, okay?" a masculine voice asks from behind us. Looking up, I spot two seriously hot guys standing there smirking. "You need some help with those?" they ask.

I'm just about to say no, we can figure it out, when Savvy says, "Yes, please."

"Where are you parked?" they ask.

"Umm, we're not. We're staying at the hotel here on base and planned to make dinner tomorrow. We didn't exactly think through getting all this back to the hotel."

"Who are you here with?" they ask at the same time. Obviously, we're not just hanging out on base for the holiday for the hell of it."

"Combs," she says proudly.

The guys nod and shift their eyes to me. "Reeves."

"And why are they not here helping you?" the taller guy asks.

"Training." I say the words a little more snarky than I intended, but I hate the thought of them thinking the guys left us to do this alone. Neither one of them would ever do that.

"Right, let us help you," the shorter of the two says. He doesn't wait for permission before grabbing two handfuls of bags and lifting them from the cart.

The other follows suit. "Lead the way, ladies." He grins.

Savannah starts walking, and I rush to catch up with her. "Do you think this is the best idea?" I ask, my voice a harsh whisper.

"What? They're being nice. They probably know the guys and just want to help."

"I don't know, Savannah."

"It's fine. We couldn't do it on our own, and it's not like we could have called the guys and asked them to come and get us. This is marine life," she whispers back, calm, cool, and collected.

I have a feeling the guys are not going to be impressed. Not that either of them have anything to worry about, but we're here to see them, and these two, whoever they are, since we don't have their names, were all too eager to help. I don't feel unsafe, but something tells me that they're not too worried about the fact that we're here visiting our guys. Not in the least. I don't say anymore as we make the short ten-minute walk back to the hotel. When I see Slade and Brandon walking up the front entrance at the same time as we do, my stomach rolls. I have no reason to feel this way, I know that, but from my past observation and experience, guys are jealous by nature. This can't be good.

"Hey, guys," Savannah says as we walk up to them.

"What's going on?" Slade asks.

"We went to the store but didn't think about not being able to carry it all back to the hotel. These two," she points over her shoulder, "offered to help."

"Thanks, man." Slade reaches out to the taller of the two and takes the bags from his hands. Brandon does the same thing. "Let us take those." His face is solid as stone, not giving anything away.

"Thanks for your help," Savannah says. "We couldn't have done it without you."

"You're welcome. You have a nice holiday," the shorter one says.

"You guys have family coming in?" Brandon asks.

"Nah," they say at the same time.

"Well, then you'll have to join us," Savannah chimes in. "We have plenty, and that's the least we can do for you helping us." I want to tell her to shut the hell up, that this is our time with the guys, but then I think about them being alone and away from family and friends, and my irritation fades just as quickly as it came on.

"You sure?" the shorter one asks.

"Positive." She sounds so sure of herself.

"You heard her," Brandon adds. "I don't know what they have planned, but you're welcome to join us."

"Room number 2016," she tells them mine and Slade's room number. Slade raises his eyebrows in question, but says nothing.

"What time?" the taller one asks.

Savannah looks over at me in question. I turn to Slade and Brandon. "Eat early like one or late around five?"

"One," the guys say at the same time and laugh.

"Looks like one," Savannah answers.

"Thanks," the shorter one says.

"We'll see you tomorrow at one," the other says with a wave, and then they're gone.

"Right, ladies, lead the way so we can get rid of some of these groceries." Brandon laughs.

The four of us make it up to our room, and the guys deposit the bags on the small counter. "What is all of this?" Slade asks.

"Well, Savvy thought we should make Thanksgiving dinner, so we went to the store, and here you have it." I chuckle, pointing to all the bags.

"That's a lot for four people," Brandon tells her gently.

"Well it's a good thing there are now six of us," she counters with a wink.

"Actually, can we make it eight?" Slade asks. We all turn to look at him. "Jeffers and Spiller are both alone too. Their families can't make it."

"Eight it is. My only concern is places to sit and plates. We might need to make another trip to the store."

"No need," Brandon says, pulling out his phone. "I'll text them to bring paper plates and drinks. I'll text Miller and Johnson too," he says.

"Miller and Johnson?" I ask.

Slade just smiles and shakes his head. "The two guys you let carry the groceries."

"Ah," I say sheepishly, the tension falling from my shoulders. I was worried that he was upset, but obviously, he's anything but.

"Come here." He grins and holds his arms open for me. I waste no time walking into them, wrapping my arms around his waist and resting my head against his chest. "I missed you," he says softly, just low enough for me to hear.

"You sure you have enough food?" I hear Brandon asks Savannah.

"Yep, we went overboard. Let's get this all put away, and we can tell for sure."

It takes us no time to get everything stored away and decide that we do indeed have plenty of food. "We need to start the turkey early," Savannah says.

"What time?"

We're eating at one, and my Internet search said it needs to cook at least six-to-eight hours. So around five."

"Why don't we just order pizza in tonight, in our own rooms?" Brandon asks.

"Great idea," Slade says before either of us can answer.

"I'll guess I'll see you bright and early." Savannah gives me a hug.

We say goodbye and walk them to the door. Once they're gone, Slade pushes me against the door, resting his palms flat against it over my head. "Four days, Austyn. I get you for four entire days."

"You do. Well, tomorrow you have to share me a little," I goad.

"I don't like to share."

"Not even with me?" I ask coyly.

"You don't count," he says.

"So you'll share your kisses with me?"

He growls, bends, and places his hands on the back of my thighs and lifts me off the ground. I immediately wrap my legs around his waist and my arms around his neck. "They're yours, angel. There's nothing to share." With that, he kisses me. It's slow at first, but the grip he has on my thighs tells me he wants it to be anything but. He carries me to the couch, sits down, and I straddle his lap.

"I can't believe you're really here," he says once he breaks our kiss. His hand cups my cheek. "Or that I don't have to leave you tonight."

"We should order food before we get carried away." I'm nervous about tonight. Not because I'm afraid to be alone with him, quite the opposite. I want to be alone with him. I want more of his kisses, and I want where that leads us. I want it all with him. That has me a nervous wreck.

"I have all I need right here," he says, pressing his lips to mine. While it's a chaste kiss, it does nothing to dampen the desire I have for him.

"You want pizza or hoagie?"

"Hoagie, sounds good right now."

"I'm thinking the same thing. A hoagie and breadsticks." I lean forward to pull my phone out of my pocket, and he palms my ass.

"Whatever you want," he says, kissing my neck.

I groan. "I'm trying to order our food."

"And I'm trying to devour you," he counters.

"There's plenty of time for that." Though to be honest, there's nothing I want to do more than to wrap myself up in him. I need to keep my head though. At least for a little while longer.

"Not really. Four days is not enough time. You know that right, Austyn?" His tone is serious. I move my eyes from my phone to his face. Warmth pools in my stomach. "Forever will never be enough time with you."

Setting my phone on the side table, I wrap my arms around his neck and kiss him. Food can wait. He's right. We only have a limited amount of time. Why waste it?

chapter 27
Slade

HOURS. I'VE BEEN KISSING HER for hours, letting my hands roam over her body, and I don't want to stop. If I had my way, I'd never stop. Kissing her, touching her is my greatest pleasure in life. I plan to do nothing but this for the next four days.

"We should eat something," she says between kisses.

"You hungry, angel?" I ask, my lips trailing down her neck. When her belly growls, I have my answer. Pulling back, I realize I've been selfish. In my need to kiss her as much as I can, to feel her in my arms, I've neglected her. What kind of guy doesn't make sure his girl is fed?

"I can see that look in your eyes, Reeves. I was just as into what we've been doing as you were. We just need to refuel before everything closes."

I grab her phone from the table; we never made it off the couch. "Hoagie, no onion with pickle for me," I say, handing over her phone. She climbs off my lap, and I dig my wallet out of my back pocket and hand her my card. She shakes her head, but I hold it out for her. "Take it," I whisper, as she starts to order our food. Reluctantly, she gives the person on the other line the number and then ends the call.

"Let me get you some money," she says, starting to stand.

"No way. I've told you. I have the money that I earn here, which I spend very little of. I also have the interest off the money I invested from the sale of Gran's house. I'm in good shape, Austyn. You're a full-time student, working part-time. Let me do this for you."

Her face softens. "Thank you," she says, leaning in for a quick kiss. "I'm going to go freshen up before the food gets here." She stands and walks toward one of the bedrooms.

I adjust my dick once she's out of sight. I'm hard as nails, but the discomfort is worth it. I can't seem to keep my hands off her, so I need to get used to it, at least while she's here. We've never talked about going further, and even though I want to more than anything, it needs to be her choice. In the meantime, I'll suffer through it.

The food arrives, and we eat it on the couch. "How are classes?" I ask her.

"Good." She takes a sip of water. "This semester it's been a constant struggle to focus, but I'm pushing though. I think it's you."

"Me?"

"Yeah, you're all I can think about. School just seems... not as exciting as it used to be."

"You like it still? Still want to be a teacher?" She shrugs, and my brows dip in concern. "Come on now, what's going on in that pretty head of yours?"

"It's nothing." She waves me off.

"It's something. I want to know. Tell me," I urge.

"Well, I'm taking this design class as an elective and I really like it."

"Okay, what kind of design are we talking?"

"Web design, like websites and some graphics like logos and stuff."

"That sounds interesting."

"It really is. I enjoy it."

"So, you want to switch your major?"

"Crazy, right? I mean, I'm almost through this semester. It would be crazy to change now."

"I think that's pretty normal, Aust. You're doing general education now, right?"

"Yeah, for the most part. I've taken two history classes that were for my teaching core, but other than that, just the basics."

"Then changing doesn't sound so bad. It sounds to me now would be the time to do it."

"I know, but Savannah and I have always said we were going to be teachers. I feel like changing that now, after wanting it or for so long is wrong or something. Like I'm betraying some kind of friend pact," she admits. "I know that sounds crazy, even to me."

"It's okay to change your mind. Maybe she will too?"

"I don't know. She's been off lately. I think being away from Brandon is getting to her. The first time around it was bad, but she knew when the thirteen weeks boot camp would be over, she would get time with him. This time's longer, you know? I think it's all just now sinking in how long of a time they will be apart. It's affecting her."

"What about you?"

When she stares down at the bottle of water in her hands, I swallow hard. "You know, it sucks to be away from you, but really, I feel this time apart means I'm getting to really truly know you. Not just Slade the Marine, but you, the man behind all that."

I nod, and a lightness fills my chest. "You are getting to know me, the real me. I've never been anything but honest with you. Hell, you know more about me than anyone else."

A small smile lifts her mouth at my words. "I feel like this time will make us strong, you know? Not that Savvy and Brandon aren't, because they are, but they've known each other our entire lives. They met as kids, and I just think… well, I think meeting now, in this way, has given us the opportunity to really dive into who we really are. While I don't want to be away from you, I feel closer to you because of it. Does that make sense?"

I love you. The words are on the tip of my tongue. That's how she makes me feel, like my heart needs her to know she's its owner. That she's everything that is good in my life. "More than you know," I say instead. "We've been together in person a handful of days, but the moment I saw you Monday night, it felt like we've been together for years." It's a struggle to not take her in my arms and tell her the words that are flashing through my mind. I finish off my bottle of water before I continue on. "I think you should go for it, Austyn." I brush a stray strand of hair behind her ear. "Do whatever it is that makes you happy. You shouldn't settle."

"It's something that I really like, and you know, I could work from home or anywhere."

My heart stutters at her words. "Is that what you want, ultimately, to be able to work from home?" She blushes a light shade of pink and tears at the label on her water bottle. "Angel," I say softly. Her eyes find mine, and she looks…worried. "You can tell me anything."

"Okay, but it was just a thought, all right? I don't want you to think that I'm trying to plan out anything or whatever…." Her voice trails off, and fuck, she looks fucking adorable as she chews on her bottom lip.

"Just tell me." I reach out and lace my fingers through hers. "There's nothing you can't tell me." Her nerves zing between us, and I can't help but think what ever she's going to say will ruin me, or make us.

"I was just thinking, not only do I really enjoy it, but working from home or remotely, I could… you know, move around a lot." She pauses, waiting for my reaction. When I don't say anything—I can't since my heart's in my damn throat—she forges on. "You know… wherever you might get stationed, I could travel to see you or… with you." She all but whispers that last part.

Her words swirl around in my mind. "You think about that? About coming with me?" My heart races with excitement. I want that. Everything she just said, I want her with me, no matter where I am. I know there will be deployments, but the thought of coming home to her each night. Fuck, do I want that.

"Yeah, I know it's too soon—"

"It's not."

"—to be thinking about it seriously, but being able to work from home would help things, you know?"

I'm pretty sure she didn't hear me. I need to remedy that. "You done eating?"

Her brows dip in confusion. "Uh, yeah."

I stand with her hand still in mine, then lead her toward the bedroom. "This one, right?" I ask her.

"Yes." That one word is a breathy whisper.

I turn out the lights as we pass the switch and lead her into the bedroom. It's dark, with nothing but the glow of the moon shining through the sheer curtains. I lead her to the side of the bed and release my hold on her. Without a word, I pull my T-shirt over my head and toss it on the floor. Next, I lose my pants and realize I didn't bring clean clothes with me. I'll have to head back to the barracks in the morning to get some for the next few days.

"Slade, I—"

I place my finger over her lips. "It's not too soon, Austyn." I shake my head, needing her to believe my words. "None of this feels too soon. What it feels is right, and right now, I want to hold you. I'm exhausted, both physically and mentally, and the thought of you coming with me, no matter where I get stationed, has me reeling. I want to hold your body close to mine and fall asleep with you. I want to wake up with you tight in my arms. I want to feel what that would be like. Pretend like you don't have to leave in a few short days."

Her breath catches, and she gives a slow nod. Wordlessly, she pulls her shirt over her head and shimmies out of her jeans. I purposely left my boxer briefs on, not sure how far I could go, should go. I want nothing more than to lie skin to skin with her, with nothing between us. When her arms go behind her back and she unclasps her bra then climbs into bed, I exhale a deep breath. I wait for her to get settled under the covers before climbing in beside her.

"Come here, angel," I say into the darkness. She settles next to me, her head on my chest, my arm wrapped tightly around her. We lie like this for I don't know how long. I'm not sure where her head is at, but mine is on what she said. I realize that my actions might have made her think that's not what I want. "You awake?" I whisper.

"Mmm-hmm," she mumbles.

"When you're ready for that, when you're ready to come with me, you let me know, okay?"

That gets her attention, and she lifts her head to look at me in the moonlight. "What are you saying, Slade?"

"I'm saying I want you however I can get you. And if and when you ever decide that you want to follow me, you let me know. I'll take care of it. All of it." She's quiet as she rests her head back on my chest. Her lips against my skin, the act sending bolts of desire through my veins. I don't know if I've overwhelmed her, but I need her to know where I am, with us.

Nothing else is said as we hold onto one another. Eventually, I drift off to sleep, only to wake a few hours later with the ringing of her cell phone. Not wanting to wake her, but afraid it might be her family, I reach over her and grab it from the nightstand. I see Savannah's name light up the screen. Swiping it, I answer, "Hello."

"Slade, open up."

"What?"

She laughs. "I need to start the turkey."

"Right. Give me a minute. I'll be right there."

"Who was that?" my girl mumbles sleepily.

"Your best friend. She needs to start the turkey."

"I feel like we just fell asleep."

"We did." I kiss the top of her head. "I'm going tell her that she and Combs can nap in the other bedroom if they want, so we can get some more sleep."

"I'm up," she says, stretching her arms above her head. Her naked breasts are on full display for me in the moonlight. Bending down, I take one in my mouth, gently nipping and soothing with my tongue. "I'm never getting up." She laughs, brushing her fingers through my hair.

I release her from my mouth and laugh softly. "I'll let them in. Go back to sleep."

"I told her I would help, even though I have no clue how to cook a turkey."

"Okay. You throw some clothes on while I let them in." With one more kiss to her head, I hop out of bed and slide into my pants from yesterday. I make my way to the door and find Combs and Savannah standing there sleepily, both with mugs of coffee in their hands.

"Our girl up?" Savannah asks.

"Yeah, she'll be out in a minute. If you all want to crash in the other bedroom, it's yours," I tell them.

"I need to run over to the barracks and grab some clothes," Combs says.

"I'm with you. Maybe we should do that now. We can be back by the time they're done."

He nods. "We'll be back." He kisses Savannah.

"Let me just go tell, Austyn."

"Tell me what?" she asks, stopping next to me.

I wrap my arm around her shoulders and pull her into my chest, kissing the top of her head before telling her the plan. "You need anything?" I then ask.

"Nope, we're good here." She looks over at Savannah. "I think."

"Ha ha, we got this."

"I got the sides. You got the bird."

Savannah holds out her fist and they bump them together and laugh. With one more kiss on the top of her head, I release her to grab my shirt from the bedroom and head to the barracks. The sooner I get there and collect some clothes, the sooner I can get back. Back to her.

chapter 28

Austyn

SAVANNAH AND I WAIT UNTIL the guys are out the door before we start cooking. She rushes around the small kitchen like she's cooked many meals there. "What do I need to do?" I ask.

"Um, can you get me the butter?"

Reaching into the fridge, I pull out the pack of butter and hand her a stick. "Aren't you supposed to, I don't know, take the insides out or something?"

She tilts her head to the side and looks at the turkey. "I think that's just if you're stuffing it. We're going with Stove Top Stuffing, so we're good. Then again maybe we should look it up," she says reaching for her phone. I watch her while she types in the question and scrunches up her nose. "Yeah, we need to take them out," she laughs.

I shrug, because honestly, I have no idea. This is the part my mom always handles. I'm usually in bed. I guess I need to get up with her the next time so I can learn. Someday, I might be making dinner at my house. "What else can I do?"

"Nothing, I'm just going to smear the top with butter, add some water to the bottom of the pan and cover it with foil."

"And then we just let it cook?" I ask her.

"Yep, easy-peasy." She grins.

"You're in an awfully good mood at this early hour," I say, holding my hand over my mouth, covering a yawn.

"I am. Last night was good. I talked to Brandon like you said. He eased my fears, and we've never been better."

"That's good to hear. I'm happy for you."

I watch as she finishes slathering butter all over the bird and then adds water to the bottom of the pan. Once it's covered in foil, I jump into action and rush to open the oven door for her. "Now what?" I ask once the bird is in the oven.

"Now, we go back to sleep." She chuckles.

"You going to take the other room?"

"Yeah, might as well so I can keep an eye on the bird. I'll text Brandon and let him know."

"Sounds like a plan," I say over another yawn, and head back to the bedroom. I burrow under the covers that smell like Slade and drift back to sleep. It can't be but minutes later that I feel the bed dip and he crawls in beside me.

"I'm back," he whispers, placing a kiss on my shoulder.

"Keep me warm," I say, snuggling in next to him.

He doesn't say anything, but then again, he doesn't need to. His arms that are braced tightly around me, holding me close, say everything. We drift back to sleep for a couple more hours, or at least I do. When I wake, I feel him watching me. When I pry open my eyes, he smiles softly.

"Morning, angel."

I offer him a sleepy smile. "How long have you been awake?"

"I never fell back to sleep."

"You should have woken me."

Reaching out, he gently moves my bangs from my eyes. "Nah, holding you while you slept and getting to watch you, no way was I missing that."

His words make me feel cherished, and not want to ever leave this bed. At least not as long as he's in it with me. "Are you not tired?"

"We get up early every day, some on very little sleep. My body's just used to it."

"What time is it?"

"A little after nine."

With a sigh and groan, I stretch. "I need to get moving."

"Yeah," he says, gripping my waist and turning me to face him. "You can do that," he says. "As soon as you kiss me good morning."

"Um, no can do, buddy. I need to brush my teeth."

"Austyn." His voice is deep, almost a warning.

"Slade," I counter. "Give me two minutes." I shimmy out of his hold, knowing damn well that he let me get away. Hopping out of bed, I rush to the bathroom and brush my teeth. I see a towel hanging on the rack and his toothbrush by the sink. He must have showered while I was sleeping. After finishing up, I race back to the bed and jump, landing softly next to him, causing him to laugh.

"That was record time." He looks so damn hot lying here grinning at me.

"I didn't want to miss out on morning kisses." I place a sloppy wet kiss on his cheek.

"We can do better than that." Before I know what's happening, he has me pinned under him on the bed. "*This* is so much better," he says, his lips a hair's breadth from mine.

"Meh," I say, giving him a hard time.

He chuckles. "I guess I need to prove it to you." With that, his lips land on mine, his tongue seeking entrance. I open for him, and leisurely, he explores my mouth. Locking my hands together behind his neck, I hold him to me, not wanting this to end. Unfortunately, a loud clang from the kitchen and a muffled "Shit" breaks us apart.

"I better get out there and help her."

He groans loudly. "I'll be out in a minute."

I don't question his delay because I felt it against me, right where he needed to be... just if there weren't layers of clothes separating us. That's something I'll have to work on tonight when it's just the two of us. No matter what happens from this point forward, I want it to be him.

I find Savannah in the kitchen, peering into the oven. "How's it going, boss?"

"Good." She hesitates. "I think. I'm nervous all of a sudden. Messing up dinner for Slade and Brandon is one thing, but the other four. What was I thinking, Austyn?"

"You were thinking anything we have, even if it's not perfect, is better than them being alone on Thanksgiving. You did a good thing."

"Right. Okay. So, what now?"

"Well, if the oven is the right temperature, we can bake the pies. Other than that, we just wait."

"Breakfast," Brandon mumbles, stumbling out of the second bedroom.

"I was just going to suggest that," Slade says, wrapping his arms around me from behind. "You hungry?" he whispers in my ear.

"Yes, but everything's closed. We have some donuts and Pop-Tarts here." I point over to the counter. "And coffee," I tell Brandon.

"Coffee." He nods, smiling in appreciation.

"You ladies need any help?" Slade asks.

"Actually, we just need to make sure we have a place for everyone to sit, either in the living room or at the table. We might need chairs from Savannah and Brandon's room."

"We have a small four-person table too. We'll just bring it over here."

"Will we get in trouble?" I ask.

"No, we'll put it back," Slade assures me.

"Great, that's your job once you've had breakfast."

"Coffee," Brandon corrects me, causing us all to laugh.

Instead of baking the pies now, we decide to set them out to thaw so we can take quick showers. I'm in the middle of rinsing the shampoo out of my hair when I feel his hands on my hips. My eyes pop open. He gauges my reaction as he steps closer. Without a word, he runs his fingers through my hair, helping me rinse out what's left of the shampoo. Grabbing my bodywash, he places a generous amount in the palm of his hand and starts at my shoulders.

Neither one of us say a word as his hands roam all over my body, washing every inch of me. It's erotic and sensual, and I've never in all my life ever been this turned on. Once he's satisfied I'm clean, he turns me front to back until all the soap is washed down the drain. Cupping my cheek, he steps closer, his hard length pressing against my belly.

He steps even closer, his lips claiming mine. My nails dig into his back as I hold him close to me, not willing to let an inch between us. Breaking the kiss, his lips trail down my neck, searing me with his touch. All I can do is hold on for the ride. He works his way over to my shoulder and buries his face in my neck. He's breathing hard and his chest heaves against me.

"Austyn," he murmurs.

Releasing my death grip on him, I wrap my arms around his waist and just hold on tight. I need to feel him against me just a little longer.

When he finally raises his head, both of his hands cradle my cheeks. "You," he says, his eyes boring into mine, "you are more than I ever expected and everything I never knew I wanted. I'm falling hard, angel." My pounding heart threatens to beat out of my chest at his words. "I'm falling hard, and damn if I want to stop it." Leaning in, he kisses my forehead and reaches behind me to shut off the water. "Let's get you dried off," he says, stepping out and holding his hand out for me.

I open my mouth to tell him that I feel the same way, but nothing comes out. Is it possible for your heart to literally stop beating in moments of pure happiness? As if it needs a minute to absorb what just happened? Somehow I manage to find my voice despite my heart and head making it difficult to form words. "Aren't you... uncomfortable?" I point to his hard length, feeling my cheeks flame in the process. It's not what I meant to say but seeing his hard length, reminds me that he has to be in pain.

"I'm fine, angel." He wraps a towel around my shoulders and gives me another for my hair.

I watch as he wraps a towel around his waist and moves toward the bathroom door. Every movement is hypnotizing. "Slade," I call out to him. My voice is gruff with emotions.

"Yeah?" He turns to face me.

"Me too, all of it. Me too," I manage to say. It's not enough, but I know from his reaction that it's enough for him. He gets me.

He nods, a smile tipping his lips. To my surprise, he blows me a kiss, then leaves the room, shutting me in the bathroom. Giving me time to get myself together.

chapter 29

Slade

TODAY HAS BEEN THE BEST Thanksgiving I can ever remember. My first with Gran was good; it was the first time I ever really celebrated the holiday other than what we did at school. But this one, it was different. It was filled with friends and good times, good laughs, good food. Well, mostly. The turkey was dry, so dry you had to take a drink to chew it in order to get it down. The mashed potatoes were lumpy, as we didn't have a mixer, and more than a little runny. The crust on the pie was burnt to a crisp, but I ate every single bite of all of it. The girls went out of their way to make this day special, not just for Combs and me, but for the guys too.

None of them complained. They shoveled it all in as if it was the best meal they'd ever eaten. It was pretty damn good, aside from the few mishaps. Good enough that between the eight of us, there were little to no leftovers.

"Ladies, that was great. Thank you," Johnson speaks up.

"Yes," the other three chime in.

"So what now?" Jeffers asks.

"Everything on base is closed. Nothing much else to do."

"We have cards," Savannah offers. "Austyn and I weren't sure how much free time we'd have on our hands until the guys were set free for the weekend, so we brought cards," she explains.

"You all up for some euchre?" Miller asks.

"We'll clean. You six duke it out," Austyn says, standing from her seat.

"I'll help." I start to stand, but her hand on my shoulder stops me.

"Relax, Slade. We've got this." She leans in and presses her lips to the corner of mine. I watch her walk away, not willing to take my eyes off her for a second.

"Hey, Romeo." Johnson chuckles. "You and Combs play the winners," he says, holding up the deck of cards.

I nod and turn my attention back to Austyn. She and Savannah have music playing from one of their phones, and they dance around the kitchen, cleaning, laughing, and having a good time. I don't even realize I'm smiling until Combs calls me out on it.

"You're sunk," he says, jabbing me with his elbow to get my attention. "You're wearing a goofy smile."

"It's been a good day. This is new for me, you know, with the holidays."

"Damn, man, I'm sorry."

"Don't be. You gave me this in a way. If you hadn't insisted I come home with you on leave, I never would have met her, and that would have been a tragedy."

"I brought the ring," he tells me. He's been holding onto it since we were on leave. I was with him at the small jeweler in his hometown when he bought it. I don't think I've ever seen him smile that big.

"Tonight?"

He nods. "Yeah, I think so, man. I'm tired of waiting. We had a good talk last night about her fears and reservations of being a marine wife. I think I helped ease some of her worry. She said Austyn really helped her too."

I nod. "They're close."

"So, yeah, I think tonight. I talked to her parents already, so I just need to jump."

"Anything I can do to help? Lure her out of the room so you can get ready? Anything?"

"Nah, I'm just going to throw it out there. Pour my heart out and pray she says yes." Even though he's laughing, I know him well enough to see he's nervous.

"You ever wonder what else is out there? I mean she's been your only one, right?" I already know the answer to this, but I also know that when he thinks about it, the answer will calm his nerves. No way is she going to say no.

He nods, understanding my question. "Yeah, and no. I've never wondered or thought about being with someone else. She's it for me." He takes a sip of his drink. "You?"

"We're not there yet," I confess.

"Really? I would have thought it was a done deal. You're tied up in knots. That much is obvious."

"Nope." I have the urge to tell him it's none of his business, but he's been friends with Austyn a long time, and other than Austyn, Combs is the closest thing I have to family. Besides, he's right. I am tied up in knots, or more like tied up in Austyn.

"She's good for you," he says, his eyes still trailing his girlfriend.

"She is."

"What are you two conspiring over there?" Savannah asks, laughing.

"Guy talk." Combs winks.

"Uh-huh." She blows him a kiss and turns her attention back to the dishes.

When the girls are finished cleaning up, they settle themselves on our laps, and we watch the euchre game unfold. Jeffers and Spiller come out on top, leaving Combs and me to play them. The girls pull up chairs and sit beside us, trying to learn how to play. That's how the rest of the day goes. We play cards, switching back and forth, and the girls ask questions, watching and learning when we play, and sitting with us when we're not.

"Well, ladies, it was a pleasure. Thank you for dinner," Spiller says, standing.

"You guys heading out?"

"Yeah." All four of them stand at the same time, and while it's been a great day and they've been good company, I admit I'll be pleased to have my girl back to myself. "We'll get out of your hair."

"Thank you for coming," Savannah and Austyn say at the same time.

Combs and Savannah call it a night as well, which is more than fine with me. It leaves me with more Austyn time. It's precious and rare, and I want to soak up as much of it as I can get.

"I'm tired." She yawns from her place on my lap.

"Want to take a nap?" I ask, rubbing my hand softly up and down her back.

"It's after five. We'll never sleep tonight if we nap now."

"And? We've got nothing to do and nowhere to be."

"You tired?" she asks, covering yet another yawn.

"Yeah, angel, up you go," I say, tapping her thigh. She stands, and I follow her to the bedroom.

"I'm going to check the door," I say to her back, as I turn and head back to the living area to double check that the door is locked. I add the Do Not Disturb tag to the outside of the door for good measure. There's nothing that we need that we don't already have. Turing off all the lights, I make my way back to the bedroom. I'm greeted with a naked Austyn climbing under the covers. "Comfy?" I ask her. My voice is calm despite the way my body reacts to seeing her like this. My cock takes notice. My palms are sweating and my breath hitches in my chest.

She shrugs. "It's my new favorite thing, to lie with you… skin to skin," she adds.

Damn. I make quick work of discarding my clothes and climb in beside her. "Come here." I hold open my arm and she takes her spot snuggled up against me, her head resting on my chest.

"Thank you for today, for cooking for everyone."

"It was Savannah's idea."

"Regardless, you did just as much, and I appreciate it." I pause, gathering my thoughts. "It was my first Thanksgiving without Gran. It's tied for my best. That first year I went to live with her, that year was like a feast. My parents never celebrated any of the holidays, so the only real exposure I had was from school, on the days they actually got me there." I hate talking about my past, but for some reason with Austyn, it comes naturally. I want her to know all of me.

"What about Christmas?"

"Nah, they spent every dime we had on their next fix."

"That's awful," she says, kissing my bare chest.

"Gran made up for it. Even though it was just the two of us, she showed me what it was about. Not just the gifts but caring enough about someone and wanting to spend time with them, and yes finding and giving the perfect gift."

"I wish I could have met her."

I smile at the thought. "She would have loved you. I'm sure of it." I brush my fingers across her naked back as I continue. "When I enlisted, they asked about being away from family for long periods of time, missing holidays, birthdays, things like that. It wasn't an issue for me, you know. I mean I had me, myself, and I. Then I met you and the thought of missing those things with you tears me up inside."

"You're always with me, knight, remember?"

"I am, I know, but physically... to be able to watch you open your present in person, to be able to kiss you at midnight on New Year's Eve... they're all things I'll miss with you."

"Well, I don't need presents and video chat takes care of that. As far as kisses, we'll just have to stock up now so we have what we need to pull us through."

I tighten my grip on her, wanting her to be tethered to me

with no space between us. Eventually, her breathing evens out, and I allow myself to fall asleep as well.

I wake up what feels like hours later. It's dark outside, and my girl is still sleeping soundly next to me. Our positions have changed, but she's still in my arms. Her back is pressed to my front, my hand resting on her belly, holding her close. Her body is warm nestled up next to mine. Unable to resist, I place a kiss on her bare shoulder. She rolls over onto her belly and I freeze, hoping I didn't wake her.

My fingers trace their way up and down her back. Her skin is smooth, and I can't get enough of her. I crave the feel of her soft skin against my lips. Leaning down, I place a tender kiss at the base of her neck and then instead of pulling back, I continue on, my lips trailing her spine. When I reach the globes of her ass, I know I should stop, but I can't, nor do I want to. I kiss each cheek. My hands roam over her, and my cock hardens with every touch.

I'm startled when she rolls over onto her back, and her hand rests on the base of my neck. She's awake. She's awake and isn't stopping me. My hand glides up and down her silky-smooth legs until I reach her thighs. I kiss her tenderly just inside her knee. Moving forward, I kiss up her thighs. When I reach her core, I move to settle between her legs. She opens for me, neither one of us saying a word.

Needing my hands and mouth all over her, I continue my exploration of her body. Slowly, carefully, I capture a nipple between my lips. Nipping and sucking, I soothe the aches with my tongue.

"Slade." My name is a whisper on her lips.

I release my friend and move on to its twin, needing to pay them both equal attention. This time when I nip the hardened bud, her hips rise, causing my cock to graze over her center. She's wet, and I thought nothing could make me harder than I was, from my need for her. I was wrong. My cock twitches between us. I feel like I could lose control any second.

"I'm ready," she murmurs. "For you," she adds, as if I didn't understand what she meant.

I understand. All too well, I understand. I also understand that I'm unprepared. I didn't expect this, not tonight, hell, not this weekend. I curse inwardly as I close my eyes and rest my forehead against hers.

"You don't want to?" Her voice is small.

I lift my head and cup her cheek with one hand, still holding my weight on one elbow, careful not to crush her. "I want." I swallow hard. "I want you more than anything, but I'm not... I don't have a condom. I didn't expect this."

"I'm on the pill, but I think it's best if we still take all precautions." I nod. Defeated. "In the bathroom, my pink bag on the sink. There's a box."

"Angel?"

"I just thought you know, that just in case we should be prepared, or I should. I didn't know what would happen, but I didn't want to be in this exact situation and not be."

I drop a kiss on her lips and climb out of bed. In the bathroom. The realization hits me that she really wants this with me. You can't change your first time, that gift that you give someone. She's giving it to me. I'm overwhelmed with emotion—fear, happiness, and most of all, love. I see the pink bag she's referring to. My hands shake as I slide open the zipper, I see a box of unopened condoms staring back at me. Opening the box, I grab one, then decide to bring the entire box. I don't know if or when we'll need them, but having them close by so I don't have to leave her is my aim.

Turning off the light, I make my way back to the bed. Placing the now opened box on the nightstand, my hands are shaking so bad. I'm not sure how I manage to tear open the one in my hand, and roll it down my length. "You sure about this?" I ask, my voice gruff as I take my place nestled between her thighs. There is a part of me that wants to rush this, to feel her wrapped around me. To finally feel what I've imagined so many times since the night we met. The other part is worried that I'm going to hurt her, hell, that I'm going to come as soon as I feel her warmth and ruin this moment for both of us. We're only ever going to have one first time, not just with each other, but in general. I want this to be memorable for both of us.

She tosses the cover over us. "Positive." There's not an ounce of hesitation in her answer, although I can feel a slight tremble in her hands as they grip my arms. Somehow, that manages to calm me a little—knowing she's just as affected by this moment as I am.

"I've never… I mean, I don't know—" I blow out a breath. Trying to find the words and not sound like a loser is difficult. "I'm not going to last," I blurt out. "I'm already hard as steel and ready to lose my shit, so I need to get you there first," I explain, my voice shaking. I'm grateful it's dark in the room, so she can't see my blush.

"It's our first time, right?"

"Yes, nothing's changed since we last talked about this. It's only you."

"It's not supposed to be earth-shattering," she says, her voice cracking. "It gets better. At least that's what Savannah says." Her hands grip tightly to my arms, bracing for what's about to happen. "It's us," she whispers into the darkness. "No matter how it turns out, it's us."

"I just thought I should warn you. I don't want you to be disappointed." Fuck, disappointing her is something I never want to do.

Her hands cup my cheeks and she pulls me into a kiss. "That's not possible, Slade Reeves." She releases me, and once again wraps her hands around my arms, digging her nails into my flesh. I welcome the feeling, knowing it's her that's marking me. That it's her beneath me.

I don't give her time to say anything else as my lips merge with hers. My tongue lazily rolls with hers as we get lost in the kiss. Moving my hand between us, I rub her clit. She gasps against my lips, and I move away, burying my face in her neck. I inhale her warm vanilla scent and push a finger inside her.

"Slade," she pants.

Her plea spurs me on. I increase my thrusts and just like that, she's digging her nails into my arms. Her pussy squeezes my fingers, and she moans deep in her throat. Hearing her need, I fight like hell not to come at the combination. I don't stop until her grip on my arm releases, and she relaxes into the mattress.

Resting my hands on either side of her head, I poise myself over her, my cock at her entrance. My arms are shaking, and I wish I could say it was from the effort of holding my weight off her.

It's not.

This moment, it's bigger than losing our virginity. It's bigger than sex; it feels like a turning point in my life. Like all the shit I had to go through to get here, brought me to this one moment. The moment where my future is defined. The moment where I hand my heart and soul to this blue-eyed angel lying beneath me. I feel it in every fiber of my being, with every steady thump of my heart against my chest, every touch of her skin. In this moment, she has all of me.

"Slade." She cups my cheek with her hand.

Turning, I place a tender kiss on her palm. "Do you know what you mean to me?"

"Tell me," she whispers.

"I don't want to scare you away."

"I'm right here." As if she needs to prove her point, she wraps her legs around me, crossing them at the ankles, holding me near.

"I don't have the words, Austyn. I can't describe all of these feelings swirling inside of me."

"Try," she pleads.

I swallow back the emotion in my throat, afraid to say the words, worried I'll lose her with my admission. Worried I'll lose her without it.

"It's you and me knight," she whispers into the darkness.

A smile tips my lips when she calls me knight. I want to live up to that, for her. I want to be her knight. I want to be her everything. "I've never felt this way, not ever." I know she wants more than that, but I can't force the words past my lips.

"Me too," she assures me.

Unable to wait any longer, I align my cock at her entrance. "I'm sorry if this hurts you."

"Just go slow."

I nod, knowing she can feel the movement from her hand that's still resting against my cheek. Slowly, I push inside, inch by painful inch. Halfway in, she winces. "I'm sorry." I lean down and kiss the corner of her mouth. Her hands slip under my arms and her nails dig into my shoulder blades.

"It's fine. I'm good. More," she instructs. "All the way."

Closing my eyes, I battle the need to thrust into her, and the need to go slow, to be tender. "You feel," I grit my teeth as I move a little further inside of her, "incredible."

"More, Slade."

"I'm sorry," I say, then push the rest of the way inside. She winces again, her nails digging deeper into my shoulders, but she remains silent.

"Angel, talk to me. I'm so sorry." I lift to pull out, but she stops me.

"No. Don't move."

Burying my face in her neck, I breathe her in. My cock twitches inside of her, wanting me to get with the program, but I need to give her time.

"Did you do that?" she asks.

"Did I do what?"

"Make it… move."

I can't hold back my laugh. "No, baby, that's out of my control. You did that. You're tight and warm, and… yeah, that was all you."

"I think that I need you to move."

Thank God. "Tell me if I need to stop." Slowly, I withdraw and then enter her, one long stroke after another. "You good, Aust? I need you to talk to me, Angel."

"So good," she murmurs. Tilting her hips brings me in deeper. "Yes," she pants.

Fisting the sheets in my hands, I keep the rhythm of long, even strokes. I bite down on my bottom lip, hoping the slight pain will help hold off my orgasm. "Austyn, I don't know—" Her nails dig into my back, and her lips touch my neck. "—how long I can hold off," I grit out. "I'm so close."

"Let go." Her soft voice washes over me.

Two more long quick strokes and fireworks release behind my eyes. My body is wracked with pleasure as my orgasm rolls through me. Pulse after pulse, my cock releases inside of her. *How will I survive without this?*

chapter 30
Austyn

WHEN SLADE TRIES TO MOVE, I tighten my grip on him. I'm not ready to let this feeling go. The feeling of being full, of feeling that he's a part of me. I can't imagine that all first times are like this one. After the initial pinch of pain, there was nothing but pleasure. It was more than sex. It was… spiritual. While it sounds crazy even as I think it, it's the truth.

"You okay?" he asks, placing a kiss at the corner of my mouth.

I chuckle. "I'm more than okay." Content, I release a happy sigh. "You? You're trembling." I felt it earlier. I thought it was more nerves than anything. Oddly enough, his reaction calmed me. It was reassuring to know he is just as nervous and affected by what's happening between us as I was.

"That—" He sucks in a deep breath. "—rocked me to my core."

I'm glad it's dark so he can't see the cheesy grin I'm sporting. "I'd say we're pretty good at that."

"Not yet, but we will be."

"Not yet? Did you black out on me?"

Soft laughter echoes in the darkness. "I was there, and I felt it all, but you didn't come, so yeah, next time. I'll do better I promise."

"I did."

"You didn't while I was inside of you. That's not how this works."

"I guess we're just going to have to practice until we get it right."

"There's not a whole lot to do here on base," he says. I can hear the humor in his voice. "I need to take care of this," he says, slowly pulling out. I miss him immediately—the feel of his weight on top of me, the feeling of being full while he's inside me. He stands from the bed. "Up you go, Angel" he says, reaching for me in the darkness. His hands roam over my naked breasts before he rolls my nipple between his thumb and forefinger. I'm ready to tell him to grab another condom when he releases me, and reaches for my hand, giving it a gentle tug. "Let's shower."

I let him guide us into the bathroom. He surprises me when he fumbles in the dark to turn on the water without turning the light on. "You want the light?" I ask, already turning to feel for the switch.

"We don't need it. Come here," he says.

I step closer to him, cautiously. When I'm close, he wraps his arms around me and kisses my neck. "My hands will find you, even in the dark." With that, he steps into the shower, and I follow after him. Luckily for us, the suite has a huge walk-in shower so we have no door or shower curtain to deal with.

Slade moves me to stand under the warm spray. I hear him open the bodywash, and then I feel him. Warm, soapy hands roam every inch of my skin. "You need me to wash your hair?"

"No. My turn," I say, turning to put him under the spray of the water. I fumble with the bodywash but eventually get a glob in my hands and rub them together. I take my time exploring the rugged muscles of his chest, working my way down to his cock. I stroke him once, then twice. He groans as my hand glides easily with the bodywash and water as lubricant.

"As bad as it pains me to say this, we need to give you some time."

"I'm fine," I assure him.

"I know you are, and I want it to stay that way." He rinses quickly and turns off the water. As if he can see in the dark, he presents a towel, wrapping it around me. I can hear his footsteps as he leaves the room. Before I can reach the bathroom light, a soft glow from the bedroom filters in through the open door. "Thought you might need to see," Slade says, stepping back into the bathroom and hanging his wet towel on the rack. In all his naked glory, he then walks back to the bed and climbs in.

I guess that's that. I try to not to feel rejected. I know that's not what's happening here, but my mind won't shut off. Did he not enjoy it? I tramp down the worry refusing to let the insecurities of my inexperience get the best of me. It's his first time, too. Neither one of us knew what to expect. Quickly, I dry off and brush out my hair. From the soft glow of the light filtering in the room, I take a look at my reflection. I don't look any different, but I feel different. I feel like my heart no longer beats in my chest for the sole purpose of keeping me alive. It also now beats for him. I don't bother taking the time to dry it; instead, I hang my towel on the rack beside Slade's and head back to bed. As soon as he sees me, he holds up the covers as a silent invitation to join him. Turning off the light, I slide under the covers and snuggle up next to him. His arms wrap around me, and his lips press against the top of my head.

"You okay?"

"Perfect." I am. I couldn't imagine tonight being any better. My first time, our first time being any better.

"Yes, you are," he murmurs.

We lay there in silence. I'm tired, yet I'm too amped up to sleep. I feel different. It sounds crazy, because I'm still me, but I almost feel as though he's a part of me. Maybe it's because it was my first time. I don't really think that's it, though. Sure, that may be part of it, but it's more than that. It's Slade. It's the way he makes me feel cherished.

"That felt like it was more than just sex." I send the words out into the darkness.

"That's because it was." We're both quiet, letting the meaning of our confession sink in.

Slade rolls over on his side and pulls me into his chest. His calloused hand traces the length of my arm, over my shoulder and up my neck before he cups my cheek. "Some might say it's too soon," he whispers. His hot breath mingles with mine.

"What's too soon?"

"Some might think it's too soon for me to tell you that I love you." My breath hitches and I think my heart just skipped a beat. He runs his thumb gently across my cheek. "Because I do, you know. I love you, Austyn. If I'm honest, that's really not a strong enough word for what you bring to my life, for what you've given me."

He loves me.

"I don't expect you to say it back, but I needed you to know where I'm at. I know we agreed to see how things go with the distance between us, but I know how they're going on my end. You are my end and my beginning, and I want all the things in the middle, only with you."

Placing my hand on his cheek, mimicking him, I say the words without reservation. "I love you too."

He exhales and then his lips are on mine. With a twist of tongues, our hands roam over every inch of our exposed skin. We kiss for hours until we're both too exhausted to go on. It's then we fall asleep tangled in each other's arms, with the security of our love wrapped around us.

When the North Carolina sun shines through the window, I groan, not ready to wake up. I hear a deep chuckle, and his body shakes beside me. "Hush," I say, burying my face in the pillow.

"You can't sleep all day. We've only got two more left after this one. And today's a big day for you."

That gets me up and moving. Removing the pillow from over my eyes, I blink them open and focus on Slade. "What time is it?"

"Just after nine,"

"What time did you get up?"

"Six."

"You've been lying here since six?"

"Yep."

"You didn't have to wait for me."

"Like I'm going to leave you naked in this bed without me. Not happening, angel. I'm going to be glued to your side until Monday morning when I have to report for training. Not to mention today is my girl's birthday. I have to give you your present."

"I'm good with this plan, well, except the present. Being here with you is gift enough. Speaking of plans, what's ours for today? This?" I motion around the room, hoping a day in bed is what's on the agenda.

"I have no idea. Have you talked to Savannah and Brandon?"

"Yeah, Brandon says they're staying in bed all day."

"I should have guessed that." I laugh. "What about you? What are you thinking for today?"

"I'm liking the idea of staying in bed all day. How are you feeling?" he asks, pushing my hair back away from my face, out of my eyes.

"Sore, but a good sore, if that's even possible."

"We should wait—" he starts, but I hold my hand up to stop him.

"I'm fine, Slade. I would tell you if I wasn't. We don't have time to wait. I'm going home soon and don't know when I'll see you again. Besides, today's my birthday and you can't say no to me on my birthday."

"I struggle with that every day of the week." He kisses my nose. "I have a small break after training is through before I'm stationed."

"What's a small break? What about Christmas?" I assume he gets time off but I'm sure it's limited.

"Five days, maybe less before we report to our permanent stations. We get a few days like we did this time. I think three around Christmas and three over New Year, but they're spread out. We have to stay close to base."

"At least you get a break. I don't know what my parents have planned, but maybe I can see you again at one of those breaks?" I ask, hopeful. "Any idea of where you're going to be stationed?"

"I hope here, but I won't know until closer to the time."

"Would that be a permanent thing?"

"Yeah, until deployment."

"Are you pretty sure you'll get deployed?"

"Yeah, not sure where or when, but that's pretty much a given. That's my job."

"You don't know when, though, right? They just give you your orders and you have to go?" I hate the thought of him shipping off to another country, the thought of him being surrounded by danger. It scares the hell out of me.

"Yeah, we might get a few days' notice, maybe a week. We might know sooner that we're going to have to deploy, but we won't know where or the exact date until right before the time."

"But you'll be able to let me know, right? You'll have time to tell me you're leaving?" My hope is that I'll have time to come to him. To wrap my arms around him, to kiss him. I want to do all those things and more to remind him what he has waiting for him here at home.

His face softens and he strokes my cheek. "I will. Most places there's Internet access so we can communicate that way. Letters take forever. At least, that's what I'm told."

"I'll do both." My chest is tight thinking about him going away, to battle or war, or whatever in the hell you want to call it.

"I don't expect that. It would be good to hear from you though."

"Look at us, talking like you're leaving next week. We still have lots of time before that happens."

"We do, but you're my life." Every time he says things like this, I melt a little more. "Other than the Marines, it's you. It's good that we talk about it. I want you to know what's going on. Even if you're not here with me, I want you to feel like you are."

I take a deep breath. He's right. I'm pleased we're open and honest about everything too. "So today? We're lounging?"

"Yes." Leaning in, he kisses me. "Time for some breakfast. You want to go out or order in?"

"We're staying in, remember?" I laugh.

"Just making sure." He pokes me in the side, causing me to laugh harder.

"We are not leaving this room. Okay, maybe we might take a dip in the pool. But we are not leaving this hotel today."

"Deal." Another chaste kiss, then he's climbing out of bed and pulling on some basketball shorts.

After I brush out my hair, and brush my teeth, I pull his T-shirt on over my head and meet him out in the small living room. "Hey, I ordered a little bit of everything from room service. Should be here soon."

"Thanks." I sit next to him on the couch, pulling my legs under me and resting my head against his shoulder. He turns his head and kisses me on top of mine.

"You still tired?" he asks.

"Not too bad. It was more that I was comfortable and warm than being tired."

"Go back to bed. I'll bring breakfast to you."

"I'm up now." I laugh just as there's a knock at the door.

Slade stands and hands me a pillow. "Hold this in your lap." He must see the question in my eyes. He bends down, bracing both of his hands on the back of the couch, caging me in. "You're practically naked. No way am I going to let whoever the fuck that is see you."

"I have a T-shirt on," I defend.

"Like I said, practically naked." He kisses me quickly and goes to answer the door.

I try to hide my smile at his protectiveness, but it's impossible. I've seen Brandon be this way with Savvy. Hell, I've seen my dad with my mom, but I've never been on the receiving end. Not like this. Not when I know it comes from deep inside and his need to protect me from prying eyes. I've had guys get jealous over stupid stuff, and they weren't even my boyfriend. I kicked them to the curb, fast, not wanting to deal with their drama.

This is different.

We scarf down our breakfast, sampling a little bit of everything. We've worked up an appetite.

"You ready for your present?" he asks pushing the cart to the corner of the room.

"It's not necessary," I tell him. This time with him is more than I ever could have asked for.

"I beg to differ," he says, placing the lid on out uneaten pieces of cake he ordered with breakfast. "Close your eyes. I'll be right back."

Doing as he asks, I close my eyes and listen as his feet carry him away and then back to me. I feel the couch dip beside me. "Open," he says excitedly.

Opening my eyes, I see a small black box with a white ribbon wrapped around it. "Happy birthday, angel."

I can't hide my smile as I take the offered box. "You didn't need to do this," I repeat.

"You might as well get used to it, Austyn." His voice is serious. "No matter where I am, you'll always get birthday presents from me.

Nodding, I pull at each end of the bow, watching as it releases in my lap. Slowly, I lift the lid and suck in a breath. Nestled inside is a white-gold diamond-heart pendent. "Slade," I breathe, running my fingers over the delicate lines of the heart. "It's beautiful."

"Not as beautiful as its owner." Leaning in, his lips connect with mine. "Turn around and I'll put it on you." Handing him the box, I turn, offering him my back. He moves my hair to one side and when I feel his lips against the base of my neck, I know the necklace is secure.

"Thank you," I say, looking down at the heart nestled against my own.

Reaching out, he traces his finger along the chain until he reaches the heart. Lifting it to his lips, he kisses it. "No matter where I am in the world, no matter how much distance is between us, my heart will always be with you. This is a symbol of that."

There's no fighting the tears that well up in my eyes. "I love you."

"Angel," he says, leaning in and pressing his lips to mine. "I love you, too."

The rest of our day is spent lounging in our room. We watch movies, laugh, talk, kiss, and order more room service. If I were to be asked to describe my perfect day, this would be it. After dinner, we decide to head to bed early where Slade makes love to me, taking his time kissing every inch of my skin. This time it's not as quick, and we both know what to expect. We're quickly learning each other's bodies. He knows that when he kisses me, just under my ear, it drives me crazy. I know that when I rake my nails across his skin, it causes him to shiver and thrust his hips a little faster. Together, we know that it's not how, but who you are with. The rest just falls into place. That's how it is between us. Since the day we met, our attraction, and now the love we have for one another, settles us. We're where we are meant to be.

chapter 31
Slade

I 'M LYING HERE, NOT REALLY awake, but awake enough to know that the feel of her hands on my cock is not a dream. Keeping my eyes closed, I focus on breathing evenly. I want to see what her plans are. Last night was, in a word… incredible. Not that our first time together wasn't, but I was more confident knowing what to expect, what it would feel like when I slid inside of her. I knew what it felt like to have her warmth wrapped around me. Yesterday, I took my time exploring her body. There's not a piece of her that my hands, my tongue, my cock didn't give full attention to.

Now, in the early morning light, my cock is hard as steel, and her small hands are stroking me. Slow, featherlight strokes have my balls tightening. I keep my eyes closed, although I want to see her with my cock in her hands. I'm sure it's an image that I'll never forget, but I hold strong, focusing on deep, even breaths.

When her mouth wraps around me, my eyes pop open, and I groan. Austyn is on her belly lying between my legs with her hand wrapped around my cock while she takes me in her hot mouth. This isn't the first time this has happened, but now we're more familiar with each other, I'm not nervous like I was then. This time, I can sit back and watch the show. Reaching out, I tuck her hair that's blocking my view behind her ear. She stops, releasing my cock with a pop, and stares up at me. I cup her cheek. "Morning, angel."

She grins, then goes right back to what she was doing. Fisting the sheets in my hands, I fight the urge to place my hand on her head and guide her. This is her show, and a damn good one at that. Taking me deeper with each bob of her head, she pushes me closer to the edge. Over and over and over she takes me into her mouth, using her tongue to drive me wild.

"Austyn, I'm close," I warn. She doesn't stop. Instead, she takes me all the way to the base, making a gagging sound. "Now," I say, and she pulls her mouth away and strokes me as my orgasm rolls through me. When the waves that rock me to my core stop, she hops off the bed and disappears into the bathroom. She's back a few seconds later with a warm washcloth to clean me up. She then tosses into on the floor and climbs into bed, snuggling up to me.

"Sorry."

"Sorry?" I huff out a laugh. "What could you possibly be sorry for? Blowing my mind?"

"I didn't swallow."

"And?"

"That's the best of the best, right? But I couldn't do it. I'm not… crazy about the taste."

This girl… doesn't she realize what she does to me? "Come here." I pull her onto my chest and my flaccid cock twitches from the feel of her naked body nestled against mine. "It was amazing, just like you are. I didn't expect to wake up with my cock in your mouth, but it was welcome all the same. Anytime you want my cock in your mouth, say the word," I tickle her sides making her laugh. "And, I have no expectations. You don't like it, don't do it, simple as that." I kiss the tip of her nose. "What do you want to do today?"

"I don't know. I guess I should call Savannah and Brandon, see what their plans are."

"Where's your phone?"

"I think I left it on the table last night."

"Stay put. I'll go get it." I kiss her because I want to, and because I can. She rolls to the side, and I climb out of bed. Her phone is on the side table by the couch, and it's vibrating and lighting up like crazy. "Babe," I call out to her as I walk back to the bedroom. "Your phone sounds like it's blowing up."

"What?" She sits up and the blanket pools at her waist, exposing her bare breasts. I hand her the phone and climb back in beside her, taking a nipple into my mouth.

"H-hey," she says, to who I assume is Savannah since that's who was blowing up her phone. "We just woke up."

Gently, I push on her shoulder, getting her to lie back on the bed and take her nipple back in my mouth. Sliding my hand under the cover, I find her wet for me. It's hot as hell that having my cock in her mouth does that to her.

"Really?" she squeals, and I'm not sure if it's from excitement or from my touch, but it doesn't sound like anything's wrong, so I keep going, running my fingers through her folds while my mouth devours her tits.

"Yeah, okay. Umm, give us an hour or so?" She says it like a question. "No, okay. Yeah. Right. Bye." She drops her phone to the bed and rests her hand on the back of my head. "You're bad," she pants.

I release her. "Me?" I ask innocently, looking up at her. My fingers slide lower as I push inside. "Everything okay?" I smirk.

"Better than okay," she murmurs.

"I meant the call, baby. That was Savannah, right?" I ask, continuing to pump my fingers in and out of her.

"I-I can't think right now."

"You ready to come?"

"Is that a trick question?"

I chuckle and press my lips to hers. I take my time tracing her lips with my tongue, then mimic my fingers, teasing her. Her hands wrap around my neck, and she holds me to her, demanding control. "Right... there," she speaks against my lips.

I cannot only see it, the way her body stiffens, the way her eyes close, the way her chest rises with her ragged breath, but I can feel it. Her walls tighten around my fingers. I know the exact moment she lets go and is consumed with pleasure.

Pleasure I give her.

"Welcome back." I grin when she opens her eyes.

"You're really good at that."

"Only for you." I kiss the corner of her mouth. "Now, why was your best friend blowing up your phone?"

"Oh!" Her eyes light up with excitement. "They're engaged."

"He finally did it." I smile a genuine smile.

"What do you mean? Did you know?"

"I did. He bought the ring when we were in Kentucky on leave."

"You didn't tell me?" She pouts.

I nip at her bottom lip. "Nope. He wanted me to keep it a secret, and you two are too close. You might have let it slip."

"I see how it is, bros before hos." She chuckles.

"No. You are first in my life, always. This was me keeping a surprise for a friend."

"I forgive you." She kisses me quickly. "They want to hang out today, grab a late breakfast, and maybe go bowling or something."

"I'm wherever you are."

"I told them we'd be ready in an hour, so I need to get moving." She hops out of bed and gathers her clothes. "Don't follow me or we'll never get out of here," she sasses over her shoulder.

I throw my head back and laugh. She's right. Now that I've had her, know what she feels like, I crave her. All of her. We'd most definitely be late. I gather some clothes and head to the other bathroom to shower and get ready. My girl is too tempting.

Thirty minutes later, we're meeting Savannah and Combs in

the restaurant of the hotel. As soon as Austyn sees them, the girls are rushing into a hug. "Let me see the ring," Austyn squeals.

When I reach Combs, I shake his hand. He's grinning like a fool, not that I can blame him. This is what he wanted, and he's getting it. He gets to keep the love of his life and call her his forever. I turn to look at the girls and see them laughing and smiling, and I can't help but hope this is where we'll end up. I want this exact scenario where it's my girl showing off the ring.

"All right you two, let's eat." Combs swoops Savannah away from Austyn and leads us to a table near the back of the restaurant.

The girls chatter on about weddings, and Combs and I are pussy whipped enough to enjoy, and sit back, listening to them. I see him every day. I want to soak up as much of her as I can. I'm sure he feels the same about Savannah. If sitting in this restaurant listening to them talk all-things wedding makes her happy, then I'm good with that. She's next to me, my hand resting on her thigh. All is right in my world.

chapter 32
Austyn

"SLADE KNEW AND DIDN'T TELL me," I tell Savannah. We're sitting at the bowling alley on base. We're on our second game, and so far, the guys are kicking our asses.

"Did he? I guess he was afraid you would tell me." She laughs.

"Gah! That's what he said. I can keep a secret."

"You can. I know that. However, you can't hide that you have one. I would have known something was up and with where my head was, it's probably a good thing you didn't know."

"You guys good?"

"Yeah, we are." Happiness radiates from her, and I honestly don't remember her looking quite this happy before. "We talked before he even popped the question. I think we both had fears. He was afraid of taking me from school and my family. He wasn't sure if I still wanted everything we talked about. I told him my fear of always being alone. He reminded me that I can go home on holidays when he's gone to be with my parents and his. And they can come to me."

"I'm so happy for you." I squeeze her hand. "You have any idea when you want to get married?"

"Now," Brandon chimes in, taking the seat next to her, and making me laugh.

"Your turn, angel," Slade says, taking the one next to me.

"I suck at this game."

"Nah, you just need some practice." He smacks me on the ass as I stand to take my turn. "Show me what you got."

"Oh, I think you already know what I got," I say in the cheesiest flirty voice I can muster.

He's out of his chair and stalking toward me. He grabs my hips and pulls me back into his chest. His lips land on my neck and he kisses up to my ear. "I know what you've got because you're mine." He nips at my lobe. "Let me help you." He positions my hips and helps me square my shoulders when I'm holding the ball. "Now, walk up slowly and release. Not too much force."

I do as he says and release the ball. It's going so slow down the lane it's as if we're watching it in slow motion. I hold my breath, waiting to see if I'm going to get another gutter ball. When the ball connects with the pins, it knocks down seven. "Seven!" I cheer. Turning, I see him still standing there wearing a sexy grin. "I think I need a kiss for luck for this next one," I tell him.

"You don't need a reason for me to kiss you." He snakes an arm around my waist and presses his lips to mine.

"Get a room!" Brandon yells out, laughing.

"We've got one," Slade fires back. He kisses me again, this time just a short peck to my lips. "Good luck, babe."

Trying to focus, I toss the ball down the lane, and this time it goes straight to the gutter, just like my mind when it comes to Slade. We finish up the game, and all agree we're over bowling.

"Now what?" Savannah asks.

"Movie?" Brandon suggests.

"There's a theater here or one over by the mall." Savannah looks over at me, and I shrug. "Let's just stay here, on base."

The guys choose an action movie, which is fine with me. I

don't really care what we're doing as long as I'm with Slade. I hate that time is moving so fast. I hate that I'm going to have to go back to sleeping without him. I hate it, but I have to learn to deal with it. After the movie, we eat dinner at a pizza place on base. The food is good, and the restaurant is packed with marines. Several of them come over and talk to the guys. Brandon introduces Savannah as his fiancé, and they both beam with happiness. I can't help but smile with them. I've been there since day one with them and never had a doubt this is where they would end up.

"You ready to head back?" Slade asks.

"Yeah, this is my last night with you."

"I know, angel." His voice dips, and I know he's dreading it as much as I am. "Let's go." He stands from the booth and holds his hand out for me. "We're heading back," he says, tossing some money on the table for a tip and grabbing our bill.

"Yeah, us too." Brandon stands from the booth as well.

We pay our bills and take the short five-minute walk back to the hotel. "I don't know why I'm tired. It's not like we did anything strenuous today," I say, kicking off my shoes.

"Bowling wore you out." He chuckles.

"Oh hush, just wait. I'm going to brush up on my skills, and when we're together the next time, I'm going to stomp your ass."

"Promises, promises," he says, pulling me into his arms. "I'm ready to hold you. This will be my last time for a while."

"I like this plan." Standing on tiptoes, I kiss the corner of his mouth and head to the bedroom to get ready for bed. I'm already under the covers when he enters the room. The lamp is on, and I have the covers tucked up to my chin. Mostly from the chill in the air without his body next to mine but also because I'm naked.

"You need anything?" he asks, standing at the edge of the bed.

"Nope. Just the light," I say.

The room is bathed in darkness. The bed then dips and he climbs in. "Come here, Austyn."

I waste no time sliding up next to him and resting my head on his chest. His strong arms wrap around me and hold me close. "I'm going to miss this."

"Me too, but hey, it will give us something to look forward to, right?"

"Right." He's quiet for a few minutes. "I know this isn't fair to you, being in a relationship with a guy who's gone more than he's there, but I promise you every chance I have to be with you, I'll be there."

"I know that. I also knew you were a marine when we met. I knew that when I fell in love with you. I'm all in, Slade. I don't want you worrying about me, about us. You need to stay focused."

"You're my family, Austyn. Other than the Marines, you're all I have. How do you expect me not to worry about you?"

"I expect you to know that I'm committed to you and what we have. I expect you to know that I'll be going through the motions each day, and not a single second of those days will be without you on my mind. I expect you to trust what we have and focus your energy on being the best that you can be. To stay safe."

"I'm not in danger here," he tells me.

"Maybe not, but you're learning the skills that could save you when you are in danger. I need you to stay focused on that."

"I thank God every day for bringing you into my life."

"I know, right? You should probably thank him at least twice a day." I say to lighten the mood.

It works. His deep chuckle shakes his chest, causing my head to bounce up and down. When his laughter calms, he kisses the top of my head. "I love you." My heart swells every time he tells me. I'll never be tired of hearing those words cross his lips.

"Love you, too." The quiet of the night surrounds our confession of love as we drift off to sleep in each other's arms.

chapter 33

Slade

I WAKE UP PISSED OFF. I had to leave Austyn at the hotel alone last night to come back to the barracks. It's five in the damn morning, and I'm running on maybe two hours of sleep, if that. We have to report for our morning run at five thirty, and all I want to do is run back to the hotel and slide under the covers with my girl. I hate that they have to go to the airport on their own. Fuck, I hate she has to leave at all. This past week with her, even on the days where we just got to meet up for dinner, has proven to me how far gone I am for her. How much I love her.

She told me to text her when I got up to make sure they're up. Their flight leaves at ten thirty, so they want to make sure they get there on time, even though I doubt there will be a crowd at the airport on a Monday morning. Grabbing my phone from the nightstand, I text her.

Me:	Morning, angel. I missed you last night.
Austyn:	I slept like shit.
Me:	Me too. I miss you already.
Austyn:	Distance makes the heart grow fonder. At least, that's what they say.
Me:	I'm not sure anything can make my heart grow any fonder than it already is.

Austyn:	Look at you being all sweet at before the sun comes up.

My girl's sassy this morning. Just one of the many things I love about her.

Me:	Is there any other way to be when I talk to the love of my life?
Austyn:	Laying it on thick! I have to get moving. Have a good day. I'll text you when we get to the airport and when we land.
Me:	I might not be able to respond right away, but I will. Be safe, Austyn.
Austyn:	My knight

I smile, remembering our exchange the first time I had to leave her. I'm sure she doesn't expect me to remember.

Me:	I'm always with you.
Austyn:	Take care of you
Me:	See you soon, angel
Me:	I love you.
Austyn:	I love you, too. See you soon.

Okay, so I changed it up a little, but since the night I told her I loved her, I can't seem to stop. I don't ever want her to go a day without feeling it, hearing it, even though I'm states away from her. Needing to get moving, I climb out of bed, grab a hoodie, and lace up my running shoes. Jeffers and Spiller are up, but not out of bed, and Combs is sitting on the edge of his, with his elbows resting on his knees. I don't say anything. There's nothing I can say that will make it better. When he finally raises his head, he catches me watching him.

"Didn't know it would be this hard."

I nod. I don't need to say or do anything else. He knows I get where he's coming from. He knows my story and how I feel about Austyn. Just when we get used to being with them, seeing them every day, we have to get used to the distance yet again. I'm sure it's a little worse for him, having her for his entire life, with her being his for the last few years to now not being with her. It has to be tough. But this is all Austyn and I have ever known. I'm grateful and pissed at the same time. I want that time with her, but I think it's a little easier on both of us not having had it before. Kind of like we're not really sure what we're missing. We have a good idea from our time together, but saying "see you soon" is our reality.

I go through the motions of the day, and it's not until we break for lunch that I'm able to check my phone.

Austyn:	Made it to the airport.
Austyn:	Getting ready to board our flight
Austyn:	Just landed. My mom's here to pick us up.

The last one was sent just a few minutes ago.

Me:	Glad you made it home safe.
Austyn:	Now to unpack, ugh. Have a great day, knight.
Me:	I'll call you tonight.
Austyn:	I have to work, but I'll keep my phone on me. Savvy and I are both working tonight, so you and B should try to call at different times.
Me:	10–4
Austyn:	LOL

I shove my phone back in my pocket and see Combs do the same. "Savannah?" I ask.

"Yeah, they made it home."

"That's what Austyn said. They're both working tonight, so we'll need to stagger our calls so they can cover each other."

"I'll be glad when we're married and can be with her every day."

"Deployment." It's something I've been thinking about a lot lately. Leaving her, the potential that I might not ever come home to her.

"Yeah, but even then she'll be my wife. There's just something about knowing she's really mine for the rest of our lives. That she's waiting here for me at home."

"You think she wouldn't be otherwise?"

"She would be." He nods. "I just need it more permanent, if that makes sense. I don't want to leave knowing she's not going to have access to my benefits or anything if something happens to me. It's all going to go to my parents, which is fine. But I want it to be Savannah, you know?"

I nod. I don't know. I've never thought about it because it's always been just Gran and me, and when I lost her, I lost that feeling... that need to take care of someone. Until I met Austyn. Now my head is swimming. If something were to happen to me, there's no one. When I signed up, they ask you to list your next of kin. I left mine blank. How pathetic is that? I had no one to list. No one who would notice or even care if I didn't come home. My situation has changed. Just another way she's brought me back to life.

"You guys talk about when?"

"Soon. She's going to wrap up this year at college, and then maybe this summer? That's what we're aiming for. She's going to look into transferring schools."

My mind races with the possibilities. Would Austyn do that for me? Could she be here where I can see her every day? It would be a lot to ask of her if we're not married, and as bad as I hate to admit this even to myself, we're not there yet. I love her, I do, but marriage is a big step. One I don't want to rush into. I never imagined myself married, now that I do, it's with her, but I only want to do it once.

"What about you?"

"Yeah, too soon for that."

"She could still move down here, transfer schools."

"That's a lot to ask of her without something more permanent behind it."

He shrugs. "Maybe so, but with what we do, there's no time to delay these kinds of things. We have to make sure that the ones we love know we love them."

"She knows."

"Oh, does she?" He laughs. "Didn't think I'd ever get that out of you."

His words register, and I realize he was trying to get me to admit my feelings for her. In doing so, he opened up a flurry of emotions, questions, yearnings for the future we could one day have. "You could have just asked me, fucker." I shake my head, smiling.

"What's the fun in that? Besides, I already knew. You can tell by the way you two are with each other. I just wasn't sure if you knew yourself or had admitted it to yourself yet."

"I told her. She told me. We're good," I assure him.

"Living the dream, man. Living the dream."

The rest of the day drags by. Combs tells me to go ahead and call Austyn first while he calls his mom and wishes her happy birthday. He gets no argument from me. Luckily, Spiller and Jeffers are out, so I take advantage and call my girl. It rings four times before she picks up.

"Hello?" she pants into the phone.

"Hey."

"Hey, sorry it's a madhouse in here tonight."

"You need me to call back?"

"No, it's fine. How was your day?"

"Long. I slept like shit last night."

"Me too. After running around here all night, I'm sure I'll sleep tonight though."

I try not to let that get to me, that she seems fine sleeping without me while I'm over here wishing she was in my arms. I should be glad she's adjusting so well; that's important for both of us. I can't imagine how hard it will be to hear her breakdown when there's nothing I can do to make it better. I just miss her.

"Yeah, I'm hoping I can, too."

"Austyn," I hear a deep voice say. "When did you get back in town?"

"Today," she says. I can tell she's turning away from the phone.

"Sorry about that, like I said a madhouse. I think half of my graduating class is here tonight."

"Oh yeah?"

"They're all home for break, and this is the go-to place in town apparently. We're all still underage." She laughs.

"This is true."

"Austyn," I hear a male voice call out to her.

"Just a second," she tells him. "Sorry, Slade. I need to go. We're slammed."

"Yeah, okay. Be safe."

"Always. Love you," she says, and the line goes dead. I pull the phone from my ear and look at the screen just to be sure. She's never raced off the phone like that before. I know she was busy, but those guys calling her name…. I shake off the doubt. I know I can trust her; that's not it. It's more the fact that I can't be there with her. She's living life, as am I, but we're in two different worlds. I send up a silent prayer that we can make this work. That the distance won't come between us.

I set my alarm to be up early so I can send Austyn an e-mail. After last night, I feel unsettled. Grabbing my laptop, I log into my e-mail and to my surprise, there's one waiting for me from her.

To: HerKnight@directmail.com
From: HisAngel@directmail.com
Time: 23:59
Subject: Tonight

I'm sorry I had to cut our call short. It's been a while since we've had a crazy night like that. I think I only sat down maybe once the entire night. My feet are killing me. It's time for some new tennis shoes. I'm going to see if Savannah wants to go shopping this week.

I didn't get to hear much about your day. I hope it was a good one. I miss you like crazy.

Love,

Austyn

Just like that the worry, the feeling of being unsettled washes away. I hit Reply immediately.

To: HisAngel@directmail.com

From: HerKnightl@directmail.com

Time: 04:45

Subject: RE: Tonight

You don't know how good it is to hear from you. I was unsettled last night, not being able to talk to you. Call me crazy, but you're an important part of my life. I needed my Austyn fix.

Hopefully, you made some good tips since you were so busy. That would at least make the tired feet worth it. If I were there, I would rub them for you. Make a note, the next time we're together, I'll do just that, regardless of how your feet are feeling.

I miss you, too. I'm getting ready to go for our morning run. Do you work again tonight? I can never seem to keep up with your work schedule. I know you have classes today, but other than that, I feel like I'm out of the loop.

Talk soon.

Love,

Slade

I close out of my e-mail and head out for our morning run. I feel as though a weight has been lifted from my shoulders, just from hearing from her. To know that as soon as she got home she was thinking of me, that alone has me standing a little taller. It's crazy that she affects me this way. She's the only one who could.

As soon as I get in from my run, I rush to my laptop to see if she's replied. Not that I expect her to this early. I hit refresh twice, just to make sure. Nothing. Wishful thinking on my part. I know she's sleeping, especially after the crazy shift she had last night. I then rush to the shower so I'm not late.

chapter 34

I WAKE TO THE SOUNDS of Dawson's feet rushing down the stairs. Peeling open my eyes, I see that it's still dark outside. Grabbing my phone, I pull up my last message with Slade and type out a new one.

Me:	Merry Christmas.

His reply comes immediately.

Slade:	Merry Christmas, angel.
Me:	Daws is up and raring to go.
Slade:	LOL. You better get moving.
Me:	What makes you think I'm not already up and moving.
Slade:	I know my girl. Now go. Enjoy this time with your family.
Me:	I'm sorry I couldn't be there with you today.
Slade:	The guys and I are hanging out. It's all good. This is what we signed up for. Now go. Enjoy. I'll call you later.
Me:	Love you!
Slade:	Love you, too.

With my phone still clutched in my hand, I climb out of bed and head across the hall to the bathroom. I set it on the counter, take care of business, then brush my teeth. I then head downstairs.

"Morning, sweetheart," Dad greets me.

I stop by the recliner and kiss his cheek. "Morning," I say, doing the same to Mom and Dawson.

"You talked to him today?" Mom asks, nodding toward my phone in my hand.

They're used to it at this point. I never know when he is going to call or e-mail or text, so I pack it with me at all times. "Yeah, he and the guys are hanging out today."

"That has to be hard being away from their loved ones," Mom says.

"Except for Slade. I'm all he has."

"You knew that this was going to be hard going into this, Austyn," she reminds me.

"I know. That doesn't mean I can't be a little sad to know he's all alone. I mean, the other guys are probably getting packages and calls from their loved ones, and he just has me."

"He has us," Dawson chimes in. "We sent him a package. You put my pictures in there, right, Aust?" he asks me.

"Yes, and I'm sure he's going to love it. Unfortunately, it's not there yet. The postal service is really crazy this time of year. I tried to time it just right so he would have gotten it yesterday but no dice."

"I'm sure he understands. Now, presents." Dad redirects the conversation.

Dawson jumps from his spot on the floor right next to the tree and starts passing out packages. One by one we take turns, the four of us opening presents. It's something we've always done. Mom likes to be able to see everyone's reactions when we open our gifts. An hour later, we're sitting in a pile of wrapping paper and boxes. Dad and Dawson are on the floor playing with a new Lego set while Mom and I are sitting on the couch, just watching them.

"Honey, we forgot one. Can you grab that card off the tree?" Mom says to Dad. He smiles over at us, hops to his feet and grabs the card off the tree. "Austyn, we have one more present for you. But first, I need to record this." Mom picks up her phone from the end table. I watch as she hits a few buttons and then smiles. "Okay, Aust, open it."

Carefully, knowing that they're all watching me and Mom is recording, I slide my finger under the lip of the envelope and pull out the card. I read the handwritten note and then read it again, tears welling up in my eyes. I look over at my mom. "Is this real?" I ask her.

"It's real." She grins, shaking her head.

"Dad?" I ask, turning to look at him. Surely this must be a joke.

"It's real, Austyn. We fly out this afternoon."

"Flying?" Dawson asks.

"Where are we going?" He looks at me for answers since I'm holding the card in my hands.

"To see Slade," I tell him.

"Say that again?" I hear his deep voice rumble from Mom's phone.

"Was that?" I point to her phone, my mouth hanging open.

"It was." She grins and turns her phone to face me, tapping the screen to switch the camera. "Merry Christmas, Slade. Are you ready for all four of the Wilson crew to be knocking on your door?"

"You're coming here, really? All of you?" Shock laces his voice.

"We are. We hated the thought of you being alone on Christmas, and it's been a while since we've seen you."

"Where are you staying?"

"On base. Brandon helped us set it all up, well, he and Savannah."

"She didn't tell me," I say, still in shock.

"Of course she didn't. That would have spoiled the surprise. She and Brandon have been helping us while she's there visiting."

"You're coming here?" Slade asks for confirmation.

Dad laughs. "Yes, Brandon and Savannah have our flight information."

"Austyn?" Slade says. I reach for Mom's phone and look at him through my teary eyes. "I'll see you soon, angel." I nod, unable to speak from the excitement and the shock of it all.

Mom takes her phone back, says goodbye and ends the call. "Our flight leaves in a few hours. You need to get packed. We're only there for two days before we fly home."

"I don't understand. I wanted to go with Savannah and y'all wanted me to stay here."

"We know how badly you wanted to go. We also know that you really like this guy and we've only met him a handful of times. We need to get to know him better. We decided to tell you no and surprise you instead. Although, I was afraid you'd tell us that you didn't need our permission and would go anyway. That's why we laid on the 'we didn't have you for Thanksgiving' guilt." Dad chuckles.

"Thank you." I lunge at Mom and hug her. Dad and Dawson are both cleaning up the wrapping paper. I walk toward both of them, pulling them both into a hug. "Thank you so much. Thank you." I kiss Dawson on the cheek and rush upstairs to pack.

I'm throwing items in my suitcase when my phone rings. Rushing to pick it up, I see Slade's name on the screen. "Hey," I answer, my voice breathy with emotion.

"I can't believe I get to see you in a few hours."

"I'm packing right now." I'm pretty sure my heart's liable to pop at any moment.

"I won't keep you, but I wanted to tell you I love you." His voice is so earnest I have to hold my breath to stop myself from crying. "Have a safe flight, and I can't wait to see you."

"Love you, too." We end the call, and squeal in excitement, then quickly finish packing. We're only there for two days so I don't need much. Grabbing clothes, I rush across the hall to shower and get ready. No way am I taking a chance of missing this flight.

chapter 35

Slade

AFTER HANGING UP WITH AUSTYN, I received a text message from Combs with Austyn's and her families flight information. I debated for all of about ten seconds on whether or not I was going to meet them at the airport. That brings me to now, standing outside their gate waiting. I've been here for over an hour. It's way too early, but staying in the barracks watching the clock was doing nothing. At least I would be here if their flight was early, which it isn't.

I'd been shocked to get a text from her mom this morning. Opening my phone, I read her message.

> **Michelle:** Merry Christmas, Slade. I'm going to call you later. It will be a video call. If you could answer, but not speak, that would be great. We have a surprise for Austyn and want you to be a part of it.

Of course, I replied that I'd do just that. Never in my wildest dreams did I imagine the surprise would be for both of us. That they'd be coming here to see me.

The crackle of the loudspeaker booms overhead as they announce that her flight just landed. I stand tall, keeping my eyes peeled for her, for them. My palms are sweaty, so I wipe them on my pants. I don't know what to do with my hands, so I shove them deep in my pockets. My eyes don't wander from the gate.

Watching.

Waiting.

When I see her, I don't run to her like I thought I would. Instead, I stand and watch her with her family. The smiles, the laughter, I envy what they have. When she sees me, she grins, and my chest expands. This is my girl. I'm ready to run to her, but Dawson spots me and takes off at a run. I crouch down to catch him as he wraps his arms around me in a hug.

"Slade! I can't believe we're here," he exclaims.

"Me neither, Daws. Merry Christmas," I say, releasing him and standing to my full height. Austyn is there, grinning at us. "Hey, angel." I hold out my hand for her, and she takes it. I pull my hand back, guiding her into my arms. She wraps her arms around my waist, and I kiss her temple. I want to devour her, press my lips to hers and never stop, but I'm trying to respect the fact that her parents are here. They made this possible. I don't want to start this trip off with me pissing them off for mauling their daughter.

"Mr. and Mrs. Wilson," I say when her parents reach us. "Thank you so much for this. I can't tell you what it means to me."

"Merry Christmas, Slade," Michelle says, leaning in to give me a hug.

"Slade." Lee holds his hand out to me, and I take it.

"Thank you both so much." I place another kiss on Austyn's temple. I can't seem to help myself. Luckily her parents just smile at us. "Luggage?" I ask them.

"Just our carry-ons. We packed light," Michelle explains.

"I brought my new Legos. You want to build them with me?" Dawson asks excitedly.

"Sure, bud. We'll definitely make that happen."

"Yay!" he cheers, throwing his fist in the air.

"We better go get our rental car so we can head out," Lee says.

"We'll have to stop at the visitors' center and get you a pass before you can take it on base, but that's not an issue," I tell him.

In the rental car, Dawson wants to sit next to me. My legs are too long for me to sit in the middle of the back seat so Austyn bargains with him. Something about taking him for ice cream when they get home. That's all it took for him to concede. I hold her hand in the backseat of the car, not willing to let go of her. Her mom looks back at us and smiles. I don't even try to release her hand. I physically can't. I get her for two days, and during that time, I have to share her with them. No way can I concede on holding her hand too.

At the visitors' center, I have to complete sponsor paperwork to get them a pass for the rental car, and for them. Once we have that all squared away, I direct them to the hotel on base where they'll be staying. It's the same one Austyn and I stayed at when she was here around Thanksgiving. Lee and I carry the bags up to the room. It's nice, with two queen beds, but it's not the suite we stayed in.

"So what's there to do around here?" Michelle asks.

"Not a whole lot. We have a movie theater and a bowling alley. There's a mall not too far from here as well. There are some pretty cool monuments about ten minutes or so down the road. Oh, and we have a beam from the World Trade Center."

"Really? That's so cool. We learned about that," Dawson says. "Lots of people were hurt from those bad men," he says solemnly.

"You're learning about that in school already?" I ask him.

"His teacher is a retired National Guard," Lee says.

I nod. It would be hard not to discuss what you've experienced in that situation for sure.

"I'm hungry," Dawson says, falling backward onto one of the beds.

"There's not much open with it being Christmas Day. There's a pizza place here on base that stays open all year round," I offer.

"Pizza's my favorite."

"Pizza it is."

"It's just down the block. We can walk if you want."

"A walk sounds nice," Michelle says.

"Yeah, it's warmer here than at home," Dawson chimes in.

"You said it was in the low teens right, babe?" I ask Austyn.

"Yep. We also got about an inch of snow last night."

"That's not enough. I need more than that to build a good snowman, right, Dad?" Dawson asks Lee.

"Right." He chuckles. "Lead the way, Slade."

Hand in hand with Austyn, I lead them out of the room and onto the elevator. Dawson rambles on about how he likes to push the buttons and that he feels like he's in a spaceship. Outside on the sidewalk, his hand slips into mine. I look down to find him smiling up at me. "Will you sit by me?" he asks.

"Hey," Austyn leans forward and mock scolds him. "He's with me."

"Slade's my friend too, right, Slade?"

"Sure am, buddy." I'm not just kissing his ass or sucking up in front of her parents. Dawson's a cool kid. I always wanted a sibling. He's the closest thing I'm going to get and maybe one day, he'll be my brother for real. At least in the eyes of the law. I can only hope that Austyn and I make it that far.

At the pizza place, we're able to find a table for six, which puts me in between Austyn and Dawson as we sit across from their parents.

"Slade, are your mom and dad here?" Dawson asks.

I swallow my pizza and take a drink of my tea before answering. "No, bud." I keep my answer simple. I don't want to darken the light in his life.

"Oh, okay. What did they get you for Christmas? I know Santa doesn't come anymore once you're big like you and Austyn."

My stomach drops. I don't want to lie to him, but I don't want to tell him the truth either. "You're my present, bud," I say, ruffling his hair. "All of you are. This is the best gift that anyone's ever given me."

"Really? But we're only here for how many days, Dad?" he asks.

"Two, Daws."

"Two days," he tells me, as if I didn't hear his dad's answer.

"I know, but to me, that's better than any gift I could have received. Spending time with those you care about."

He nods like he gets it and goes back to eating his dinner.

Dawson tells me about all his presents and reminds me that I promised to build Legos with him. Michelle and Lee smile indulgently at their son as he rambles on. I try to pay for dinner, but Lee waves me off.

All the way back to the hotel, I hold onto Austyn's hand like it's my lifeline. I don't want to say goodnight, but I'm sure they're tired from getting up so early and the flight. I want more than anything to curl up beside her and hold her in my arms. If I thought I could sneak her in, I'd take her back to the barracks with me. Then again, not a good idea, not with Spiller and Jeffers there. Combs is here in the hotel somewhere with Savannah. I bite back my jealousy and remind myself to be thankful that she's even here. That they all are.

"So, Slade, how about a tour of those monuments tomorrow?" Lee asks.

"Sure. You tell me when to be there, and I'll make it happen."

"You have anything you have to do tomorrow?"

"No, sir. I'm off for the next two days."

"How about nine? We can grab some breakfast here at the hotel before we head out?" Michelle suggests.

"I'll be here. Thank you both again, so much for this."

"You're welcome."

I turn to Austyn. "I'll see you in the morning."

"Yeah." I can see it in her eyes she doesn't want to say goodbye either.

Mindful that her parents are watching, I press my lips to her forehead. "Goodnight, angel."

"Night."

With that, I turn and walk right back out of the hotel. I want to stand there and watch her until the elevator doors close, soak up as much of her as I can, but that would be creepy as hell, so I force myself to keep walking.

chapter 36
Austyn

TODAY IS OUR LAST DAY here. Slade has to report to training tomorrow and our flight leaves later today. Yesterday, we spent the day with my family seeing all the sights. Dawson loved it. I did too. I liked getting to see what he does every day. Well, not really what he does, but get a better glimpse into his world. Last night, Savannah and Brandon went to dinner with us. Savannah's flight left early this morning.

"Our flight leaves at six," Mom reminds me.

"I know. We have to leave here at four, right?"

"Yes," she confirms.

"I'll be here. I promise."

Slade and I are spending the day together without my family. Yesterday was great, but I need time with him not under the watchful eyes of my parents. Not that we have anywhere to go, but he's not kissed me since I've been here. Sure, there have been kisses but not on my lips. Sweet, innocent kisses are all he's given me, which I love, but it will be a few weeks before I see him again, maybe longer, and I need to feel the press of his lips against mine before I leave. I told my parents Slade and I were going on a day date today before we leave. They were fine with it. They're not stupid; they were young once. Dawson, on the other hand, wasn't impressed. He wanted to spend more time with his buddy Slade. I'm glad they get along, but I'm not giving in. Not today.

Slade arrives at a little after eight and we head down to the restaurant to eat breakfast with my family. "So what are we doing today?" I ask him.

"It's a surprise."

"Tell me," Dad says, trying to get a rise out of me. I watch as Slade leans over and whispers his plans, *our* plans for the day, leaving me out of the loop. "Good choice." Dad grins at him. "Is that close?"

"Yeah, about twenty miles or so. We'll be back in time for her to make the flight."

"Ready?" I ask, sliding my plate away from me. I'm ready to be alone with him and see what this big surprise is.

"When you are."

We both stand and say goodbye to my family. Slade laces his fingers through mine and leads me to the front of the hotel, and my excitement amps up. "No hints?" I ask sweetly.

"No, babe. You'll find out soon enough."

"Fine," I concede, and climb into the back of the waiting cab he previously organized.

"Your parents are great, Aust. I can't believe they did this."

"They are pretty great," I agree. "They knew how badly I wanted to be with you, and I was upset they didn't let me fly out with Savannah. Of course, now I know it's because we were all coming to see you."

"You're lucky to have them. I'm glad to know you have such a great support system when I'm not here." He pauses, placing our entwined hands in his lap. "You know, when I deploy, because it will happen, I'm glad you have them."

I fight back the worry that bubbles up every time I think of him deploying. "Do you know how soon that will be?" This is a question that crosses my mind several times a day. I dread that day we get that call.

"No, we find out where we're stationed in a couple of weeks. After that, it's just a waiting game for me anyway. I wait for the Marines to tell me where I'll go next."

"But Marine deployments are short right, like six or seven months?"

"Yeah, unless it's a forward deployment. Those can be longer."

I nod, taking it all in. "Then you go back to where ever it is you're stationed, right?" On the outside, I'm the model of "put together," on the inside, I'm freaking out and crossing my fingers it's not forward deployment.

"Yeah."

"I hope that you and Brandon are stationed at the same place. It would be nice to get to see my best friend when I come and visit you." It's going to suck when she moves away. I'm going to miss her, but I'm happy for them.

"So this summer, huh. They set a date for June?"

"Yeah, they're going to do it here. Just a small ceremony. Her parents and his. You and me, and I guess maybe some of the guys, if Brandon decides to invite them."

"How do you feel about that?"

"About what? Them getting married? I'm happy for them."

"About them doing it here."

"Oh, that." I laugh. "I think it's fine. It's not about the location or guests. It's about the two of them. They're getting their fairy tale ending. That's what matters. If they're happy, we should all be happy for them."

"That's a good way to look at it."

The cab stops, and I survey the area, trying to see where we are. When I see a horse and carriage sitting out front of an old rustic barn, I turn to look at Slade over my shoulder. "Is that for us?" I try to hold in my excitement, not wanting him to see the disappointment if it's not for us.

"Yes."

Unable to find the handle fast enough, I climb out of the cab and rush to the horses. I can hear Slade chuckling behind me. "Good surprise?" he asks, resting his hands on my hips, pulling me back into his chest.

"Very good surprise."

Slade introduces himself and takes care of the ride, while I take my time petting the black beauty that's hooked up to a beautiful white carriage. "Ready?" Slade asks, drawing my attention from the horse.

"Yes!" I say, and the horse nudges me with his nose. It's like he's just as excited as I am. Slade takes my hand and helps me into the carriage, climbing in after me. There's a blanket inside that he lays over our laps.

"There's a thermos of hot chocolate if you want it. It's warmer today, but just in case."

"This is awesome," I tell him.

He laughs. "Angel, we haven't even started moving yet."

"I know, but the thought alone is so sweet."

"Come here you." He places his arm over my shoulders, and I go willingly, burrowing into his chest.

"Finally," he exhales. "I've been waiting to get you in my arms since you got here."

We fall into comfortable silence. Slade keeps me held tightly in his arms as we enjoy the ride. It's a perfect ending to this trip. Just the two of us. No words need to be said; we know how the other is feeling. We tell each other every day. This is more to soak up each other's warmth and living in the moment. These times are few and far between for us, and each one is just as precious and memorable as the last.

When the carriage turns to take us back, I lift my head to look up at Slade and find him watching me. "Thank you for this."

His answer is to lean in and press his lips to mine. It's soft and slow, just like the ride we're on. He kisses me, his hands cupping my face until the carriage stops. After thanking the driver and giving him a tip, we go inside to warm up a little and wait for our cab.

"Now what?" I ask him.

"We don't have a lot of time. I thought we could stop and have lunch on the way back. I wish I could take you to the barracks, but that's out. Not to mention the other guys are there."

"I don't care as long as I'm with you. Are you going to the airport with us?"

"Do you want me to?"

"Yes."

"Then I'll go."

That's how it is with us, easy. I'm sure the day will come where we disagree, but we're still so new, the feelings so strong that it's not happened yet. The foundation we're building is solid. I can only hope it's enough to pull us through his future deployments.

chapter 37

Slade

W E'RE STANDING JUST OUTSIDE OF the security gate at the airport. This is as far as I can go. I have let her go, but for some reason, I can't seem to do it. My grip on her hand is firm, then again, she's gripping mine just as tightly. I hate this part, saying goodbye to her. I have this ache in my chest, and there's a lump in my throat. I'm not usually one to show my emotions but having this time with her, with all of them, means the world to me. Saying goodbye to not just my girl, but her family, is a hell of a lot harder than I thought it would be.

"Slade," Lee says, shaking me out of my thoughts.

"Yes, sir?"

"Lee," he corrects me. "It was good to see you. Stay safe," he says, holding his hand out to shake. Luckily, it's not the hand that's holding Austyn's I'm not sure I would have let go to shake his. Yeah, I know I've got it bad.

"Thanks for showing us around," Michelle says, hugging me. I hug her back with one arm, still not willing to break my connection with Austyn just yet. I know it's coming.

"Thanks for building Legos with me. When you come home, can we do it again?"

My heart stutters in my chest.

Home.

"I don't know when I'll be… there," I tell him.

"But you have to come home, right, Aust? He's going to come home?" Dawson asks her.

Lee places his hand on my shoulder. "He'll be home," he assures his son. Then he focuses his attention on me. "Remember what I told you. Regardless, you're always welcome."

I nod. "Thank you."

"All right, let's give them a minute to say goodbye." With a wave from her family, they walk away giving us time.

"God," Austyn says. I cup her face in my hands, and that's when her first tear falls. "I hate this, Slade. I hate saying goodbye to you. I know I need to be strong because it's harder on you if you see me cry, but I miss you and I want to be with you."

I wipe her tears with my thumbs. "You are always with me," I say adamantly. "Just like I'm always with you."

She clutches onto me, fisting my shirt in her hands. Wrapping my arms around her, I hold her close. My hold on her is tight as I bury my face in her neck. We stand there oblivious to those around us. After a moment, I pull back and stare into those baby blues. "I love you, Austyn. With every breath I take, I love you. I know this is hard, baby, but I need you."

"I love you, too. I'm sorry."

"Don't. Don't ever apologize for showing me how you feel. We have to be open and honest to get through this." I brush my mouths against hers. "Call me when you land."

She gives me a watery smile. "Take care of you."

"I'm always with you."

She nods. "I love you. I'll see you soon."

"See you soon, angel. I love you, too." I press my lips to hers tasting her tears. I can feel the emotion welling up in my eyes, and I squeeze them shut to keep them at bay. Breaking the kiss, I lace her fingers through mine and lead her to her family.

"H—" My voice cracks and I clear my throat. "Have a safe flight. Thank you again, so much for coming here. I can't even tell you…." I choke up again. "I can't tell you what this means to me."

"You're family." Dawson says it so simply.

I nod at him and ruffle his hair. I want nothing more than to be a part of this family. For that warm feeling that's currently swarming my chest, covering the sadness of her leaving to be permanent. After another round of hugs, I watch them go through security until I can no longer see them.

I'm in the cab on the way back to base when my phone vibrates. Combs's name pops up on my screen.

Combs:	You get your girl dropped off?
Me:	Yeah, headed back to base now.
Combs:	Hoops?
Me:	I take it you need a distraction, too?
Combs:	Yep.
Me:	Count me in.

It's New Year's Eve, and the four of us are holed up in our room. We went for pizza and just got back. Drinking is out of the question as we're underage. We get caught, we pay the consequences. None of us feel like pissing off the Marine Corps or pissing away all of our hard work these past several months. So here we are, living it up playing euchre.

"What are your lady friends doing tonight?" Jeffers asks as he deals the next hand.

"They're out with some friends. Then going back to Savannah's house," Combs tells them.

"That sucks. They're out living it up, and you two are stuck here. You worried at all?" Spiller asks.

"About what? They'll more than likely be home early. The party scene is not one either of them are fond of," I tell him.

"Yeah, but they're both hot as hell." He holds up his hands in defense. "Just saying. You know they're going to get hit on if they're at a party."

"Fuck off. We don't need to hear that shit. Besides, Savvy has her ring on. I'm sure of it," Combs fires back.

Jeffers laughs. "You think a ring is going to stop some douchecanoe from hitting on her when he sees she's there alone?"

Combs looks over at me, and I'm pretty certain the pained expression on his face matches my own. This shit is hard enough without these two putting ideas in our heads. I know I can trust Austyn, other guys not so much. Combs reaches for his phone, and I do the same. Jeffers and Spiller don't say a word as they get up from the table in our small living area and disappear.

"Hey," Austyn says after three rings.

"Happy New Year, babe." The noise in the background is so loud I can barely hear her.

"Happy New Year. I thought I was calling you at midnight?" she asks over the music.

"I couldn't wait that long," I tell her honestly. I just leave out why the sudden urgency. "Having a good time?" What I want to ask is if any assholes have hit on her.

"Not really. This isn't really my scene. Savvy and I are getting ready to head to her place."

"You didn't drink, right? I mean, not to sound like your dad or anything, but I need you safe."

"Nope. Not a drop, hence the reason this party is probably lame. We're both stone-cold sober."

"That's good. Be careful driving home." She starts to speak but is interrupted. "Hey, sexy, let's dance," I hear some drunk asshole slur.

"No, thanks, talking to my boyfriend," she tells him. I smile at that. "He's not here. I am. I can show you a good time," he says loudly. It's so loud it's as if he's talking directly into the phone. He must be close to her.

"Angel," I say, pulling her attention back to me.

"Yeah?"

"Stay on the phone with me and find Savannah." I look over at Combs, and he raises his eyebrows in question.

"She's right beside me."

"Good, ignore that guy and head outside to your car. Wait, is it lit? Are there lights outside?"

"Slade, it's fine. We're fine. He's just some drunk guy. He's harmless."

Harmless, she says. "Stay on the phone with me. You need to be alert to your surroundings. Make sure he's not following you."

"Slade, seriously, you're starting to scare me. It's fine."

"Reeves?" I turn to face Combs. "Talk to me." I quickly relay the info and hear him start to give Savannah the same speech.

"We made it to my car," Austyn tells me.

"Good. Lock the doors once you're both inside."

"We did. What's gotten into you?" she whispers, and I can hear the panic in her voice mixed with uncertainty.

Fuck! Resting my elbows on the table, I hang my head, keeping my phone pressed tight to my ear. "I'm sorry. I didn't mean to scare you. Jeffers and Spiller were talking about you two getting hit on with us not there, and then that guy was pushy asking you to dance, and I freaked out."

"I'm okay. He was so drunk he could barely stand. I was never in any danger."

"If I were there, I would have known that. No, better yet, if I were there, that fucker would have never approached you."

"Are you done?" she asks, her voice louder than before.

"What?"

"You heard me. Are. You. Done?" She repeats her question slowly. I'm silent, not sure what to say. "I'll take that as a yes. Now, it's your turn to listen to me. I'm not incapable of taking care of myself, Slade. I won't, nor will Savannah, ever put ourselves in a position where we'd be in danger. Frankly, it pisses me off. I know the distance is hard, but it's as if you don't even trust me. This will never work, Slade Reeves, if we don't have trust."

"Austyn—" I start, but she cuts me off.

"I've gotta go. It's late, and we want to go home. I'm not going to talk to you when I'm upset and chance saying something I'll regret. Not to mention trying to drive."

"Call me when you get home."

"Why don't you try asking me instead of telling me?" I don't get the chance to reply because the line goes dead.

chapter 38
Austyn

I SLAM THE PHONE DOWN in the cupholder and start the car. I hear Savannah tell Brandon she's gotta go and she'll call him back.

"What's wrong?"

"Slade."

"I gathered that much. What did he do?"

"He heard Tommy ask me to dance. Sure he was rude." I sigh then tell her the conversation. "Slade gets all, 'go to the car,' 'make sure there are lights on,' 'watch your surroundings,' and freaks me the hell out." I pull up to a stop light and loosen my grip on the steering wheel. My knuckles are white.

Savvy reaches over and places her hand on my arm. "Aust, you need me to drive?"

"No."

"You want my opinion? No, you know what? You're getting it anyway." She turns in her seat as much as the seat belt will allow and starts talking. "He was being protective, Austyn."

"Right. Possessive is more like it."

"What are you upset about? Let's start there."

"He can't call me and tell me what to do when he's hundreds

of miles away. That's not going to work. I have to live each day without him. He has to trust me to do that." I take a breath. "And he scared the hell out of me. Why would he do that? Make me think the situation is worse than it is with him yapping all these instructions into my ear. How in the hell can I stay alert with all that yapping?" Savannah throws her head back and laughs. "It's not funny."

"It really is. You're being irrational."

"Irrational? Really? Like you wouldn't have done the same thing to Brandon." I'm angry, so damn angry. I can't believe he would get me all worked up like this.

"Actually, Brandon pretty much said the same things to me that Slade said to you."

"How are you not mad?"

"Because I know why he said it. Not because he doesn't trust me or because he's trying to control me. He cares, Austyn. He was worried. That's what you do when you think someone you love is in danger. Especially guys like Slade and Brandon. They're the problem solvers. He was trying to remove you from what he felt from the information could have been harmful.

"Shit," I murmur. With it laid out like that, I get it. Savannah's right. That's what he does, especially when it comes to me. Slade would give anything to protect me and with him not being here, I'm sure it sounded a lot worse than it was.

"Yeah, shit." She laughs. "You need to apologize."

"I hate this," I admit.

"It's not a walk in the park by any means, but you have to know that he was coming from a good place. My guess is he's beating himself up over it now."

I pull into her driveway and turn off the ignition. "I thought I could do this, Savannah. I thought I was strong enough, but what if I'm not?"

"It was an argument, Austyn. You really ready to give up what the two of you have, what you've been working for these past few months because of one argument?"

"No. Hell no, but what if I'm not what he needs? He doesn't need to be worried about me while he's there. I mean, what happens when they get deployed? Then what? He needs his head in the game."

"Austyn, can you seriously look me in the eye and tell me that even if things are all fluffy puppies and unicorns with the two of you that you think he's not going to worry or think about you?"

"Well, when you put it that way," I admit just as my phone rings. His name flashes on the screen.

"Answer it and apologize. I'm going on inside to call B back. Come in when you're done."

I nod and swipe the screen as she exits the car. "Hey."

"Angel," he sighs. "I know you're mad, but I can't help it. I have this... need to protect you, keep you safe. And I wasn't there. I admit I should have let you handle it without barking orders, but I won't apologize for taking care of you. Yes, even hundreds of miles away, I want to take care of you."

"I'm sorry," I say once he's done.

"What?"

"I overreacted. This is hard, Slade."

"It is, so fucking hard, but the alternative is that I lose you. I can't lose you."

"You won't."

He exhales his relief. "I was sure this was the end, you know? That you were going to tell my crazy overprotective ass to take a hike."

"Nah, I love your crazy overprotective ass."

"I trust you. I do. It's those drunk assholes who I don't trust. It's not just because you were at a party. I worry while you're at school. I worry about you leaving work late at night. I can't stop it. I can't be with you or even close to you, so telling you to remove yourself from the situation was the best I could do. I trust you," he says again, and I melt a little at his words. "You have all of me, Austyn. My trust, my heart, my soul, every single piece of me."

Emotion clogs my throat. "I love you, knight."

He chuckles. "That couldn't be more fitting for this moment. I love you, too, angel."

It's starting to get cold, so I put the keys back in the ignition and start the car.

"What are you doing?" he asks.

"Starting the car."

"Are you going somewhere?"

"No. You called as soon as we pulled into the driveway, so I've been sitting in my car talking to you."

"Go get inside, crazy girl."

"I like having this time with you all to myself."

"It's cold as hell there. Go inside. Take me with you."

"Fine," I grumble playfully. When I walk in the door, I see the light on down in the basement, and I know that's where Savannah is. I drop my overnight bag at the bottom of the steps and head downstairs.

"What are you doing now?" He laughs. "It sounds like you're running a marathon."

"Hush." I giggle. "I'm walking down to the basement to find Savannah.

"Over here," she yells out. I take a seat next to her on the couch.

"Found her," I tell him. "I'm going to go so we can get some food. Savvy is giving me her 'I'm starving' look. We'll call you guys closer to midnight."

"Sounds good. I'm glad we made up, Aust."

"We're good," I reassure him.

"All better?" Savannah asks as soon as we end the call.

"Yeah, all better. I apologized and so did he, even though he didn't need to. I get that he was worried, and I need to be more understanding of that. Thanks for setting me straight."

"What are friends for?" She nudges me, and I smile over at

her. "I ordered pizza. We better take this party upstairs so we don't miss the delivery guy."

We settle in to watch the New Year's Eve special on TV and devour almost an entire large pizza. At ten minutes before midnight, we call the guys. Slade and I talk about their euchre game and how he and Brandon are undefeated. When the ball finally drops, his deep sexy voice washes over me.

"Happy New Year, angel."

"Happy New Year, knight."

We talk for a little longer, about everything and about nothing. That's the way it's always been between us. Conversation is easy, and I feel like I can just be me. I don't have to worry that I'm going to say something and make myself look bad in front of him. I can just be.

chapter 39
Slade

I GOT MY ORDERS TODAY. I finally know where I'm going to be stationed and I couldn't be happier. The icing on the cake is that Combs, Jeffers, and Spiller are all at the same location with me. We all received our top pick. I've been sitting on my bed watching the clock on my phone as the numbers roll past. I can't wait to call Austyn and tell her. She has a late class this semester. I started to send her a text and tell her, but I need to see her face when I do. We've talked about this, and we both knew the odds were even for the three places I could be stationed. This time the odds were in our favor.

The clock hits six, and I pull up her contact and hit the button for a video call. "Hey, you." She grins down at her phone. "I'm just walking to my car. Give me a sec."

I should have waited to let her get to her car, or even get home, but I couldn't wait.

"Okay, sorry, that wind is wicked. How was your day? That's an awfully big grin you're wearing."

"I got my orders today."

"And?" Her big blue eyes are wide, waiting to hear.

"Camp Lejeune!"

"What? No way!" she practically screams her excitement.

"That's awesome. I swear I was scared to death it was going to be Japan. No way could I just drive or fly there. California was even iffy, but at least it's in the USA."

"It puts me here, which is the closest to you. That's all I wanted."

"What about the other guys?"

"Combs, Spiller, and Jeffers are all here as well. Miller and Johnson are off to California."

She squeals and bounces in her seat. Laughter bursts free and happiness races through me. "That means you'll be there for the wedding and I'll get to see you, and if I come spend a week or so with them, I can see you and oh my God, I'm so excited!"

I don't even attempt to hold back my big-ass grin. I love that she's as excited as I am. "I don't know if Brandon's got ahold of Savannah yet. He's not in our room. So maybe wait to speak to her until you know for sure."

"She'll be pissed, but she'll get over it. B needs to be the one to give her the news. So, what's next?"

"Well, training is over soon, and we get five days liberty to get settled. This will be my permanent home until we get deployed."

"How long... I mean do you know if or when?"

"No. I know that we'll find out in advance, usually a few months, but we won't know the exact date until about a week or so before we ship out."

"You ready for that?"

"I am. This is what I'm trained to do. The only part I'm not looking forward to is being so far away from you."

"Pft, don't worry about me. I'll be here when you come home. Or probably there when you get to come home. I'll definitely need to wrap my arms around you after all that time."

"You and me both."

"This is great news, Slade."

"It is. This is definitely the best-case scenario, for all four of us."

"I wish I was there to celebrate with you."

"Me too. How are your classes? You're almost through with your first year of college. You excited?"

"Meh," she says. "I still have a few months to go."

"Maybe, but it's getting closer. Are you still thinking about changing your major?"

"I am. I haven't mentioned it to Mom and Dad yet."

"You know they're going to support you no matter what you want to do, right?"

"Yeah, I just hate that they already paid for this year and I won't be using it."

"We talked about this. In your last e-mail, you said that there were only two classes that you took that wouldn't transfer to your graphic design degree."

"That's a lot of money, Slade."

"I know that, angel. But think of it this way. Better than four years' worth of classes that you'll never use. If you don't love the career you've chosen, switch now before two classes turn into twenty. Talk to them."

"I know you're right," she sighs. "I'll talk to them tonight. It's time to register for classes for the summer and fall, and I really want to make the change."

"How's wedding planning going?" Sure, I'm interested because it's our friends, but honestly, I just want to keep her talking. I'm not ready to let her go, and hearing about it all makes me feel as if I'm there with her.

"You know, surprisingly, not bad. I thought Savannah would be picky about everything, but she really just wants a small gathering. She wants to be married so she can be there with him."

"We both can understand that."

"Yeah."

I can tell by the tone of her voice something is up. "What's wrong?"

"Nothing really. I was just thinking about how the three of you are going to be there in North Carolina, and I'm still going to be here in small-town Kentucky."

I want to tell her to move here, to transfer schools. That I'll put her up in an apartment close by. Anything so I can see her every day. It's not fair of me to ask her to do that, but fuck if the words aren't on the tip of my tongue.

"Slade? Did I lose you?"

"You could move here." The words fall from my lips before I can stop them.

"What?" She laughs.

"You could transfer schools, move here. I could see you every day."

"Yeah, then when you deploy, I'll be all alone."

"You'll have Savannah. The two of you could lean on each other."

"We could," she says slowly. "But that's crazy, right? To just up and move?"

"Not to me. I'd give anything to have you close to me." We're both quiet. I can only assume she's processing all of this in that gorgeous mind of hers. "Talk to me, angel. It's just a dream, okay. I don't expect you to move and nothing changes between us if you don't. I just... I was thinking it, and the words just came out. I don't want to pressure you." I'm rambling, trying to backpedal, afraid I've scared her off. "Austyn?"

She clears her throat. "I've thought about it. Moving there, even more so since Savvy and B got engaged. I never mentioned it. I didn't want to assume, and it's a huge step, and we're still new."

"We've been together for months now."

"Yeah, but—" She stops. "It's a big deal."

"It is. That's where I see us ending up. We've not talked about it, but I want to be where they are—Savannah and Combs. I want that to be us one day."

"Slade," she whispers.

"I love you, Austyn. Regardless of where you live, you have all my heart. Think about it. You let me know what you want to do. I'll find an apartment close to base. Whatever I need to do, I'll do it. I can even stay with you as long as I report to base when I need to. Most of the single guys choose to live on base because it can be expensive, but I've invested well."

"It's out-of-state tuition."

"Not if you move here before you apply."

"You've thought about this?"

"Every day since the first day I had to say goodbye to you."

"You'll still have to say goodbye when you deploy."

"I will, but I'll also get to see you every day while I'm here. Get to hold you and kiss you, and our goodbyes will be few and far between."

"I—"

I stop her. "Think about it. Look at the local colleges here. Look at their programs and see if it works for you. Talk to your parents and think it over. Don't just do it to be with me. I want you to be able to pursue your education. I want you to follow your dreams, and hopefully your heart at the same time."

"I love you. Give me some time." Her voice is soft, almost a reverent whisper.

"You have a lifetime, angel. I'm not going anywhere."

chapter 40
Austyn

I'M SITTING IN CLASS WHEN my phone vibrates in my pocket. Pulling it out, I check the screen and see a message from Slade.

Slade:	Hey, angel. What time do you get out of class today?
Me:	This is my last one. I should be out of here in about 30 minutes.
Slade:	Call me on your way home.
Me:	K

I slide my phone back in my pocket and try to focus on class. This is English, and I need this one regardless of what my major is. Ever since our conversation a couple of weeks ago, I've been looking online at colleges in North Carolina. UNC Wilmington has a digital arts degree. It's exactly what I want, and it's less than fifty miles from Camp Lejeune. I've talked to their admissions department and my parents.

Just as Slade said they would be, Mom and Dad were on board with whatever makes me happy. They did like the savings of moving and paying instate tuition. It's more expensive, not living at home and paying room and board. Then there's the option of an apartment. That idea is the one that appeals to me the most. The college is within the distance Slade is allowed to travel, and if I were to get an apartment in between the two, I could have a twenty-minute drive to the base and to school. He could stay with me. No more rented hotel rooms. Not that I have anything against them, but having my own space, *our* own space would be nice.

I can't believe I'm thinking of moving there, living with him. It all feels like it's someone else's life. I never would have imagined this is where I would be the second half of my first year of college. Switching majors and wanting to move just to be near a guy. He's not just any guy though.

This is Slade.

My knight.

My heart.

Class ends, and I rush to pack up my stuff and head to my car. As soon as I'm on the road, I dial Slade.

"Hey," he greets me.

"Hey, yourself. Having a good day? I thought you were in training all day today?"

"Change of plans," he says, not offering more information.

"This is a treat to get to talk to you in the middle of the day."

He chuckles. "It is. How was class?"

"Same thing another day."

"You thought any more about your major?"

"Yeah, they have a good program here, and they also have a good one at UNC Wilmington." He's quiet on the other end of the line. "Slade?"

"I'm here. I'm just trying not to influence your decision. Staying quiet is my best bet." He laughs.

"You think so?" I know he wants me there with him. If I'm being honest with myself, that's where I want to be too.

"I know so."

"So if you didn't stay quiet, what would you say?" I ask,

pulling into the driveway.

"I'd say lots of things, but I'd much rather say them in person."

"I just got home. We can hang up and I can call back on video chat," I tell him, climbing out of the car and heading inside.

"We could do that or I could just tell you the next time I see you."

"Slade," I sigh. "We don't know when that's going to be."

"No?" he asks. "Try looking up."

It takes me a minute to decipher what he said. When I look up, I squeal and drop the phone. Slade is standing in the doorway of the kitchen, my parents' smiling faces standing behind him. I rush to him and he catches me. He holds me tight as he buries his face in my hair.

"I missed you," I say, trying to fight the tears. "What are you doing here?"

"I missed you, too," he says, kissing my forehead and setting me back on my feet. "I might have maybe told a little white lie about when my leave was."

"But Brandon, he's not on leave either."

"Yeah, about that, he's here too. He surprised Savannah."

"I can't believe you're really here," I say, wrapping my arms around his waist and hugging him tightly.

"We need to get back to work. We'll see you both tonight," Mom says, placing her hand on my shoulder.

I nod, not willing to break my connection with Slade. As soon as the front door closes, he cups my face and presses his lips to mine. "I missed you."

I kiss him back before pulling back for air. "How long are you here for? Where are you staying?" I rattle off questions.

"Three days. I have five, but I have to get settled into my new room at the barracks, and we have to be ready to report on Monday." Lacing his fingers through mine, he leads me to the living room. He sits on the couch and tugs gently on our combined hands, pulling me into his lap. "I'm staying here."

"What?" I sit up straighter and turn to look at him. "Here?"

"Yeah, when I called your mom and asked her about surprising you, she offered to let me stay here. I'll be sleeping on the pull-out couch in the basement."

"Three whole days!" I say excitedly.

"Three." Kiss. "Whole." Kiss. "Days." Kiss. He melds his mouth to mine, his hand gripping my thigh.

Somehow, without breaking the kiss, I move to my knees and straddle him. My hands rest on his shoulders, and I rock my hips as his tongue slides against mine.

"Jesus, Austyn," he pants, resting his forehead against my chest. "We can't do this here. Not on your parents' couch."

"Then let's go to my room." I rock my hips again for good measure. It's been so damn long.

"I want nothing more than to be buried deep inside you right now, but Dawson will be home soon."

"How do you know that?" I ask, pulling back.

"Your mom told me what time he gets home."

"Damn little brothers," I mutter.

He offers me a sexy grin. "You know you'd miss him. We have two more full days together. We'll make time," he says, tucking my hair behind my ear.

"Thank you." Grabbing his wrist, I place a kiss on the center of his palm. "So you're here, in front of me, what were you going to say earlier?"

Both of his hands cradle my face, and his dark brown eyes capture mine. "I want you close to me. I want you to transfer schools and live in North Carolina. I've been looking at apartments, and there are several halfway between the base and UNC Wilmington. I even researched the school and the digital art program."

"Really?"

"You're my future, Austyn."

"I talked to Mom and Dad again last night. They support me."

"Yeah?" he asks, his eyes wide and full of hope, the hint of a smile lifting the corner of his mouth. "Does that mean you've made a decision?"

"Not yet. I know what I want. I just need to take the leap."

"I'll catch you, baby. Every damn time I'll catch you."

I'm choked up thinking about what our future might hold. Words escape me, so I lean in and kiss him. That's how Dawson finds us when he comes barreling through the door after school not long after.

"Slade!" he cheers and rushes to the couch. He completely ignores me and the way I'm straddling his lap and throws his arms around his neck. "You're here."

Slade chuckles. "Yeah, bud. I'm here for a few days." He ruffles his hair.

"Yes!" He throws his hands in the air in celebration.

"Homework, Daws," I say, partly because he needs to do his homework and partly because I want all of Slade's attention.

"Do I have to?"

"Yes. Hurry and get it done. That way you can show Mom and Dad when they get home."

"I want to see Slade," he whines.

"I'm staying here, bud. You'll have plenty of time to see me before I go."

That's good enough for Dawson. He jumps off the couch and races up to his room to do his homework. Slade and I settle on the couch to watch a movie. I stretch out and lay my head in his lap. He immediately runs his fingers through my hair. I can't remember a time I've ever felt more content.

chapter 41
Slade

I WISH I COULD SLOW the time. When I'm with her, it flies by. My three days are up. I fly back to North Carolina early in the morning. I feel like I've barely blinked an eye and the time just disappeared. I've enjoyed my time here with her, and her family. They've welcomed me with open arms and accepted that I'm a part of her life. In turn, I consider them a part of mine.

"Dad likes to cook on the grill all year long," Austyn tells me.

We're sitting at her kitchen table discussing dinner. "There's nothing like a steak on the grill," Lee chimes in.

"Steaks it is." Michelle smiles at her husband. "Did you ever get another tank for the grill?"

"Shit," he murmurs, causing us all to laugh. "I'll go get one now. I'll be back in no time."

"I'll come with you," I say, standing from the table.

"Can I go, Dad?" Dawson asks.

"Not this time, bud. We'll be right back." He looks over Dawson's head toward me, and I give him a slight nod.

Austyn looks at me in question, and I throw her a wink. "We'll be right back." I bend down and kiss the top of her head. Thankfully, that's something that they've all grown accustomed to by now. I can't not touch her, not when she's this close to me.

I follow her dad out to his truck. He waits until we're on the road before he breaks the silence. "What's on your mind, son?"

Son. "I wanted to ask you something. Just before I left base, my captain came to me. When I enlisted, we had to fill out mounds and mounds of paperwork. In that paperwork, I didn't list a next of kin. At that time, I didn't have anyone to notify." I look over at him, and he nods, not taking his eyes off the road. "Now I do. I have Austyn, but I'm struggling with listing her. I love her, Lee, and the thought of her being alone when she finds out that something happened to me, I can't bear it. I can't get past it."

"What do you need from me?"

"I know she's strong enough to handle it. It's my hang up. I just… don't know what to do here. I know that when we get married, it will be her, but again, that scares the hell out of me. I don't want her to be alone if that day ever comes."

"When you get married?" he asks.

I can't tell what he's thinking, but that doesn't stop me from forging ahead. "When," I say again. "I guess since we're here and all alone, I can go ahead and ask you for her hand in marriage. I'm not proposing anytime soon," I rush to say. "She still has to decide what she wants to do with college. I don't want to pressure her."

"So you're telling me you haven't told her to move to North Carolina?"

"Oh no, I told her if I had my say, that she would already be there. But I also told her that no matter what she decides, where she wants to go to school, that she and I are in this together. We'll figure it out no matter what she wants to do."

He nods. "I appreciate you not pressuring her."

"Pressuring her just puts more stress on her. I want her to follow her dream, do something she loves and get a good education. I did tell her that I would pay for her to have an apartment." I don't tell him that I'd live there too. I don't want him to discourage her in any way.

He's quiet for a few minutes. "So we have a couple of different things going on here, Slade. First, let's get back to this marriage thing. You asking?"

"Yes, sir. Lee, I would love your blessing to one day, when she's ready, to marry your daughter."

"I like you, Slade. I do. I think you're a good kid, with a good head on your shoulders. Giving you permission to take my baby girl from me is something I'm not sure I'm ready to do."

I nod, defeated. "I understand that. Just know that I don't need your blessing, and even if I don't get it, I'm going to ask her. She's my entire world. There's nothing I wouldn't do for her. Without her, I'm not me. She's the missing part of me that I didn't know I was missing. I love your daughter, Lee. Nothing's ever going to change that. Meeting Austyn changed my life."

He's quiet for a few minutes. I let the silence stretch between us. Letting my words sink in. "I'd be honored to have you as a part of my family. Just don't pressure her, okay? Give her time."

"I'm not in a big rush, but it's going to happen. When she's ready, it's going to happen."

"You think she'll say yes?" he challenges me.

"You think she'll say no?" I fire back.

We both laugh. "She loves you," he finally says. "Now the second issue. What are you thinking?"

"If I don't list someone, no one will be notified. Of course, Combs, I mean Brandon will be there too, but if he's hurt as well or if communication is scarce, she won't be told that I'm hurt or worse." I swallow back the lump in my throat. "That I'm gone."

"Let's just think about you coming home safe."

"I do, but I'm not naive enough to think I'm indestructible." He pulls into the local convenience store and turns off the engine. He turns to face me, and I rush to get the words out. "I was wondering if maybe, if I could list you? I don't have any family. It's just Austyn, and like I said, the thought of her being alone when she gets the news doesn't sit well with me."

"If you two get married, like you say that you are, you'll have to list her eventually."

"No, I could keep you on the list."

"She's not going to like that too much. I'm sure she's not thinking about it now, but by then, especially with Savannah and Brandon getting married this summer, those girls talk, and it will eventually come to her."

"Maybe. I'll cross that bridge when we get there. I just... I don't know. The thought of being so far from her and leaving her, it kills me. I didn't have anything to lose when I enlisted. Now I have everything."

"What if she moves to North Carolina? You still want it to be me?"

"I do. I don't want her there alone. I mean, yeah, she'll have Savannah, but I just... I don't know. It's a feeling I have deep in my gut telling me that this is the way I can support her in the event something does happen. It's my way of making sure she's got her support system surrounding her in the event of... something bad."

"I can respect that. I can see how much you love her, Slade. You two can get through this, but if it's me you want to list, I'm fine with that. You're family now, and from what you're telling me, that's not going to change."

"No, sir. Not if I can help it."

"It's settled then." He reaches for the door handle and climbs out of the truck. An exhale whooshes out of me. That went much easier than I thought it would, on both topics. It's been weighing on my mind a lot lately. Combs has been talking a lot about the wedding and changing all his stuff to Savannah, and it hit me: I have no one listed. I know Austyn won't get any benefits unless we're married, but she will get all that I have otherwise. I've already made the call to list her as my sole beneficiary on all my accounts and investments. I haven't told her, and I don't know that I will. In the event that something does happen, she'll be notified.

After grabbing the new tank for the grill, we head back to the house. Austyn gives me a "how did it go?" look, and I smile and pull her into me, kissing the top of her head. I don't say anything because I don't know how to. How do I tell her that she's my world and that she's given me so much these last few months? How do I tell her that I'm scared as hell that I won't come home to her, that I'll leave her broken? Not only do I not have the words, but I don't want to worry her.

We spend the rest of the night laughing and joking with her family. Dawson steals the show with his talk of a field trip he's going on this week. The kid's excitement is infectious.

Lee and Michelle put Dawson to bed and wish us goodnight. Austyn and I head down to the basement to watch a movie. We're curled up on the couch, her back to my front as we watch TV. When her breathing evens out, I know she's asleep. "I love you." I kiss her shoulder and let sleep claim me.

chapter 42

Austyn

I N THE LOCAL COFFEE SHOP with Savannah, we're going over her wedding plans. While it's going to be a small intimate affair, there's still the dress, flowers, lodging for the guests, and the reception to get organized.

"So you think the local steakhouse is sufficient?" she asks.

"I do. There's going to be less than twenty people. I think if you call ahead, maybe talk to the manager and explain, they will easily accommodate us."

"Three more months. I just have to get through this semester and then I can work on transferring schools."

"It's all going to work out. We have all summer to take care of that."

"I'm getting married, Aust. We're really doing it."

"Never doubted it." I can't stop the smile from spreading across my face. I've always known those two would go the distance.

"When Brandon and I started dating freshman year, I never would have guessed this is where we'd end up. I can't wait to start our lives together."

"You don't have long to wait, future Mrs. Combs." She beams

at that.

"Are you going to come with me?"

"Yeah, I told you I'd stay the week of the wedding."

"That's not what I meant, and you know it."

"I think I am," I tell her. "I love him, you know? And teaching isn't for me, not like I first thought it would be. That was my dream when I was younger, and I never really let myself consider anything else."

"You've always liked graphic design. Hell, you led the yearbook committee junior and senior year. That's your passion. I don't know how either one of us didn't see this sooner." She laughs.

"Yeah, I really think it is."

"So, you're moving to North Carolina, moving in with Slade? How'd he take it?"

"I haven't told him yet," I confess.

"What? What are you waiting for?"

"I don't know, honestly. I guess I'm just giving myself time to adjust to my decision. This is a huge step for us. We've only been together a few months."

"Six months," she corrects me. "That's half a year."

"Yeah, and we've been together a handful of times. What if he leaves his dirty socks lying around or the seat up on the toilet and I can't deal?"

She throws her head back in laughter. "Come on, Aust," she chides. "Do you not think that every couple goes through that? Hell, I've been with Brandon for five years and we're going to be dealing with the same stuff. We've never lived together before."

"What if he changes his mind?" I whisper. "I know he loves me, but living together is totally different. I'd be there all alone."

"First of all, you're not alone. I'll be there and so will Brandon. Second, you can always go home or switch to the dorms. You will be an instate student at that point. Third, he's not going to change his mind. Do you even see the way he looks at you? Hell, the way he talks about you…. Brandon said from day one that he was a goner for you. You two are the real deal. Don't let fear keep you from following your heart."

I let her words sink in and I know she's right. I'm sure that this is the correct decision for me, and no matter what happens between us, UNC Wilmington is a great school and their program is stellar. "I'll tell him. I know I should have already, and I will. I mean, I'll have to, right? We're moving in together." I can't hide the smile the forms. "What about you? Married housing?"

"Yeah, they give an allowance to married couples. It makes the most sense, at least until I graduate from college." She looks at her watch. "Crap, I'm gonna be late for class. Thanks for meeting me. I can't believe I'm getting married in three months," she says excitedly. I help her gather her things and shove them in her bag. "I'll call you later," she says, and flies out the door.

On the drive home, my phone rings. Seeing that it's Slade and it's the middle of the day, I wonder if he's surprising me again. "Hey, handsome," I greet him.

"Hey, babe. How was class?"

"Good. I met with Savvy after to go over the wedding details. I'm headed home now. What's up? Are you waiting for me on the front porch?" I ask, hopeful.

He chuckles. "I wish. No, I have some news. I'll wait until you get home to tell you."

"Tell me now."

"It can wait. You're almost home, right?"

"Yeah, about three minutes away. You're scaring me."

"That's not my intention."

"I was going to call you tonight with some news of my own."

"Oh yeah?"

"Uh-huh."

"Care to enlighten me?"

"Oh, I think I'll wait until I get home."

He laughs. "I get it," he says.

We make idle chitchat about what's been going on in our lives. He's settling into a routine, and I couldn't be prouder of him. "All right, mister. I just pulled into the driveway so spill."

"There's no easy way to say this, so I'm just going to tell you. I got word today. It's happening. I'm being deployed."

My heart stills in my chest before it kickstarts into a heavy rhythm beating harshly against my ribcage. I knew this day would come, but I thought we had more time. I'm not ready.

"Austyn?" His voice is pained.

"I'm here," I manage to croak out. "Why so soon? I mean, I thought we had more time?"

"That's just how these things work, angel. There's no rhyme or reason to it. They say when and where I go."

"I know that, I just thought…. When do you leave?"

"July. That's all we know. We won't have the exact date until right before we deploy. A week or so notice maybe?"

I'm quiet, biting hard on my bottom lip to keep the sob that so readily wants to break free from my chest. I'm so not ready for this.

"Say something."

A lone tear falls, trailing down my cheek. Sucking in a deep breath, I put on my game face. I need to be strong for him, for us. He needs to know I'm good, that we're solid while he's gone. He needs to focus on staying safe and coming back to me. "We knew this was part of it, right? We'll get through it."

"When I signed up for this, I had nothing and now, with you, I have everything. This is my job, but you are my fucking heart and soul."

"I'll be here when you come home to me."

He exhales heavily. "I love you."

"I love you, too."

"What was your news?" he asks.

I swallow hard. "Well, I was going to tell you that I was coming to you. That I'm going to transfer schools so we can be together, but with this news, maybe I should stay here another year? I don't know what to do."

"As much as I want you here, I think the idea of you being close to your family is a good one. Savannah, she might do the same. I don't know. They have to apply for married housing, so maybe they'll do that and put the target date of when they need housing as the date we're supposed to come home."

"When is that? I mean how long are you going to be gone?"

"Six months."

"If I move now, I'll get all that time with you before you leave. School is out in late May. That would give us an entire month, maybe longer, depending on when you deploy."

"I want that, Austyn. I do, but I like the idea of your family being close to you while I'm gone. We'll figure something out. I don't get leave, but we'll figure something out."

His words wash over me. We'll figure something out. We have to. "So," I change the subject, "how was your day?" There's no sense in letting the news keep us from being real. The news is real. He's being deployed. We can't stop it, and he wouldn't want to. He loves being a marine, and it's my job to support him.

He chuckles. "Other than the deployment news, it's been good."

"This is what you're trained to do, Slade. You're going to be great, and when you get home, I'll be there. I'll be packed and ready to go. We'll start the next phase of us when you get home."

"I like the sound of that."

"Good. It's done."

"I need to get back. I just stepped out so I could give you the news. I don't know if Combs has called Savannah."

Just then I get a text. I pull my phone away from my ear, and I see a text.

Savannah: Have you talked to Slade?

"She just texted me," I tell him.

"Call her. You two will need each other when we go. She's going to be married weeks before he has to deploy."

"I'm going to try and talk her into staying here. I hate the thought of her being there all alone."

"I'll call you later," he says.

"I'll be waiting. Love you, knight."

"Love you, too, angel."

As soon as we hang up, I dial Savannah. "Hey," she says. I can tell she's been crying. "You talked to Slade?"

"Yeah, he just called."

A sob comes through the line, and it takes all I have not to join her. "Are you okay to drive? I assume you left class?"

"Yeah. He called right before I went in. I knew I'd never be able to focus."

"You okay to drive? You need me to come and get you?"

"No, I'm good."

"Come here. I'll make us some buffalo chicken dip, and we can veg out in front of the TV."

"I'm on my way."

Jumping into action, I head to the kitchen and start the dip. By the time she arrives, I have it in the oven. I cheated using canned chicken. "Hey," I greet her, giving her a big hug.

"I don't know how to handle this, Austyn. How are you so calm?"

"We have to be, Savannah. This is who they are. This is their job. We knew that going into this. We have to be strong and support them. That's our role right now." Even as I say the words, and know they're true, I'm freaking out on the inside. This is a day that I've dreaded. I don't want him to go. I want him here where I know he's safe.

"God, I don't want him to go."

"I know the feeling, but the reality is they are. We'll get through this, together."

"What would I do without you?"

"You'll never have to find out." I take a seat next to her at the kitchen table. "Listen, I want to run something past you. It's something for you to think about. I know you said that you and B have to apply for married housing. Why not apply for an opening date of when they come back and stay here while they're gone. Don't transfer yet."

"Why?"

"So you're not there alone," I say gently.

"I'll have you."

"I'm gonna wait until they come home to move. I can change my major here, and I've already talked to the schools and my gen ed classes transfer. I'll just work on those while I'm here." She's quiet. I'm sure processing what I've just said.

"You're not coming?" she says brokenly.

"Not yet. I am, but I think being here at home it would be… easier while he's gone. I know one day, if I get to be in your shoes and we're married, that option won't be as easy, but we're so new, and he'd be leaving almost as soon as I got there. I just think it's best to wait."

"I want to be with him as much as I can before he goes. We can't stay at the barracks."

"No, and I know. I want the same thing. There has to be a solution." I go to the oven to check the dip, and it's ready. We serve up huge helpings, grab a bag of chips and a couple of bottles of water, and head to the living room.

"There has to be something," Savannah says, taking her first bite of dip. "Gah, this stuff is so damn good."

"I could eat it all day every day," I agree. We finish off our plates, and that's how Mom finds us.

"Hey, you're home early," I tell her.

"Yeah, I brought work home with me." She points to the bag on her shoulder. "What are you girls doing?"

"The guys got word they deploy this summer," I tell her. Saying it out loud to my mom causes an onslaught of emotions

I've been trying to push back to break free. I'm scared as hell for him. Even though I try to fight it, a tear slips down my cheek.

"Oh no." She drops her bag to the floor and sits in the recliner. "That changes your plans?" she asks me.

"Yeah, I was going to tell him today, and I did, but we talked about it and we both agree not making the change yet is the best option."

Mom nods her agreement. "What about you, Savannah?"

"It makes sense, but I want to be with him before he goes. We'll be married, and even if it's only a couple of weeks, I want that time with him."

"So we need a solution."

"Exactly." I laugh. "We've been thinking and eating on it all day." I point to our empty plates.

"Your dad's gonna love to see you made that."

"We better get more before he gets home," I say, only half joking.

"You know, what if the two of you moved down there temporarily. You could share an apartment. I'm sure the guys would be all for this and help out financially. Rent would be cheaper if you get a two bedroom and split it."

"What about our jobs? No way we can both take leave from the diner that long," I ask.

She shrugs. "Sometimes you have to pick your battles. What's more important? I would say you both give notice now and give her time to replace you. When you get back, you can apply again, but chances are you'll have to find another job somewhere else."

"It would be worth it." Savannah perks up for the first time since we heard the news.

"You think we can find a place for two months? I mean, Brandon said July, but they don't know when. I don't want to leave until he does."

"I'm sure you can. There are a few short-term stay places that are fully furnished," Mom says casually, as if we're discussing the weather.

"How do you know this?" I ask her.

"I've been looking online and even called a few since I knew what you were going to do."

"Thank you." I jump from the couch and hug her. "I don't know why we didn't think of this." I can't believe that she did. Then again, I can. This is my mother we're talking about. She knows how I feel about him and that my decision to move to North Carolina and switch schools is not one I came to lightly.

"You're too close to it. The pain of them leaving. Call the guys and see what they say. I'll give you the information of the places I checked out. Fingers crossed they have an opening when you need it."

Immediately, we're both on the phone calling the guys. They're together and are on board before we can finish explaining. Just like that, a shit day turns not so shitty. He's still leaving, but I get a good month, hopefully two with him before he has to go. That's the best-case scenario.

chapter 43
Slade

S INCE THE MOMENT I FOUND out the girls will be moving here temporarily, it's all I can think about. I told her not to work while she's here, that I can cover the cost. Combs agreed. Between the two of us, we can easily afford the rental on the apartment. It's two months; I don't care if I go broke because of it. Not that I will. The girls are driving their cars, and I've been checking my phone all damn day. Austyn has been checking in every few hours when they stop for food or gas. I hate the thought of her driving this far on her own, but she was quick to remind me she's a big girl. They're following one another, and if I know them, they've been on the phone talking all-things wedding since they pulled out on the road early this morning.

My phone rings and I rush to pull it from my pocket and answer it. "Hey, you okay?"

She laughs. "I'm fine, Slade. Just wanted to let you know the GPS says we're about ten miles out."

"Ten miles." My hearts pounds in my chest. Just ten miles and I'll see my girl. I sit up from where I was lying on the bed in our new apartment. Yes, ours. No way am I not staying here with her. Combs said the same thing.

"Yep. You are at the apartment?"

"I am. We're going to order some pizza. We figured you guys would be tired and hungry."

"What? You're not making dinner?"

I laugh. "Nope. I don't plan on taking my hands off you when you get here."

She sighs. "Yeah?"

"Uh-huh. Be safe, babe. I'll see you in a few." I end the call and open the bedroom door the same time Combs does. "Your fiancée call you?" I ask him. His face lights up when I call her that. Can't say that I blame him.

"Yeah, what kind of pizza you want?"

"Anything. Austyn likes pepperoni," I tell him.

"She was mine first, Reeves. I know what she likes on her pizza." He says this to get a rise out of me and even knowing that, it's still gets to me.

"She was your friend. She was never yours. She's only ever been mine," I remind him.

He just shakes his head and smiles, while pulling up the number for the pizza place and ordering dinner. "Thanks for doing this, man. I don't know that we could have afforded to otherwise."

"Are you kidding? Pass up the chance to spend every night with her? No thanks needed, my man. Enjoy your time with your future wife. I just hope it's the end of July before we leave. The more time we have with them, the better."

Combs and I head outside to wait for the girls. I don't know about him, but I've felt like a caged animal pacing, waiting for her to arrive. Austyn pulls in first, and I'm moving. My feet carry me toward her car, and by the time she stops and puts it in Park, I'm opening her door. I don't give her time to get out. Instead, I drop to my knees and pull her into as much of a hug as I can with the seat belt between us.

"Slade." She laughs.

Pulling back, I frame her face with my hands and kiss her, deep and slow, trying to show her how much I missed her, and how much it means to me that she's here. She quit her job to spend a month with me. I can't even explain what that does to me—knowing she's in my corner and that we're in this together.

"I love you. I missed you," I mumble against her lips, before going in for another taste.

She's smiling when I pull away, and those blue eyes of her are sparkling. "Can I get out of the car?"

"Good plan." I reach over and unbuckle her seat belt. Standing to my full height, I offer her my hand and help her out of the car. This time, I wrap my arms around her, bury my face in her neck, and lift her feet off the ground. "You're really here," I murmur.

Her hold on me is tight. "I'm really here. I'm not leaving until you do."

"I missed you so fucking much," I tell her again.

"I missed you too, knight."

I set her back on her feet with a quick kiss. "Let's grab your bags. Pizza should be here soon."

"How is it?" she asks, referring to the apartment.

"Good. It's not the Ritz, but it's clean, and there are two bedrooms. Fuck, Austyn, it could be a cardboard box, and as long as you're with me, I'll be a happy man."

"Yeah, no cardboard boxes, though." She pokes my side.

"Not for you, angel. Never for you." I kiss her temple and grab three of her five bags. "Leave those. I'll come back and get them."

"I'm capable of carrying them, Slade."

I don't argue with her. I know I won't win. Besides, I don't want her first day here to be about a silly argument.

By the time we have her bags in our room, the pizza is delivered. The four of us sit around the tiny four-person kitchen table and eat. The girls talk about the drive up, and just as I guessed, they talked on the phone the majority of the time.

When Austyn yawns for what seems like the tenth time, I

stand and offer her my hand. "Let's get you to bed."

"I'm sure you're exhausted too," Combs says, standing and doing the same.

I tune them out and focus on my girl. Reaching for her, she laces her fingers through mine, and I lead her to our room. Once inside, I lock the door. I want to ravish her, but I can see the exhaustion. "Let's get you undressed." I reach for the hem of her tank top and pull it over her head. She reaches behind her and takes off her bra. Meanwhile, I unbutton her shorts, tracing my hands up her sides, loving the feel of her skin against mine. She drops her bra to the floor and shimmies out of her shorts and panties.

"Your turn," she says, huskily lifting my shirt. I have to bend to help her get it off, making her laugh.

I take over and quickly discard my shorts and boxer briefs. Grabbing her hand, I lead her to the bed and hold the covers up for her. She climbs in, with me following after her. She snuggles in next to me. With my arm around her, I release a sigh of contentment. Kissing her temple, I enjoy the feel of her silky-smooth skin against mine.

"I can't believe I'm here."

"Here in North Carolina or in our bed?"

"Our bed. I like the sound of that."

"Me too."

"Both. The last time I saw you it was when you surprised me and stayed with us. I didn't get to lie with you like this. It's my favorite thing."

"Anytime I get with you is my favorite thing."

"Aww," she says through a yawn.

"Get some sleep, angel." I kiss her temple one last time, then close my eyes, drifting off to sleep with my entire world in my arms.

chapter 44
Austyn

IT'S HOT, TOO HOT. I go to move the covers and feel a heavy hand holding me still. Slade. I can't believe I just fell asleep on him. That's not how I planned our reunion to go. Carefully, I lift my head to look at the clock. It's three in the morning. We went to bed fairly early, but now I'm wide-awake. How can I not be with his naked body snuggled up against mine? Tomorrow is Saturday, and he's assured me that he's off all weekend. Waking him up shouldn't be an issue.

Rolling over, careful not to wake him just yet, I rest my hand on his chiseled chest. He's more defined than the last time I saw him. That's saying something. I can't imagine the workouts he's put through as a marine, the training. I close my eyes and feel his heart beat against my palm, praying he returns to me, safe and sound.

My hand roams down his chest until I reach the V at his waistline. Going lower, I palm him in my hand, loving the velvety feel of him.

"Austyn," he murmurs.

I'm not sure if he's asleep or awake, but I don't stop. I want him. No, I need him. It's been too long, and I need him to fill me. I need to know this is real. That I'm really here with him until he has to leave. I pump him a few times, slowly, leisurely.

"Love your hands on me," his sleepy voice greets me.

"Yeah?" I whisper into the darkness.

"Yeah, only one thing I love more," he says groggily.

"What's that?" I ask, still stroking him.

"My hands on you." He rolls me over and settles himself between my legs. When his lips find mine, I open for him, letting his tongue caress mine. "God, I fucking missed you," he breathes into me.

"Make love to me."

"Let me get a condom," he says, kissing me chastely, then moving out of my embrace.

"Hurry," I whisper, causing him to chuckle. I hear him open the nightstand and the tear of a wrapper before he's back where he was. Not missing a beat, he captures my lips with his once again.

"I can't believe you're really here," he says, pushing inside.

My back arches off the bed, and he captures a nipple between his lips. He lavishes my breasts, one then the other, with attention while I hold on, digging my nails into his back and he thrusts over and over again. Each time is better than the last. I don't know if that's how it's supposed to be from my limited experience or if it's the love we have between us. Either way, it's us, and it's real, and I want more.

So much more.

"I don't know how much longer I can hold off," he murmurs, his face buried in my neck.

"I-I'm there," I tell him, locking my legs around his waist and digging my nails into his back.

"Ready, baby?" he asks, his breaths short, quick pants and his thrust long and deep.

"Sl—" I start to call out his name, but the fire coursing through my body as my orgasm takes over stops me.

His hips pump into me, his face buried in my neck. He bites

down on my shoulder, and it causes a tremor to race through me. "Jesus, Austyn," he says, lifting his head to look into my eyes.

"I thought maybe it was just me," I confess.

"Oh, it's you," he says, pulling out of me. "I'll be right back." With a quick kiss, he climbs out of bed and disposes of the condom in the small trash can by the dresser. Before I know it, he's back in the bed. "It's all you," he says, picking up where he left off. "The softness of your skin, the feel of your nails on my back, the way you let me in. It's all you, angel."

"I like to think it's us together. We just seem to fit, you know?"

"We do. Just think, we get to spend the rest of our lives feeling this."

"The rest of our lives, huh?" I ask coyly.

"You know that's where we're going right, Aust? You know that's our end game. I want you to have my last name. I want you connected to me in every way imaginable."

"I like the sound of that." I do. It's what I want for us, and my heart swells knowing we're on the same page. He's hinted around but never came out and said it before.

"Come here." He opens his arms, and I rest my head on his chest. "Let's get some more sleep."

Closing my eyes, I let the soft stroke of his hand tracing up and down my spine, and the sound of his heart lull me to sleep.

When I wake a few hours later, the sun is shining, and the same soft stroke is tracing along my spine. "Good morning, beautiful," his deep voice greets me, alongside a kiss on my bare shoulder.

"Morning," I mumble into the pillow.

"We need to get you unpacked."

"I can do that while you're at work this week."

"Nope, I need to see your stuff lingering with mine. Up you go." He smacks me on the ass.

"What, no sleepy morning sex?" I say, only half kidding.

"Oh, that's going to happen, angel. Just not today. We have things to do, and I need to see you. It's been too damn long, up and at 'em, angel." He climbs out of bed.

I roll over and pry my eyes open to see he's already dressed for the day. "How long have you been up?"

"I never went back to sleep."

"Seriously?"

"I'm used to getting up around that time. My body's just trained for it. Besides, I win, getting to watch you sleep and not because I knew it was going to be weeks or even months before I had the chance again. This time, I knew when you woke up today and fall back asleep tonight, you're not going anywhere. Not for a while at least."

Content. That's how I feel knowing what he said is true. Content that we're where we want to be, together for more than just a couple of days. Sure, there's an expiration date, but this is more than we've had till this point, and nothing is going to damper my excitement of being here with him. "So, what's the plan for today?" I ask, leaning up on one elbow as he pulls one of my bags from its spot on the floor, then sets it on the bed.

"We get you unpacked and then nothing. I just want to be with you. We can do anything you want."

"Then come back to bed," I say, my voice husky with desire.

He chuckles. "We can do that, too, babe. But we're not sleeping. I'm not sleeping my day away when it's been weeks since I've seen you."

"Who said anything about sleeping?"

He leans over my bag on the bed, slides his hand behind my neck, and pulls me into a kiss. "We can make that happen," he says against my lips. "First, we get you unpacked. I need to see it, your stuff with mine."

I don't understand it, but I can tell it's important to him. Climbing out of bed, I pick up his T-shirt from the night before and slide it over my head. That's when I notice all of our other clothes are missing. "Where are the rest of our clothes?"

"I picked them up. Habit I guess, from being a marine."

"But you left this," I say, plucking the shirt from my body to show him.

"Yeah, I left that. I wanted you in my shirt."

I look down at the shirt again and realize it's a USMC shirt. "Any reason?"

His heated stare bores into me. "My name's on the back of that shirt. You're mine, Austyn, and seeing you in my shirt, with my name, that turns me the fuck on and ignites a fire inside of me." My body reacts to his words, and I have to remind myself that we have time. There's no need for me to pull him back into bed with me no matter how badly I want to. We're more than just sex. I just need to remind my libido of that small fact.

"You got more of these?" I ask. The thought of keeping this one, the one he wants me to wear... something of his, that he wore to get me through the nights when he won't be here. Something warms in my chest, and for the first time in my life, I'm thinking about stealing. My fingers are crossed that he has more.

"Yeah."

"Good. This one's mine now. That way, when you're gone, you'll know I'm sleeping with you when you're not there."

In two long strides, he's standing before me. He bends, placing his hands on the backs of my thighs. "Around my waist," he says, and that's my only warning when he lifts me in the air. I wrap my arms and legs around him and bury my face in his neck. We don't say a word. We just hold onto each other as if this could be our last chance. I plan to do this exact thing as much as possible the next few weeks.

I finally pull back, clasping my hands behind his neck. "I love you, Slade Reeves."

"I love you, too." He kisses me, just a quick peck on my lips. Then carefully, he sets me back on my feet.

After unpacking my bags, we head out to the kitchen to make

some breakfast. Nothing fancy, just a couple of cans of cinnamon rolls. The guys went to the store and bought the basics, but we'll need more than just frozen pizza, chips, and cinnamon rolls to eat. We don't see Savannah and Brandon before we lock ourselves back in our room. I left the cinnamon rolls on a plate on the counter. They'll find them.

Back in our room, Slade locks our door, turns on some low music on his phone, and proceeds to undress both of us. We spend the rest of the day in bed, not sleeping, and it couldn't be more perfect.

chapter 45
Slade

I T TURNS OUT SOMETIME IN July was actually July first. We got our orders a week ago. One short week after Brandon and Savannah's wedding. The two of them spent every waking minute behind their bedroom door. Then again, so did Austyn and I. I was hoping we would have until the end of July or at least another week or so. Unfortunately, that's not the case.

Austyn sits on our bed, legs crossed, hands laced together in her lap. Her head is down, and I know my girl is fighting back her emotions. I'm packing for deployment. I'm headed to Afghanistan for six months. Six months of sketchy Internet service and a communal phone with a service just as sketchy. There's snail mail, but it could be weeks before we get mail delivered. Basically, I'm going to have limited communication with her.

It breaks me seeing the pain in her eyes. She's trying to be so strong for me, for us. I can see the battle she's fighting, though. Her smile is there, but her crystal blue eyes are filled with fear, sorrow, and pain. I don't know how to take that from her. Hell, I know that I can't, and that's like a dagger to the heart.

"How will I know when you get there? I mean, can you call me and tell me you're safe?"

"I don't know, angel. There is a phone and Internet, but the service is spotty at best, or so I hear."

"I'll write to you every day," she says, still looking at her hands that are folded in her lap.

"Hey." I place my index finger under her chin and lift her eyes to mine. "I promise you, I'll fight to come home to you. I'm trained for this, Austyn. This is what I do."

She nods. I see her swallow hard and I know she's not able to speak right now. Not unless she wants to show the pain I see in her eyes. I know my girl, and she's tough. She's going to fight it. I can't let her keep it bottled up inside, though.

"Baby," I whisper, sitting on the bed next to her. "Talk to me." She shakes her head. "Please." I pull her into my arms.

She climbs onto my lap and clutches me. "I'm not ready for you to go," she says, a sob breaking free from her chest.

I swallow hard fighting my own emotions. "I have to go. This is my job."

"I know that, but I want you here, in this little apartment. I want you in this bed with me at night."

"Me too, angel. I want that more than anything, but I have a duty to uphold. We knew this would happen."

"I know. But that doesn't mean that I'm ready for it. I hate the thought of you being over there. It's dangerous, Slade."

"Babe, I'm a marine."

She lightly smacks my chest. "I know that."

"No matter where I am, how many thousands of miles away from you I am, my heart still beats for you. Nothing can change that. Not distance, not time, nothing will change the way I love you."

"I'm sorry. I know that. I'm just... missing you already I guess."

"Don't apologize. Never hide how you're feeling from me. Never hide from me, because regardless, I can see all of you."

"I don't want to leave this room until we have to. I have

twelve hours with you and I want them all."

"I want that too," I say, pressing my lips to hers.

She turns so that she's straddling my lap, taking control of our kiss, and I let her. She needs this, and I'll never deny her anything that's within my reach to give her. Her hands grip my shoulders as she grinds against me. "I want you," she says against my lips.

I stand with her in my arms and rest her back against the bed. Slowly, I unbutton her shorts and slide them down her legs. She sits up and raises her arms over her head. Lifting her tank, I remove it from her body. She's in black scraps of lace, a vision that will be sure to get me through long lonely nights in Afghanistan.

Reaching behind her, I remove her bra, then lower to capture one hard nipple and then the next between my lips. "Lie back." My voice is gruff. She complies, lying back on the bed, her gorgeous body on display for me. I play with her nipples a little more, sucking one, gently squeezing and tugging on the other with my thumb and forefinger. My mouth trails down her belly, kissing, nipping, not leaving a single inch untouched.

When I reach the scrap of lace that is her panties, I rip them from her body, causing her to suck in a surprised breath. Tentatively, I run my fingers through her folds. Needing my mouth on her, I lean in close and trace her the same way my fingers just did, only this time with my tongue. She squirms underneath me, so I place my hand flat on her belly at the same time my mouth covers her clit. I suck and tease her with my tongue, sliding two fingers inside of her.

"Slade." My name is a whispered plea.

I don't stop. Tasting her, touching her, feeling the way she responds to me. When her pussy squeezes my fingers, I know she's close. I pump them faster and suck a little harder. Her hands are on the back of my head, holding me to her. Within seconds, she falls apart.

I settle on the bed next to her, my hand resting on her

stomach, just holding her, letting her come down from her high. "Your turn," she says, grabbing my dick through my shorts.

"Not tonight," I tell her. "I need to be inside of you," I whisper in her ear, nipping her lobe.

"You're wearing too many clothes."

She's right. I am. I know I needed that barrier, need to take my time with her, worship her body. "Let me fix that." I kiss her hard, then stand to quickly discard my clothes. Before I join her on the bed, I reach for the nightstand for a condom, but her voice stops me.

"Wait." I stop and turn to look at her. "I'm on the pill, have been for years." I nod. This is not new news to me. "I don't want anything between us, not tonight."

Fuck, I want that. More than anything, I want that. "You sure?" I ask, even though I want nothing more than to slide into her heat.

"Just you and me," she says, holding her hand out for me. "I need this tonight. I need it to just be about us, nothing else, nothing more."

Taking her offered hand, I climb onto the bed, settling between her thighs where I belong. My hands are braced on either side of her head as I hold my weight off her. Her hands slide under my arms. Softly, her nails trace up and down my back, causing me to shiver. Looking down at her, my chest swells with emotion. This angel is my life. I can't imagine living a day in this world without her.

She lifts her hips, and I grind into her. She closes her eyes and tilts her head back on the pillow, enjoying the feel of our bodies united, skin to skin. Holding my weight on one hand, I align my cock at her entrance. Fuck, I can already tell this is going to be quick. "Open your eyes, Austyn."

Her eyes pop open and bore into mine. I hold her stare, trying to see if there's an ounce of hesitation. Her eyes are lit by the soft rays of the sunset shining through our bedroom window. "I'm sure," she says, reading my own hesitation.

Resting my weight on my elbows on either side of her head, I press my lips to hers while slowly, I push inside, then still.

"What's wrong?" Her hot breath caresses my cheeks.

"Nothing, you just feel like… heaven. I need a minute, or this is going to be over way too quickly."

She giggles. "Yeah?" She lifts her hips, driving me insane.

"Austyn," I warn her.

"What?" She tries to sound innocent, but we both know better.

"This is the first time my cock has felt your warmth. You need to give me a minute here."

"We can do it again," she says, wrapping her legs around me and holding me tightly against her.

"We will," I assure her. "But this time…" I move her hair out of her eyes so I can see her. "This time is special."

"It always is."

"Yes." I slowly pull back then push back in. "Always, but this is another first for us. I've never made love to you like this. I need to take my time and savor every memory." I ease out again and push back in just as slowly, starting an unhurried and steady rhythm. "Every pulse, every moan, every kiss." I press my lips to her softly. "I never want to forget this moment."

A tear slips from her eye, and she shakes her head. "I can't lose you," she murmurs.

"I'm right here, angel. I promise you, I'll do everything in my power to come home to you." With the onslaught of emotions, the fear, and the love, my libido is calm as I steadily make love to her. I kiss her everywhere my mouth will reach. My hands roam over her body and hers on mine. We make love for hours until we both succumb to exhaustion.

chapter 46
Austyn

T HE ALARM BLARES AT SIX, but I've been awake for a few hours. My hand rests over his heart as I feel its steady rhythm and watch the gentle rise and fall of his chest with each soft breath. I let the tears fall. I'm sure my eyes are a mess from all the tears, but I can't seem to stop them. My fear for him, for what he's about to face… my fear that this will be the last time I'll ever see him… it was all too much, so in the quiet of the night, I let them fall.

"Morning, beautiful." He kisses my shoulder.

Taking a deep breath, I gaze up at him. "Morning." I lean in and kiss his chest, right over his heart.

"I need to get moving," he says, climbing out of bed.

My heart cracks. We have one hour. Sixty minutes is all I have with him. Just us. Wrapped up in our love. I climb out of bed and begin to get dressed. I pull out my T-shirt that Savannah and I got the other day when we went shopping. It's gray and says *I love my marine* with a heart at the bottom with the USMC emblem in it. I slide it over my head and pull on a pair of khaki shorts. Slade and I move across the hall together and brush our teeth at the same time. I don't bother with makeup, knowing it's all going to be gone. Plus, there's no fixing my swollen face from my night of tears. I brush out my hair and leave it down. I don't have the mental energy to do more than that.

"Come here." Slade tugs me into his chest and the dam breaks.

"I'm sorry," he whispers. "I hate leaving you. You're everything to me." He pulls back and bends down so we're eye to eye, his big hands cupping my face. "You're everything. Do you hear me? There's nothing I won't do to come back to you. I'll fight with everything in me."

"I wish you could tell me it was going to be okay," I say through my tears.

"I won't do that to you, Austyn. It's dangerous, but me and my brothers, this is what we're trained to do. We've got each other's backs. In six short months, you'll be right back here, in my arms where you belong. I'll do everything in my power to make that happen."

"I love you," I sob. "I need you to know how much. Not a minute goes by that I don't think about you, won't think about you. Something good happens, you're the first person I want to tell. Something bad happens, you're the first person I want to run to. I need you, Slade."

"You've got me, angel. Come on." He leads me out of the bathroom and back to our room.

I hear Savannah and Brandon in the hallway, but I ignore them. I know her heart is breaking just like mine; she's been married for two weeks and he's leaving too.

"I love you," he says, embracing me. "So fucking much it hurts to breathe. Every second I'm gone, I'll think of you. I'm already counting down the hours until I get to hold you again, just like this."

"I'll be here when you get home. You're taking my heart with you over there. I'm gonna need you to bring it back."

"That's easy, baby. I'm leaving mine here with you."

I give him a watery smile, trying to be strong. "Get ready, Marine. You don't want to be late." I pull away from him and let him finish gathering everything he needs. While his back's to me, I slip out the letter I wrote for him out of the dresser drawer. When he turns, I hand it to him the same damn time he hands me one. We both laugh. "You can't read it until you're in the air.

"That goes for you too. Wait until we're gone." He cups my face in his hands. "Fuck, Austyn, it's going to break me getting on that plane today."

"This is what you're trained for," I remind him, remind myself. I know we're on repeat, but the words are our mantra. "To serve and to protect. Go be amazing, and come home to me."

"I love you." He kisses me quickly then grabs his bag. I follow him out of our room to the small living room. Savannah and Brandon are there waiting for us. We agreed to ride together so that Savvy and I are not alone on the way home.

"You guys ready?" Brandon asks. His tone is somber matching the rest of us. I'm terrified to look at him and see the sadness reflected in his eyes. I know if I do, I won't be able to stay brave. To stay strong for Slade, for all of us.

Slade nods and holds his hand out for me. I take it and follow him out to my car. Tossing his bag in the trunk, he slides behind the wheel. Reaching over, he tangles his fingers with mine and rests them on my thigh. The ride is silent. The four of us not willing to talk about what's about to happen. Instead, we hold steady to one another all the way to the base.

When we arrive, there are people everywhere. Kids hanging on to their mothers and fathers, and my heart breaks for them. Do they understand what's happening today? Do they know that their mother or father is putting their life on the line for our freedom? Do they know that there's a small chance that this might be the last time they ever see them? I bite down hard on my bottom lip to keep the sob from escaping. I want to cry for me, for Slade, for Brandon and Savannah, and for everyone here. Anyone and everyone who's sending their loved ones off to the land of the unknown. To a country in battle.

Slade drops his bag at his feet and pulls me into his chest. His hold is tight, so tight I can barely breathe, but I say nothing. Instead, I bury my face in his chest and grip him, holding onto him with all that I am. Bending down, he places his lips next to my ear. "No matter what happens, I need you to tell me you know what you mean to me. You've given me life, Austyn. I had nothing before you. I'm leaving you with my heart, my soul, and I'll be back to get it," he says, kissing just below my ear.

Not caring who's watching, I jump into his arms, and instinctively he catches me, just like I knew he would. "The only clear vision of my future is you. Take care of you," I say as the tears begin to fall. He kisses my lips, just a peck.

"I'm always with you." He wipes away my tears with his thumbs.

"I love you, knight."

"I love you, angel."

He rests his forehead against mine. "I'll see you soon."

"I'll see you soon."

He kisses me. Just a firm press of his lips to mine before setting me back on my feet. They announce overhead that it's time for him to go, and it takes all my strength to not pull him back to me. To beg him to stay.

"I'll be home soon." He picks up his bag and walks away.

Tears roll down my cheeks unchecked. It's not until I hear a sob and feel a body collapse into mine that I remember Savannah. We hold onto each other as we watch them, our men, our marines, the owners of our hearts walk away to face battle head-on.

Numbly, we make our way to my car. I have to sit there for a few minutes getting myself together before I can drive. The ride back to our apartment is just as quiet as the ride there. The only difference is, this time you can hear the pain, feel it in the air. When we make it back, we both go to our rooms, just needing some time. I assume she has a letter just like I do, and I can't wait to rip it open and read what it says.

Austyn,

Walking away from you today is going to be the hardest thing I ever do in my life. Yes, I know I'm headed to Afghanistan. Yes, I know the risks; it's my job. It's what I do. All of that, none of that holds a candle to the sorrow of leaving you behind.

I've spent many nights watching you sleep, holding you close, feeling your hot breath against my skin. Those moments are the ones I live for. Those moments are fuel for my fight to come home to you.

I can't make promises that I'm not certain I can keep. What I can promise you is that you are my heart. I can promise you that you will always be with me and are never far from my thoughts. I can promise you that when the times comes and I make it home, I want you to be my wife. I want you to share my last name, be the mother of our children, and most of all, I want to know that no matter where this career might take me, you'll always be there.

Stay strong, angel. I'll write, call, e-mail... whatever I can, as much as I can. Just know that even if you go a while without hearing from me, I'm always with you.

I love you, angel.

Slade

After reading the letter twice more, I burrow under the covers that smell like him, like us, and cry myself to sleep.

chapter 47
Slade

I HAD TO MAKE MYSELF turn and walk away from her. My features remain as stone; there's no other option. I'm a United States Marine. I'm trained for this. I know my job. I'm confident in my skills. They trained me for that. My brothers and I, we're ready. What they didn't train me for was the way my heart would feel like it was splitting in two when the tears coated her cheeks. They didn't train me with the words to tell her what she means to me. I must have said "I love you" a hundred times in the last two days, but I couldn't seem to find the words to tell her any other way.

Stepping onto the plane, I strap in and pull her letter out of my pocket. I keep it gripped in my fist, both eager to read it and dreading it at the same time. I'm not so sure I'll be able to keep from losing my cool. Looking around, I see many of my fellow marines—hell, most of them—have envelopes or papers gripped in their hands. Oddly enough, it makes me feel marginally better that they too didn't know how to express how they were feeling. I can only assume their wives, husbands, boyfriends or girlfriends, even their parents and siblings, struggled the way my girl had. Hence the reason we're all clutching letters as if it were them.

I wait until the plane takes off and open her letter. I take a deep breath before I let my eyes roam over her words.

Slade,

I can't tell you how many nights I've woken reaching for you, fearing you were already gone. Tonight's going to be hard. After sleeping in your arms every night for the past few weeks, it's going to be hard to adjust.

I've tried to memorize everything. The way your heartbeat feels against the palm of my hand, the hugs from your strong arms, your kisses against my skin. Every laugh, every smile, every "I love you," all of it. I've tried to memorize it all.

I worry I didn't stay strong enough, that letting you see my tears will worry you, but I assure you, I'll be okay. I know you're coming home to me. I can feel it deep inside. Our story doesn't end here.

I worry I didn't say I love you enough. Do you know how much you mean to me? Just in case, let me tell you again. You're my entire world, my heart, my soul, my knight. I love you. I love you. I love you.

Remember that. Don't let a second pass by while you're there not remembering how much I love you. When times get tough, because we both know they will, close your eyes and feel the love I have for you. Let me be the one to pull you through the chaos and bring you home safe.

I love you,

Closing my eyes, I clutch her letter in my hands. I want to demand they turn the plane around. Demand they let me stay with her. Don't get me wrong, I love being a marine; it's who I am. The Marines gave me something more when I had nothing at all. Friendship, brothers, and that led me to Austyn. I feel prepared for my duty. I'm proud to serve my country. That doesn't mean I'm not going to be counting down the days until I get to hold her again. To press my lips against hers and to ask her to be my wife. I'm proud to be a marine, but the emotions, the pride, the love that flows through my veins at the thought of her being my wife, they surpass all others.

Flying to Afghanistan is not my idea of a good time, but finally, we arrive. We set up camp and are shown where the computers and phones are. We're told we can call our families, give them our address, and tell them we've arrived safely, and to keep it to one call and under five minutes. I want to race to the phone, to the computer, but I don't. I take a cot next to Combs and wait for the crowd to die down.

"It was cleared out when I left," Jeffers says.

"You two better go call the ball and chains," Spiller chimes in.

"Fuck off," Combs fires back. "You try leaving your wife of two weeks and tell me how you handle it." He stands from his cot and storms away.

"That's low, man. Just because you choose to stick your dick in any willing female and we don't, doesn't make it right. One of these days you're going to fall, and then you'll understand what we're going through." I stalk off after Combs. It's time to call my girl.

I dial her number, and it barely rings before she's answering, her sweet voice greeting me. "Slade?"

"Hey, Aust."

"Hey." Her voice cracks.

"I only have a few minutes, but I wanted to tell you that we made it and give you our address. You got something to write with?"

"Yeah, let me grab it." I can hear her rustling around. "Okay."

I rattle off our address, and she repeats it back. "Thank you for your letter."

"I've read yours a hundred times." She laughs softly.

"I love you, Austyn. I don't know when I'll get to call again. We can e-mail for sure, but the connection is bad, and if we are out in the field, it might be a few days. Just know as soon as I get the opportunity, I'll reach out, okay?"

"Yeah, okay. I love you, too. Be safe. Take care of you."

I smile. "I'm always with you. I gotta go."

"Okay." Her voice breaks. "Love you."

"Love you." After ending our call, I head back to my cot. The guys are all subdued. This is our first deployment. No matter how much we've trained, we're still in the dark about what the reality of our next six months are going to look like.

In the silence of the room, Spiller shouts out, "Oorah!"

"Semper Fi, baby!" Jeffers shouts after him. Their outburst causes us all to laugh and breaks the tension, and the sadness we're wallowing in. It's time to man up and be the Marines we're trained to be, so we can get the fuck out of here, and go home.

chapter 48

Austyn

Letter #1

Hey, handsome,

I read online that I should number my letters both inside and on the envelope, that way when you finally get them, you can read them in order. Kind of like a book. So this is letter #1.

Last night was my first night to sleep without you and let me tell you, it sucked. I'm not trying to make you feel bad, but I want you to know that I miss you. I missed your arms around me.

Savvy and I haven't talked much since we got back to the apartment. She's hurting. Savvy has never been as strong as she leads people to believe. We need to decide when we're going back home. I'm going to try and convince her to go out to dinner tonight. The faster we lose ourselves in school, moving home, and anything else we can, the faster time will go and the sooner you'll be home.

Take care of you.

Love,

Austyn

Letter #2

My knight,

Another lonely night without you. I miss you so much. Yesterday I convinced Savannah to go to dinner, and we talked about when we should go home. We decided to drive to the beach for a few days. We both have some money saved, and I think it'll do us both some good. We talked about getting jobs but figured it would be shitty to work for four weeks and then quit. So after a few days at the beach, we're going to pack up and head back to Kentucky. I'm taking your stuff with me. We didn't even think about that when you left, but don't worry, it's safe with me. You can get it when you stop by to pick up your heart. << See what I did there?

Stay safe out there.

Love,

Austyn

Letter #3

Slade,

Not a lot to report today. Savvy and I are packing to go to the beach for a few days. I plan to kick back and read a good book or ten. LOL. You know, however many I can work in while we're there.

I miss you.

All my love,

Austyn

Letter #4

Hey, you,

The beach is so nice. We've had perfect weather. I'm currently sitting beside Savannah soaking up some rays. I didn't sleep great again last night, but that's to be expected. One of these days, I'll just crash from exhaustion. Savannah is sleeping next to me. She's been sleeping even less than I have, and that's saying something. I talked to Mom and Dad, and of course, Dawson this morning. They send their best. Daws said to tell you to kick butt.

Counting down the days.

Love,

Austyn

Letter #5

Slade,

The beach was relaxing, but I missed you. You don't know how many times I wished you were there with me. Savannah finally broke down last night, and I'm glad. She needs to feel it, all the fear, the pain, all of it. She seems better today. She's been talking more, and she even smiled today. We're making progress. I'm glad she decided to come back to Kentucky while you guys are away. I never could have left her like she's been these past few days.

This is our last night at the beach. There's a concert at the pier that we're going to check out.

Wish you were here.

Love,

Austyn

Letter #6

Dear sexy boyfriend,

I miss you. I miss the feel of your hands against my skin. I miss the taste of your lips. I miss the feel of you over me, pushing inside of me.

My heart misses you.

My body misses you.

My mind misses you.

I just miss you.

All of you.

I love you.

Austyn

Letter #7

Love of my life,

Yesterday was exhausting. We turned in the keys to the apartment and drove all day. Last night was the first night I've slept clear through without you. That doesn't mean I don't miss you; it just means I'm staying busy, keeping myself occupied, so I don't worry. Because I do, you know. I worry about you, about Brandon, about all of you.

I'm trying not to worry that I haven't heard from you. I know you said it could take some time, but I still worry. I'm holding down the fort here at home. I've checked into my classes to make sure what will transfer so the transition when you get home and I move will be easier. Did I tell you I'm counting down the days? I miss you so much.

All my love,

Austyn

Letter #8

Mr. Reeves,

I'm beginning to wonder if I should be e-mailing you? I know you said the connection was spotty at best, and there's just something about letters that's more personal. When I hear from you, you can tell me which you prefer. Until then, I'm going to keep writing these, and mailing them, hoping they arrive to you, wherever it is you are.

It's been two weeks since I last talked to you. I pray all is well.

Stay safe, Mr. Reeves.

I love you,

Austyn

Letter #9

Slade,

I really didn't know what to send, so here is a box full of items I think you might like. I can only imagine what the MREs are like. I added some beef jerky, some gum, and mints. There are baby wipes again. I don't know if you need them, but it was on the list in an online forum I found. Pretzels and your favorite, ranch Fritos. When you get this and can reply, tell me what you need, what you would like to have, and I'll send it. I'm new at this loving a marine thing.

Enjoy your snacks. I hope you're safe.

I love you.

Austyn

chapter 49

Slade

THE LAST THREE WEEKS HAVE been hell, pure fucking hell. They can't train you to deal with the desert, the heat, the dry. The constant hours of being awake. The sounds of bombs, and semi-automatic weapons firing at all hours of the day. They can't train you for that shit. They can tell you about it. They can tell you what to expect, but none of it, not a single word of what they warn you compares to the real thing.

We're finally back to base for what I hope is a few days of rest. I want to call Austyn, and sleep. Lots and lots of sleep, and a shower, what I wouldn't give for a long hot shower.

I drop my gear on my cot and head toward the makeshift office. There's a line of guys waiting, just like me. Funny, just a few short weeks ago, I was willing to wait, to have privacy to talk to her. Now I couldn't give a fuck who hears me. I need to hear her voice.

"Reeves." I hear my name called and turn toward my captain. "This is for you." He hands me a box and a stack of letters that are rubber banded together. He goes down the line calling out our names, giving us a little piece of home. Before Austyn, this would have been a sad day for me. There's no one but her who will be writing me. I'm torn between rushing back to my cot to tear into them or holding my place in line to talk to her. The need to hear her voice wins out. We get three minutes, but that's more than nothing.

When it's finally my turn, I dial her number, and it barely rings before the sound of her sweet voice washes over me. "Slade." My name is a plea, as if she thinks it might not be me.

"It's me, Aust."

"Are you okay?" Her voice is shaky.

"Yeah, baby. I'm good. We've been out in the field since we arrived. We just got back to camp."

"I sent you letters, and a package, did you get it?"

"I'm holding them now. They just gave them to me. I can't wait to read them."

"Should I e-mail instead?"

"No, this is good. The connection is too spotty. You can hear the crackle on the line now."

"Yeah. So you're safe?"

"I'm safe, angel. I don't have much time. How are you?"

"I miss you."

"I miss you, too, so damn much. I'll call again as soon as I can. I don't know when we're going back out, but I'm good here," I assure her. I don't bother to tell her I'm so exhausted I can barely stand. I haven't showered in three weeks, and there are blisters covering my feet. That truth will only make her worry more.

"Take care of you."

"Always, baby. I'm always with you. You know that, right?"

"Yeah. I know. I love you, Slade."

"I love you, too." I can barely get the words past my lips from the emotion clogging my throat. I knew this would be hard, but being this far away from her, it's taking its toll on me. I would give anything to hold her in my arms right now. After ending the call, I take my package and my letters back to my cot. We have makeshift showers here at camp. They're pointless for the most part, but I need to get out of these clothes and wash away some of the sweat and sand from my body. I rush through the process, knowing there's a line of my fellow marines waiting to do the same thing. Even though the shower was lacking, I feel a thousand times better.

Sitting on my cot, I stretch out and hold her package and the stack of letters in my hands. I go to the box first. I know my girl, and there's bound to be some food that isn't a MRE inside. Opening the lid, I feel like I've hit the lottery. Ranch Fritos, baby wipes, jerky, gum, socks, which I needed, and a letter. It's labeled number nine, so I put it to the side and dig through the box. I grab the pictures she sent and a few snacks for later and set the box on the end of my cot. "Hey, guys, help yourselves," I tell my brothers. Tearing into the Fritos, I pick out letter number one and begin to read. I don't stop until I've read them all twice. It's then that I open the papers that were in the box. A picture from Dawson and a card signed by both her mom and dad, telling me to stay strong and be safe.

I'm thousands of miles from home, well, Austyn, because technically I don't have a home. Sure, I have a place at the barracks, but that's not a home. A home is what I plan to make with her. Even thousands of miles away, she makes me feel as if she's right here with me, holding my hand through all of this shit. And her family, their support is something I've never had, that of two loving parents. That's just another way that meeting Austyn has changed my life. I fold the picture that Dawson drew and place it in my pocket. I stare at the pictures she sent. Some are of her and Savannah on the beach, others are of her and Dawson acting silly. Then there's one of us. I remember the day it was taken. We were sitting in the living room, and Savannah gave us maybe a second's notice telling us to smile before she snapped it. This too, I fold carefully, making it smaller, but not altering the image, and place it in my pocket next to the picture I had developed from my phone that I took of her at the fair, all those months ago when we first met.

Grabbing the paper and pen she sent in the box, I write her back. I don't know when we're going back out, and even though I'm exhausted, she's more important. I know she's worried and getting a letter from me will help ease some of her fears.

I hope.

> *My angel,*
>
> *I like how you got creative at the beginning of each letter. I bet you thought I wouldn't even notice. Well, I've read them all twice while I snacked on my ranch Fritos. Thank you for that, and the package, the letters. I shared some of my goodies with the guys.*
>
> *I'm glad both of you are close to your families too. I'd hate to be thinking about you being all alone while I'm here.*
>
> *That's great that your classes are going to transfer. Have I told you that I'm proud of you for chasing your dream? I am, so damn proud.*
>
> *Tell Daws I love the picture and I'm carrying it with me. Please thank your parents for the letter. I'll write to them, but right now, I'm dead on my feet. I didn't want to risk getting called back out to the field without replying to you.*
>
> *Things are okay here. It's hot and dry, and really sandy. Nothing much else to report. Lots of long tiring days. I think about you every second of every one of them.*
>
> *I love the letters. I love getting a glimpse of what's going on in your life. I miss you more than you know.*
>
> *I love you, angel.*
>
> Slade

I seal the letter in an envelope, address it, and put it in the bin to go out in the mail. I barely remember climbing back on my cot as sleep claims me.

We were back at camp for two days when we got word we were going out again. We had to be boots on the ground in two hours. We barely had time to pack our gear and gather what we needed. There was no time for a letter, or a phone call, not even a quick e-mail. Luckily for me, I wrote Austyn, her parents, and Dawson the day before. I had a feeling we would be going out again soon. The sounds of the battle going on all around us was a pretty good indication. I mean, that's what we're here for.

I'm starting to lose track, but this is day ten or possibly eleven of our second trip out. We're exhausted, cranky, hot, sweaty, dirty, and we have no idea when we might get a break. We're doing our route clearance. Spiller and Jeffers are in the Humvee, while Combs and I walk along behind. We switch off every couple of hours, giving us all a break from being on our feet. The Humvee is about a hundred yards ahead of us at all times. Combs is telling me about how Savannah sent him a letter saying how they were approved for married housing on base. He's pumped up. I don't think I've seen him smile this much since we've been here.

I'm just about ready to tell him that Austyn and I will hopefully be following in their footsteps very soon when a loud explosion rocks the ground under our feet. We drop to our bellies and look around, and that's when I see it. The Humvee up ahead. The one with Spiller and Jeffers inside is hit. Flames encased in a black cloud of smoke roar into the air.

A scream rips through my throat as I climb to my feet. Combs is hot on my heels as we race toward the burning vehicle. My heart pounds in my throat as I try not to let the fear take hold. Not only are we spotted, meaning the enemy is watching, but two of my brothers are in there, and by the looks of it, they'll be lucky to be alive.

By the time we reach the Humvee, we're both running on pure adrenaline. "We gotta get them out!" Combs screams over the roar of the fire. The machine is hot, too hot to touch. Using my gun, I beat on the handle. The heat is unbearable, but I do my best to ignore it, pretending it's not there. I ignore the way flames dance toward me with every thrust of my gun against the handle. Instead, I focus on the screams that are coming from the inside. A mix of terror and pain, a sound I'm certain to never forget. I continue to beat on the handle until it jars loose and the door flies open. Spiller falls out, barely missing me and rolls on the ground. Combs and I rush to him and use our packs to pat him down to put out the flames. He's screaming and writhing in pain. The smell of his skin from the fire causes my stomach to roll.

"You got him?" I yell over at Combs.

"Yeah, what are you — Reeves!" he shouts after me, but I don't stop. I rush around the Humvee to the driver's side and start beating on the door. The longer he's in there, the less chance of survival. I get closer, the heat searing my skin, but I keep at it, beating against the handle. I'm lost in my mission to get him the fuck out of there when the Humvee explodes, and I'm thrown from the blast. My body lands on the unforgiving ground as if I'm a ragdoll.

I hear Combs yell out for me, but I can't make my mouth move to answer him. Pain sears my leg. My arm is twisted to hell, and my entire body is numb. I know I need to try and move or at least call out for him and tell him where I am, but all I can think about is Austyn. Her blue eyes smiling up at me. This can't be it for us. I need to fight for her. I told her I would fight my way back to her, and I will. With all my strength, I lift my arm that's not twisted like a fucking pretzel into the air and yell for Combs. The pain from that simple act alone nearly has me blacking out. My head is ringing from the explosion, so I don't know if I'm truly screaming or if it's all in my head. I don't get time to figure it out when everything goes black.

"Reeves." I feel a slap to my face. "Wake the fuck up, man. Come on, you've got to wake up."

"Austyn." I push the words past my lips. My head is foggy, and I can barely make out what he's saying. I can smell the fire and feel its after math down to my twisted bones. I can taste blood and ashes, but the only thing I can think of is her. She's all I see as I close my eyes. My angel.

"Austyn," I croak. When I close my eyes, I can see her. She takes me away from this war, this hell that I'm currently lying in broken and battered.

"Thank fuck," I think I hear him say. I can tell he's scared; the ringing in my ears is softer now, allowing me to hear his panic. "We'll call her, okay? We'll let you talk to her, but you have to stay awake, man."

"I—" My mouth's dry, as if I've eaten a pound of sand. The taste of blood, and ash gagging me. The pain from my injuries is excruciating. "I love her," I grit out. "T-t-ell her."

"Fuck that." Combs leans in close. "You're going to tell her. You're going to stay awake until the medic's flight gets here, and then you're going to tell her. You hear me? You're going to be okay. Stay with me. You're going to tell her."

"Angel," I try to say, but I'm not sure if I do. Everything is starting to blur.

"Open your fucking eyes, Reeves! Open them," Combs says.

I want to. I want to open them and see her face, I want to open them and make him promise to tell her how much I love her, but I can't make it happen. No matter how hard I try, they just won't open.

My entire body hurts. The pain is all-consuming as I lie here in the sandy desert waiting for help to arrive. "Slade, stay with me!" Combs yells, and that's the last thing I remember before darkness takes over yet again.

chapter 50
Austyn

I T'S SATURDAY AFTERNOON, AND WE'RE just lounging around the house. Classes start next week, so I'm taking a break before my life gets crazy again. I worked the morning shift at the diner. Turns out, good help really is hard to find, and Margaret welcomed Savannah and me both back with open arms.

"Aust, I say we draw more pictures for Slade," Dawson suggests.

I can't help but laugh. He's drawn almost as many pictures as I've written letters. I've mailed every single one of them too. I hope a little piece of home will keep him going. "Sure, bud. We can do that. Why don't we watch a movie first?"

"*Transformers!*" He cheers, and we all groan because we've seen it hundreds of times.

"Why don't we watch *The Avengers* this time, bud?" Dad asks hopefully.

"Fine," he grumbles. "We need popcorn." He jumps off the couch and races to the kitchen.

"I better help him." Mom laughs and follows him to the kitchen.

Dad pulls up the movie and hits pause, waiting for them to come back. "You heard from Slade?" he asks.

"No, it's been a couple of weeks. He's out in the field like last time I'm guessing."

Before he can reply, his phone rings. He looks at the screen as if he's not sure he should answer it, but then swipes the screen and puts it to his ear anyway. "Hello," he says, still looking not uncertain about whoever's on the other end. "This is Lee," he confirms.

I pull up my phone and text Savannah, asking if she wants to come over and hang out with us.

"What does that mean?" I hear dad ask, pulling my attention back to his call. "Yes, I see. Where?" He's quiet, listening I assume. He's staring straight ahead at the wall. His stare is laser-focused on… nothing. "Can you please send me that information? Yes, that's my e-mail. Thank you for calling." He hangs up the phone and rubs his hands over his face.

"Popcorn!" Dawson exclaims, coming back in the room, Mom on his tail, laughing.

"Dawson, I have an idea. Why don't you take the popcorn up to your room and start on those pictures for Slade? I need to talk to your mom and your sister for a few minutes." His shoulders are tense, and it feels like something is wrong.

"Ah, man, I never get to hear the good stuff," he whines.

"Dawson," dad warns in a stern voice. I'm now certain that whatever it is, is bad. Fear clutches my chest as I wait for Dawson to go upstairs.

"Fine. I wanted to draw a picture for Slade anyway," he grumbles, taking his bowl of popcorn and stomping up the stairs.

"Dad?" I ask, rubbing my sweaty palms on my legs. I take a deep breath and slowly exhale to attempt to calm my suddenly frazzled nerves. Something from that call upset him. He stands from his chair and moves to sit next to me on the couch. Reaching over, he takes my hand in his. "You're scaring me," I tell him.

"Austyn, I need you to listen to me, okay?"

I nod, the fear capturing my ability to speak.

"When he was here, Slade asked me if he could list me as his next of kin. He didn't have anyone else, and his fear was you being alone if you got the call. There was an explosion."

"Oh, God." Dad squeezes my hands a little tighter, I'm sure because of the way I'm trembling. "Tell me he's okay. Tell me!" I scream, as a sob rocks through my body. "What did they say? What happened?"

He glances over at Mom, and she comes to sit next to me on the other side of the couch. Her hands rest on my thigh. "That was the Marine Corps. All they could tell me was that there was an explosion, but he's alive and stable. They're taking him to a hospital in Germany for further treatment."

My hand grips my necklace that I haven't taken off since the moment he put it on me. My breathing is labored; I can't seem to be able to pull in enough oxygen.

"I need you to calm down," he says soothingly.

"He's alive?" I repeat his words as my mind races to process everything he's said. *There was an explosion.* "Stable, what does that mean?" I'm somehow able to ask through the fear that's gripping me.

"Yes. He's stable, but they couldn't tell me more. They're sending me the information via e-mail of where he's going to be. As soon as we get it, we'll go to him."

"We need to go now." I try to stand, but his hand on my shoulder stops me.

"Austyn, listen to me. I need you to calm down. I know you're scared. As soon as we get the information, we'll book a flight." He looks over me at my mom.

"Please," I beg him. I need to go now. I can't just sit here and wait. I need to go to him. My phone vibrates on my lap, and I grab it, hoping it's him, hoping that this is all some big misunderstanding. It's not him. It's Savannah. "Brandon?" I ask him.

"They didn't say, sweetheart, and even if he was hurt, they

wouldn't tell me. They will only tell those who are listed as next of kin."

"I can't tell her," I sob. "She'll worry. What do I do?" My phone rings again and my pulse races. "It's Savannah," I show them the screen.

Mom takes the phone from my hands and answers the call. "Hello." Her voice is soft. "Yes, she's here, but we've just received some news." She listens intently. "That's good to know. I'm glad they called you." She listens again. "I'll tell her. They're going to be leaving as soon as we know where he is for sure. We'll keep you updated. I'll tell her. Thanks, Savannah." She hands me back my phone. "Brandon was with him," she tells me. "He insisted he gets to call her and let her know he was safe. He's still out in the field, but he knew she'd worry once you told her about Slade. His captain called her to tell her he's unharmed and he'll be in touch soon."

I exhale in relief that he's not hurt too. "What about the other guys? Did she say anything?"

"No, they won't give her that information," Mom reminds me gently.

"So what do I do? I can't just sit here when he's God knows where and all alone."

"You need to go upstairs and pack. That way, when we find out where he is for certain, we can be on the next flight out," Dad says.

"I'll be right behind you to pack myself."

"You're going?"

"I have to, Austyn. You're not listed, I am. They're not going to tell you anything once you get there. Besides, no way am I letting you fly out of the country on your own, especially when your emotions are all over the place."

"Come on, sweetie. Let's go pack a bag so when Dad gets the information, you guys can go."

I allow her to pull me off the couch. Blindly through my tears, I follow her up the steps, holding her hand. I sit on the edge of the bed, while Mom pulls a bag out of my closet. "I'll pack a hoodie. I'm not sure what the weather is like in Germany, that way you'll be covered," she rattles on.

I don't respond. I'm numb. He's hurt and alone, and they said he was stable, but is he? Is that what they tell families, so they don't worry until they get there? What am I going to find when I get to him? How bad is he? An onslaught of questions filters through my mind.

"Austyn?" Dad says from the doorway. I shake away my thoughts and look up at him. "They sent me everything. I'm going to go book our flights and pack." He doesn't wait for a reply. Instead, he gives me a sad smile and walks back downstairs.

Dad was able to get us on the next flight out. We had two layovers, but finally, after hours and hours of traveling and worry, we're here. The cab pulls up in front of the hospital, and we climb out, our bags in hand. He tried to get me to go to the hotel first to check in, but I begged him to take me to Slade. It didn't take much to convince him. I can tell he's just as worried as I am.

"Hi, we're here for Slade Reeves," Dad tells the receptionist.

"Are you family?" she asks.

"Yes, ma'am. I should be listed as his next of kin." He goes on to give her his name and ID.

"Of course, he's on the fifth floor." She looks over at me. "Only immediate family can go in," she says apologetically.

"She's his fiancée. Is he awake?" Dad asks.

"I'm not sure. You'll have to ask the nurses on that floor."

"Thank you." With his hand on my shoulder, he guides me to the elevators. "He'll be asking for you," Dad tells me. "That I'm certain. They won't refuse you to enter when he asks for you."

I nod. I want to see him, but even more than that, I need to know he's okay. I want to hold him, kiss him, touch him, but the need to know he's going to be okay, that he's going to make it out of here and come home to me, trumps it all.

We exit the elevator and Dad leads us to the nurses' station. He asks for Slade, and after confirming that he is indeed on the list, we're told to have a seat, and the doctor will be out to talk to us soon.

"That's bad, right? Why can't we go in and see him?" I ask Dad.

"Honey, I'm sure he just wants to update us on his condition before we go in."

"Why? We should be able to go see him, and he can tell us himself."

"Austyn." Dad turns in his chair to face me. "I need you to take a deep breath." He waits for me to do so.

"The family of Slade Reeves?" an older gentleman in a white coat asks from the doorway.

"That's us." Dad stands, pulling me out of my chair by my hand to stand beside him.

"Mr. Wilson?" the older gentleman clarifies.

"Yes, this is my daughter, Austyn. She's Slade's fiancée."

"Right, I'm PFC Reeve's physician. Let's go to a private room." He turns and walks away leaving us to follow along behind him.

I grip Dad's hand with all I've got. This can't be good. Why are we in a private room? My palms are sweaty, and my heart's beating so fast I know they can hear it. My belly feels like there's a pound of coal just sitting deep in its pits, heavy fear like I've never felt before.

"Mr. Wilson, Private First Class Reeves has sustained multiple injuries. He's undergone two surgeries since his arrival and is being prepped for number three."

"Oh God," I sob.

The doctor continues. "There are risks to any surgical procedure, but he's young and healthy, and we do expect him to recover." Some of the dread lifts until he says, "However, it's going to be a long road to recovery. PFC Reeves shattered his leg. We've attached rods and pins, His arm is broken, and his rotator cuff is torn. That's his next surgery. We're going in to repair it. In some cases, tears can heal on their own in time, but we feel it will aid his recovery if we surgically repair the cuff as well."

"Can we see him?" Dad asks.

I'm gripping onto his arm, tears rolling down my face as I listen to the doctor tick off his injuries as if he were reading from a textbook.

"I'm afraid not until he's out of recovery. The surgery is normally done via outpatient and is a quick procedure. I'll send a nurse to get you once he's back in his room."

"Please." My voice is raspy and thick with emotion. "Can I see him?"

He gives me a sad smile. "I'm sorry." He shakes his head. "I'll be sure to have you updated when he's out of surgery and in recovery." He turns and walks away, leaving us to stare after him.

"Let's go check into the hotel. It's just down the street. We'll grab a bite to eat and head back," Dad suggests.

"No. I'm not leaving until I see him. What if he wakes up and asks for me and I'm not here?"

"Austyn, sweetheart, he's in surgery. He's not going to be asking for you."

"You heard him. It's a quick procedure. I'm not leaving. You go get us checked in."

"I don't want to leave you here alone. Not to mention they won't tell you anything."

"I'm not leaving."

"Okay," he concedes. "I'm going to get us checked in and drop off our bags. I'll keep my phone on. I shouldn't be gone more than twenty minutes."

"I'll be here," I assure him. Nothing is going to pull me from this hospital until I see him.

chapter 51

Slade

BEEP. *BEEP. BEEP.*
The annoying sound is what greets me. What the fuck is that? I try to open my eyes, but they won't open. They feel like they're matted shut.

Beep. Beep. Beep.

It won't fucking stop. My body feels like I've been hit by a truck. What the fuck happened?

"Mr. Reeves, can you hear me?" A female voice asks.

Who is she? It's not Austyn, I would know her voice anywhere. Oh shit, where am I? I try again to pry open my eyes, and when they open, I'm greeted with bright white lights.

"Sorry, let me turn those off." I hear her feet rustle across the floor, then her hands, cold as ice, nothing like Austyn's, touch. "Try again. The lights are off."

Doing as she says, I force my eyes to open and find a woman in blue scrubs standing over me. "Welcome back. I'll let the doctor know you're awake. First I need to check your vital signs."

"Where am I?" I croak out the words, my voice raspy and dry to the point of pain.

"You're at a hospital in Germany. You have quite a few

injuries, but I'll let the doctor explain."

Closing my eyes, I try to remember what happened, how I got here. That's when I remember. We were on patrol, the Humvee, Jeffers, and Spiller. I feel like I'm going to be sick. The beeping grows louder.

"Mr. Reeves, that's your heart monitor. Take a deep breath in and slowly exhale. You need to stay calm."

"My brothers, where are they?"

"I'm sorry, but I don't know. I can try to find out for you. I'm going to get the doctor. I'll be right back." She leaves the room and me to my thoughts. I remember getting Spiller out; he was on fire. Combs and I got the flames extinguished, but Jeffers.... I swallow back the lump in my throat, the explosion.

"PFC Reeves, I'm Dr. Craft. How's your pain on a scale of one to ten? Ten being high and one being low."

"Ten." My throat feels like I've swallowed a bed of nails. "W-what…" I try to speak but the pain searing my desert-dry throat is too much. A nurse, who I didn't see, places a cup and a straw to my lips and I sip greedily. The cold liquid is soothing.

"What happened?" I ask the doctor. "My brothers, there were four of us on patrol. How are they?" I close my eyes as memories of the explosion play like a highlight reel in my mind.

"I'm not certain. You were brought in yesterday. You've undergone three surgeries since then. One, to remove your spleen, the second was to repair your leg. The bones were shattered. We had to use rods and pins during the repair. Your final surgery was just about an hour ago. We had to go in and repair your torn rotator cuff. The one on the arm that is broken."

I try to keep up with everything he's saying. "My family, Austyn?" I ask.

"There is a Mr. Wilson here and his daughter, who claims to be your fiancée, in the waiting room. They arrived just before you went into surgery."

"Can I see them?"

"I'll have the nurse send them in. I'm going to give you

something for the pain, which will make you drowsy."

"Wait, let me see her first. Please. I can handle the pain, just let me see her."

"A few minutes. I'll have the nurse send them in."

I close my eyes and wait. The beep, beep, beep is the only sound in the room, and it's about to drive me mad. The sound is doing nothing for my frayed nerves. The panic of what happened to the others. Tears prick my eyes when I think about Jeffers. Is it possible he was able to also survive the second explosion? What about Combs and Spiller? Are they here too? The pain that has taken over my body tells me I'm lucky to be here. To have survived.

Faintly, I hear what sounds like the door opening. I force my eyes to open, and that's when I see her. My angel. Her eyes are cloudy with tears, but I've never seen a more beautiful sight. With my one good arm, I lift my hand and hold it out for her, fighting back the cringe of pain. My entire fucking body hurts to move, but there is no amount of pain that will keep me from holding her. Standing behind her with his hands on her shoulders is her father. I want to thank him for bringing her to me, but right now I can only focus on her.

A sob rips from her chest, and her hand covers her mouth. "Angel," I call out to her.

"Go," her father whispers.

Slowly, she takes tiny steps toward me where I lie broken in this bed. When she gets close enough to reach out for my hand, she takes it softy, and I let my arm drop, causing her to move forward. "I missed you," I tell her.

She smiles through her tears. "I missed you, too." She takes the chair next to the bed, and her father comes to stand next to her.

"Slade," he greets me.

"Hey. Thanks for this." I move my eyes back to Austyn.

"You're family. The doctor says you should make a full recovery, but it's going to be a long road for you."

"I didn't really ask." My first thought was her, and then the others. I know I'm alive. I don't need them to tell me the recovery is going to be a long road, I can feel it from the pain that courses through me from head to toe. There is not a single inch of my body that doesn't hurt. Once he told me you and Austyn was here, that's all I cared about.

"No, he didn't," I hear the doctor's voice behind him. He steps into view. "He was more worried about seeing you." He looks at Austyn. "Mr. Reeves, we should really give you something for the pain. There is no sense in you suffering, and it hinders the healing process. Your body is fighting the pain on its own."

"Slade," Austyn scolds me, and despite her tone, I've never heard a sweeter sound. "You need to take something for the pain," she says, wiping her tears.

"I know." I turn my head to face her. God, she's fucking beautiful. "I told him I would. I just needed to see you first. It's been too long." I lift our combined hands and kiss her knuckles.

"Take care of you," she whispers and gives me a watery smile.

"I love you," I tell her.

"I love you, too." She faces the doctor. "Give it to him now."

"I'm sorry, but you're not on the list to make decisions."

"She is the decision. She's my life."

The doctor nods. "All right then." He moves to my IV and administers the medication. "I'll put in orders for the nurses administer new meds every four hours. You get some rest." He turns to leave then stops. "The pain medication will cause him to be drowsy. He needs his rest."

"Got it." Austyn nods. She watches him leave then turns back to me. "You heard him, you need your rest." Her eyes are fixed firmly on me, her eyes roaming over my injuries. There's a beautiful determination in her stare, as if it's her new mission in life to make sure I'm resting. "I mean it."

Already my pain is easing and my head's becoming hazy. "I

had to see you first," I murmur.

"Well, I'm here and I'm not going anywhere." She brushes her soft hand over my cheek, and I close my eyes a moment.

Forcing them back open and fighting the drugs, I turn to Lee. "Thank you, for bringing her here." I close my eyes again. "I was with Combs, and Spiller, and Jeffers. I don't know how any of them are and they won't tell me anything."

"Brandon's okay. He wasn't allowed to call, but they did call Savannah and tell her he was safe and unharmed," Austyn explains.

With effort, I swallow the lump in my throat. "That's good," I practically slur. The pain meds are really kicking in. I can also feel the bile rising in my throat as I think about my brothers.

"Sleep, knight," her sweet voice whispers. "I'll be here when you wake up."

My eyes are too heavy, so I squeeze her hand; at least, I think I do. I'm not sure it actually happened as the meds take over and I drift off to a painless sleep.

chapter 52
Austyn

I FINALLY CONVINCED DAD TO go to the hotel and get some sleep. The nursing staff brought in a chair that leans back into a bed of sorts, as well as a blanket and a pillow. I'm good with that. I'm not leaving him. When I walked into his room and laid eyes on him for the first time, I had to fight to keep my composure. He's battered and bruised. His arm is in a sling, his leg the same, lifted into the air.

Sitting here holding his good hand, I thank God for keeping him safe. He's lucky, so damn lucky to be alive. I want to crawl into bed with him, rest my head on his chest and hear his heartbeat. But I can't; there are too many wires, and I'm scared to death I'll cause him pain, so I settle for holding his hand and placing my other on his chest, right over his heart. I feel its steady rhythm, not that the annoying beep of the monitor would let me forget. But he's breathing on his own, he knows who we are, and he's going to recover. He's battered and bruised, but he's still my knight.

"Hey, beautiful," his sleep-laced voice greets me.

"Hey, handsome." I stand and kiss his forehead. "How are you feeling?"

"I'm okay," he assures me.

"You will be, but that's not what I asked. I asked how you were feeling?"

"Hurting a little," he confesses.

"I'll get the nurse." I turn, and his grip on my hand and the wince of pain from the act stop me in my tracks.

"I'm okay. Right now, I just want to see you. How are you holding up?"

"Me?" I laugh. "Now that I know you're going to be okay, I'm perfect."

"You always have been," he flirts.

"Look at you, lying here after you've been through hell and all you can do is charm me." I shake my head at him.

"You're all that matters."

"What matters is that you're okay. That I still have you here with me."

"The explosion, you were my first thought."

"You want to talk about it?"

"Nothing to say. It happened. I'm here. I'll recover."

"Slade."

"Honestly, I'm good. I need to know how the guys are, but other than that, I'm good. Promise."

"I'll let it slide, for now. But eventually, you're going to have to talk about it. I'm here for you, no matter what you need."

"What I need is a kiss."

"That I can do." I press my lips softly to his.

"Just as sweet as I remember." He moves his position and winces in pain.

"Knock, knock." The nurse enters the room. "I have orders for more pain medication. What's your number, PFC Reeves, one to ten, ten being high, one being low?"

"Ten," he says, closing his eyes.

"He just tried to move, and winced," I tell her.

"You can expect that for a few more days at least. Once you're stable with your pain management, we'll transfer you back to the States to a veterans hospital to finish your care. You're going to need lots of physical therapy on that leg and shoulder."

"Do you know if he gets to choose where he goes?"

"Usually a VA hospital closest to home so that loved ones can help take care of him."

Mentally, I'm already planning for him to come home to Kentucky. We have a VA hospital just about twenty miles from Mom and Dads.

"Where's home?" the nurse asks Slade.

He looks over at me. "Where ever she is."

"Kentucky," I tell her. "There's a VA Hospital close to us."

"That where you want to go?" she asks Slade.

"I just told you that," he snaps at her.

"I'll make a note," she says, not letting his attitude faze her. She pushes his meds into the IV and leaves the room quietly.

I want to scold him for how he treated her, but I'm sure it's the pain talking; he's been through so much. "Get some rest. I'll be here when you wake up."

His eyes close and his rapid breathing evens out. I sit there next to him, holding his hand, watching him sleep. "I love you," I whisper, knowing he can't hear me, but needing to tell him all the same.

"Hey." Dad walks slowly into the room. "How is he?"

"Good, they just gave him more pain meds about fifteen minutes ago. He's out for the count."

"Let's head down and grab a bite to eat."

I waver, but I know the meds knocked him out. I feel better knowing he's going to recover. "Yeah, maybe a bagel or something," I concede. We grab some food in the cafeteria. We both end up with turkey subs and a bag of chips. "The nurse was saying that once his pain and injuries are stabilized, he'll be transferred to a VA hospital in the States," I tell him.

"Does she know where?"

"Yeah, she said they usually get them into a VA hospital close to home, so their loved ones can be a part of their recovery."

"We have one in Lexington," he tells me.

"We do, but where will he stay? He can't take care of himself. At first, he'll be in the hospital, I realize that, but after, he's going to have months of physical therapy once he's released. Where will he stay?"

"With us."

I stare at him. "He can't do stairs."

"Well, your mom and I will just move up to the spare bedroom or better yet, the one down in the basement. We'll figure it out, Austyn."

My eyes well up with tears. "Thank you. I just don't want him to be alone, you know? I can see the pain he's trying to hide. Not just the physical, but the mental. I want to be there with him, through all of this." I choke back a sob. "I love you, Dad. You and Mom have always been there for me, no matter what the situation, but these last several months since meeting Slade... I can't thank you enough for all that you've done.

"We all will be. He probably needs to talk to a counselor too. I'm sure that's mandated by the Marine Corp for injured marines."

"I'm sure. He's in for a long road of recovery. He keeps asking about the guys he was with. I'm going to message Savannah later and see if she can find anything out the next time she talks to Brandon."

"I'm sure they'll tell him. Aust, you need to keep in mind there's a chance they didn't make it. That they weren't as lucky as Slade."

"That will crush him."

He nods. "You need to be prepared for that. He's been through so much and seen things we can't even begin to imagine."

"I'm going to pull him through this," I say with complete certainty.

"If anyone can, it's you," he assures me.

We finish our food, then head back up to the room. Dad goes back to the hotel to get some more rest, and I settle in for the night on my makeshift bed, right next to his. I'll be here when he wakes up and every day moving forward.

chapter 53
Slade

I WAS ONLY IN THE hospital in Germany for a week. They transferred me here, to the veterans hospital in Lexington, Kentucky. Austyn and her dad stayed with me until I was ready to be transferred. I don't know how I'll ever be able to show them my gratitude for what they've done for me.

I've been here for two months, and the pain is less each day. However, my physical therapist reminds me that once we start progressing my rehab, it's going to be a bitch. He assures me they'll give me something to ward off the pain, but it won't be nearly as strong as what they were giving me in Germany, or when I first arrived here. He's a real ball buster who's already rehabbing my shoulder. He assures me my leg will be much worse.

"Hello, knight," Austyn says, breezing into the room.

"Hey, angel." I hold my good arm open and she leans into me, letting me hug her the best way that I can at the moment. She tries to pull back, but my hand on the back of her neck stops her as I press my lips to hers. "I missed you."

"You just saw me yesterday and every day before that." She laughs, and I love the sound. It overrides all the others that play like a highlight reel in my head. The sound of Spiller screaming, the sound of my own screams, Combs telling me to get back, the explosion. It's all like one very bad movie that I can't turn off.

"I know, it's been almost twenty-four hours. I missed you." I kiss her again then let her go.

"I came right after class."

"How was it?"

"Meh, general education classes are a bore. I can't wait to start on the good stuff."

"I'm excited for you, babe."

"How was rehab today?"

I lift my arm, showing her my progress. "Gets a little better every day."

"That's great. Did he get you up on crutches today?"

"He did. I walked the hall outside my room twice."

"That's good to keep your noninjured leg in shape as well."

"You sound like him. Did he pay you to say that?"

"No," she says, laughing. "We got the rooms all changed out for when you get released. We finished it up last night."

"Are you sure they're okay with this? I can just get an apartment." We both know I can't.

"Positive. The room in the basement is actually bigger and the bathroom is better too. Mom has always said she wished that the one in their room was as nice. Now she has it."

"Thank you."

"They love you, almost as much as I do."

"Yeah?" I ask her.

"Mmm hmm." She leans in and kisses the corner of my mouth. "Now, for today's dining pleasure, I have…." She reaches into her bag and pulls out a bag of ranch Fritos.

"You really do love me," I say, taking the bag from her.

"So you hear anything about Spiller or Jeffers?"

"No."

"I hate that they're keeping you in the dark."

I don't tell her that my gut tells me it's bad. The longer I'm lucid and off the heavy dose of pain meds, the more details I can remember. No way Jeffers could have survived both explosions, and Spiller, he was badly burned. I can remember the smell of it; it will haunt me for the rest of my life. I don't tell her any of that, or about the nightmares that keep me up at night. I don't know how I can hide it once I'm living with them, unless I give in and take the sleeping pills they've prescribed me. I hate that I need them. I hate that my mind won't shut off. I hate that I'm keeping this from her, but she doesn't need to see this, to see the ugly that I have.

"Aust, it's not good," I confess. "I just have a feeling it's not good news."

"We have to have faith."

I change the subject. "How did Dawson do on his math test?" Her parents and Dawson stopped by last night, and he was telling me how hard he had been studying all week.

"I haven't heard yet. He was pumped up for it. I swear that kid is as smart as a whip."

"That he is."

"You know, I can see it." She pauses a moment and strokes my forehead. "The pain behind your eyes. I can see that you try to hide it from me. I love all of you, Slade. Even the broken pieces."

"I'll be okay," I assure her. She's right. I'm broken. But that's for me to deal with. She doesn't need to know the details of how I ended up a battered version of myself. Those are better left unsaid. "It's just the memories sometimes are hard to fight off."

"You want to talk about it?"

"No."

"Okay. I'm here when you do."

"I'm good, babe. Trust me." I don't need to talk about it. I need to forget. I need to erase that day from my mind. The sounds, the smells, and the heat, all of it. I just want it gone.

She stays well past visiting hours, like always, but the nurses just look right past her as if she's not even here. I'm thankful I have her. There any many here who don't get a single visitor. That was my life, that's where I would be, just like them, if I hadn't met her. I don't even want to find out what life without her would be like.

chapter 54
Austyn

S LADE HAS BEEN HOME NOW for two months, after three months in the hospital. By home, I mean here, at my parents' house. He's quiet most of the time, respectful. He watches TV with Dawson, compliments Mom on her cooking, and hangs out with Dad in the garage. We snuggle on his bed and watch TV at night. He then kisses me sweetly, and I head upstairs to my room. That's become our routine. I schedule his therapy around my classes, and he's getting better every day.

But he's also just going through the motions. Literally. He says and does the same things every day. I worry about him constantly, but I hate bringing it up. I know he hates to talk about it and even though I wasn't there, I can only imagine what happened. We found out the day he came home, to my parents,' that Jeffers didn't make it. Spiller suffered severe burns to most of his body and was still in Germany. When we found out, that night he was quiet, claiming to have a headache and disappeared into his room. When I checked on him, he was lying on the bed staring up at the ceiling. I didn't even try to get him to talk to me that night. Instead, I crawled into bed beside him and rested my head on his chest, thankful for its steady beat.

He's still my Slade, handsome as ever, scars and all. He's still in great shape as he works out every day before therapy. His dark hair has grown out from his buzz cut, and his face is covered with stubble. He still holds me like I'm the air he breathes, and he still loves me. Of that, I'm certain. However, that's the physical parts of him. The emotional, on the other hand, he's... hurting.

He still tells me that he loves me. He still kisses me any chance he gets, but the light that used to shine in those big brown eyes has dimmed. Nothing seems to excite him anymore. I wish there was something I could do to help him. He's seeing a counselor as a mandate from the Marine Corps, but it doesn't seem to be helping. I don't know what to do. I'm at a loss. I just want him back. I want my Slade back. I'll love the scars, both physical and emotional, if he would just let me.

My parents are taking Dawson and a friend to an indoor water park for the weekend. It's Dawson's ninth birthday, and he's pumped. He begged Slade and me to go, but I made excuses that I had too much schoolwork to catch up on. I didn't want to blame it on the fact that Slade isn't ready for wet surfaces and lots of kids racing around. He's doing well, but I don't want anything to slow his progress.

"We have the entire house to ourselves all weekend," I say, bouncing on the couch beside him.

"We do," he agrees. No emotion. If I had said that exact same thing before he deployed, there would have been fire in his eyes. His hands would have been on me in seconds. Not this time. This time he acts as though we're discussing the weather. I've been patient with him, up to this point. I know he's been through a lot, but unless he talks to me, hell, talks to someone, my fear is that he will never dig himself out of this rut he's found himself in. My heart constricts in my chest just thinking about it.

"So, what are we going to do about it?"

He never takes his eyes off of the sports channel he's watching. "I don't feel like going out," he says absently.

"Slade!" I say his name louder than I intended. Reaching over him, I grab the remote and turn off the TV. He doesn't yell at me to turn it back on; he just stares at the now blank screen. "Did you hear me? No one is here but us all weekend long."

"I heard you."

"I miss you."

"You see me every day."

"You're right, let me rephrase that. I miss being intimate with you."

"I'm sorry, babe." He puts his arm around me and holds me close. I take a deep breath, breathing him in. "Let's go take a nap."

A nap? I try to not be offended. I know therapy takes a lot out of him. Besides, once I get him in the bedroom, I can have my way with him. I stand from the couch and offer him my hand to help pull him to his feet. He waves me off and struggles to stand on his own. I don't argue, knowing he feels helpless enough already.

In his room, he strips out of his clothes, leaving his boxer briefs on. I slide out of my shorts but opt to leave my tank and panties on. He settles himself on the bed, under the covers and holds them up for me. I take my spot beside him and snuggle into his chest. I place soft kisses against his heated skin.

My hand follows the ridges of his abs taking my time. I explore his body. Before I can go any further, he captures my hand with his and brings it to his lips, kissing my knuckles. He then rests our combined hands on his chest. I fight back tears of frustration, tears of sorrow for the amazing man who can't seem to get past the hell that he's gone through. I wish I could take this from him, that I could shoulder the pain, the memories.

If he would only let me.

His breathing evens out and I know he's asleep. Snuggling in a little closer, I soak up his warmth, letting sleep claim me.

When I wake sometime later, I'm cold, and I know he's no longer in bed with me. Prying my eyes open, I see him standing by the window. His arms are at his sides as he stares off into the distance. He's slipped his pants back on, and that alone fills me with defeat. I don't know how to get through to him. I don't know how to help him. He kisses me, holds me like I'm still this precious gift, but I miss the feel of him over me when he makes love to me. I'm selfish for even thinking it. Deep down, I think he needs that connection too. But it's as if he's too scared to feel.

Climbing out of bed, I approach him slowly. He doesn't move, doesn't speak, just continues to stare out the window. When I reach him, I rest my forehead against his shoulder blades, and my hands grip his back. I try to give him my strength. "Slade." His name is barely a whisper, but I know he hears me. His body tenses. "Let me help you."

"You can't," he says brokenly. "You can't fix me."

"Let me try."

"You can't erase that day, Austyn. You can't take those memories, the smells, the sounds, you can't erase those from my mind. I'm captured in this hell, and there's no way out."

My heart cracks. His voice holds so much pain, so much agony. "I'm here." I press my lips to his heated skin. "Let me pull you through the darkness."

He's quiet for several minutes, and I just hold him. My grip is firm, needing him to know I'm here. "I don't know how," he finally says.

"I know, babe. We'll get through this, together. I promise you. I think talking about it will help you. Maybe we can visit Spiller. I hear he's home. He lives in Illinois. We could drive there in a few hours."

"I can't bring you into this hell, Austyn. I won't do it."

"That's what you don't understand. I'm already here. I'm living it with you every day. I just don't know the details of why. You can push me away all you want, but I'm not going anywhere."

"Of course you're not." He says it like it's the craziest thing he's heard.

"I wasn't so sure," I confess.

He turns and wraps his arms around me. "What are you talking about?"

"I wasn't sure you still wanted me." My voice is soft as fear grips my chest. Fear of his response to that statement. It's something I've thought multiple times since he's been home, but one I've just now been brave enough to speak aloud.

His big hands cradle my face. His eyes, such a dark brown they often appear black, peer into mine. "You are everything. Do you hear me? Everything."

"Prove it," I say. I'm terrified this will push him too far, but something has to give.

"What do you mean, prove it?"

"Make love to me."

His face softens. "Austyn."

"I think I know, at least a little." I'm going out on a limb with my guess, but from the research I've done and the way he's been acting, I think I have a good idea. "I think you feel guilty."

He scoffs.

"I think you feel guilty that you survived and Jeffers didn't. I think you feel guilty that you didn't get to Spiller sooner."

"You don't know what you're talking about." He drops his hands from my face and turns back toward the window.

"You were all there, Slade. Spiller doesn't blame you, and I can guarantee that Jeffers…" My voice cracks when I say his name. "If Jeffers were here, he would tell you to man the fuck up."

He's silent.

"You need to face this, Slade. I know you. I know that you're not talking to the therapist like you should be. He's there to help you. But in order to do that, you have to be open and honest. And me, I'm here for you. I'm standing right here."

He remains silent.

"Look at me!" I shout at him. Slowly, he turns to face me. "I'm right here." I point to my chest. "My heart breaks for you and all that you've been through. I know it was hell. I also know that you can't keep it bottled up inside. It's going to eat you alive, Slade. It's going to tear us apart."

I see it now, the crack in his armor. Finally, if this is the angle I need to play, fine. Tough love and all that. "I'm losing you, slowly. Day by day, I'm losing the man I love, and it's killing me, Slade Reeves. Killing me." My tears fall unchecked down my face.

"I love you, you know that."

I nod. "I know that, but is that enough? You've been up on your feet for a few weeks, yet you still only manage to give me chaste kisses."

"Excuse me, I've been learning how to walk again. Fucking you was not high on my list of priorities."

"It's not just that. You kiss me, you tell me you love me, but it's more of a routine than a feeling. You've closed yourself off. You won't talk to me. Hell, you won't talk to anyone. That's no way for either of us to live."

"What are you saying?"

"I'm saying that I love you. You're my heart, Slade. I love all of you, the broken pieces, the you that plays with my little brother, the you who spends time with my dad in the garage. The you who committed his life to the Marine Corp and came out battered and bruised because of it. The you who loves me like I'm the air he breathes. You spoiled me." I laugh humorlessly. "You showed me what it's like to be cherished, and I want that. All of it. If you can't give me that, then I don't exactly know where that leaves us."

"Austyn." He reaches for me, but I step just out of his reach. I'm risking pushing him too far, I know this, but I don't know what else to do. I've given him time and space. I know there is a chance he's going to tell me that I'm no longer what he wants, and if that's the outcome, I'll have to learn to deal with it. However, if there's a chance that he's so lost in the forest that he can't see the trees, maybe my confession will ignite him. Bring him back to me.

"I know you're hurting. I do. I've seen the hell your injuries have been, and my worst nightmare is the reality of what put you in this position. I also know you're hurting and you can't get through this darkness alone. You have to let me... hell, let anyone... someone help you. I need my Slade, my knight to come back to me." I turn to leave the room.

"Angel," his voice cracks.

I turn to look at him over my shoulder. "I'm going upstairs to my room." Without another word, I walk away from the man I love, praying to God I didn't just make things worse. This is the first time he's shown any emotions whatsoever. I hope that it works, that maybe I got through to him, at least a little. Maybe gave him something to think about. When I get to my room, I slide under the covers. I'm not tired, but I need to be alone to let the tears fall. I cry for him, for his brothers. I cry for me.

Dear God, please let us get through this.

chapter 55

Slade

I T TAKES ME ALL OF five minutes to realize that I need to get my shit in order or I might lose the only good thing in my life.

Austyn.

As quickly as I can with a bum leg, I make my way up the stairs. As soon as I reach the top, I hear her soft cries, and it guts me. Pain lances through my chest. I hate that I did that to her, caused her pain. I'm trying to spare her. She has to understand that. Pushing open her door, my heart cracks right down the middle. I have to place my hand on my chest to make sure it's still beating. My beautiful angel is lying in a ball in the center of her bed, sobbing, almost uncontrollably.

"Angel," I whisper. Hobbling to the bed, I settle in behind her and wrap my arms around her. "I love you. I'm sorry." I kiss her shoulder.

"I don't know how to do this. I-I-I can't watch you self-destruct into your pain. Please. Please let me help you."

"I'm trying to protect you, angel. I don't ever want this darkness to touch you."

"It's too late for that. We are one, Slade. My heart for yours. We traded them a long time ago. What touches you, touches me."

"I'm sorry," I say again. I thought I was protecting her, keeping her from this darkness, not wanting it to touch her. I thought that's what I needed to do, but her tears tell me otherwise. I've been pushing her away and I'm scared as hell that I pushed her too far. That she's giving up on me. Giving up on us. "I don't know what do to. Tell me what to do to make this better?"

She turns in my arms, and the sorrow in her eyes guts me. "Get help. Let me in, open up to the counselor, try, for me. Please, can you just try?"

The alternative is losing her, and that's worse than any hell I've been through being a marine. "Okay, baby. I'll try. For you, I'll try."

"For you, for us," she corrects me.

"I love you." I kiss her lips and taste her tears. "I'm sorry I hurt you."

"You hurt you too. We can do this together."

For the first time since I've been home, I believe we can. This beautiful woman in my arms is stronger than I give her credit for. In my quest to keep her from the darkness, I created a new realm all on my own.

Leaning into her, I press my mouth to hers. My tongue traces her lips, and she opens for me, moaning deep in her throat. Her hands rest on the back of my head, holding me to her.

Desire.

Need.

With just a kiss, I know what she's been saying. I've been blinded by the nightmares, by the guilt. I know I need help, and it took her talking like it might be the end of us to open my eyes. How could I have let her be this close all this time and not touch her like this? Not caress her soft skin?

"I'm so sorry," I murmur, kissing down her neck.

"I miss us." Her voice is soft. Fragile.

"I'll do whatever I have to do to keep you from feeling like this again." My hands slip under her tank top. My fingers stroke over her bra, her nipples hard at the simple touch. I need more of her, all of her, and I need it now. Standing, I pull my pants and boxer briefs down, kicking them to the side. Grabbing onto her legs, I pull her to me and make quick work of ridding her of her panties. She sits up and holds her arms in the air. She's letting me take the lead, something I've always done with us, up until I let myself get lost in the haze.

Lifting her tank over her head, I toss it on the floor. She reaches behind her back and unclasps her bra, tossing it over the side of the bed. "You're so fucking beautiful," I say, taking her in. She's my angel.

"I'm sorry I shut you out." I place a tender kiss on her lips. She scoots back on the bed, and I follow after her. "I don't know...." My voice trails off. My leg is complete shit still. Yes, I'm walking, but my mobility is not yet what it used to be, if it ever will be.

"It's you and me," she whispers, pushing me on my back and straddling my hips. "I don't care about your leg or your scars. I care about what's here." She leans down and kisses my chest, right over my heart. "I love all of you," she says, sitting back up. I watch with rapt attention as she fists my cock and strokes me, root to tip, her eyes never leaving mine. Lifting, she guides me inside of her.

I moan, closing my eyes and just feeling her. Feeling us. It's been too long, too fucking long without this. I'm an idiot.

"You good?" she asks. Her voice is nothing but a whispered breath, telling me she's enjoying this.

"So good." I grip her thighs as she rocks back and forth. "I'm sorry." I choke out yet another apology.

"We've got this," she moans.

I lift my hips, pressing off the bed with my good leg, causing her to throw her head back. Her pussy tightens around my cock; she's close. Already. She's not the only one. One hand remains gripping her thigh, holding her to me, while the other slips between us finding her clit.

"There," she moans. Her hips rock faster. "Slade, I can't hold off...," she pants.

"Let go, angel. I'm right here with you. I'll always be with you," I say, my words having a double meaning.

"Yeeesss," she moans, deep in her throat. Her pussy convulses, squeezing me, and I don't fight it as I release inside her.

She falls forward, and I wrap my arms around her. "I love you, Austyn, So much. I'm sorry, and I'm going to try. No, I'm going to do this. I don't ever want to be the reason for your tears."

"That sounds like my Slade," she whispers, moving to lie beside me.

Her head is resting on my chest, my hand tracing up her spine. "We were on patrol," I say, then stop. I fought telling her, telling anyone except for my commanding officers what happened that day. This feels wrong, to give her the details, but I refuse to lose her. I *can't* lose her. "I never wanted this to touch you, Austyn. I don't know what my future is with the Marine Corp with my injuries, and if I were to deploy again... I don't want this to be all you think about when I'm gone."

"You think I won't? Just because I don't know the details doesn't mean that if and when you deploy again this will not be in the forefront of my mind. It's not that I need the details, Slade. *You* need to speak them aloud. *You* need to process what you went through, so you can start to heal not just physically, but emotionally."

"We were taking shifts a—couple hours in the Humvee, a couple of hours walking. We'd just switched about fifteen minutes before. Combs and I were walking." She's quiet as a mouse. I can feel her hot breath against my skin and the warmth of her hand resting over my heart.

"I'm right here," she whispers. "No matter what you tell me, I'm right here."

"It came out of nowhere, the bomb. It hit the Humvee. The

sounds… Combs and I were screaming as we hit the ground." I swallow hard but push on. It's like I'm living through it all over again. "We scrambled to our feet and ran to them. The Humvee was on fire. We had to beat the door handle to get the door open. When it finally broke free and we pulled…" I close my eyes briefly. "Spiller… we had to pull him out. He was on fire. The smell, his skin." I swallow hard again, fighting back nausea. "The other door was the same way. I was beating on it, trying to get it open to get to Jeffers, and it exploded." Her hands clutch me tighter. "The Humvee exploded and threw me. The pain was unlike anything I've ever felt. I knew my leg was fucked, my arm too. I remember thinking about the promise that I made you. That I would fight to come back to you. I told you I loved you… because I wasn't sure I'd ever get to say those words again."

Her tears wet my chest, but she remains silent. "The next thing I remember is waking up in the hospital in Germany and asking for you. You were there," I say in awe. "It's like I wished for you and you appeared."

"Nothing would have kept me from going to you," she whispers, her voice thick with emotion.

"I'm sorry for shutting you out. I'm sick of the pills, but I'm scared to death that if I don't take them, the nightmares will start again, and you, your family, fuck, Dawson doesn't need to see that."

"They love you, too. They want you to get better. Let us be there for you."

"I can't do this without you, Austyn. Not just deal with my issues, but life in general. I can't do life without you."

"You don't have to. I'm right here."

We spend the rest of the day and night making love and talking. For the first time since I made it back home, I feel like there's light in the darkness, like this hell that I've been living in is not as hot as it was just a few days ago. The answer was there all along. I just needed to give into her. Give my angel the power to pull me through.

chapter 56
Austyn

I T'S BEEN THREE MONTHS SINCE the night Slade finally had a breakthrough. A lot has happened since then. He was medically discharged from the Marines. With all the hardware in his body from his injuries, it's not safe for him to be back in the field. He had a hard time with it, but we were there for him, and he was able to keep the darkness at bay.

He's still seeing a counselor at the VA hospital and day by day, he grows emotionally stronger. He's off the sleeping pills as well. The first couple of nights was pure agony for all of us. He would wake up screaming and crying. I even found him cowered in the corner of the bedroom, calling my name. Turns out, the solution was me, well, not all me, but I like to tease him and take credit for it. About four days in with no medications, we fell asleep watching a movie. He whimpered in his sleep, waking me up. I wrapped my arms around him, and he settled down. That was the worst of it. We tried it the next night and same thing. I've slept beside him every night since.

My parents have been supportive of us, of him. I never imagined I'd be sleeping in my parents' old room with my boyfriend, with them and my little brother in the house, but that's what he needed. Not that I object.

Today is another huge day for him. He graduated from physical therapy. It's been a long road, and he still needs to work on his own, but he's determined. He's stronger than ever, and I couldn't be prouder.

We're currently sitting around the dining room table of my parents' house. Savannah is here, Brandon too. He asked for leave to be here for this, and it was granted. B and Savvy are doing well. She moved to North Carolina when their tour ended just a few weeks ago.

"I'll be right back," Slade says, kissing my temple and standing from his chair.

"It's so cute," Savannah says about their small condo on base. "You guys need to come and visit."

"We'll have to do that soon."

"Austyn!" Slade calls out for me. "Can you come here for a minute?"

"Be right back." I slide away from the table. "What's up?" I find him standing in the living room holding my coat.

"I want you to walk outside with me."

"You are aware that it's freezing-ass cold outside, right?"

"I'm aware." He laughs. "Just humor me."

He bats his eyelashes, that encase those big brown eyes that he knows I can't refuse. I hold out my arms, and he helps me slip on my coat. When we reach the front door, he leans in close. "Close your eyes."

"What?" I laugh.

"Just do it, Aust." Shaking my head, I close my eyes and let him lead me out to the front porch. "Watch your step," he cautions. We take a few more steps and stop. I feel his hot breath against my ear. "Open."

Slowly, I open my eyes and gasp. There, sitting in front of my parents' house, is a horse and carriage, just like the one we rode in North Carolina. This one is all lit up, glowing in the night. It looks magical.

"Slade, how did you do this?"

"I have my ways." He grins. He offers me his arm. "Care for a ride, my lady?" He changes his voice, making it even deeper.

He helps me into the carriage and covers us with a blanket. I snuggle into him, and he wraps his arms around me. "You know, this is one of my favorite memories of us. We knew where we were going and we were determined to kick ass and take names to get there."

"It was a great day. I was desperate for time alone with you that trip."

"You know, we might have got derailed, but I still want to get there, with you. I still want the life we planned. I know that my future is you."

"So you think we can still kick ass and take names, huh?" I ask.

"I do, but there's one thing I think will help us with that."

"Oh yeah? What's that? We can use all the help we can get." I chuckle.

He takes my hand in his and drops to his knees.

"Slade, what are you doing? You'll hurt your leg."

"I love you. When I first met you, you reminded me of an angel, with your blonde hair and baby blue eyes. From that moment, you were my angel. Little did I know that it would be your light that pulled me through the darkness. I've given you my heart, and you captured my soul. Now I want to give you my name. Austyn Michelle Wilson, will you do me the incredible honor of being my wife?"

Tears are flowing down my cheeks, and I feel as through my face might crack from my huge smile. I've imagined our lives together, but somehow, I never imagined this moment. Nothing I would have thought of would have been better that this moment here with him. He opens his palm and there, nestled inside, is a heart-shaped diamond solitaire. I nod, unable to speak from the emotions clogging my throat. Of course, I'll marry him. He's my heart.

"I need your words, angel. Will you marry me?" he asks

again.

"Y-y-yes," I sob, wrapping my arms around him. He climbs to his feet and takes my hand, pushing the ring onto my finger. He brings it to his lips and places a kiss there.

His lips then find mine and he doesn't stop kissing me until the carriage stops in front of my parents' house. I expect them to all be standing outside, but it's just an empty front porch that greets us.

"They know I'm going to ask, but they didn't know when. I wanted it to be us. Although I have their permission, I don't need it. All I need is you." I love that he included my family and got their blessing, but like he said, we don't need it. I would have said yes, no matter what. We're two pieces needing the other to be whole.

Slade helps me out of the carriage and talks to the driver, then turns back to me. "Ready, fiancée?" he asks.

"Yeah, I think we should wait and see how long it takes them to notice the ring."

"Babe, we were gone a while. I'm sure they realize something's up."

"Let's see how long it takes them," I say, smiling up at him.

"Anything you want." He kisses me quickly and opens the door.

We walk into the living room, following the voices. Slade sits on the loveseat beside Dawson and pulls me into his lap.

"You two were gone forever," Dawson says like it was years.

"It wasn't that long." I reach out and run my fingers through his hair. He tries to duck, but I'm faster than he is and get my hand buried in his locks.

"Yeah, what did you do anyway?" Savannah asks. I can tell by the look in her eyes she knows something's up. Not to mention I can't stop smiling.

Pulling my hand from Dawson's hair, I set it on my lap, and she screams.

"No way!" She stands and rushes toward us, pulling my

hand from my lap. "You're engaged?"

"We are," Slade answers, gripping my waist. Cheers of excitement ring out. We're swarmed with one-sided hugs for me, because Slade refuses to let go of the hold he has on me, and handshakes for him. Everyone is genuinely happy for us, but their happiness doesn't hold a candle to ours. I can feel it deep in my soul, feel it in the way he looks at me, the way he grips my waist, holding me to him as if I'm his lifeline. In a way, I guess I am. We anchor each other.

I turn to look at him. My fiancé. We're surrounded by those we love, those who have been with us on this journey of love and happiness. It's the little things in life that are important. Love is a guiding factor, and if you let it pull you through, it will never steer you wrong.

epilogue

Slade

ten years later...

A S SOON AS I WALK through the door, the pitter-patter of little feet greet me. I bend down and catch Corey, my son, in my arms. "Hey, little man, were you good for Mama today?"

He nods. "Yep."

"I see you had spaghetti for lunch," I say, pointing to his shirt. He pulls out his shirt and looks down. Looking back up at me, he grins. "Where's Mama?"

"Working."

"Right here," my wife says. She's leaning against the doorway, her rounded belly on display.

"How are my girls?" I ask her, rubbing her belly and kissing her quickly. Corey wiggles to get out of my arms and I set him down.

"We're tired," she says, grinning. "How was your day?"

"Good. Let me wash up and change, then I'll start dinner."

"Have I told you you're the best husband ever?"

"You have, but I won't stop you from saying it again." I bend to kiss our daughter.

"You're the best husband ever." She laughs, and her belly

jiggles with her.

"Love you, angel. Go put your feet up. I'll wrangle Corey into helping."

"Should I be worried? The last time you and our three-year-old son made dinner our kitchen looked like a tornado had blown through."

"Hey, he was helping."

"Uh-huh."

"Love you."

"Love you, too."

I watch her waddle back into the living room, grabbing her laptop, and slowly lowering herself onto the couch. She completed her degree in digital arts a few years back, and now she works from home. She designs websites, makes custom logos, and a multitude of other things. It couldn't be more perfect for us as she wanted to stay home when Corey was born. When we found out we were having a boy, she wanted to name him after Jeffers. It was a good tribute, and we both happened to like the name Corey Slade. And Corey Reeves just has a nice ring to it.

Our baby girl is due in two months, and her name will be Grace Austyn Reeves. Austyn says baby number two is the end for her, but I want more. I want a house full. I'm sure she can be persuaded.

Being medically discharged from the Marine Corps, was a hard pill to swallow. That is until I decided where I wanted my future to go. Gus, my physical therapist, inspired me, he was incredible. He never let me slack off and pushed me when I needed to be pushed. So, after talking with Austyn's parents, and moving Austyn and me into the basement—giving them back their first-floor room—I enrolled in college. It took me seven long years to become a physical therapist, but I love what I do. We live comfortably on my salary so Austyn can take as many or as few jobs as she wants. Being a full-time mom is her number one priority. I support her, even offered to hire a nanny, but she refused. The money I invested from selling Gran's house all those years ago is still sitting in the bank, drawing interest. It's there for a rainy day if we ever need it. Corey and Gracie will need to go to college and who knows, we might travel the world someday once our kids are raised and on their own. I don't know what our future holds, but I do know that no matter how our story unfolds, my angel will be right by my side.

contact
kaylee
ryan

I cannot thank you enough for taking the time to read
Pull You Through.
I appreciate each and every one of you.
I'd love to hear from you.

Facebook ~ http://bit.ly/2C5DgdF

Reader Group ~ http://bit.ly/2o0yWDx

Goodreads ~ http://bit.ly/2HodJvx

Twitter ~ http://bit.ly/2w6rVYy

Instagram ~ http://bit.ly/2reBkrV

Pinterest ~ http://bit.ly/2wbOCuu

BookBub ~ http://bit.ly/2KulVvH

Website ~ http://www.kayleeryan.com/

other works by kaylee ryan

With You Series
Anywhere With You
More With You
Everything With You

Soul Serenade Series
Emphatic
Assured
Definite

Stand Alone Titles
Tempting Tatum
Unwrapping Tatum
Levitate
Just Say When
Unexpected Reality
I Just Want You
Reminding Avery
Hey, Whiskey

Southern Heart Series
Southern Pleasure
Southern Desire
Southern Attraction

acknowledgments

I needed some help with this one. It was important to me to get the details of military life as accurate as possible. Sure I could have made it up in the name of fiction, but I wanted it to be real. *Toni* and *Lauren*, you ladies and *your amazing husbands* helped me so much. Thank you for taking the time to answer my questions and guide me through military life. I could not have done this without you.

These are my words, but my team helped me make it what it is.

Sara Eirew produced an amazing image of *Mike Chabot* and *Carolyn Seguin*. The three of you together created an image that brought Slade and Austyn to life. Thank you to all of you for doing what you do.

Sommer Stein, Perfect Pear Creative Covers, never ceases to amaze me with her designs. I give her the basics, and she gives me a cover that surpasses my expectations. Thank you for being kick ass at what you do. I'm honored to work with you.

Hot Tree Editing, your team is my lifeline. You make me work for it, to make each book the best version it can me. Thank you for not taking it easy on me.

Tami, Integrity Formatting, I never worry about what the final product is going to look like with you at the helm. Thank you for making each book beautiful on the inside.

Give Me Books, you never fail me. You take the stress and worry out of release day. I cannot thank you enough for all that you do.

Becca the Bibliophile, you nailed the trailer! Thank you so much for bringing Pull You Through to life.

Me beta team, *Stacy, Jamie, Lauren & Ashley*. You ladies are not just my beta's, but my friends. I truly value the friendships we've created throughout this journey. I would be lost without you. I will never be able to thank you enough for the time you put into reading my words over and over. *S. Moose*, our talks keep me moving forward when the plot pushes me backward.

Bloggers, there are so many of you who take the time away from your lives, time away from your families to support authors. Thank you, doesn't seem like enough. You don't get paid to do what you do. It's from the kindness of your heart and your love of reading the fuels you. Without you, without your pages, your voice, your reviews, spreading the word it would be so much harder if not impossible to get my words in reader's hands. I can't tell you how much your never-ending support means to me. Thank you for being you, thank you for all that you do.

My readers, I love you. Not only do you buy my books and read them, you message me along the way. I love hearing from each and every one of you. I love hearing your thoughts as you read, and how the story as a whole touched your life. I'm grateful for ALL of you more than you will ever know. Thank you for taking the time to read my words.

My family, your continued support is beyond measure. I'm so thankful to be living this life with you. I love you.

My Kick Ass Crew, the name of the group, speaks for itself. You ladies truly do KICK ASS! I'm honored to have you on this journey with me. Thank you for reading, sharing, commenting, suggesting, the teasers, the messages all of it. Thank you from the bottom of my heart for all that you do. Your support is everything!

With Love,

Kaylee Ryan
AUTHOR